Also by David Ebsw
The Jacobites' Appre

David Ebsworth is the pen name of writer Dave McCall, a former negotiator and Regional Secretary for the Transport & General Workers' Union. He was born in Liverpool but has lived for the past thirty years in Wrexham with his wife Ann. Since their retirement in 2008, the couple have spent about six months of each year in southern Spain. Dave began to write seriously in 2009. For more information on the author and his work, visit www.davidebsworth.com.

Map designed by Cathy Harmon Helms (Avalon Graphics) and based on the original leaflet produced by the National Spanish State Tourist Board in 1938.

the Assassin's Mark

DAVID EBSWORTH

SilverWood

Published by the author in 2013 by SilverWood Empowered Publishing

SilverWood Books
30 Queen Charlotte Street, Bristol, BS1 4HJ
www.silverwoodbooks.co.uk

ISBN 978-1-78132-100-3 (paperback)
ISBN 978-1-78132-101-0 (ebook)

British Library Cataloguing in Publication Data
A CIP catalogue record for this book is available from the British Library

Set in Bembo by SilverWood Books
Printed on responsibly sourced paper

Dedicated to Marc Tortosa García, Pedro Carayol García,
and all the future generations of Spain

In memoriam to Jack (James Larkin) Jones and Frank Deagan

Reflection

Saturday 1 October 1938

Sydney Elliott discarded yet another attempt – his fifth – at writing the obituary. He slammed aside the carriage release and dragged the sheet of blurred typeface from the platen of the emerald green Royal, reminding himself that he would need to change the ribbon. He balled the thing in his hand, flicked it towards the over-sized waste basket that filled the far corner of his office, and took another drag on the Capstan. He looked at it, removed a strand of the tobacco from his lower lip. Medium Strength. Not like those rot-gut things that Jack Telford smoked.

Bloody Telford. He could be an annoying bugger when he chose. But Elliott missed him.

He still did not fully understand what had happened, and maybe he never would. He supposed that he should feel guilty, having sent Jack off on the crazy assignment in the first place. Yet there'd been nobody else who could have gone. Not himself, that was for sure. Not all the way to Spain when, as Editor, he had the paper to run.

The dirt-streaked window showed street lamps already burning outside, an ochre and orange aurora distorted by the autumn drizzle, fog seeping through the ill-fitting sash.

The details are so vague, he thought. *The accident in San Sebastián. Damned curious. Positively gruesome.* Then the events at Covadonga. Wasn't that the name of the place? Elliott had never heard of it before. And Sheila's account of the weird conversation she'd had with Jack when he wanted to file his copy. *What was that all about?*

Telford's article. There it sat. On the other side of his desk. Not what Elliott had wanted at all. But…

It had been quite a day. The competition all falling over themselves to pat Chamberlain on the back. *Peace for our bloody time indeed!* Well, the Prime Minister was in for a rude awakening if he thought *Reynold's News* would toe the same line.

Elliott glanced at the wall clock. Two hours before the Composing Room needed to begin putting the weekly to bed. The advertising pieces were all ready to go, but he knew that the copy-cutters would be keen as mustard to make an early start, to begin dividing up the work between the linotype operators, or to get the hand compositors cracking on the main headings. With a bit of luck he might see the first proofs by ten-thirty and have the final form in the press room by midnight.

But, first, there was the obituary to write.

Chapter One

Thursday 15 September 1938

Jack Telford met the newly-weds on the Night Ferry train. They had, it seemed, selected this tour of Franco's recently won battlefields as their ideal honeymoon destination.

They were a complete contrast, of course, to the travelling companions of his previous journey to Dover, twelve months earlier. On that occasion he had been chasing interviews with those volunteers still heading to Spain in defence of the Republic, pledged to fight – an entirely illegal enterprise, made so by this Non-Intervention Agreement that the British Government had brokered to theoretically prevent foreign interference in Spain's own affairs. But the volunteers had gone anyway. First to London. Twenty-eight and sixpence for the weekend ticket to Paris. No passport needed. The *Golden Arrow* to Dover, boat train to Calais, and then the journey through Paris, Lyons, Beziers and Perpignan. An eighteen-hour climb in the French Pyrenees to the Spanish border. And finally to Barcelona, where they would be enlisted with the International Brigades of the People's Army.

Jack, though, had accompanied them no further than Dover, sometimes securing a story, more often failing in his endeavours. But he recalled standing with one of them, a casual dock labourer from Liverpool, grumbling as the First-Class carriages alone were loaded onto the ferry whilst all the other passengers had been forced to brave the wind and rain of the boat's boarding bridge.

'You see, comrade?' the fellow had said. '*That's* what Spain's all about! No more class system and better bleedin' weather.'

Well, the class system was still alive and kicking in Britain alright. Yet here was Jack Telford, now himself a First-Class on this occasion, aboard the Southern Region's Night Ferry train rather than the *Golden Arrow*, dressed for dinner but feeling less than comfortable. So when he entered the restaurant car he had hesitated for a few moments, unsure whether he should wait to be seated and, too late, realised that he had caught and held the gaze of a man at the nearest table. Held it for just too long. The man jumped to his feet, disturbing the place settings as he did so, apologising to the lady sitting next to him.

'My dear chap,' said the man, 'you seem quite lost. Forgive me, but do you have a reservation?'

The fellow was older than Jack by perhaps ten years. Forty maybe. Short and overweight. Thinning hair and moustache. Two fingers of his left hand thrust into the fob-pocket of his waistcoat.

'No,' Jack replied. 'I didn't realise one was needed.'

'Of course, it is not. Not necessary at all. A simple enquiry about whether you already have arrangements or whether you should care to join my *wife* and I.'

The man turned to his wife, obviously pleased that he could use the term in public. A novelty, it seemed, and Jack knew them at once for recently married although the woman's expression was hardly welcoming. She was younger than her husband, closer to Jack's age but dressed almost in widow's garb, purple lipstick and pale make-up generously applied.

'Thanks,' said Jack, 'but I've no wish to intrude.'

'No intrusion whatsoever, I assure you,' said the man. 'Truly. And there's little time to quibble about the thing when all's said and done. We shall be in Dover just after ten-thirty. Only just time to eat. Besides, between you, me and the bedpost,' he lowered his voice, 'the service is not exactly top-notch. Still, you *shall* join us, surely? What do you say, Mrs Moorgate? We should enjoy the gentleman's company, should we not?'

'It's all one to me!' said the wife. 'But please, if you intend to do so, perhaps you might care to be seated…?' She glanced over Jack's shoulder, and Jack did the same, apologising to the white-liveried waiter whose progress through the carriage he was evidently blocking. Another apology, and Jack sat at the table. The train lurched, the double-headed engines pulling them away from Victoria Station's Platform Number Two. There was a ritual checking of watches throughout the carriage, a nodding chorus of approval for the punctuality. A billow of steam curled past the windows and a gust of outside wind from the open corridor brought them a particularly pungent waft of coal-smoke, causing Mrs Moorgate to wrinkle her nose.

'Forgive my enquiry, but do I take it that you are newly married?' Jack said to her.

'Why, however did you guess?' she replied, the words dripping sarcasm. 'My husband already so tired of me, it seems, that he invites a total stranger to dine. And not even the benefit of an introduction, Bertie.'

'Tired of you, my sweet?' said the man. 'Gracious, how could you think such a thing! But my *wife* is quite correct.' He half stood again, more careful this time, extending his hand to Jack. 'Albert Moorgate, sir. Delighted to make your acquaintance. And my wife, Frances.'

'Jack Telford,' Jack said, exchanging a handshake with Bertie, the briefest touch of fingers with the new Mrs Moorgate.

I thought that the fashion for black nail varnish faded two years ago, he thought. But then the *Wagons-Lits* waiter returned to take their orders and Jack, having barely glanced at the menu, opted quickly for the Italian soup followed by the turbot and green sauce.

'And where are you bound, Mister Telford?' asked Frances Moorgate, trying to ignore her husband's futile attempts to outplay the *sommelier* and his wine-list recommendations.

'To the south,' Jack replied. 'To catch the last of the fine weather, you know. Oh, and some work as well. Not too much. And yourselves? Honeymoon in Paris?'

You were never the best of liars, Jack, were you?

'You do not seem like a man who would take the sun for frivolous pleasure, Mister Telford,' said Frances Moorgate. And he thought that her voice had the same tone of ivory cream as her complexion. Gardenia.

'And not Paris, dear fellow,' said her husband. 'Gracious no! Somewhere more...'

Jack imagined that he was about to say *exotic* but then, to his astonishment, Moorgate produced the familiar leaflet from an inside pocket of his jacket. It was folded, of course, but there was no mistaking the thing. Jack had a copy of his own within the luggage back in his sleeper compartment and he cursed himself again for accepting their invitation.

'Ah!' he said. 'The War Route. You're bound for Spain then?'

Bertie Moorgate had barely begun to unfold the two-sided brochure and looked at Jack over the top of his spectacles, amazed that he should have recognised it so readily. Yet he passed it across the table anyway, while the waiter served their first course.

'You're familiar with the excursion, Mister Telford?' he said.

'More than simply familiar, I think,' said Frances. 'Unless I am mistaken, Mister Telford is a fellow-traveller.' She took an oyster, tilted her head and swallowed, closing her eyes, so that the green lids and false black lashes accentuated the waxy pallor of her skin.

Jack set down his soup spoon, accepted the leaflet and read the familiar opening line.

'National Spain invites you...' and that strange assortment of alluring beaches above, shell-shattered cities below.

He turned it over.

'The Path of War in Spain...' and the photo of General Franco, front and centre, his principal commanders beneath, the edges set with scenes of Nationalist victory. Tanks and guns.

'Yes,' said Jack. 'It seems that fate will carry us much further than Paris together. Though we might not be booked on the same trip, I suppose.'

'We begin on the Seventeenth,' said Moorgate as Jack handed back the brochure.

'Then a remarkable coincidence. Me too,' Jack replied.

'Thank Heaven that we shan't be the only English on the trip,' said Frances. 'Bertie tells me that Spain is a strange place indeed. And the work that you mentioned, Mr Telford?'

'I'm a journalist, Mrs Moorgate. My newspaper asked me to write a piece on the venture. There's a lot of interest in the idea. It's unusual for battlefield tours to be organised while the war's still being fought, don't you think?'

'Journalist, you say?' said her husband. 'Oh dear, we shall have to mind our Ps and Qs. We should not want to be quoted, Mr Telford.'

'You have my word that I shall not steal a word until we reach Spain.'

Oh, Jack, you almost sounded convincing!

'And might we enquire which paper you write for?' said Frances. 'Or are you a freelance, as they say?'

'I've done freelance stuff in the past, but I'm working for *Reynold's News* just now.'

'My goodness, are you a Socialist then, Mr Telford? How very quaint!'

'The *News* does lean toward the Labour Party, that's true,' said Jack, 'but only in so much as it tries to provide some balance.'

'Not too much *balance* so far, I imagine,' said Albert Moorgate. 'Has it covered anything except the Reds' side of the story? We don't read it, mind. But the occasional headline, naturally...'

'Though a friend has shown me those new cartoons from time to time,' said Frances, the dark rosebud lips hesitating towards a smile.

'*Young Ernie*? Yes, they're clever, aren't they? It's surprising how he can make them so funny without using any dialogue. Carl's a great fellow. Wonderful artist.'

Frances favoured him with an enthusiastic grin.

My God, she could be quite attractive if she'd only practise those facial muscles some more!

'All the same,' said Bertie, catching the conspiratorial exchange, 'I am surprised that *Reynold's News* would be interested in this tour, Mister Telford. Or are you only intent on sniping at General Franco's efforts?'

Jack held up his hands in mock defence, while the waiter cleared their first course dishes and set their places afresh.

'I'm under the strictest instructions from my editor,' he said, 'to tell the tour's story exactly as it happens.' *Too bloody true! If I get half a chance I'll drive a coach and horses through this shit that Franco and the* Daily Mail *have been peddling.* 'But what about you two? What made you choose this instead of Paris or Biarritz?'

'Well, I'm not certain that we *should*...' said Albert Moorgate, and he turned to his wife for reassurance.

'Mister Telford seems an honourable man, Bertie,' she said. 'And what could he print that would be so terrible?'

'The Bank would not wish to be mentioned, my dear, I'm sure. That's all.'

'The Bank?' said Jack, as their main course arrived and the *sommelier* brought a fine Chablis. Albert Moorgate tried the wine, signalled that it passed muster and insisted that their guest should try a glass.

'My husband works for the Westminster,' she said, while the glasses were filled. 'Manager of their London Foreign Branch.'

'Really?' said Jack. 'My father worked in a bank. The Old Worcester. Before the war, of course.'

Jack recalled the Grammar School's Roll of Honour. Ex-pupils who had fallen in the Great War. *Telford F.W. 1894-1899.* Jack had passed it every day that he, himself, had spent at the Grammar. The daily remembrance. The tangled truth.

'Your father fought in the war?' said Moorgate. As always, there was the unspoken question. *And did he survive?*

'He died in 'Fifteen, Mister Moorgate. Hardly a glorious death. A gunner. But he caught a chill, somewhere in Flanders. Complications set in. They sent him back to the Red Cross Hospital at St Albans. He died there.' The practised art of omission came easily to him after all those years. *Simply forget to mention the details, Jack.*

'My dear fellow! I am so sorry. We all lost so many friends and family, did we not? For my own part, I was lucky. I volunteered and ended up a Lieutenant. In the Intelligence Corps. But saw no real action. All administrative work. My background, I suppose. I could have become Lawrence, perhaps, but I lacked the fellow's sense of adventure.'

'They also serve…' Jack began. But, he thought, Lawrence too had been mostly forgotten until his death, three years before, in a motorcycle accident. *Another accident.*

'Yes, quite so,' said Albert Moorgate. 'Anyway, I always promised myself that I would go back. To visit the war graves, that kind of thing. And when the Westminster gave me this position, in '34, I decided to celebrate. Took the Michelin Tour the following year. Ypres. The Menin Gate and so on. You would not believe how many thousands of people signed the Visitors' Book there in that one year alone. But what a stroke of luck! Met Frances. She was with Thomas Cook, but all the same…'

'You lost somebody in Flanders too then, Mrs Moorgate?'

'Goodness no,' said Frances, and seemed shocked that he should suggest such a thing. 'But I do have a fascination for history, Mister Telford. And some professional interest in the matter.' Jack raised an eyebrow for clarification. 'I am a librarian,' she whispered. 'And the tour of the battlefields was so edifying.'

'Excuse me for saying so, Mrs Moorgate, but you don't quite fit my image of a librarian.'

'Oh, Hampstead Library requires a somewhat different mode of attire than this when I'm working, Mister Telford. You should hardly recognise me.'

'But Spain…?' said Jack.

'I spent a couple of years there,' said Albert Moorgate. 'The Bank opened branches all over Europe after the war and they made me sub-manager at Barcelona. It was quite an upheaval, to be sure. But it was never going to work. Their economy was a total mess. Their army was being hammered by the Rif tribesmen in Morocco. The Government pressing more and more conscripts. And Barcelona? A beautiful city. Beautiful, Mister Telford. But full of anarchists, communists, republicans. All protesting about this and that. A weak king. The unions promoting general strikes at the drop of a hat. Street fighting. You would still have been at school, I imagine?'

'Yes, I was,' said Jack, 'but I know the story.'

'Yes, I suppose you would! Anyway, we thought things might get better after Primo de Rivera's coup. King Alfonso made him Prime Minister but he was dictator in all but name. Exactly what the Spanish needed, we thought. But it was clear, soon enough, that he would bankrupt the Government. So we pulled out. Closed every Spanish Branch.' He counted them on his fingers. 'Bilbao. Madrid. Valencia. And Barcelona, of course. I helped to write the report. The Bank was very pleased. A shame, but there you are! By the beginning of '24 we were well shot of them all. And good riddance. But I always had a hankering to go back. Nothing wrong with the country. Beautiful. The cities, at least. Countryside still in the Dark Ages though, eh Frances?'

'So you keep telling me, my sweet. I am so looking forward to it. Imagine, Mister Telford. Battlefields where the blood is barely dry. Beaches and excellent food too, so they promise. Though I'm sure it will all seem very foreign.'

Jack tried to imagine the milk-white Mrs Moorgate taking the sun at a Spanish seaside Lido but the thought, difficult enough in itself, troubled him at some deeper level.

'To be honest, I'm not sure about the battlefields,' he said. 'My mother raised me with such a hatred of war. I can't shake it off. If it wasn't for my editor, I wouldn't be here. It all seems just a bit, well, macabre, doesn't it?'

'Macabre, my dear fellow?' said Albert Moorgate. 'Not at all. War touches us all, does it not? We need to understand it. The horror of the thing. We watch film and newsreel about it. We read your newspapers. So why should we not visit the places where these things really happened. It is simply a tourist commodity, Mister Telford. And everything's a commodity these days. At least we do not indulge in watching the battles themselves – though I fancy that Frances might quite enjoy that. What do you say, my dear? Would you have wanted to stand with the spectators that watched Waterloo unfold? Or Borodino?' Frances smiled at her husband, steak knife cutting a bloodied slice through her medium-rare sirloin. 'And do you know, Mister Telford, that during the Boer War, Thomas Cook ran excursions to South Africa so that people could see some of the action there? Simple sensationalism, sir. But is that not the role of journalists also? To sensationalise war in exchange for increased circulation?'

'It seems to be the preoccupation of certain competitors, Mister Moorgate,' said Jack. 'Although *Reynold's News* is, naturally, above all that!'

'Oh, naturally,' said Frances. 'Yet given your commitment to peace, should you not be in Germany today, rather than here?'

'I'm sure that Mister Chamberlain will manage very well without me,' said Jack.

'A bold move, I thought,' said Albert Moorgate. 'The idea of meeting face to face like that. I am perfectly certain that Hitler is a reasonable fellow. I always thought that most international differences could be better resolved if only we removed so-called diplomats from the process. Don't you agree, Telford? Face to face, that's the way to do it. Man to man. It's the way we do things at the Bank.'

Not a bad comparison, thought Jack, as an image of the sober and unimaginative Prime Minister came into his head, cast now in the role of bank manager. *'Sit down, my dear fellow. Now, tell me what this Sudeten business is all about and let's see if we can help.'*

'Well,' said Frances, 'I, for one, am profoundly relieved. The whole country's been *so* unsettled. Hooray to Mister Chamberlain, I say. Or are you one of those who think that we shouldn't talk to the Germans, Mister Telford?'

'No, I don't think that at all. But I don't see the German Chancellor as some harmless innocent either. The man is a bully, plain and simple. Mussolini, too. Hirohito and those who pull his strings. Bullies, all of them. And like any bullies, if you stand up to them early enough...'

'Oh, we've heard the argument over and over again, Mister Telford,' she replied. 'But these aren't school bullies, surely. These are serious men trying to restore some order in countries with deep problems. We should leave them to their own affairs. Now, shall we take dessert?'

But Jack chose to excuse himself. Notes to write, he said. And then wished to see the train loaded aboard the ferry.

'Indeed,' said Albert Moorgate. 'They tell me that the new dock is quite the thing! Double lock gates so the ships can be kept at one level with the train tracks. Remarkable. But you know, Mister Telford, that there will be another of your profession on our little excursion?'

'Another journalist?' Jack said.

'Oh yes. A young woman. Miss Carter-Holt. Joins us in Paris, I understand.'

Paris, thought Jack later, lighting a cigarette while Dover's lights faded into the distance. *Will I have nobody but fascists for company on this whole bloody trip?* But images of Valerie Carter-Holt, recollections of her picture in the papers, unsettled him in ways that were also entirely non-political.

But leave the Germans to their own affairs? he thought. *That way lies war.* And his mother was right. Another war, like the last one, was unimaginable. *Anyway, I've already been to Germany. Wouldn't want to go back in a hurry, either.* He remembered January '35. Jack had been with *The Observer* then and sent to work alongside Sheila Grant Duff on the Saar Plebiscite.

And so, Jack, what brings the fabulous Carter-Holt on our little foray?

The Reuters journalist had been wounded during the previous winter while covering the fighting in Spain from the Nationalists' side. A fellow-writer had been killed in the same incident. And Franco had been so impressed by Carter-Holt's work, her dedication to duty in the face of extreme danger, that he had awarded her a medal.

Jack looked at the brochure again, his own copy. The crude but effective attempt to re-write history.

It's the way Carter-Holt will write up the tour, I guess. Another 'Christian Crusaders against Murderous Reds' story.

It had been his editor, Sydney Elliott, who first put the thought of an alternative version in his head. Elliott had been with *Reynold's News* since it was bought by the National Co-operative Press in '29 while Jack had only been with the paper since the previous autumn, October '37. He had left *The Observer*, enticed by a post at the *Mirror*. But he resigned from the *Mirror* too when their anti-appeasement stance veered towards re-armament and a war-mongering editorial line. So he had been doing freelance work when Sheila introduced him to Sid. They took to each other straight away and Elliott had hired him. And when Sid had seen this bizarre brochure in a local travel agency window, he had brought it into the office. July. The first tours had only just taken place.

'You know, Jack,' he had said, 'I don't think people give a shit any more about whether the Popular Front is fighting to defend democracy or whether Franco is fighting to stop the Bolsheviks. Maybe *both* of those things are true anyway. They're not mutually exclusive, for Christ's sake! At least, both true in part. But why don't any of us write the third story? Here's the thing, Jack. The Popular Front gets elected in '36. It's a coalition of Left groups that don't like each other very much. Then along comes Franco. He incites most of the army to revolt against the elected Government. But who jumps up to stop him? Not the Government itself, that's for sure. Not in the beginning. Not the army commanders who remained loyal either. No, it's the workers, Jack. Ordinary people. Tens of thousands of them. No weapons at first. Just their own guts. And why? Because, Jack, Popular Front or no Popular Front, the people of Spain had started their own revolution. It didn't rely on the Communist Party either. It didn't need to. Did you know Spain before the war started, Jack? It was feudal. Feudal. It could have been Nineteenth Century Russia. You never saw such a gap between rich and poor. Most of the land owned by robber barons and all of them sanctified by the Church – for a fee, of course. So the people started taking the land back for themselves. And Franco was going to put a stop to *that* alright! And *there* is the third version that not a single British newspaper has bothered to tell, Jack. How this is a war in which ordinary Spanish workers have defended their fight-back against a feudal aristocracy and a feudal church. So go tell it, Jack. It's Pulitzer stuff!'

The lights of Dunkerque were showing as Jack flicked the end of his cigarette out over the water, a tiny red flare spinning towards the stern.

A distress signal, thought Jack. *My own private distress signal. How am I going to catch that story, Sid, sitting on a bus full of fascists – even if they're classy beauties like Carter-Holt? Christ, I'll be lucky if I haven't killed half of them before we even get to the Spanish border!*

Chapter Two

Friday 16 September 1938

The two Sisters of Our Lady of the Holy Light joined the *Sud Express* at Bordeaux. Jack, sipping a strong French *café* at the station's buffet, watched them pass their modest, much-travelled suitcases to the attendant. There was a forty minute halt that allowed an additional dark green 2-D-2 'Pig Nose' electric locomotive to be coupled for the extra traction needed on the journey's final section through SNCF's South-Western Region and across the Atlantic shoulder of the Pyrenees.

So far, the journey had gone exactly to schedule. A transfer by taxi from the Gare du Nord to the Gare d'Orsay, great baroque cavern, glass-domed, the first electrified urban rail terminal in the world. His trunk had been loaded aboard the baggage wagon, the train's *fourgon*, and Jack, along with his day bag, had then been shown to his seat in the second of four *wagons-salons*, the blue liveried day saloon carriages bearing a double-lion insignia in gold.

Jack had done his best to avoid spending more time with the Moorgates but it was almost impossible, and Bertie had several times come to find him, so that he might be presented to others who, the bank manager had discovered, were also due to join them on their adventure. Amongst them, Albert Moorgate had met the blind pianist, Julia Britten, and as they crossed the river east of Tours at Montlouis-sur-Loire, Jack had been persuaded to join her during a period when her companion was engaged elsewhere.

'Your friend has a busy social life, doesn't she?' he said, after Moorgate had made the introductions and left them. Jack settled in the plush armchair alongside her.

'Nora?' she said, turning her face towards that end of the compartment, and through several of the open teak partitions, where the tiny woman was engaged in three or four loud conversations with people she barely knew, as though they were all lifelong acquaintances. She was so small that Jack was hardly able to see her any better than could Julia Britten, but there was no mistaking the shrill voice nor, indeed, the frizzy white hair that appeared occasionally above this seat or that. 'She never stops,' the pianist continued, 'but she keeps me young. And she *does* look after me.'

'Keeps you young?' said Jack. 'My goodness. You don't look as though you need any help in that direction, Miss Britten.'

'I see that you are a *roué*, Mister Telford. But I assure you that everybody needs a Nora Hames in their life at times. She can be infuriating but you should see her at a reception or party. Always the first on the floor. Always the last to leave it. And she could easily drink any amount of your journalist friends under the table. She will be sixty-seven this year yet she shows no sign of tiring. She inspires me, Mister Telford.'

So far as he could recall, Julia Britten was at least twenty years younger than her companion, though her short-cut auburn hair had begun to show its own grey streaks. *How long has she been blind?* he wondered. *Since birth? I'm damned if I can remember. But didn't she make her debut at the age of eleven or something similar? With Beecham, I think. And she was definitely blind then.*

'Well,' said Jack, 'we're all in need of inspiration from time to time. Certainly in my profession. Which I suppose means that I'm obliged to ask what brings you on this strange excursion. I was going to say "*Not that it's any of my business*", but I think our readers will be fascinated that you're here. You're quite a heroine to many of them, I think.'

'Surely not!' Julia Britten smiled, lowered her head in embarrassment and pressed the knuckle of her index finger to her eyes. Then straightened her light tweed jacket, her skirt too. 'I seem to be cursed by a certain talent for those sonatas and concertos favoured by dictators, Mister Telford, if the truth be told. Beethoven, Wagner and Bruckner have taken me to Vienna recently with Herr Hitler in the audience. Then Milan and a Giuseppe Martucci concert for Il Duce. And now…'

'And now…?' Jack said when Julia Britten faltered.

'And now Mister Telford,' said Nora Hames, appearing unexpectedly at his side, 'you must let an old lady sit down. Or can I call you Jack? I had a friend called Jack once. Jack Crossfield. In Manchester. Oh, he was lovely!'

'Yes, of course,' said Jack, surrendering the seat. *You seem to have upset Miss Britten, Jack,* he thought.

'Oh Nora,' he heard her whisper as he left them. 'You rescued me just in time, as usual!'

Rescued her? thought Jack. *From what? She's performed for Hitler and Mussolini. And now…?*

The railway turned south again, crossed the Cher and the Indre, and followed the right bank of the Vienne upstream beyond Maillé. At Châtellerault it crossed the Vienne and continued to the city of Poitiers.

Jack buried himself in his book for the most part, although the unfolding panorama was an easy distraction from *The Hobbit.* It had been Sheila's recommendation and she had assured him that it was *not* a children's book, though Jack had been drawn to it by an interview he had read in which the author professed himself an avid reader of William Morris. A shared hero, therefore. But he had found something grating in John Tolkien's over-simplified views of good and evil and, worse, the central characters' apparent reliance on luck for their salvation. Still, it had protected him from another intrusion.

They had followed the Charente valley from Saint-Saviol downstream, the tracks crossing the river several times before slowing to pass through Angoulême. And there, Albert Moorgate had appeared once more, come to tell him that two further members of the tour had been discovered.

'Husband and wife,' he said, whispering to Jack. 'Remarkable story. He lost his brother in the fighting at Bilbao.'

'English?' said Jack.

'Yes, of course.'

'And fighting for the Nationalists?'

'Come now, Telford. I see that Socialist bias creeping in again. Well, he was hardly alone, was he? It may be a nice fable that you've sown about your precious International Brigades but General Franco has plenty of supporters at home too, you know. What's that you're reading, by the way?'

'This? Oh, nothing. A friend asked me to review it. A silly thing, really. So how did this fellow come to be fighting for the rebels then?'

'For National Spain, dear boy. You can hardly call them rebels at *this* stage, now can you? Anyway, their name is Kettering.' He whispered again, bending closer to Jack's ear. 'Catholic, I imagine. Joined some Carlist unit and then transferred to the Spanish Foreign Legion. Come and meet them.'

'No, I don't think so,' said Jack, as politely as he was able. 'Plenty of time to chat with them during the journey.'

Moorgate left him to his book and while Bilbo the Burglar made his way with Thorin's Dwarves to Rivendell and the Misty Mountains, the *Sud Express* pressed through the Dordogne and eventually found the Garonne.

Jack had seen and heard Valerie twice during the journey but she had ignored him. For his own part it occurred to him that, whatever hardships she might have suffered, they had done nothing to damage Carter-Holt's good looks. All the same, by the time they reached Bordeaux, just before five in the evening, he was badly in need of a stretch. The thought of bumping into the woman held some attraction, but having to endure more chatter with his fellow-travellers had constrained Jack from walking the corridors as he might otherwise have done. So the buffet at the Gare de Bordeaux-Saint-Jean was a welcome relief. The coffee too. And the opportunity to buy a paper perhaps.

But here he had been disappointed, for the kiosk's only useful international offering was a copy of yesterday's *Times*. He bought it anyway. Interesting to compare its coverage of Chamberlain's planned trip to Germany with the version in *The Manchester Guardian* that he had studied on the Night Ferry crossing.

Nothing new, however. The headlines almost identical.

DRAMATIC BRITISH MOVE FOR PEACE
Mr Chamberlain to Confer with Herr Hitler
Flying to Germany Today
A CORDIAL WELCOME FROM THE FÜHRER

Jack knew Germany relatively well, but he was not sure that he could put his finger accurately on a map to show the area occupied by Sudetenland, although several of the quality dailies had taken up pages of newsprint so that readers might understand the location of this minor racial dispute which, once again, threatened to plunge the world into the bedlam of global war. *Only, my God, what a job we can make of it this time! Civilian bombing now the order of the day. The Germans and Italians already masters of the new art, practising on the Spanish. And we won't be far behind them. No use pretending that the British, French and Russians will have any qualms about following suit.*

He searched in vain for a while seeking news of Spain itself, but the Battle of the Ebro, having raged already for two months, had slipped from the pages.

Yet there was good coverage of other items. The maiden flight of the Graf Zeppelin, the second giant airship of that name, from Friedrichshafen, across Munich, Augsburg and Ulm. Over nine hundred kilometres in less than six hours. On the other side of the world, at Bonneville Salt Flats in Utah, John Cobb was expected to break the World Land Speed Record in his specially designed Railton.

He would probably have continued daydreaming until after the *Sud Express* pulled out again had it not been for the nuns, for they almost missed it themselves, running from another platform and a connecting train. Jack threw some coins on the table and ran too, for his own carriage, settling himself back in the plush fabric and using *The Times* to hide his secret reading matter for this next portion of the journey. He gave a cursory thought to how Cobb and Chamberlain might have progressed and then turned his attention to Eggo the Ostrich, Lord Snooty and Morgyn the Mighty.

It must have been twenty minutes later when he became aware of somebody looking over his shoulder and he almost jumped up when he realised it was the younger of the two Sisters, dark-robed and with a stiffly starched white coif framing tiny Mediterranean features.

'Ay, *Señor!*' she cried, her words heavily accented. Spanish or Portuguese perhaps. 'You have a secret. And I am caught out in a sin.'

'It is a very small secret, Sister. I should have given up comic strips years ago, but they remain a vice. And you? You wouldn't have read *Oor Wullie* I don't suppose?'

'I don't think so.' She tried to form her lips around the strange words.

'But it was me that was caught out, I think. How could that be a sin on your part?'

'The sin of curiosity, *Señor.*'

'My goodness,' said Jack. 'Have they made that a sin too now? I didn't know.'

'Sister Berthe Schultz...'

'You're not going to tell me that Sister Schultz is Dutch, I hope?' Jack said, smiling at the speed of his own humour.

'*¡Qué va!* Why should you think so? She is Swiss, of course. She says that curiosity is a sin. To be interested in something useful is good. But to look at things, to listen to something, not meant for us. It is a thing...*entrometida*. Such people, we poke our faces into everything. We make it difficult for people to live with us. Those of us who live in communities, we ruin. Because community must have trust. Trust and curiosity do not go together. We insist upon knowing everything that is going on. To find out about others. And when the urge is strong, it is a sin.'

'Well, that was some speech. I should hate to have the full thrust of it from Sister Schultz.'

'Sister *Berthe* Schultz. In the Order, we must use each Sister's full name.'

'And which order might that be, Sister?'

'The Order of Our Lady of the Holy Light,' the nun replied, apparently dismayed that Jack should not already have known.

'An Order that considers curiosity a sin?' He was aware of her hand clutching the back of his seat as she swayed to the movement of the train.

'Sister Berthe Schultz says so. She says we must always seek the motive for our curiosity. If we are always curious, perhaps we seek attention for ourselves. And pretending to be important, we pass on the information we have discovered even when it might not be correct. We talk about things in the wrong place. If we are only sometimes curious, if we read another's documents perhaps,' she coloured deeply, 'then our curiosity usually stems from jealousy, or a thirst for power over that other person. We have to know everything, every secret, so that we can have control over this person. It must not be confused with concern, of course. Concern is good. But we should never use secrecy to show our concern. *Nunca*.'

'No, of course not!' said Jack. 'I had not realised that curiosity was such a great sin, I must admit. But what if I lent you my copy of *The Beano*? No sin in that, surely?'

'*Beano?*' she said.

Ah, she thinks I said 'vino'! thought Jack.

'This.' He lifted the comic from within the folds of *The Times*, offering it to her.

'*¡Bendita Madre de Diós!* How could that be, *Señor*? If I have seen something that does not belong to me and I have coveted that thing, it is a sin. If I then accept that thing from your hand I am also a thief. A trespass against the Seventh Commandment. For I will have gained this thing dishonestly.'

'Yes,' said Jack, 'I understand the problem. And we have Sister Berthe Schultz to thank for saving us both from this sin?'

'Oh, *Señor*, I do not think that you have any part in this sin. It is entirely my own.'

'But was it not I that put the temptation before you, Sister?'

She looked thoughtful for a moment.

'Yes,' she said, at last, 'I think that Sister Berthe Schultz would agree that you must share some of the burden.' The train lurched once more and she almost lost her footing entirely.

'From what you've told me,' said Jack, 'I could not imagine it otherwise. But won't you sit for a while, Sister, while we consider how we might best absolve ourselves?'

'I am not sure...'

It was clear that she was contemplating the possibility that an acceptance of his invitation might constitute another infringement of Sister Berthe's harsh code but she finally agreed to join him. She thanked him, sat demurely.

'You know, Sister,' he said, 'I was just thinking that if curiosity is a sin, then the whole of my profession must be damned.'

'Your profession, *Señor*?'

'I am a journalist, Sister.'

'But that is noble work. Sister Berthe Schultz says so. At least, for those who write the truth. Who write to shed light in dark corners. Who write to educate others. It is the work of my Order!'

'Journalism?'

'*¡Hombre. Por favor!* The Order has two Mother-Houses. One helps to provide teachers. Our own is at Axenstein. For nurses.'

'You are a nurse, Sister?'

'Oh, no. I am Sister María Pereda.'

'Jack Telford, Sister María Pereda.'

'I am pleased to meet you, *Señor* Telford. And no, I am not a nurse. But I work mainly at the Sanatorium Deutsches Haus. In the office there.'

'It's famous,' said Jack, with delight. 'I've heard of it! But you're Spanish! How did you end up in a Swiss Religious Order?'

'The Order is *also* famous, *Señor*. It was my mother's wish. But now, you see? I am going home.'

'It's not the best of times to be returning to Spain, Sister.'

'No? Why is that? *El Caudillo* has almost won the *Reconquista* against the godless heathens.'

'But the war's not over yet. You might be in danger.'

'Oh, *Señor*, how could I be in danger? I have the Holy Mother on one side and Sister Berthe Schultz on the other. *Además*, we go to the north. Only to the north. It is safe there.'

'To the north?' said Jack. 'Where exactly? Or do you think I am risking the sin of curiosity by asking?'

'It might be so,' she replied. The nun thought seriously for a moment. 'But Sister Berthe Schultz says that we are only in real danger if we persist in the sin. And the sin is worse for Christians who know the sacrifice made by our Lord, Jesus Christ, but deny his Redemption by continuing to practise sinful ways.'

'Well, I'm not a particularly good Christian either, but it sounds like that might favour me. So I'll risk it, Sister María Pereda. Just a couple of curiosity questions maybe?'

'*Vale*. In that case, we are going to Santiago de Compostela.'

'This journey is full of coincidences. I'm going to Santiago too. Well, eventually.'

'You are going on the tour of *El Caudillo's* fields of glory?' she said.

'You and Sister Berthe Schultz too?'

'*¡Qué suerte!* Oh, I am so pleased.'

'Well, I see that you are correct, Sister. My own curiosity has now plunged me into confusion. I understand that you think General Franco a great man. But a tour of *battlefields*?'

'We are sent to visit the sites of the Holy Martyrs. Those who have given their lives so that Spain might be free once more.'

'Sent?'

'Yes. By the Director of the Sanatorium. Herr Alexander. He is a National Socialist. A good friend of the Führer. He has made many changes at the clinic.'

'What, no more Jews?'

'Oh, I was not thinking of *that* change. I meant medical change. You think it is *good* that Herr Alexander has banned the Jews? I was not sure. But Sister Berthe Schultz says that it *is* good.'

'Well, perhaps I should speak with Sister Berthe Schultz about this. I don't really understand how anybody who could make such a meal of curiosity...'

'Make a meal...?' The nun laughed.

'Turn curiosity into a sin,' he said. 'Anyway, how could she not see that Hitler's and Mussolini's treatment of the Jews isn't a sin too? There are thousands being forced to leave their homes. And we hear terrible stories about thousands more. Persecuted and put in ghettoes. Worse.'

'Oh, Sister Berthe Schultz says that this is all a lie. *Una mentira.* That the Jews run away from Germany because Herr Hitler is creating a better society, and *they* want to keep all the wealth that they have stolen from others.'

'But the President of the United States was here in France, just two months ago. With thirty-two other countries. A huge conference at Évian to discuss the crisis. Because *they* all believe that the Jews are being persecuted.'

'I see,' she said. 'And what did they decide?'

You led with your chin there, Jack, didn't you? Go on, tell her the truth. That they decided bugger-all!

'You're changing the subject,' said Jack. 'I'm sure that there must be something in the teachings of Sister Berthe Schultz about the sin of changing subjects. You were telling me how the Herr Director sent you both to Santiago. But I thought that you would be under a Mother Superior or something?'

'But of course, *Señor.* Mother Superior Inge Rolfe. But she works very closely with Herr Alexander. It was his suggestion that two of the Order should go to Berchtesgaden, with flowers for the Führer.'

'Flowers for the German Chancellor?'

'Yes, two of the Sisters have gone there this week.'

I wonder if they'll bump into Chamberlain while they're there...

'But yourself and Sister Berthe Schultz are bound for Santiago. If two others of your Order have gone with flowers for Hitler, then...?'

'*¡Qué va, Señor!* You see? Sister Berthe Schultz was correct. You have been curious and now you persist in your curiosity. Your questions have turned to sin and now you stray into the forest's edge. Yet I cannot stray there with you.' The young nun hoisted herself from the armchair. 'But I look forward to speaking with you again during *El Caudillo's* tour. Perhaps next time Sister Berthe Schultz may also join us.'

'Yes, I can hardly wait,' said Jack as Sister María Pereda made her way into the next carriage.

Well, there's somebody else in a hurry to get away from me, he thought. *It looks like the nuns and Julia Britten both know more about this trip than they're letting on!*

With the western tip of the Pyrenees unfolding to the left, the train ran towards the coast at Biarritz where, after a brief halt in the busy resort, the tracks looped back and forth between sandy beaches and rocky foothills until, finally, they arrived in the border station of Hendaye-Plage. It was two minutes before nine in the evening, and the *Sud-Express* was a mere three minutes behind schedule.

Albert Moorgate had found him again as Jack peered through the windows, craning his neck so that he could see the arches of the International Bridge spanning the Bidasoa River and the border with Spain. He was surprised to find that he retained the Englishman's wonder at any frontier which could be crossed without a sea voyage.

'Is that Fuenterrabía?' Jack said, pointing at the lights on the Spanish side and to the north.

'Yes, I think so. To tell the truth, I expected more formality that this.'

But there was none. At least, they were told, there would be none until they were in Irún itself. A few passengers descended at Hendaye, although the train had mostly emptied, first at Bordeaux and then at Biarritz. So it looked as though most left aboard were those destined for the War Route as the train slowly hauled its way onto the bridge and crossed from the edge of France – warm bread, strong coffee, each laced with essence of *Gauloises* – into the entirely distinctive soul of Spain. Freshly-fried fish, jasmine, scorched olive oil.

'I hadn't given a thought,' said Jack, 'to how we're going to get across. The border was closed in '36, wasn't it?'

'Oh, Franco made some sort of deal with your French Socialist friends, I think. Their trains now run down into Irún so that any transit passengers can swap onto Spanish trains without having to walk across, and Spanish trains can do the reverse, heading up into Hendaye. Damned efficient.'

'Yes,' Jack replied although he did not really care. He had been thinking about Sister María Pereda. About Julia Britten too. He seemed to have struck a nerve with each of them. 'But I say, Mister Moorgate. Do you mind if I ask you something?'

'Of course not, my dear fellow. So long as it's not a request for an unsecured loan, eh?'

'No, perish the thought! It was something else. About this trip. Have you heard of anything planned to take place other than what's on the official itinerary?'

'Why, Mister Telford,' said Moorgate. 'Whatever can you mean?'

Chapter Three

Saturday 17 September 1938

The tour guide, it transpired, came from County Sligo and wore the black dress uniform of the Falange. He was in his mid-twenties, did not seem in the best of health, but he met them at four the following afternoon, as arranged, in the reception area of the Hotel Jaúreguí.

It was a five-storey stone building dating, Jack guessed, from the early part of the century, in the relatively more modern section of Fuenterrabía, on the northern side of the old town. From its half-timbered balcony fluttered the red and yellow flag of National Spain.

They had been conveyed there by taxi and Jack had initially hoped that he might get to share one either with Sister María or with the blind pianist, so that he could probe them further. On the other hand, he was not entirely sure that he wished to share a cab with Valerie Carter-Holt but, as things transpired, he need not have worried on either count.

The passport control at Irún had seemed rudimentary in the circumstances with a customs official and a couple of Guardia Civil troopers giving nothing but a cursory glance to each traveller's papers. The Moorgates first. Then Julia Britten with Nora Hames declaring that she would faint from the heat but, oh dear, what a handsome young policeman!

Carter-Holt next. Twenty-six years old, the youngest daughter of the Honourable Ursula Uxbridge and Sir Aubrey Carter-Holt, then Secretary to the First Lord of the Admiralty. She had apparently excelled at Oxford and later been taken on by Reuters as a foreign correspondent, rising to fame almost immediately by her brush with death and her lurid attacks on Spain's Popular Front Government. She still looked, thought Jack, like a hardened yet seductive version of Fay Wray. But she received the deference due to her from the officials, producing her papers efficiently from the leather saddlebag shoulder purse. Even a salute from one of the *Civiles*.

The two nuns were processed quickly as well and, finally, the Ketterings. Catherine and Peter. They had shaken hands with Jack as they left the train. Apologised that they had not introduced themselves earlier. Not a problem, Jack had said, surprised to find that he took an instant liking to them, and they had exchanged a few pleasantries while standing in the queue. They seemed nervous, out of place here, but they went through the control quickly enough and he had looked forward to travelling with them to their hotel – only to find that, as the last in line, there seemed to be some difficulty with his own documents.

The customs officer conveyed them to a small office. Five minutes went by.

'Is there a problem?' Jack had said in his slow Spanish to the sergeant.

'Wait!' said the older Guardia Civil. *¡Espera!*

Jack shrugged. He had not planned to do anything *other* than wait.

The customs officer appeared again in the doorway, now accompanied by a more senior representative. They looked at the passport and travel papers together, studied *Señor* Telford carefully, whispered for a moment, and returned to the office. Jack could hear the telephone in operation and began to experience that cold loneliness he had experienced so often in Germany. He dismissed the idea of any further exchange with the *Civiles*, who stared at him impassively, dark eyes below the polished black crowns of their distinctive uniform hats. Another five minutes went by.

'*Hay un taxi…*' Jack began. There is a taxi.

'*¡Espera!*'

'Fine. I´ll wait then.'

But not for long. The customs official returned, as did Jack´s papers. A cursory nod. No explanation. And a Guardia Civil pointed to the door.

'*Gracias,*' said Jack, with as little sarcasm as he could manage. '*Muchas gracias.*'

The warm September evening air was filled with crickets and the scent of unknown flowers, a pleasant change from the slightly bitter atmosphere of the ochre station building, a stench of blocked drains, and he had been relieved to find that there was, indeed, an ancient taxi still waiting, Jack´s trunk alongside it. The equally ancient driver had a copy of the War Routes brochure with him and waved it towards Jack.

'*¿Usted, Señor?*' he said.

'Yes,' Jack replied, and climbed onto the worn leather back seats while the old fellow removed his cap, using it to give himself a better grip on the starting handle. The engine fired easily and they drove onto the dirt road up into town. It was difficult to see in the dark but Jack could make out that only a few houses were intact, wood-shuttered, like images of Swiss chalets, whereas the rest were in ruins, stone gate-posts standing sentinel over vacant lots. They made a circuitous journey before, apparently, leaving the town behind.

'The Hotel,' said Jack. 'Not in Irún?' His Spanish was limited but accurate enough if he chose his words carefully but, as so frequently happens with noviciate linguists, it was certainly not adequate to deal with the lengthy response. He gathered, however, that Irún had been destroyed by Anarchists and the reply quickly developed into a rehearsed speech, presumably part of the tour's script.

So they headed north, but not for long, until they skirted some dimly perceived town walls. Fuenterrabía, explained the driver. *Preciosa*. Nice place. Beaches. Good food.

They had stopped outside the Hotel Jaúreguí where Jack had been obliged to help the old man manoeuvre the travelling case inside until the well-dressed concierge finally deigned to offer some assistance in the absence of a porter. He pointed at a notice board with an announcement that on the following morning, Saturday the Seventeenth, travellers on the War Routes Tour were free to explore the town but might wish to be present for an information meeting, here at the Hotel, beginning at four p.m.

A porter finally appeared in response to the reception desk bell and Jack was escorted to his room, borne to the top storey in an elegant paternoster elevator but disconcerted, as always, by the absence of any elevator doors. He had to restrain himself at the second *and* third floors from poking out his head as they passed. It was no surprise to him that the contraption had not caught on at home. *Give me a proper lift any time*, he thought. But they were popular enough on the Continent.

He smoked a *Capstan*, then slept badly, partly due to being in a strange room and normally needing a day or two to settle anywhere new. But partly the result, too, of that form of embarrassment which his limited circle of school friends would have described as a 'wet dream.' Carter-Holt, damn the woman! So he was up early. The hotel reception seemed happy to exchange a small amount of sterling for local currency, the Burgos pesetas of National Spain, naturally, and then he was out on the streets, ignoring the basement dining room and avoiding fellow-guests in favour of a bar near the church, up the hill in the old town. The entire location seemed, to Jack, as though it had been pickled during the Thirty Years War, remaining that way throughout the ensuing three centuries, and he admired the half-timbered façades, the colourful wrought-iron balcony grilles, the bougainvillea and hibiscus, the elegance.

What did you expect, Jack? That it would be like the newsreels? Grey and grainy. A war zone. Or filled with donkeys, maybe. The fact is, I'm not sure what *I expected. Just...Well, not this.*

He searched for an English newspaper without success and eventually picked up a Spanish daily. The front page was taken up with photographs of Nationalist aviators, smiling, victorious. Over the page, Chamberlain's docile face gazed out at him. Mention of the Berchtesgaden. Hitler. It all looked very amicable. *And London. Chamberlain returning to London? Is that what it says? It was a quick visit then.* But he could only pick out odd words. *Sudeten.* No imminent hostilities anyway, it seemed.

Jack visited the town walls, the old gateway, and then sat on the beach for a while, at the farthest end away from the Hotel. He read some more of *The Hobbit*, dazzled by the light and frequently setting down the book to squint across the modest bay of the Bidasoa river mouth to Hendaye-Plage on the French side. The tide was out but the central channel still had ample width for the small boats that plied its waters. The place reminded him of a trip to Salcombe that he had taken with his mother. It would have been in '20 or '21, a year or so after Jack had been awarded one of the scholarships at the Grammar. But Salcombe was home to several aunts and uncles, as well as a collection of cousins. The eldest of the girls was older than Jack by eighteen months, an impossible gap at that age, but she dutifully took him to the beach each day while the adults engaged in the serious business of post-war adjustment. She took pity on him.

'How awful,' she had said, 'that your poor father should have been so disturbed.'

And Jack had learned the truth for the first time. That war was so terrible that his father, even having escaped its clutches and been returned to St Albans, had still taken his own life rather than face any prospect of return to the trenches. A view reinforced time and time again, subsequently, by his penitent mother, contrite that she had not been honest with her son.

But, even then, Jack mistook the cousin's obedient pity for affection. It was a flaw which he had never overcome. If any woman of a certain age and appearance showed him more than a passing interest, he generally mistook it for attraction.

Why, Jack, you even imagined Sister María to be a little smitten by you!

But it was not Cousin Betty's lime-green frock or her revelations that he remembered best from Salcombe but the ghost of his father that he was sure had appeared to him there for the first time, standing beside a favourite rock pool. The first time, but not the last. Seeking something from him. But what? He had never been sure.

The memory was packed back into its box, however, and Jack went to find lunch. A small *taberna* near the front, falling silent as he entered but offering *pintxos* from which he chose a selection. Salted cod, anchovy, stuffed pepper, each skewered with an olive to its own oval of oiled bread and served with the smallest glass of beer that he had ever seen. His serenity was shattered only when he returned to the Hotel and found the tour group already assembled in the reception area, plainly waiting to begin. Jack checked his watch, holding it to his ear to confirm that it had not stopped when he saw that it said only a quarter to four.

'You must be Mister Telford,' said a neat, middle-aged woman with a shrewish voice. She advanced and shook his hand. 'We were becoming quite concerned. And our friends here were anxious to start early.'

She introduced herself as Dorothea Holden, and she pointed out her husband, Professor Alfred Holden, a swaying willow of a man with a Hitler moustache who Jack recognised from pictures in the newspapers. The Professor was once a darling of the Right-wing press and had helped Mosley establish the British Union of Fascists. He had written whole sections of the party's programme and ideology, they said.

Professor Holden now bobbed and wove a path from table to table, as forced *bonhomie*, jocularity, pumped his Adam's apple back and forth. His turtle's neck stretched impossibly from an over-sized collar, while his wife took up a lecturing mother's stance in the centre of the gathering.

'Ladies and gentlemen, good afternoon,' she began. 'Shall we commence?'

Jack received a few raised hands, the occasional smile, from the Moorgates, the Ketterings, from Sister María – whose flippant behaviour was instantly corrected by Sister Berthe Schultz. A piercing 'coo-ee' from Nora Hames brought a frown of reproach from Dorothea Holden.

'*My* name,' she said, 'is Dorothea Holden.' Nora tutted. 'My good friend, *Señor* de Armas Gourié, has asked me to say a few words of welcome.' An immaculately dressed Spaniard rose and bowed. 'My husband and I have been working through the Friends of National Spain, an entirely non-aligned body, to help bring these tours about.' *Ah,* thought Jack, *so we know who's paid for your trip, Mrs Holden.* 'They are arranged, naturally, by the Tourist Department here but our own organisation has certainly helped to spread the word, as you might say. The trips have been running since the beginning of July. Several times each week, as a matter of fact. And we are so *very* blessed that we can see history in the making. Just think what it would have been like to ride with the banners of Ferdinand and Isabella as they re-conquered Spain from the dreaded Moors. And *that*, my friends, is the treat in store for *you*. But much more besides. Because on *this* trip you will also enjoy some of the world's most elegant beaches. Scenery of unsurpassed beauty. And time along the way, for those so inclined, to play a round of golf. To practise your fly-fishing. To hunt the elusive chamois.' Dorothea Holden paused for effect, seemed disappointed that nobody clapped, then pressed on. 'Now,' she said, 'you will all have many questions, I am sure, but first I shall invite the Hotel Manager, *Señor* Molino, to say a few words.' They were few indeed. A welcome, clumsily translated by Mrs Holden, and Molino hoped that they would enjoy their stay in his fine establishment. Then he begged that they would excuse him, offered them the most formal of bows, swept aside the long tails of his evening jacket, and made his exit through the large double doors at the back, where Jack could see a pleasant terrace and fountain. Dorothea thanked the Manager as he withdrew, before saying, 'And a short contribution, I think, from *Señor* de Armas Gourié. We are so privileged to have him with us this afternoon.'

She began to applaud enthusiastically so that the rest had little option except to do likewise, and the tall Spaniard stood, tidied his cravat and ran a finger along his waxed pencil-moustache.

'I thank you,' he said. 'Too kind. Please. My name is Laureano de Armas Gourié. Well, I am architect and designer. But now I working also for the State Tourist Department of National Spain. I bring greetings from the Department Head, *Señor* Bolín. Yes. That is correct. Bolín. Like your English Queen. So you see. Many links between Spain and England.' There was a moment's silence. 'Well…'

'Oh!' cried Nora Hames. 'Anne Boleyn. He means Anne Boleyn. Yes, very good, *Señor*.'

'Thank you. Very much,' said the Spaniard, pleased to have begun so well. 'Yes, Ana Bolena. All true Castilians still despise her, you know? For the way your King Henry set aside our Catherine of Aragón. We have long memories.' More smiles. 'Now, I work for State Tourist Department, like I say. But we want that you form your own judgement of the real situation here. In National Spain. I say *National* Spain because now we work for *one* country again. Just one. The Republic has destroyed Spain identity.'

Jack raised his hand, causing Dorothea Holden to take the floor again.

'I *did* say, Mister Telford, that we would take questions later, did I not? Please, *Señor.* Continue.'

'Yes, good,' said the Spaniard. 'Well, this week you will visit many places. To see the situation and to enjoy the country. To San Sebastián. Durango. Bilbao. Santander. Gijón. Oviedo. You will stay in the best hotels. Eat the finest food. And then, at the end...'

This is clever, thought Jack. *They name all these holy sites so that, when we get there, we're already half-conditioned to accept whatever tripe they want to feed us.*

Dorothea Holden jumped to her feet again.

'Perhaps, *Señor,*' she said, 'we should save that little surprise for later. Oh, *two* surprises, actually. Yes?' Laureano de Armas Gourié hunched his shoulders, took his seat again as Dorothea indicated he should, and received a polite burst of applause. 'Yes,' she continued. 'Well done, *Señor.* Now, the route. She unfolded her copy of the brochure, displaying its map. 'Here *we* are,' she pointed to the French-Spanish border, 'and here is Santiago de Compostela. The towns marked in red are the places where we shall stay overnight. But we'll be making lots of additional visits each day. We've had to make a tiny adjustment towards the end of the week...'

'Saboteurs, my sweet,' added her husband – unhelpfully, thought Jack, since his intervention elicited several gasps from the group.

'Yes, but nothing to worry about,' said Dorothea. 'Absolutely nothing. A minor detour, that's all. Now, I know that this is a lot to take in but you must not worry. We have an excellent guide with us. And English in the bargain.'

The black-uniformed guide stood stiffly and with some difficulty.

'Well,' he said, without a trace of good humour, 'I'm a County Sligo man, as it happens. But I *speak* English well enough, to be sure. And God's blessing on you all. My name's Brendan Murphy. We'll get to know each other just fine as the week goes by. Please ask me anything. Anything mind.'

He sat down again.

'Now,' Dorothea continued, 'Mister Murphy is fully trained and qualified. He has been strictly tested on his knowledge of history and geography. He is the only non-Spaniard amongst fifteen guides. Besides that, he is himself a serving member of General Franco's forces – who saw action with General O'Duffy's Fifteenth *Bandera,* if I'm not mistaken?'

'Indeed, ma'am,' said Murphy, 'and not to be confused with the so-called Fifteenth International Brigade fighting for the heathen Reds – but not for much longer, so we hear.'

Now what does that mean? If only we could get some decent bloody newspapers.

'Quite so,' said Dorothea. 'Well, any questions?'

Jack raised his hand, but Nora Hames was less disciplined.

'I wonder whether somebody might tell us more about these saboteurs?' she said.

'Miss Hames,' said Dorothea, 'there really *is* nothing...'

'If I might?' said Murphy. 'Mrs Holden is quite right. These self-styled partisans sneak down from the mountains now and again, blow up a bridge and then disappear back to their holes. It only means that we have to change the route while we make repairs.'

'And have they ever attacked the tours?' asked Nora.

Murphy snorted with laughter.

'Bless you, no, ma'am,' said the guide. 'But it raises an interesting point, Mrs Holden. Everything is perfectly safe but the tour *does* go through recent war zones. We can talk about this again tomorrow but we do ask our guests to remember that you must be accompanied by myself or some other official representative at all times. That way we can guarantee your safety. Oh, and photographs only where they're permitted.'

'Thank you,' said Dorothea. 'A timely reminder. Now, more questions?'

'Yes, I have one,' said Jack. 'For *Señor* de Armas Gourié. You mentioned that the Republic has destroyed Spain's identity. Can I ask which identity you meant, *Señor*?'

'Yes, of course,' said the Spaniard. 'My country has always been a Monarchy, supported by the Catholic Church. We are a Catholic nation. And over centuries we have fought to make this one country. Strong. United. The Republic has spat on the Church. On the Monarchy. It has given power to the regions so that we are not one country anymore.'

'But doesn't Spain also have a different identity? Liberal and enlightened? The Spain that fought for a democratic constitution? The Spain that recognised the very real individuality of its various parts? The Basque country is a good example, isn't it?'

The Spaniard was about to respond, but Dorothea Holden stopped him.

'Mister Telford,' she said, 'this seems to be a speech rather than a question. Perhaps you might speak with *Señor* de Armas Gourié later about this. I'm sure that he will satisfy you.'

'Then can I ask a more relevant question?' said Jack.

'If you must,' she sighed.

'English newspapers,' Jack said. 'Is it possible that we might receive one or two regularly?'

'Ah,' said Professor Holden, 'you want to know about the crisis. I have a copy of yesterday's *Times* in my room. Nothing to worry about, Mister Telford. The Prime Minister is already back in London but will be trotting off to Germany again next week. He enjoyed a delightful tea party with Herr Hitler apparently. Mister Chamberlain said that he had enjoyed his first experience of air travel and they chatted about the weather, it seems. Whitehall is returning to normal and the markets are getting over their jitters. That's about it, I think.'

'But yes, *Señor*,' said the Spaniard, 'we will make sure that there are English newspapers at your hotels as quickly as possible each day.'

Valerie Carter-Holt lifted her hand, and Jack experienced a moment of consternation, recalling his night's erotic fantasy.

'Yes. Miss Carter-Holt,' said Dorothea.

'You mentioned a couple of surprises, Mrs Holden. Might we know what they are?'

My God, what's happened to her voice? She didn't sound like that on the train. Pretentious bloody woman. Putting on airs and graces for the plebs. All the same, I wouldn't mind betting that these 'surprises' have got something to do with Julia Britten and the nuns.

'Well, I think we should wait a little longer,' Dorothea Holden replied. 'For one thing, we are still waiting for two more members of the group to arrive. And we need *Señor* de Armas Gourié to make our special announcement – but he can't do it just yet. Am I being a terrible tease? Yes, I think I am…' The double doors to the terrace opened slightly and the Hotel Manager's head appeared. He gave a discreet cough. She made a hand gesture in return and Molino pulled the doors together again. Dorothea Holden beamed with pleasure. 'Now,' she said, playing the drama for all that she was worth. '*Who* can tell me the name of General Franco's favourite British film actor?'

It seemed that the whole group was stumped on this one, so Mrs Holden called grandly for *Señor* Molino, who dutifully threw open the doors. The travellers waited in stunned expectation until, finally, they heard the unmistakeable catch-phrase, the famous West Country voice loud and clear.

''Ang about, me 'ansum!'

And the tousled head, the absurdly wide gap-toothed grin of Max Weston appeared from around the door-frame.

The two Sisters of Our Lady of the Holy Light seemed none the wiser, and Valerie Carter-Holt, like Jack and Julia Britten, remained unimpressed, but the others all got to their feet in delighted surprise as the funniest man in England waddled, Chaplin-like, into the reception area, followed by his wife and manager, the almost equally famous Marguerite Weston.

'So, Mister…Telford, isn't it?' said Brendan Murphy, taking the seat next to Jack. 'Did you know beforehand that we were to be honoured with Mister Weston's presence?'

If anybody had told me that I'd be sitting in Spain chatting with one of Franco's Blackshirts about the biggest buffoon in Britain apart from Chamberlain…

'I wouldn't have agreed to come if I'd known.'

Jack watched the Westons. Max with some stupid jokes. Marguerite, a large woman, a seaside postcard bosom, arranging the autographs. Signed photos of the great man. *So,* he thought, *Julia Britten plays concerts for Nazi dictators. The nuns come from a Sanatorium that sends flowers to Hitler. And now Franco's favourite comedian turns up. I think I can see where this is going…*

'That bad?' said Murphy. 'Worse than spending a whole week with our gaggle of fascists, eh?'

'Is that how you think of yourself, Brendan?'

'Not on your fecking life,' whispered the guide. 'I joined Eoin O'Duffy because I'm an active Catholic, Mister Telford, and I couldn't stand by and watch what the Reds were doing to my Faith here. Though there were certainly plenty of hard-core Hitler fanatics in the Bandera.'

'And you think that everything the *Irish Independent* told you was true?'

'No more nor less true than the rubbish fed to the Reds at home by the *Daily Worker*, my friend. Or by *Reynold's News*, eh? We read what we read and choose our sides. I'm proud that I fought for Franco.'

'So what have you read about the International Brigades, Mister Murphy? You implied that they wouldn't be fighting for the Republic much longer.'

'Just a rumour. But the word is that Negrín is going to announce the withdrawal of all foreign troops on their side.'

'Unilaterally? Without a reciprocal arrangement for Franco to kick out the Germans and Italians?' Murphy was non-committal. 'Well,' Jack continued, 'the International Brigades have at least stayed the course better than your Irish Bandera, I suppose. And they won't be sent back in disgrace like O'Duffy's crew, will they?'

'O'Duffy was a fool.'

'But you decided to stay after the rest sailed back to Dublin?' said Jack.

'I didn't have much choice. But it's a long story.'

'And speaking of rumours, Mister Murphy. Did *you* know that Max Weston would be along for the ride? And for what purpose, exactly?'

'Not really my place to say,' smiled the guide. 'And...'

'Ah, *Señor* Telford.' It was the Spaniard. 'You were asking about newspapers. You need more information about the crisis?'

The Westons' circus act was still in full swing.

'To be honest,' Jack replied, 'I was hoping to find out what happened with the Land Speed Record.'

Señor de Armas Gourié seemed perplexed and Brendan Murphy spoke to him in rapid and fluent Spanish.

'Ah!' said the Spaniard. 'You mean Cobb? I can tell you myself. Two days ago, he broke the record. Record, yes? Three hundred, fifty point two miles per hour.'

'My God,' said Jack. 'That's amazing.'

The Spaniard laughed.

'More amazing still, *Señor*,' he said. 'He only hold for one day. Yesterday your George Eyrton beat by another seven miles per hour. But his Thunderbolt twice as heavy than Cobb's Railton, and more than twice as powerful. Best engines in the world. Rolls-Royce V-Twelve.'

'You know your engines then? You race?'

'A little,' said the Spaniard. 'I fly too. I was first President of Royal Flying Club, in Las Palmas.'

'And you have another surprise for us?' said Jack.

'Now, now, *Señor*!' The Spaniard wagged a finger at him.

'Come, come,' shouted Dorothea Holden. 'Shall we discuss arrangements for dinner, and then for tomorrow's departure?' She began to herd the group together and Jack moved to join them, but he was restrained by Brendan Murphy's hand on his arm.

'Mister Telford,' he whispered, 'just a reminder, sir. No wandering off on your own, now. And photographs only where they are permitted.'

'Are you guide or guard, Mister Murphy?'

Murphy smiled at him, released his arm.

'Now,' said Dorothea. 'Dinner! We will be eating at a very nice restaurant.'

'I 'opes they got scrumpy!' called Max Weston. Nora Hames slapped her thighs, tears running down her face, he had made her laugh so much.

'I'm sure they have! But they have also prepared some local delicacies.' Dorothea read from a sheet of paper. '*Bacalao al Pil-Pil.* That's spicy cod, I think. And...What is this, Mister Murphy? *Cocochas*?'

'Yes, ma'am,' said the guide. 'Throats of hake.'

There was a chorus of complaint, expression of distaste, query about decent English food.

'Thank you,' Dorothea continued. 'I'm afraid you may find the food a little different here. But perfectly delightful, once you become accustomed. And for those who prefer their meats, there is Grilled Goat.'

Frances Moorgate looked up with interest. 'Sounds delicious.'

Dorothea smiled. 'But we will also be joined by the Mayor and his good lady wife. And they are bringing one or two friends.' *Probably all the leading lights in the local Falange,* thought Jack. 'So does anybody else have a few words of Spanish. Sister María Pereda, of course. Anybody else?'

Jack decided to keep his limited Spanish to himself but suddenly noticed Sister María looking at him sternly, gesturing surreptitiously for him to raise his hand. He shook his head, feigning ignorance. *Did I speak with her in Spanish? I don't think so but...*

Dorothea Holden had forgotten to mention the currency. She understood that a few people had exchanged money back in Britain and been issued with Republican pesetas. No use in *this* part of Spain, of course. But while she was explaining the process of swapping these for acceptable Burgos notes, a uniformed messenger, a motorcycle army courier, came into the reception area, spoke quietly to the concierge and was pointed towards *Señor* de Armas Gourié. A telegram was delivered and the Spaniard read it quickly, then nodded to Dorothea Holden. She beamed with delight.

'So, no more Spanish speakers then? Very well, let us proceed to some exciting news.' There was a slight buzz of excitement. 'You may have realised that our little group is slightly larger than we might normally expect for this particular Tour, and there are some special reasons for this. Mister Weston was specifically invited, for example, because he is so appreciated in the very highest circles of National Spain's new Government.' More West Country nonsense from the comedian. Dorothea Holden smiled, waited for the obligatory titters to subside. 'Mister Kettering because he is due to receive a medal in honour of his brother's sacrifice.' The Ketterings slumped a little lower in their chairs. 'The good Sisters because they have been chosen to make a very special presentation.' They both sat straighter in their own. 'All of these things will take place at an event when we reach Santiago de Compostela. There we shall be entertained by Miss Britten. Some pieces by Albéniz, I think?' Julia Britten nodded and Nora Hames clapped her hands together. 'But this will also mean we may have to tolerate a slightly more stringent level of security than that to which one is perhaps accustomed. For in Santiago we shall be received by none other than *El Caudillo* himself. Here is the confirmation.' She waved the telegram. 'Captain-General Francisco Franco y Bahamonde. Supreme Leader of the National Movement of Spain.'

Chapter Four

Sunday 18 September 1938

The yellow bull-nosed Dodge school bus was part of the fleet purchased directly from the Chrysler Corporation and shipped to Spain in time for the start of the War Route tours back in July.

Of course, thought Jack, *Franco probably had no more money for these than he had funds to pay the Germans and Italians for their planes and pilots. But no problem for* El Caudillo, *eh? Just let Hitler have the rights to all the Spanish mineral wealth he needs for his arms industry. All the iron, the mercury, the tungsten, the antimony, the pyrites. But what in God's name did Franco give Chrysler for their twenty buses?*

It was standing outside the Hotel Jaúreguí, engine ticking over and driver clutching the steering wheel, gazing through the windscreen with a look of such rapture that it was clear he had now reached the pinnacle of his life's ambition.

For this was no ordinary bus. The distinctive bright yellow had been retained but a sign-writer had carefully painted the name *Badajoz* in blue along the length of the bonnet, while above each of the rear windows a Thermador *Kool Air* cylindrical unit had been fitted.

'Cumbersome but effective, they tell me,' said Albert Moorgate, as they shared a cigarette and admired the vehicle. 'No expense spared, Mister Telford. I understand your question now, by the way.'

'On the train?' Jack replied.

'Yes. Bit of a shock, this business with Franco. Exciting though. And how did you sleep after all that strange food?'

'It was a bit late for me, to be honest,' Jack said, 'but I slept well enough, I suppose. Considering. The food was fine. But all the excitement, as you say. There was a mosquito or something in the room too. I've got a few bites but nothing to worry about. Do you know how they work?'

'Mosquitoes?' said Bertie, and Jack thought that it must be a rare attempt at humour until he realised the bank manager had been distracted by the sight of Marguerite Weston's substantial figure crossing the street towards them.

'No,' said Jack, 'the coolers.'

'Ah, yes. Evaporative coolers. Don't need them much in dear old England, eh? Mrs Weston, good morning. I was just explaining the vehicle's cooling system to Mister Telford.'

'I'll be a'needin' it, an' all,' she replied, mopping her brow. 'Not much room though, be there?'

'It's a good job there's a roof-rack,' said Jack. 'It would be a bit cosy if we had all the luggage inside as well.'

Most of the larger travelling cases and trunks were already stowed in the rack, while the concierge and two local boys struggled with the last of them before fitting and securing a tarpaulin.

Brendan Murphy emerged from the hotel with Professor and Mrs Holden.

'Good morning, gentlemen,' she cried. 'And Mrs Weston. Another fine day, is it not?' In truth, she seemed less than enthusiastic about the comedian's wife, who was still grumbling about last night's meal. 'But where are all the others? We said nine o'clock sharp!'

'Shall I wander back and see what's keeping them, my sweet?' said the Professor.

I can't tell whether the fellow is genuinely deferential towards her or if he's taking the Mickey, thought Jack.

'Yes, Alfred, of course. But don't get lost yourself, will you? He gets easily distracted, you know.'

'Of course, petal. Straight back, eh?'

And he made his strange, bobbing way back across the road, adjusting his blazer as he went and standing aside to let the Sisters of Our Lady of the Holy Light pass.

'Good morning, Sisters,' said Mrs Holden. 'Find seats wherever you like for now. We'll get everybody organised later.'

The nuns climbed aboard, Sister María risking the slightest of smiles to pass conspiratorially between herself and Jack. Then the Ketterings appeared, said hello, and took up two of the front seats.

'You see,' said Dorothea Holden. '*There* is the problem. Once people have sat in the front seats they always think they can keep them for the whole trip. It causes *such* a commotion.'

'Oh, I can imagine,' said Moorgate. 'Ah, here comes my dear wife, at last.'

Frances Moorgate had been irritable at the evening's dinner but she seemed recovered now, her pale gardenia complexion enhanced by the full-skirted black cotton dress and her lips glossed to match. She applied a little more from her jet and gold thread purse.

'I was sayin',' said Marguerite Weston, 'that there's not a lot of room on the bus, Mrs Holden.'

Dorothea looked her up and down. 'No,' she said, 'I suppose not. But we should have just enough to allow you a double seat to yourself, I think. Would that help?'

''Appen it will, too!' said Marguerite and clambered aboard, taking up the remaining front seats, at the driver's back. The Moorgates followed and Julia Britten emerged from the hotel, her elbow held by Nora Hames. More greetings, and they occupied the seats behind the Ketterings while Brendan Murphy and

Dorothea Holden shared grumbling concerns about the time.

Jack decided that he would sit near the pianist and her companion, so climbed aboard after them, said hello to the driver and made his way down the central aisle. At the back, he noticed, the grey moquette seats had been removed apart from one in the middle, to allow room for the Thermidor water reservoirs but also for a bank of red *Coors Beer* travel coolers.

'Free beer, you think?' he said to Albert Moorgate, sitting opposite them and just behind Nora.

'Never touch the stuff,' said the bank manager. 'Gives me wind.'

The town's church bells kept up a discordant note and the street began filling with people, workers mainly but all dressed in good Sunday clothes. Talking loudly they stared at the bus, although it did not seem to be an unusual sight, particularly as the tours ran so often.

Valerie Carter-Holt was next to appear, clutching a box camera. She nodded a greeting to everybody, smiled at Brendan Murphy and sat behind Jack, settling down with a copy of *McCall's*. Then Max Weston at last, sharing a story with Professor Holden. Weston looked about for a seat, almost ignoring his wife.

'Sit down, Max,' she snapped at him. 'Or we'll never get goin'!'

The comedian performed a couple of the Morris dancing steps that he had made famous in the film. Jack had seen it, of course. He could still remember sitting in the packed cinema, the only member of the audience, it seemed, who found nothing funny about the thing.

''Appen you should lighten up, me 'ansum,' Weston said to him, nudging Jack in the ribs as he took the seat alongside him.

Jack smiled, and Brendan Murphy took up the makeshift dickie between the coolers.

'Very good, driver,' shouted Dorothea Holden. '*Adelante!*' There was a strident complaint from the three-speed box, a jarring crash as the straight-cut gears attempted to mesh, and the bus lurched forward, Dorothea grabbing for the overhead strap to steady herself. 'Well, good morning again, ladies and gentlemen. I hope you enjoyed yesterday evening as much as *we* did. And such charming company!' *Oh charming*, thought Jack. *Must have been every leading fascist in the town.* 'But this is the start of the tour itself, of course. A very full day ahead of us. Which is why I *must* stress, once again, the need for punctuality. Today, for example, we are going to visit Irún itself. Now, *Señor* de Armas Gourié sends his best regards, by the way, and may rejoin us when we reach San Sebastián. Meanwhile, in a few minutes, I think that Mister Murphy will explain the background to the Battle for Irún. Is that correct, Mister Murphy? Yes, good. And then we have been invited to join a special church commemoration service. Mister Murphy will give us the details.'

Albert Moorgate raised his hand from the seat immediately in front of her.

'It's RC, I imagine?' he said.

'A Roman Catholic service? Yes, of course.'

'Ah! We are C of E, Frances and myself.'

'Yes, Mister Moorgate,' said Dorothea, plainly perplexed. 'I'm sure that several others on the trip are likewise. But we are only asked to observe the proceedings. We shan't find an Anglican service, I'm afraid. And this is a Sunday, after all.'

'What if we are expected to...Well, join in?' he replied. He placed a finger inside his collar, easing it away from his reddening neck.

Poor Bertie, thought Jack. *Whatever does he imagine they will force him to do?*

'Well,' said Dorothea, 'I'm sure that nobody will be offended if members of the group choose not to attend the service itself. That's right, isn't it, Mister Murphy?'

'Yes, ma'am,' said Brendan. 'But I'll need to make some separate arrangements. Nobody goes off on their own, remember? Don't worry about it though. We'll sort it out once we're in Irún. Just a few minutes now.'

An anxious few minutes, however. All eyes were averted as they passed two men, neatly peeling the intact skin from a dead calf suspended below a tree branch. Then they all lurched forward as Mikel stamped on the brake pedal, narrowly avoiding a donkey cart that had swung in front of them from a dirt-track side road. The horn blared. Mikel swore, first to himself, then to the old man on the cart. The old man swore back, frantic with rage. The guide restored order, and the bus eventually continued along the dusty highway.

'Good,' said Dorothea, checking that her hair was still in place. 'Well, what can I say? Anybody hurt? No? Right, then after church it's coffee and a tour of the city. At least, what passes for coffee in Spain these days. Then a meeting with the Mayor at the Town Hall. Lunch there too. Afterwards, a visit to some of the Red defensive positions south of the town before we run on to San Sebastián. Very nice hotel. Good dinner. Plenty of time to relax.'

'And dinner a bit earlier tonight?' said Nora Hames.

'Oh,' said Mrs Holden, 'it's that Spanish thing. They eat at the most uncivilised hours. But yes, we'll try to bring dinner forward. Now, anything else?' Marguerite made another unsuccessful bid for some plain English cooking. 'Ah!' Dorothea ignored her. 'The seating arrangements. What would you think about more or less sharing the seats as presently but rotating around the bus clockwise each day? That way, by the end of the week, everybody should have had the chance to enjoy the front seats. Mister Murphy, I assume, will keep his seat at the back?'

Yes, he would indeed. And the passengers were generally agreed, although it did not prevent Dorothea from a lengthy description of how the rotation system would work in practice.

'So, tomorrow Mrs Weston will move across to here. Mister and Mrs Kettering will move back...'

'Well, Miss Britten,' said Jack, leaning forward and ignoring Max Weston's attempts to confuse Dorothea's calculations, 'we are to hear your Albéniz then? When we were on the train I thought you had some darker secret.'

'Well, we were not so intimately acquainted then, Mister Telford. And it's not always easy to explain that one is favoured by so many of Europe's Axis rulers.'

'She gets *hate* mail, Jack,' said Nora. 'Can you believe it? How do people expect her to make a living if she picks and chooses where to perform?'

'If war comes,' said Jack, 'it will all become much simpler, I suppose.'

'Oh, don't say such a thing,' said Nora, her small features wrinkling in disgust. '*Nobody* wants war, do they?'

'Well, they seem to be making a decent fist of it here. And the Germans and Italians wouldn't be rehearsing so hard unless they had a full-blown concert in mind, I imagine.'

'And where do you stand on the matter, Mister Telford?' said Julia Britten. 'An anti-appeasement man, I suppose, from your paper's editorials.' She sensed his unspoken query. 'It is Nora's job to read the newspapers carefully to me for a spell each day.'

'Then I clip any articles about dear Julia,' said Nora. 'We've got quite a scrap book now.'

'You must let me see it some time. But anti-appeasement? My own stance is purely anti-war, Miss Britten.'

'And isn't an accommodation with Herr Hitler the way to ensure peace?' said Julia.

'People accuse me of over-simplifying. But Hitler is a bully, hungry for more power. I never knew a bully yet whose nature was soothed by accommodating his demands.'

'Oh,' said Julia. 'He didn't seem like a bully at all when I met him. He was charming. But I suppose that's no real way to judge. Have you met him yourself, Mister Telford? And if we don't accommodate the Chancellor, will that not also lead to war?'

'I was in Germany for a while,' said Jack, 'but I never met him. And, to be honest, if I thought anti-appeasement would lead to war, I'd be against that as well. No, I think there must be a third way. A more united front against Hitler and Mussolini. Economic sanctions to stop their worst excesses.'

'That would work, d'you think?' Julia said. 'I do hope so. You might take exception to those who enjoy my music, Mister Telford, but I assure you that I do not necessarily share their politics.'

They were entering the outskirts of Irún, the driver hammering at the horn to scatter a score of chickens from the rubbled road.

'So,' shouted Max Weston, 'what sort of bird lays electric eggs?'

'Ooooh...' said Nora, searching hard for the answer.

'Battery 'ens!' said Max.

Dorothea Holden looked puzzled.

'It's a new thing, my petal,' said the Professor. 'You keep the birds in cages. Sloping floors. Eggs roll gently to the front for collection. Interesting book on the subject by Milton Arndt...'

The bus had passed some fire-blackened apartment blocks but came to a halt at the end of a broad open square, the arched façade of Irún's Town Hall at the far side, the now familiar flag of National Spain flying from its upper storey. It was just after nine-thirty but the sun was already strong and Brendan Murphy suggested they gather in the shade that the bus provided.

'Well, ladies and gentlemen,' he began, 'good morning again. I hope you all slept well. Yes? That's grand, sure. Now, we've arrived in Irún and, as you know, we're just across from the French border here. So imagine that we're back in '36. Spain has been taken over by the Reds...'

'You mean, I think, that a Popular Front coalition had won the General Election in February of that year, Mister Murphy,' said Jack.

'A coalition of lefties, communists and freemasons, Mister Telford,' Brendan replied. 'Like I say, Spain had been taken over by the Reds.'

'But the Popular Front had a mandate to govern...'

'They may have won by a handful of votes but they had no mandate for an atheist revolution. Within weeks the country was crippled by strikes. With workers demanding higher wages. And the unions setting up armed militias everywhere. It was like Russia in 'Seventeen. The Church repressed. Bolsheviks in control. Assassinations taking place. The forces of law and order had to take charge. And they asked their most loyal army officers to lead the Reconquest. General Sanjurjo. General Mola. General Franco.'

'The French call that a *coup d'état*, I think.'

'And I think, Mister Telford,' said Dorothea Holden, 'that we are all capable of putting our own interpretation on these things. *Most* of us would like to hear what Mister Murphy has to say.'

'Quite right, my dear,' said the Professor, and Jack saw that several of the other group members were also nodding their agreement. He let it go.

'Thank you, ma'am,' said Murphy. 'Well, as I'm sure you all know, poor General Sanjurjo was killed in a plane crash, but *El Caudillo* had soon established a strong base in the south-west, based on Sevilla, and General Mola in the north, based on Burgos.' *Which means, Brendan my lad,* thought Jack, *that at least half the army failed to support these military plotters and they ended up without a single one of Spain's principal cities.* 'Now, as I said, we are here on the French border and the Reds were being constantly supplied with arms by their comrades in France itself. In addition, this is Basque country. Many of the people that we'll meet over the next few days are proud to call themselves Basques, but *they* are good and loyal people. Not to be confused with those who wanted to create a separate country here. Of all the traitors in Spain, the Basque Nationalists are the worst. Because they, professing themselves to be good Catholics, conspired with the atheists – yes, ladies and gentlemen, with the *atheists* – to set up their own independent state.'

Poor Brendan. He's genuinely astonished that such creatures as atheists can possibly exist. How strange it must be to have Faith like that.

'So General Mola devised a daring plan that would serve three purposes. He would thrust up across the hills and mountains of Navarra to cut off the Basque traitors from the French. At the same time this would stop the flow of illicit arms across the border. And, third, it would cut off the north coast from the rest of the territory still held by the Reds and allow its liberation. Without the capture of Irún, the reconquest of the North might not have happened.'

'When you say *liberation*, Mister Murphy,' said Nora Hames, 'from whom do you mean?'

'From the Reds, ma'am.'

'But I don't understand how these Reds came to be here. Oh, am I asking stupid questions? It's my age, I think.'

'Not at all, Miss Hames,' said Brendan. 'They were already here, you see? Spanish people, but traitors who'd been infiltrated. Led astray by Marxists and Freemasons.'

'So they were liberated from themselves then?'

'Yes, in a way. Just as Our Lord was sent to liberate Mankind from its sins.'

Dorothea Holden shone her most patronising smile upon Nora Hames, though the old woman still seemed puzzled.

'But this General Mola wasn't the Lord Jesus, *was* he?'

Dorothea glowered at Jack as though, somehow, he had encouraged Nora's questions, her impertinence.

'Really, Miss Hames,' she said, 'we *must* get on. Time is so very short. Please, Mister Murphy. We have to be at the church by ten, I think?'

'And what about the C of Es, Mrs Holden?' said Albert Moorgate.

'All sorted out, sir,' said Murphy. 'Well, on the eleventh of August, General Mola sent one of his finest officers, Major Beorloguí, to drive a wedge between San Sebastián,' he pointed away to the west, 'and Irún. The town was defended by about three thousand Reds, anarchist militiamen, Asturian miners, Basque separatists, and a gang of French communists. Beorleguí's force was smaller. Much smaller. But it included some artillery, some light tanks, and a Bandera from the Spanish Foreign Legion.'

The Ketterings looked particularly interested at this mention of the Legion.

'Do you know if Peter served here?' said Catherine Kettering.

'I don't, ma'am, but it's likely that he did. The Legion fought bravely here. And they had air support too.'

'These tanks and planes,' said Jack. 'A purely military question, Mrs Holden, but were they German by any chance?'

'I believe so,' said Brendan Murphy. 'Yes, almost certainly. But as you'll see, the Reds left this city a burning ruin when they finally abandoned it. By then it was the middle of September. The battle had lasted four weeks. Poor Major Beorloguí had sacrificed his life in the process too. Shot by some cowardly Red snipers as they fled across the river to France.'

And the dead, of course, thought Jack, *must be venerated. The symbols of martyrdom. Look at them. One mention of some named individual and Brendan's job is half done already. We're all suckers for it. Nobody would take the name of the dead in vain, would they? The dead are sacred. Impartial. Unbiased. So Franco runs his tours on the strength of them. And just being able to run them shows that the Nationalists are legitimate. Winning, damn them!*

'Now,' said Dorothea Holden, 'I think I'm right in saying that the town was finally liberated on the fourteenth of September. And it so happens that today the local people are celebrating the second anniversary of their freedom. At the church of Santa María del Juncal. It's the reason we've been invited, I believe. Is it far, Mister Murphy?'

'No, ma'am. Five minutes, no more. If I lead the way, we can talk as we walk and I can explain the arrangements for those who don't want to attend the service.'

In fact, Brendan had decided not to attend the service himself. He had already been to Mass, he said, and would therefore spend some time with the Moorgates. He showed them a bar which served half-decent coffee, in the square and alley that led down to the church. They all agreed to meet there at eleven. He would watch for them coming out. He introduced Dorothea Holden to a priest on the fringes of the crowd that had gathered outside the column-flanked entrance.

It was a solemn gathering, almost silent by Spanish standards. All men out here, no women. Either young, early twenties, or an older generation, past fifty. But Jack noted that there seemed to be very few of middle-age. Most wore dark suits, hats and a profusion of berets while many were dressed in black jackets, polished Sam Browne shoulder belts and holsters, red berets in place of the normal black. And a visible tremor ran through them as the procession of officiates appeared from the side of the building. The crowd parted to form a passage. Eager hands shot out in Nazi salutes.

The group was ushered to pews inside and Jack saw that Brendan Murphy had left them now. The Moorgates too, of course. They were each provided with a Missal, and Jack gave the order of service a cursory glance whilst peering along their own row, past Julia Britten and Nora Hames, past the Holdens, to where Valerie Carter-Holt stood. She was dressed in a simple summer suit, navy blue with a discreet white trim. A beret too, a shade darker than her suit. But it was the medal that drew attention, of course. The Red Cross of Military Merit on its white and red ribbon. *The perfect Falangist, Miss Carter-Holt!*

As the service progressed, Jack managed to take a few notes for later. He was no stranger to Catholic Mass but he had no true interest in the proceedings. So through the reverences to the altar, the greeting, the Act of Penitence, he conjured up the forms of words that he might use for his article until, at last, the *Agnus Dei* was sung and Communion distributed to the congregation, with the Ketterings, the two nuns and Nora Hames going forward to accept the flesh and blood of Christ.

More prayers and a few brief announcements, thanks given for the city's deliverance. The concluding Rites, the retiring procession and then filing out into the dazzling sunshine again. Blessings from the Archbishop, more fascist salutes.

Jack saw the black uniform of Brendan Murphy hovering on the edge of his vision, up the steps, near the bar. He declined a *cafe con leche*, opting instead for the tiny thick concoction that Brendan had selected. It was a well-known fact, said the guide, that the English could not stomach anything except the weakest coffee. But given the shortages here, beggars could not be choosers.

'*¡Vale, guapo!*' said the woman who delivered the drinks to his table. She smiled at him.

'*Guapo*?' Jack enquired when she had gone.

'It means *handsome*,' said Murphy. Jack looked at the woman with fresh eyes. 'But I think she says that to *all* the lads.'

'Your Spanish is excellent,' said Jack.

'There were times at the Front, I reckoned that if you couldn't speak the lingo, you'd never get to eat. And you, Mister Telford? You speak a bit?'

'No, none at all. Just *gracias* and *adiós*'

'Only thanks and goodbye, is it?' said Brendan. 'Well, that's polite at least, sure.' Then he raised his voice so that the rest of the group could hear. 'Shall we get going in, say, five minutes?'

The waitress, assisted by Murphy, showed people to the toilets and Jack finished his coffee before venturing a comment to Carter-Holt.

'It was a nice touch,' he said. 'Wearing the medal, I mean.'

'Are you being ironic, Mister Telford?' She swept the beret from her head, ran fingers through the dark waves, then scratched gently at one of the thick eyebrows that described a curving arch on her long forehead. Her voice, he thought, had returned to the way he recalled it from the train too.

'Oh, I can safely leave all the irony to Brendan Murphy on this trip, I think,' said Jack. 'No, I meant it. You wear Franco's honour with pride. And you can call me Jack.'

'Because we're colleagues, you mean? You write for *Reynold's Weekly*, Mister Telford. It is a Sunday entertainment sheet, owned entirely by the Co-operative Movement on behalf of the Labour Party.'

'And your own writing is impartial, I suppose? Is that why you were accredited by the Nationalists?'

'Mister Telford,' said Carter-Holt patiently, 'I am a Reuters correspondent. There is no news agency in the world, no newspaper either, which so scrutinises the work of its journalists to ensure balance in their copy. I could not pretend to impartiality in Teruel last winter so I wrote exactly and only what I observed with my own eyes. They were descriptive reports. They almost cost me my life. But I was always certain that, whatever I wrote, line for line, word for word almost, would be matched by a similar report from a colleague correspondent over in the Republican lines. Might I venture to ask who it is that's writing the reverse side of your presumably left-biased account of our excursion, Mister Telford?'

She stressed his surname, stood and joined the toilet queue.

Well, that went better than you expected, Jack.

He smoked a *Capstan* while he waited, glanced at the notes he had made in the church.

Is she right? he wondered. From Worcester Grammar School he had won a scholarship to the Owens College of Manchester University. With its strong links to the Mechanics' Institute, the politics of the faculty were certainly Left-wing, and Jack had been sucked into flirtations with various groupings, largely through his editorial responsibilities for the college magazine and, later, through his Presidency of the Esperanto Movement. He had graduated with a First Class Degree in History, and then gone to London University where he studied for a Diploma of Journalism, the only one then available in Britain. He had been forced to read every cynical comment ever written on the subject. By Twain, Chesterton, Wilde, Schopenhauer, Yeats. It was difficult to find a *positive* opinion about his chosen profession. But it was Thomas Jefferson's simple epigraph that he wrote in the front of every note-book. *'Whenever people are well-informed, they can be trusted with their own government.'* He should have known better. For that which had seemed such a trite one-liner at University had haunted him ever since with all its contradictions.

Brendan Murphy gathered them together, a collie snapping at the heels of his flock.

'So,' he began, 'you've already seen the inside of the Parish Church. It's impressive, isn't it? Parts of the building date back to the sixteenth century but most of it is later.'

He led them back up Calle Sarasate, towards the Town Hall, then turned into the Calle Mayor, heading west, with damaged buildings on either side and, frequently, yawning spaces left where some had been demolished entirely. There were a few, built of solid stone that, though smeared with soot, at least retained their shell.

'What a terrible waste,' said Nora Hames. 'I imagine it must once have been very beautiful.'

'Indeed, ma'am. But the Reds are no respecters of property. Of history or culture neither.'

'But why would they burn their own town?' said Nora.

'It's a mystery to me too, ma'am,' said Brendan. 'But they are natural arsonists. You'll see the same wherever we go this week. Here, when they knew the battle was lost, they fired the town and then swam across the Bidasoa into France.'

'Perhaps,' ventured Albert Moorgate, 'they took a leaf from the citizens of Moscow in 1812. Eh, my dear?' He turned to his wife. 'She is quite the expert on all things Napoleonic.'

'The Russians, I think,' said Professor Holden, 'were practising a scorched earth policy in order to prevent much-needed supplies falling into the hands of French invaders. A very different situation. In any case, there is a real controversy amongst academics…'

But the tour had already moved on and by the time they had returned to the Town Hall, Nora Hames was complaining of the heat. She looked exhausted, but Brendan Murphy made one final stop at the Column of San Juan de Harria, erected to commemorate the valour of the townsfolk in defending themselves against their invaders and thus securing liberation from the French.

'It's such a beautiful country,' said Dorothea. 'You can't help but feel for the Spanish. They've had to free themselves so many times from so many that would enslave them. The Moors. The French...'

'The French on more than one occasion too, my petal,' said the Professor.

'Yes. And then the Reds.'

'The landowners too?' offered Jack.

'Oh, *please*, Mister Telford!' said Valerie Carter-Holt. She had assumed that exaggerated upper-class tone again, Jack noticed. 'May we take photos here, Mister Murphy?'

'Indeed, miss,' said Brendan. 'Now, would you like me to take one of yourself, sure?'

She seemed surprised by the question, looked down at the camera.

'Well no,' she said. 'But thanks awfully for the offer, all the same.'

The return to the Town Hall, just a few steps across the *plaza*, was punctuated by Brendan's explanations that the ruins around the outside of the square were all the result of the fire. It was due simply to the grace of God, apparently, that the eighteenth century *ayuntamiento* itself had survived.

The party was met with great ceremony at the main door by the Mayor and they were led into a small room on the ground floor where a photographic display demonstrated the devastation caused by the Reds. As they would see, said the Mayor, much had already been done to repair the damage but there remained such a task ahead of them. They had a fund, naturally.

Jack examined the snaps. A group of Carlist *Requetés* receiving benediction from a priest before their attack. The Civil War's press coverage had made these fiercely Catholic fighters instantly recognisable. And there were photos too of once tall apartment blocks, now merely burned-out shells. The sepia-shaded city burning, taken from across the river. Troops in tasselled forage caps searching houses.

The Ketterings stood whispering together in front of this particular batch, Catherine's slender finger tracing a path across the faces of marching soldiers as she searched for some familiar feature.

'Spanish Foreign Legion?' said Jack.

She jumped, startled.

'Yes, it looks like,' said Peter Kettering, taking his wife by the shoulders.

'You think that your brother was here then?'

Peter Kettering said *no* at precisely the moment his wife said *yes*. They smiled weakly at each other, looked apologetically at Jack.

The Mayor was deep in conversation with Sisters María Pereda and Berthe Schultz while, near the door, a heated exchange was taking place between Julia Britten and Max Weston.

'If you please, Mister Weston,' Jack heard her whisper, 'just a *little* decorum, if we may!'

'Aye, Max. Give it a rest, will 'e?' snarled Marguerite.

Weston can't resist it, can he? thought Jack. *But it's hard to blame him. A whole week of this stuff and we'll all be suicide cases.* The word had escaped its box before he even knew it. That hurtful word. The pain of the abandoned child.

Brendan began to interpret again. The Mayor was showing them a photo of a school that had recently been built. There were so many *analfabetos*, the illiterate, in town. But the Government of National Spain had begun to deal with the crisis, of course. Restored the links between education and the Catholic Church. And Sister Berthe Schultz responded with a glowing account of the Führer's own education programme, the value of the Hitler Youth.

Upstairs, an elaborate lunch was arranged for them. Rice and fish. A suckling pig. Cheeses from the region. Apart from the rice, it was all so much more familiar. But there were wines and *refrescos* too. Further speeches. From the Mayor, the Archbishop, the Minister.

''Ere,' said Max Weston, when the pork was finally served and he himself was restored to his normal affability, 'there was this old farmer and 'is wife in our village. One day, the old woman remembers they be married almost fifty years, so she says to 'e, *It's our anniversary next week, me 'ansum. Let's kill the pig!* But 'e just scratches 'is head, see? *I don't know about that*, 'e says. *Why should the poor old pig 'ave to take the blame for what 'appened fifty years ago?*'

But even this gem did nothing to revive poor Nora Hames. She looked entirely exhausted and Julia Britten was clearly concerned about her.

'Perhaps she'd feel better on the bus,' suggested Jack. 'She could rest for a while before we carry on.'

Julia thought that it was a good idea, although Nora herself insisted that nobody should fuss over her.

'I can't possibly leave poor Julia,' she said.

'I managed perfectly well,' Julia Britten replied, 'all the time that I was in Austria. Somebody will see me back safely, Nora, I'm sure.'

Even Brendan Murphy agreed that the old woman did not look good and, yes, there was no problem if Mister Telford wanted to escort her. They had passed the bus already, waiting at the far side of the *plaza*. Jack promised that he would take Nora directly to the vehicle and would stay with her, thankful for an excuse himself to escape the Town Hall.

Nora Hames protested all the way back across the square, between protestations about what a good boy he was, but Jack was more taken with the yellow bus itself.

More precisely, he was taken with the driver. He was about Jack's age and had seemed permanently afflicted with a wide grin. A mop of brown hair fell across the left side of his face. But the grin had disappeared now, that was certain, for he was standing in front of the Dodge's bonnet, deeply engaged in an intense argument with a coarse man, heavily stubbled chin and cheeks, a striped suit, a shirt with no collar.

'Oh dear,' said Nora, clinging tightly to Jack's arm. 'I don't like the look of *that* chap! He seems a real *desperado*. Do you think our luggage is quite safe, Jack?'

'Yes, I'm sure everything's fine. Probably just some beggar.'

But there was an air of menace about the man that belied Jack's words.

The pair had not initially seen Nora and Jack approach but, when they did, the stranger fixed them with an insolent stare, turned again to the driver, prodding him once with a finger to his chest. Then, pushing his hands deep into his trouser pockets, the man set off into the neighbouring streets with all the appearance that it was he, and not the Mayor, that ruled Irún.

Chapter Five

Sunday 18 September 1938

The driver's habitual smile had returned by the time Jack and Nora reached the bus, but his expression was nervous, edgy.

'Everything OK?' said Jack. '*Bien*?'

'*Sí, Señor.*' The man shrugged, pushed the hair from his eyes, tugged at the front of his blue uniform shirt. '*¡No pasa nada!*'

Jack nodded. So it was all fine. He handed Nora Hames up the step with some difficulty, worried for a moment that the heat inside might be too much for her. But no, she assured him, she was just happy to sit for a while. Perhaps forty winks. But not before she had powdered her nose, taking an ancient compact from her handbag.

He returned to the driver, noticing a newspaper on the dashboard.

'*¿Se puede?*' Jack asked, picking up the copy. May I?

The driver shrugged again and Jack offered him a *Capstan*, lit it for him. The driver coughed, made a chopping gesture with his right hand in appreciation of the tobacco's strength.

'*¿Cómo se llama?*' Jack asked.

The driver beamed, something simple about him, a delighted puppy.

'Mikel,' he said.

'Mikel,' Jack repeated, careful to mimic the sound as accurately as he could.

The driver smiled and Jack returned to his seat with the paper. Nora Hames was already dozing so he sat quietly and studied the front page. It was the *ABC*. Monarchist he thought. Anti-Republican. And this was a Sevilla edition.

Why Sevilla? I must remember to ask Murphy.

The front page confirmed the price, at twenty *céntimos*, but was otherwise entirely taken up by an etching of Mussolini, arm raised in fascist salute and a legend confirming that the *Duce* was due to speak at some gathering in Trieste.

And then headlines that Jack, with some difficulty, could translate as:

> *Chamberlain and Lord Runciman report in detail to the British Cabinet on their trips to Germany and Czechoslovakia. French Ministers will travel to London today to consult with Chamberlain.*

He looked up to see his fellow-travellers coming back across the square but all was evidently not well. The Holdens were remonstrating with Marguerite Weston about something while Max tried to placate her and received a slap to the face for his troubles. The Ketterings, meanwhile, were escorting a distraught Julia Britten to the bus, and the nuns, Valerie Carter-Holt too, seemed entirely above the whole situation, climbing aboard without any comment. Simply a smile for Brendan Murphy.

The disturbance woke Nora Hames, however, who instantly began to fuss about her 'poor lamb.'

'I am perfectly fine, Nora,' Julia insisted as she took her seat. 'I merely trod on Mrs Weston's foot. A simple accident but the damned woman seems to have taken the matter personally, as though I had chosen to injure her deliberately.'

'Some folks should mind where they be steppin',' shouted Marguerite, taking her seat again at the front.

Nora had to be physically restrained from going forward to give the woman a good thrashing and Jack decided that, despite the old lady being half Marguerite's size and twice her age, his money would probably go on Miss Hames if the bout ever occurred. Max, meanwhile, had politely asked whether he might sit by the window. *As far from his wife as possible*, thought Jack and stood in the aisle to let him through, wondering whether he should tell Brendan Murphy or the Holdens about the insolent-looking fellow who had been harassing Mikel. But, in the end, Nora Hames took the decision from his hands.

'He was a surly brute,' she exclaimed, once she had been diverted from thinking about Marguerite Weston and had recalled the earlier incident. 'Thank goodness Jack was able to see him off!'

'I did absolutely nothing,' Jack protested, while Murphy questioned the driver.

'Mikel says he was just a local beggar looking for tobacco,' said Brendan.

'Well,' said Nora, 'I've never seen a beggar physically assault somebody when they simply wanted a cigarette!' She continued to give a lurid account of the man and Mikel accepted that he had been prodded, but insisted that the beggar was drunk and best ignored.

Murphy looked far from well but, once everybody was settled again, he stood by the driver to make his announcement.

'Ladies and gentlemen,' he said. 'We'll head to San Sebastián now, but we'll drive south first, on our way out of town, to the Puntza Ridge where our soldiers fought for a week to capture the Reds' positions. Did everybody enjoy lunch?'

Yes, they all agreed, although Dorothea Holden thought that, in future, it might be best to have the political speeches, important though they certainly were, *after* the food rather than before.

'Oy,' said Max Weston. 'There be this busload o' politicians, see, drivin' down a lane when suddenly they runs off the road and crashes into a ditch. The old farmer sees the whole thing an' goes to investigate. 'E digs this big 'ole and buries the politicians. Driver too. A few days later, the local constable comes past, sees the crashed bus and asks the old boy where all them politicians be gone. The old farmer tells 'im that 'e buried 'em. The constable says, "Lord in 'Eaven, be they ALL dead, then?" The old farmer says, "Well, some of them *said* they wasn't, but you knows what them crooked politicians be like."'

'I *hope* you're not implying...' said Dorothea Holden.

The bus climbed a narrow, bone-rattling route into the hills beyond Irún while Sister Schultz maintained a monotone monologue towards the younger nun who responded only the occasional *Ja, Schwester Berthe Schultz* or *Nein, Schwester Berthe Schultz.*

Max Weston's full-moon face stared amiably, vacantly, at the scenery while his fat fingers tapped out a beat upon the hand-rail at the back of Nora's seat, keeping time to the tune that he whistled through the considerable gap between his front teeth. The tune, Jack realised was *Three Blind Mice.*

'So, Mister Weston,' he said, anxious only to stop him as quickly as possible. 'You have another film planned?'

Jack learned, without any true interest whatsoever that Weston's wife was indeed in the process of negotiating a contract with Ealing for their third film. The title was likely to be *Mexican Max* and would take the hapless character off on holiday to Jack Dempsey's Hotel Playa in Ensenada, with most of the action taking place in the heavyweight boxer's world-famous casino. Dempsey was apparently thrilled with the idea and had met Marguerite in person to discuss the possibilities. Well, a few times, actually.

Now, what was that look, Max? Jealousy? Or are you really as stupid as you seem? And what about all these rumours that Capone is Dempsey's partner in the casino business? Maybe if Marguerite could arrange to get him out of Alcatraz for a couple of weeks, Alphonse could put in a guest appearance. A cameo role, maybe.

The bus wound its way up a mountain pass and halted where the track widened slightly. There was a steep drop below them.

'So,' said Brendan Murphy when they had all gathered in the shade of some sweet-scented pines, 'we're on the side of Mount Zubeltzu, just above the Puntza Ridge.'

'I think I saw this on the Pathé News, Mister Murphy,' said Nora Hames. 'Would that be correct?'

'Most likely, ma'am. It was a heroic struggle. Beorloguí pushed the Reds off the ridge, all except for the Convent over there. Twice, as it happens. But each time the Reds counter-attacked. The third time it was the same story. The Reds were driven back but held on to the Convent. In the end, some *Requetés*, our Carlist troops, had to storm the place. The Reds were just about out of ammunition by then, so took to throwing rocks and sticks of dynamite instead.' Murphy snorted in derision.

'Well,' said Nora Hames, 'that sounds very brave of them *too.* How many soldiers were defending the Convent, Mister Murphy? Do you know?'

'Oh, they weren't soldiers, Miss Hames. Not proper soldiers anyway. A mixed rabble of militiamen and miners, ma'am.'

'And they fought off General Mola's tanks for a whole week? My goodness!'

'Well,' said Murphy, 'it's hard to deploy tanks in mountainous terrain like this. No, it was the bravery of the Carlists that finally drove them out. Bayonets against dynamite, Miss Hames.'

Nora muttered something about sticks and stones, while the guide reminded them of the battle's aftermath. The Red arsonists, he said, had fallen back on Irún and fired the town before fleeing across the Bidasoa into France. And Beorloguí, of course, had been cruelly killed, just before realising the fruits of his victory. Like Sir John Moore at Coruña, he stressed.

The group was invited to spend a few moments enjoying the panorama, and Jack moved to the back of the bus so that he could enjoy a *Capstan* in peace. Slowly, the article that he must write for the paper was coming together in his mind, but needed a lot more work. He noticed the Ketterings just ahead of him, climbing down a path into the trees.

They'll be in big trouble with Brendan if they wander off, he thought. *Better warn them.*

But as he reached the top of the path, Jack saw that they had stopped. He was about to climb down and join them, feeling a bit guilty that he had not yet spent more time with the couple, but they also seemed to be taking advantage of their momentary privacy.

'Well, was he here, d'you think?' Kettering was saying.

'I *know* he was, Can't you feel it?'

'Not really. We shouldn't have come, Cath,' he replied.

'Yes we should! But, God, I am *so* afraid now.'

'Me too,' said Peter. 'We'd better get back though. We'll have that fascist bloodhound on our trail if we're not careful.'

'Hey, you two!' called Jack, as though he had just come up. 'I think we're on the move again.'

'I was just saying to Catherine,' Kettering called back, 'that Mister Murphy will have a search party out looking for us.'

It was only about ten miles from the ridge to San Sebastián, but the descent was marked by Mikel's personal struggle to maintain second gear, using it to reduce speed on the tight bends.

'Good driver,' said Albert Moorgate. 'Drums will seize up if he's not careful.'

At that moment, Mikel also applied the hand-operated prop shaft brake so that he and his passengers jolted back and forth in unison, synchronised metronomes to the engine's rumba rhythm, and it took some time for the bus to negotiate the treacherous descent before reaching the village of Sagasti and heading west, past a farm of bulls clearly bred for the *Corrida*, for bullfighting.

Rural Spain, thought Jack. *The French countryside looked poor enough. But it was positively prosperous compared to here.*

'Why did the bull rush?' said Max Weston. No answer. 'Because 'e saw the cow slip!'

'You've been reading *ABC*,' said Brendan as he passed Jack's seat to have a word with Mikel. 'I thought you didn't have any Spanish?'

'Oh, I don't,' Jack replied. 'Just looking at the pictures. But tell me, Brendan. *ABC* is printed in Sevilla?'

'It's a bit more confusing than that,' Brendan smiled. 'The paper was always printed in Madrid so the offices are now in the hands of the Reds. It's a scandal. They've turned it into a Republican rag. But there's also been a Sevilla edition for a long time too. So the owners decided they'd shift their operations *there*, give the southern edition a more national flavour. Printed in Sevilla, naturally.'

Jack turned to page nine.

'They specialise in illustrated news?' he said.

'To be sure,' said Brendan. 'They employ some fine artists. Photographers too.'

'German, it seems,' said Jack. 'I've never seen such clear aerial photography.'

'Technology, Mister Telford. A wonderful thing, sure.'

'You think it's possible to pinpoint bombing on military targets alone then?'

'Well!' said Brendan. 'You worked that out just by looking at the pictures?'

'Intelligent guesswork, Mister Murphy. I'm in the business, remember?'

The guide looked at him, calculating, ducked his head to peer through the windscreen as the bus lurched on the uneven road, but effectively bringing his face close alongside Jack's own.

'War kills all manner of innocents, Mister Telford. It tends to disillusion folk though, if you talk about it too loudly, do you not think?'

'War disillusions everybody but those with the blindest faith – and thank God for it!'

'You think so?' said Brendan. 'Then why do we keep doing it? And so readily too. We'll have the whole of Europe at war again before long unless people see sense and allow the Führer to take those Sudeten Germans into the Reich. With the Bolsheviks massing on the Ukrainian border to stop him, Europe needs to make up its mind which side it's on.'

'It sounds like more innocents die whichever of your two choices we take. And which side will *you* be on, Brendan, if it *does* come?'

'Well, that depends which side *England* is on, does it not? And only the very safe or the very naive think there's a third choice, Mister Telford. No offence, mind.'

Oh, none taken, thought Jack, as Murphy continued down the bus. *Interesting little threat though, if that's what he intended.*

They crossed and re-crossed the railway, bounced through the potholes of several villages, drab industrial areas, over a river into the dull-looking town of Rentería, a large harbour, fishing boats. Then uphill, through the eastern suburbs of San Sebastián itself.

So, thought Jack. *The Ketterings. Peter thinks they shouldn't have come, and Catherine is afraid? Of what, for God's sake? How very odd.*

'Ladies and gentlemen,' Brendan announced, 'welcome to San Sebastián.

The city *has* been burned in the past, but not by the Reds on this occasion. No, it was the English, when they took it back from the French in 1813. The Duke of Wellington's army looted the place for a full week, and the fires that they started destroyed everything except two churches and thirty-five houses.'

'But the Duke,' said Frances Moorgate, 'was not here in person, was he? And, overall, the Spanish recognise the huge role played by Wellington, surely, during the Peninsular War – their War of Independence?'

'Which makes the point, Mrs Moorgate, that the most well-intentioned actions in war can sometimes go wrong. We must always keep our eye on the larger picture and atone in due course, if we can, for any mistakes that we might have made. The English and Portuguese were, indeed, instrumental in helping to restore Spain from the travesties of the French, but not without cost. Similarly, *El Caudillo* relies on the support of friends and allies in the Crusade to drive out the Reds and regain the true identity of this country.'

Oh, congratulations Brendan. A neat point. To associate Franco with one of England's finest and, at the same time, to absolve him from any mistakes that might be made along the way!

'But it's so elegant,' said Nora.

'So it is, ma'am. As you can see,' the guide continued, 'the whole city was rebuilt during the last century. A blank canvas, so to speak. The Basques call it Donostia, of course. And from the turn of this century, San Sebastián has enjoyed a real heyday.'

'A true *Belle Époque*,' said the Professor. 'The most cosmopolitan city in Europe, they say. Did you know, my petal, that on one night in '14, the Casino was host – at the same time, mind – to Mata Hari, Romanones, Ravel *and* Trotsky...?'

'And here is the Hotel María Cristina,' said Brendan. 'You'll be staying here two nights, as you know, so I'll leave the manager to tell you a bit more about the place once you're settled in.'

A swarm of bell-boys appeared and, under Mikel's guidance, the luggage was unloaded, the guests ushered into the fine main entrance on the Paseo República Argentina, facing the bridge and the Urumea River.

The interior was white. Marble and Mudéjar-patterned floor tiles. Palm trees in pots swaying in a cool breeze. Iced *refrescos* were waiting for them, lemon or grenadine, while a surprisingly young hotel manager regaled them with stories of the María Cristina's history as though he had been present to witness the events in person.

'But the Hotel has seen bad times too,' Brendan interrupted. 'In '36, when the *Reconquista* began, the Basques declared a Republic of their own. There were plenty of Red Anarchists around too, of course, but here in San Sebastián it was the separatist traitors who had the upper hand, calling themselves good Catholics but actually working hand in hand with the Freemasons and Marxists. The local army commander, Colonel Carrasco, tried to hold the town for National Spain but the Reds attacked his troops. They were forced to fall back here and the old

Casino building. They held out for as long as they could, and you can still see the damage on parts of the outside walls. But, in the end, hoping to save the lives of his men, Carrasco was forced to surrender. A few days later, the Reds shot him. Then, on the Thirtieth of July, the Anarchists stormed the prison where the Nationalist prisoners were held. They killed fifty innocent men in cold blood. Next day, twelve more were shot on the Paseo Nuevo. Thankfully, those Basques still left with some sense of morality were also disgusted by the excesses of their Red friends, so when General Mola surrounded the city in August, they at least had the decency to surrender San Sebastián intact, rather than let the Anarchists burn it down, like they'd done at Irún. So...' Brendan Murphy, Jack had noticed, possessed the disconcerting ability to switch seamlessly between the darkly macabre and the sunny travelogue at a moment's notice. 'What time is it? Four-thirty. Dinner's at nine.' There was a collective groan. 'In the main dining room. Early start in the morning but if anybody fancies a swim, the Hotel has the use of some bathing huts. They can provide towels too, but you'll need to take one of their boys with you. Otherwise, you can just relax on the terrace or in any of the lounges. And they do an excellent Pimm's Royal Cup, they tell me.'

'Newspapers?' said Jack.

Brendan exchanged a few words with the manager.

'A selection in your room apparently, Mister Telford. Yesterday's, naturally.'

'Naturally. And they don't have a tennis court, I suppose?'

'As a matter of fact they do! And if you're a tennis fan there's a real treat in store for you tomorrow.'

'Really?' said Jack. 'I'll look forward to it. Now all I need is a partner for a set or two this evening.'

'I'll give you a game, Mister Telford,' said Julia Britten. There was a barely constrained chuckle from Marguerite Weston. 'Nora and I play a fair hand of doubles though I would expect you, as a gentleman, to play solo for your own part.'

Jack smiled.

'Of course,' he said, and bowed, knowing that she would expect the gesture even if she could not see him.

They agreed to meet an hour later and Jack was shown to his room on the third floor where his trunk and day-bag were waiting for him, as well as the promised papers. He unpacked some of his things between glancing at Saturday's news.

The *Daily Mail*, never to be trusted for objectivity, still carried a page nine exclusive on Chamberlain's proposal that Czechoslovakia should become a neutral state, with Britain, France and Italy standing as guarantors of her neutrality, and with the Sudeten District becoming a distinct canton.

Not a bad idea, thought Jack. *Looks like a third way, if everybody will accept it. But this is clever stuff in the* Guardian. *It's always worth looking at what the foreign press has to say.*

And here was *The Manchester Guardian* providing some examples of how the Sudeten crisis was being reported in Germany.

Jack washed, changed into his tennis whites, recovered his racket from the bottom of the trunk and tightened the wing-nuts on its press.

What are you playing at, Jack? Tennis challenge from a seventy year-old and a blind woman. Let them win? Then you'd be obliged to put up with whatever tennis jokes Max Weston might have in his repertoire. No, Julia Britten is a good woman. You owe it to her to play well. Just play normally. See what happens.

He found the two women warming up on the clay court, both suitably attired.

'So here are the rules, Mister Telford,' said Julia. 'First, whenever you are about to serve, you must call *Ready*. You may not serve until I have shouted *Yes* – or something clearly similar. You must then serve within five seconds. Nora will act as umpire if you are agreeable and, if you have not served within the allotted five seconds, the shot will count as a let. Is that understood?'

'Perfectly.'

'Good. Second, I am allowed a second bounce.'

'I'd be happy to give you three.'

'What do you think I am, Mister Telford – an invalid?'

'I apologise, Miss Britten.'

'Good. And, third, neither yourself nor Nora are allowed to volley. Does that seem fair?'

'Eminently. Would you like a knock-about before we start? Just to get the feel of things?'

'Do you need one, Mister Telford?'

'No, not really.'

'Then we shall begin. My service, I think.'

Julia Britten edged back from the net, keeping the soles of her shoes flat to the ground until she reached the baseline. She reached down until she could physically feel the textural difference of the white paint.

'Centre, Nora?' she said.

'Two feet to the right, my lamb.'

Julia edged to the correct position and served an ace that sped past Jack's racket before he could even blink.

'Fifteen love,' said Nora.

'You didn't say *Ready*!' Jack protested.

'Are *you* blind, Mister Telford?' said Julia. 'I really had no idea.'

'Never mind!'

His opponents took the first set by six games to four, Julia using the double-bounce advantage to good effect, playing close to the ground for the most part, often bent almost double, and Jack forfeiting point after point by forgetting that he was unable to volley. On occasion, Julia would ask Nora for measurements if she had faulted in her service or her own volleys had been called out, and on each of those occasions she managed to rectify the error perfectly with her next shot.

A waiter, entirely unbidden, appeared with jugs of barley water while they rested and, to Jack's chagrin, he saw that an audience had also gathered. Marguerite

Weston and Valerie Carter-Holt. The Moorgates too. He suddenly found that he did not want to lose face in front of Carter-Holt, though he was unsure why it should matter.

'Do you mind if I ask where you learned to play?' said Jack.

'At the Guildhall School of Music. I haven't always been blind, Mister Telford. Some rare form of glaucoma when I was five.'

'I've been with Julia ever since!' said Nora.

'Ma and Pa employed Nora as my companion. It helped the Guildhall to accept me. But they insisted that I should undertake the full curriculum, including sports activity. I was also fortunate to win a scholarship to the Royal Academy. I bullied them into letting me have a tennis coach. Now, do you intend to sit here all evening?'

Fortunately, Jack managed to win the second set by seven games to five, but he was sweating like fury by the time they were finished. There was some polite applause from the spectators, except for Carter-Holt, and an appreciative glance, he thought, from Mrs Weston.

'You're a very good player, Mister Telford,' said Julia.

'Thank you, Miss Britten,' Jack gasped. 'That is praise from the praiseworthy, I think. I'm still not sure that you didn't let me win a couple of those final games. Anyway, I must have a smoke and a swim. In that order.'

'Then we may see you later. I'll find out whether Nora would like a stroll to the beach, assuming that's where you're headed?'

Jack confirmed that he would be wherever the Hotel's bathing huts might be located, then went to reception, told them that he would like to use the beach facilities. There was no problem, and a boy would be waiting for him, here at the desk, whenever he was ready. Jack returned to his room by way of the enormous and luxurious main elevators, threw his racket on the bed, and smoked a cigarette while picking up his swimming shorts as well as *The Hobbit*.

When he came out of his room, however, instead of turning left to retrace his steps, he decided to go down the corridor to his right. It was the main corridor for this north wing of the Hotel and, as he had suspected, there was another set of lifts much closer to him. But it was a paternoster, similar to the one in the Hotel Jaúreguí, although on a larger scale. The cars moved continuously on an endless belt, down to the ground floor or beyond on one side, then up to the top on the other. He stepped into the next downward car, stood back from the edge and watched the walls pass before his eyes, waited for the sign that said *Ground*, in English as it happened, and walked smartly out as though he had practiced this arcane form of travel all his life.

He felt quite pleased with himself as he navigated back to the reception desk, to find a towel and boy waiting for him as promised. The youth was a brass-beaming pantomime Buttons with green uniform and knee-length laced boots, and he was being admired by Marguerite Weston, who also seemed to be waiting for Jack.

'I 'opes you don't mind,' she said. 'But I couldn't 'elp 'earing you say as you was going for a swim. Well, I thought, you don't swim, Marguerite Weston, but it'd be a treat to see the beach an' all. An' what better than that nice Mister Telford for company, eh? You could take me for some proper food too, Jack. There must be somewhere that does proper food. In a place this size. What d'you think?"

'Max not joining us?' said Jack. *Oh God*, he thought. *The last thing I want is to be stuck with Marguerite Weston for the evening. Or worse! Christ, what would Jack Dempsey say?* He smiled at the image.

'Well, I'm glad to see as I can put a smile on your face, me 'ansum,' beamed Marguerite. 'And no, Max 'as a headache. Poor bloke, eh? Any'ow, three's a crowd, don't 'e say?'

The boy led them through the terrace at the rear of the Hotel, and one block south before they turned right into Calle del Camino and the Calle Andía, following the tramlines on the right side of the street, past the pale stone façades of banks and offices, hotels and restaurants, archways and awnings.

Marguerite kept up a continuous chatter, hanging on Jack's arm while the bell-boy maintained a steady pace ahead of them. She was wearing a frock that would have graced Ascot. White, with diagonal stripes of royal blue forming a V-pattern from the middle of the ample skirt upwards. It seemed to have been designed with the intention of accentuating her surprisingly narrow waist, but instead it served simply to magnify the width of her hips, while the buttons from neck to midriff were open at the top, either with the intention of being provocative or, Jack imagined, because they would simply not close over that cleavage. Her tight curls were topped by a white slouch Fedora, with a matching blue hat-band, worn Garbo-style.

'Never wear a hat then, Jack?' she said, suddenly.

'It's the rebel in me,' he replied.

'You must be the only man in this entire street that don't 'ave one.'

He caught their reflection in a series of shop windows, his own pinched features contrasting strongly with Marguerite's full but attractive face.

Well, Jack Telford, he thought, *you seem to have made a conquest. Or is it the other way around? And do you want to be saddled with the famous Marguerite Weston? Nice that she's shown an interest though. I wonder what Sydney would say if you turned in* My Seven Nights of Lust with Wife of Madcap Max *instead of this third way thing. Sheila would beat me half to death!*

'It makes me distinctive,' he said.

'It makes you look like you 'aven't got two 'alfpennies to rub together! Would 'e like me to *buy* you a hat, Jack? A nice Panama would suit 'e just fine, my lad.'

She squeezed his arm, pressed herself against him.

'You buy clothes for Max?' he asked. 'Does he suffer from headaches very often, by the way?'

'All the time,' she said. 'The headaches, I mean. An' Max...well, he isn't a *real* man, if you takes my drift?'

'He's not?'

But if Marguerite expanded on the point, Jack certainly missed it, for they had reached the end of the street where it opened out near the pier of the Real Club Náutico to display the whole vista of the bay. The double towers of the former casino, now Town Hall, stood to their right. The beach curved away from them, a crescent moon of fine golden sand flanked at both ends by round-topped hills separated by an island, the Isla de Santa Clara, where the mouth of the bay opened to the sea. The promenade was busy with trams, motor vehicles, horse-drawn carts, carriages and was distinctive with its twin clock towers backed by a row of impressive palaces. Children flocked in cheerful droves. And the entire town seemed to have turned out for the evening *paseo.* The green waters of the sheltered bay itself were busy with lateen-sailed boats, rowing skiffs and bathers, while the beach was still decked with a thousand square canvas canopies, white and reflecting the sun that had now begun to sink in the western sky.

'We're not so different, you an' me,' Marguerite was saying. 'We believes in the same things, more or less. You mustn't be fooled because we're on this silly trip, Jack.'

'So what are you, Marguerite? Spy for the Popular Front? Secret mission for the Republic?'

'What? You think I be another Mata Hari? Oh, how flatterin', Jack Telford. But it were the last thing I was expectin'. An invitation for Max from Franco 'imself. Only two months notice an' all. 'Ardly time to pack!'

The bell-boy had steered them to a row of wooden huts on the edge of the promenade, enquired by gestures whether they needed one or two.

'Oh, we can share, can't we?' Marguerite giggled, but he gently pushed her aside, entered and changed. He left *The Hobbit* with his clothes and emerged again, suddenly embarrassed by Marguerite Weston's presence. She made some seductive comment about his physique, never Jack's strong point, he felt, for though his shoulders were broad enough, his ribs protruded just a bit too much. She insisted, also, on joining him all the way to the water's edge, removing her shoes on the warm sand.

Marguerite shouted an encouragement, while Jack waded out into the shallow water. The tide was coming in but it still took him several minutes before he reached swimming depth, cooling any ardor that he might have felt towards Mrs Weston as it reached his private parts, the familiar chill on his stomach before he ducked beneath a slight swell and struck out, breast-stroke, in the direction of the island, breathing quickly as his body adjusted to the temperature.

He swam for maybe twenty minutes, returned to find Marguerite still waiting for him, as well as the bell-boy, towel at the ready. He wrapped himself, and their strange procession headed back up the beach, stopping at one of the small troughs with a pump so that he could wash sand from feet and legs. As they reached the changing hut again, however, Jack heard a familiar and welcome noise.

'Coo-ee,' cried Nora Hames from a hundred yards away. She was leading Julia Britten, following yet another bell-boy along the *Paseo,* and she turned to speak in the pianist's ear.

'That old witch will be bad-mouthin' me again,' said Marguerite. 'I don't know why you encourage 'er, Jack, I really don't. Or do you fancy the blind 'un, eh? Bit old for you though, me 'ansum, ain't she?'

And before he knew it, she had thrown her arms around his neck, pressing her purse against his shoulder and her bosom against his chest, kissing him with a passion, flicking at his lips with her tongue. He took her shoulders, pushed her away, but feeling the colour rise in his cheeks, his eyes fixed on the damp discolouration of her frock from his wet body.

'You!' Jack said to the bell-boy. 'Take this lady,' he gestured towards Marguerite, 'to the Hotel. Hotel?'

The lad changed his leering grin to an apologetic frown. It was not possible, Jack understood him to say, without first locking the hut.

Dammit, thought Jack. He saw that Julia Britten and Nora had both stopped, the older woman gesticulating towards them, the pianist attempting to placate her.

'I thought that would put a stop to 'er gallop,' laughed Marguerite, as Jack eased past her and locked the bathing chalet door behind him. But when he emerged again, only a minute later, Nora and Julia had both disappeared. He had to endure Marguerite's suggestive banter all the way back to the Hotel but he stopped at the terrace when he saw Julia sitting alone, sipping a glass of wine.

'Well, thanks for the walk,' Jack said.

'You could buy me a drink, if you like,' said Marguerite.

'No, I want to get some air.'

'Suit yourself then!' she snapped, giving Julia a murderous look as she flounced up the steps.

'Well,' said Julia Britten, 'you *are* the ladies' man, aren't you, Mister Telford?'

'I couldn't get rid of her. She's like a limpet.'

'Oh, that's not the way Nora told the story. She was quite outraged. Passion on the prom, that kind of thing.'

'It wasn't like that.'

'There is absolutely no need to explain yourself to *me*, Mister Telford. I already have the measure of Mrs Weston. But Nora is another matter. She has been hoping for the past twenty years and more that I might meet some eligible bachelor – a suitable one, naturally. I fear that she added you to her list of possible candidates. She has such fancies, I'm afraid, but she means well. It will take every ounce of our joint diplomacy to restore you to her good books, I'm afraid.'

'Will she join us for dinner, d'you think?'

'I doubt it. Apart from anything else, she's having trouble adjusting to the *cuisine*. Which means that, if you wouldn't mind, I need an escort to my room. I need to change. By the way, I meant to thank you for this afternoon.'

'What for?' said Jack.

'You know fine well, Mister Telford. For stopping Max Weston whistling that awful tune. Though it didn't bother me. He is a total fool, isn't he?'

Jack laughed. 'Yes, he is!'

He took her elbow and guided Julia Britten through the Hotel to the lifts.

'Thank you, Mister Telford. I normally take the stairs when I'm on my own. I am constantly amazed that quality hotels find themselves unable to either arrange their lift buttons consistently or to have them labelled with Braille. Hardly a great expense, I wouldn't have thought.'

'It's no trouble. But you said something interesting just now. You said you had the measure of Marguerite Weston. What did you mean?'

'About Mrs Weston?' said Julia. 'Don't be silly. You have the measure of her yourself. But I have to be honest with you, Mister Telford. There *is* something that troubles me deeply about this trip. And I can assure you of one thing, at least. That not everybody on this little adventure is exactly what they seem.'

Chapter Six

Monday 19 September 1938

'Ladies and gentlemen,' Brendan announced, with a flourish when breakfast was finished, 'your carriages await.'

'No bus this morning?' said Jack.

'Since we're spending the day in San Sebastián,' said Dorothea Holden, 'we thought we might furnish transport more in keeping with the town's elegance.'

And elegant they were, indeed. Four horse-drawn open landaus, gleaming black with yellow spoked wheels and a green fringed awning to keep the sun at bay – a somewhat unnecessary addition this morning since the sky was almost entirely obscured by grey Atlantic cloud, though it remained warm.

'Am I allowed to take a picture, Mister Murphy?' said Valerie Carter-Holt, holding up her box camera.

'Of course, miss, so long as the horses don't mind.' He offered her a rare smile that the journalist almost managed to reciprocate.

'Then have I got time for a call of nature?' said Jack, before taking himself off to the gentlemen's cloakroom near reception. At first it seemed a big mistake though, for when he returned the first three carriages were already full and the only available space was in the final vehicle with Brendan and the formidable Carter-Holt. Jack had clearly interrupted some profound discussion, then belatedly realised that he was rather exhilarated at the prospect of sharing the ride with her.

'Better now?' said the guide. 'Good. In that case, enjoy the journey. First stop, the Aquarium. *¡Adelante!*'

'Will Reuters pay you for the photographs too, Miss Carter-Holt?' said Jack, sitting across from her.

'Do you *always* indulge in questions to which you already know the answer, Mister Telford?'

'I always imagined that the pictures used by the News Agencies are provided by freelancers,' said Brendan.

'Yes, of course. For the most part anyway,' she said. 'I think it was simply Mister Telford's attempt at chit-chat.'

Jack peered beneath the awning to give him a better view of the architecture gracing the commercial buildings on his left as they turned onto the Alameda del Boulevard.

'And that elegant camera,' said Jack, 'that's German as well, isn't it? Gift from a grateful Führer?' *My God, Jack, that's the first time she's even flinched. Looks like you struck a nerve there. Nazi bitch!* 'Might I see?'

But Carter-Holt placed a protective hand on the square black-fabric case.

'It's a simple Agfa,' she said. 'The Box Forty-Four. It takes One-Twenty Rollfilm. Eight exposures on each. And I bought it in London. Is there anything else that *Reynold's Weekly* needs to know about me?'

They were approaching the port with its grey protective sea wall. It narrowed towards the farther end, past the harbour entrance, while a second quay split this nearer section, providing an even more secluded inner haven. There were some expensive private yachts here, white and varnished wood, many smaller boats too. But no fishing vessels. Just heaps of nets to mark the berths they would normally occupy.

'The fleet would have been out at the crack of dawn, I suppose?' said Jack.

'Hard life,' Brendan replied. 'Fourteen hours, fifteen, every day. That's their *lonja*.' He pointed to a substantial building to their right, back from the quayside.

'*Lonja*?' Jack asked.

'Fishermen's guild. It serves as a meeting place. Social club. They sell their catches there too. But here we are! The Aquarium. The wonder of San Sebastián.'

And a wonder it was. Opened in '28. But the place disturbed Jack. Inside the grey stone building, perched above the breaking waves, he found himself sharing some affinity with the shoals of fish trapped in their subterranean tanks. The place was humid, filled with a spectral yellow light that he somehow associated with the atmosphere of the tour itself.

'Which fish can perform operations?' shouted Max.

'Sturgeon!' came a chorus of replies, bored, exasperated.

Jack returned to the entrance, lit a cigarette, looked across the sweep of the city's beaches. The long curving line of the *malecón*, the esplanade, white archways above the sand, white balustrades, white hotels and palaces, almost unbroken around to the opposite end, where the hill of Monte Igueldo rose, topped by its tower. He took out his notebook.

San Sebastián is magnificent, he wrote, *but it is not the war!*

It was a terrible paraphrase but it would suit the tone of his blossoming article.

'You really *should* wear a hat, Mister Telford,' said Carter-Holt as they climbed steps to rejoin the carriages. The drivers, all decked-out in traditional dress, had taken the opportunity to head up onto the higher *paseo* at the Aquarium's rear. 'You are becoming preposterously pink!'

He thought of Marguerite Weston. She had shunned him at breakfast and declined to join the group that took Brendan Murphy's after-dinner stroll around the river promenade, the visit to Admiral Oquendo's memorial, to the modern Cathedral, to the former Casino where the leaders of Spain's various Republican parties had met in '30 to agree a common front, the famous San Sebastián Agreement that had paved the way for their eventual victory in the polls during '36.

Julia Britten had joined them, however, though without Nora Hames. She was spurning Mister Telford's company too, it seemed. A punishment for his shameless behaviour with "that hussy."

Jack had promised to build bridges at the earliest opportunity. Though what had she meant earlier? Jack had pressed her. *'Not everybody on the tour is exactly what they seem.'* Yet she would not be drawn. Simply another enigma.

'Living in this luxury inoculates us from the horror of it all, don't you agree, Mister Telford?'

And she would not explain *that* comment either, though Jack suspected that it held some meaning beyond the obvious.

Beyond the obvious. Beyond the port. Beyond the old town itself. There stood Monte Igueldo's twin, the hill that sheltered this eastern entrance to the bay. Mount Orgull. And around its seaward edge ran yet another esplanade, the Paseo Nuevo. The carriage-drivers negotiated their way to its concrete surface, above the tide-line, and then proceeded around the hill in a clockwise direction, stopping where a broad path cut up through the woodland slope on the right.

'Time for the first of Mister Telford's surprises for the day,' said Murphy. 'Or do you already know what we'll find up there?'

'The castle?' Jack replied.

'You can see the castle plain enough. No, not the castle. You don't know, sure?'

No, Jack did not know. And then the guide gave them choices, always a mistake with any tour group, he joked. But they were going to climb half-way up the hill to see something special. Those who did not want to do the walk could stay and enjoy an extended carriage ride. Those who wanted to make this initial climb could, if they chose, then come back down to the vehicles, while those who wished to see the castle could continue with Brendan to the summit, picking up the carriages again on the far side.

They all chose to make at least the initial climb, and were joined by the drivers, who carried long canteens of water for their refreshment. It was shaded but steep in parts so that Marguerite Weston, Albert Moorgate and Nora Hames were all sweat and agitation by the time they stopped at a low, moss-covered stone wall. There was still no direct sun but the effort was clearly enough for them, though they were somewhat recovered by the *cantinas* of water that the drivers brought to their rescue.

'It's a cemetery,' said Professor Holden, his Adam's apple bobbing with excitement. 'More of National Spain's heroic fallen, Mister Murphy?'

'These stones are a bit old for that, sir, aren't they? No, there's nobody buried here but the English.'

'Peninsular War?' asked Frances Moorgate.

'Ah, of course!' said Holden. He gave her an appreciative glance. 'You are a natural scholar, Mrs Moorgate!'

'I think we *all* gathered that they must be Napoleonic,' said Dorothea.

'Most of them are a bit later, actually,' said Brendan Murphy. He led the way through a gap in the wall, to a reddish stone monument, military figures and the dedication. *In memory of those courageous British soldiers who gave their life for the flag of their country and for the independence and the freedom of Spain.* 'They cleaned and opened the cemetery about ten years ago,' Brendan continued. 'The graves were all but forgotten until then. But come and see this one...'

Brendan led them to a cluster of small tombstones, pointing at one in particular. There were a few gasps of surprise and Jack found himself almost overcome by an unexpected shiver of emotion.

'What is it?' said Julia Britten.

'It says,' Nora began, 'Colonel F.C. Telford...Died on the fourth of July, 1837.'

'Oh, my goodness,' said Julia. 'What a coincidence!'

'The First Carlist War,' said Professor Holden.

'Yes, sir,' said Brendan. 'Everybody forgets but, for the Carlists, this particular war began a hundred years ago.'

'But who was he?' said Jack.

'I was hoping you could tell me!' Brendan replied. 'I remembered the name from the last couple of trips. But the only thing for certain is that this particular Telford must have been sent as part of the British Legion which came here in 1835.'

'But why?'

'Why?' said Brendan. 'Well, the Spanish King – Ferdinand – died in 1833. He had two possible heirs. His daughter, the Princess Isabella, who was supported by all the Liberal factions. And Ferdinand's brother, Carlos, who was supported by the Traditionalists. Staunch Catholics. The supporters of Carlos – the Carlists, naturally – also claimed that the rules of succession had been made clear in the previous century and should give the crown unequivocally to Carlos. When they didn't get their own way, a civil war broke out. The First Carlist War, as the Professor says. As usual, the English sided with the woolly-minded Liberals and sent a Legion of Volunteers out. Ten thousand of them. All professional soldiers and all keen for glory. The Carlists laid siege to San Sebastián and the British Legion helped to defend it for Isabella. Lots of them died in the process, as you can see. They held the town though and they were disbanded not long afterwards. Your ancestor must have been one of the last to be killed, Mister Telford.'

'Extraordinary,' said Jack. 'I had no idea.'

'No missing family members then?' said Albert Moorgate.

'None that I know of!'

Brendan was already sorting the walking wounded from the hale and hearty who would continue to the castle. In the end, only Albert Moorgate and Marguerite returned to the carriages with the drivers, Nora Hames clearly preferring to suffer discomfort than the close proximity of Mrs Weston.

'So there were more Carlist Wars?' said Jack once the smaller party had resumed its climb.

'By their reckoning,' said Brendan, 'this is the fourth. They still hope that, when this is all over, the throne will pass to Carlos's descendants.'

'The British have such a *penchant*,' said Professor Holden, 'for involving themselves in causes, don't you think? The French think that they have a monopoly on romanticism but we have a particular streak that's run through our own veins ever since the Crusades. Look at Byron…'

'Look no further than our own guide,' Dorothea interrupted.

'I wish that you wouldn't…' said her husband.

'Why, it was devotion to *this* Crusade, surely, Mister Murphy,' Dorothea continued, 'that brought you to Spain? And poor Mister Kettering's brother too.'

Peter Kettering smiled, but it was a weak attempt.

'Well, sure, that's a different story,' said Brendan. 'And you'd have to ask Mister Kettering for his brother's reasons, I guess. But it wasn't romanticism that brought me, Mrs Holden. There's nothing romantic about fighting for your beliefs. That fashion is dead, is it not? The Great War killed it. Everything that it brought in its wake too – including the Bolsheviks.'

'And you, Mister Telford,' said Frances Moorgate, 'as a keen supporter of the Popular Front, were you never inclined to volunteer?'

She had dressed today in a pair of black trousers and a black silk blouse with puffed short sleeves. The low collar, the broad lapels, were embroidered with chinoise flowers and leaves in pastel-coloured thread, predominantly pink. The blouse accentuated her figure and gave a startling effect to her pale complexion, as did the deep crimson lipstick. She carried an umbrella too, he noticed. *Against the possibility of sunshine, presumably,* he thought. *But why does her question trouble you so much, Jack?*

'Oh, you could never accuse me of romantic tendencies, Mrs Moorgate,' he said. It was a clumsy, useless response, simply inciting a sneer from Carter-Holt and some aside from Nora to Julia Britten that he could not quite catch.

The path had taken them up and around the side of the La Mota Castle, much of it fallen into ruin and disrepair but, from its southern, landward rampart and the site of an old chapel there was a memorable view down through the trees to the town and the bay.

Max Weston had been unusually quiet since the Aquarium visit but seemed to rally with each minute spent away from Marguerite.

''Ere,' he said. 'That flamin' burial ground reminded me. There's been this terrible disaster in Dublin. Some two-seater biplane 'as crashed into a cemetery there. They've 'ad Irish rescue workers out lookin' for the bodies it seems. They reckons they've already recovered nearly five 'undred!'

Then he looked at Brendan, suddenly wishing that he had remembered to set the joke in Wales, perhaps.

'It's alright, Mister Weston,' said the guide. 'They tell the same joke here about Andalucians. Even the Irish make jokes about Andalucía. Always *somebody* further down the food chain, eh? And the English *do* like their jokes, don't they? But you won't find many in San Sebastián who think the English are funny. They'll be polite enough. But memories like elephants, these *Donostiarras*.'

And he described the town's siege in 1813. Napoleon's armies all but driven from Spain by Wellington and the Allies. San Sebastián holding out under a French garrison. The English commander, Graham, and his bombardment of the city. The firestorm that followed. The French retreat here, to the castle. And then six days during which the Spanish townsfolk were left to the tender mercies of the English. The atrocities that they inflicted on the inhabitants, said Murphy, some of the most gruesome of an already brutal Peninsular War.

'Can you give some examples?' said Frances Moorgate.

'Best not to go into detail, ma'am,' said Brendan. 'But I could share them privately with anybody who has the stomach for it.'

'I should like that,' she replied.

I bet you would, Mrs Moorgate, thought Jack.

'And there's a moral to the tale, Mister Murphy, I assume?' said Jack. 'That in the heat of battle, even the English are capable of atrocity? That, when you fight a crusade to liberate Spain from whatever afflicts her, some innocent blood is bound to be shed?'

Brendan Murphy laughed, though it seemed as though the act caused him some pain.

'Oh,' he said, 'my job is simply to fill in the historical gaps, Mister Telford. Morals are not on my agenda, sure. And anyway, to an Irishman the words *English* and *atrocity* go hand in hand. Ah, now. I see I may have over-stepped the mark. My apologies, ladies and gentlemen. But Mister Telford has raised an interesting point. You really can't make an omelette without breaking eggs.'

They descended through the zigzag of woodland paths, to a street of the old town where the carriages had arrived ahead of them. Marguerite Weston was sprawled on one of the seats, uncomfortably close to Albert Moorgate, her fingers resting on his arm.

'This is the start of the Calle San Jerónimo,' said Brendan when the couple had joined the main group again, and he had led them to the beginning of a narrow alley that ran southwards. 'I was just explaining to the others about the fires that almost entirely destroyed the city. And here's a plaque that lays the blame fairly and squarely on the English, I'm afraid. But let's head back up here.'

Brendan took them on a cursory visit of the *barrio*. The bars of the Fermín Calbetón, each brightened by its trays of preening *pintxos*. There were street sellers too. Women in traditional tapestry dresses, holding out wide semicircles of skirt material, a smaller semicircle cut into the straight edge to fit any size of waist; market trestle tables spread with broadsheets, pottery jugs and gewgaws; and a black-garbed woman who Jack pictured in the role of Madame Défage sneered at him whilst simultaneously enticing him to buy the high-crowned straw bonnet to which she was stitching scallops of ornamental blue felt.

But the guide did not delay in any of these locations, steering them instead back to the Calle San Jerónimo, where they arrived at a pinched tobacconist's shop, with the new flag of National Spain on one side of the door – the red horizontal sections at top and bottom, the yellow stripe between bearing the eagle of John the Evangelist – and the standard of the Falange on the other.

'We're going inside,' he said, 'to meet a couple of very special ladies. But there's not a lot of room, so we'll need to squeeze ourselves in a bit. All ready?'

Inside, the *estanco* was clean, modern, and they filed towards the back of the shop with its familiar tobacco smells while, behind the counter, a full-faced woman stood, sad eyes, probably in her late-twenties.

'This is *Señorita* Dolores Alisa,' Brendan Murphy informed them, and they in turn murmured their greetings in English or Spanish while the guide spoke with the woman at some length. Jack made out the words *grupo especial* and *El Caudillo*, looked around at the stock. A large dispensing rack to hold a dozen different brands of cigarettes, each brand to its own compartment, but the only 'foreign' varieties that he could see were *Gauloises* and *Gitanes*. The rest he did not know at all, but their packaging was all similar, twenties wrapped in squat oblongs of gummed heavy paper. Cigars too, mostly wrapped in bundles of five or ten but some, the more expensive ones, in a large cabinet, a *humidor*.

And there were newspapers in bundled abundance. No copies of *ABC*, for some reason. But *El Heraldo de Aragón* alongside *La Gaceta del Norte* and *El Pueblo Vasco*. Plenty of *El Correo Español* too, the official organ of the Falange. A dozen others, although it was impossible in this particular press to reach any of them and none of the headlines looked especially interesting. Yet the item which held Jack's attention most were the postcards. An entire stand of them with attractive photographic views showing the various tourist sights of San Sebastián. Of all the incongruous things that he had seen so far on this strange tour, nothing had surprised him so much as this.

'*¡Mamá!*' called *Señorita* Alisa, drawing aside a curtain of strung beads.

I must ask whether the tobacco is rationed, Jack thought, with a moment of panic, since he had only brought a limited supply of *Capstans* with him. He caught some of the others – the smokers, of course – whispering the same thing to each other.

An older woman appeared from the curtain. *Señora* Emilia Alisa Pedrón, Brendan told them. More Greetings.

She had the same face as her daughter, though twenty years older, and her eyes were melancholy, hair matted to her head in damp, greasy curls. She was a widow, from her black dress and matching shawl.

'The *Señora* apologises,' said Murphy, although Jack had heard her say no more than *Buenos Días*, 'if she appears a little less than her best. Her husband died when her children were young and she has had to work long hours at the hospital, besides running the *estanco*, so that she could raise her four kids. But there aren't four any longer. Besides her daughter, she'd had three boys too. Jesús, Augusto and Mario.'

At the sound of her son's names, *Señora* Emilia spoke for a few seconds.

Dorothea Holden nodded wisely with each sentence.

'She says,' Brendan translated, 'that her sons were like those in the parable told by Saint Matthew. The Kingdom of Heaven is like the master of a family, who went out early in the morning to hire labourers for his vineyard. And having agreed with the labourers that they would work for a penny a day, he sent them into the fields. Her sons were like those labourers, she says, working from the early hours, from the very beginning, for National Spain.'

The Sisters of Our Lady of the Holy Light exchanged some German on the subject, and the word "labourer" seemed to spark one of Max Weston's recollections too, although Marguerite restrained him from pursuing the story. She was standing, Jack now realised, immediately behind him and, in the confined space, she was gradually edging closer. Professor Holden was making some absurd observation about vineyards, while Marguerite whispered in Jack's ear.

'I'm sorry if I've been a bad girl, my lovely,' she said.

Brendan had cut the Professor short, explaining that Señora Emilia's sons had kept much of their devotion to National Spain as a matter of private conscience.

'She knew that Jesús was well respected in the local ranks of the Falange, but she had no idea that he had actually become chief of the Party here in San Sebastián. At least, the poor woman didn't know until the day when Jesús went off to a friend's house. It was on the Twenty-Third of July. '36. The Reds caught him there and shot him.'

Jack made a quick calculation. The Generals had launched their bid to seize power on the Seventeenth and Eighteenth, supported here in San Sebastián by Colonel Carrasco and he, in turn, had been defeated by the local militia during the following week. By then, Jack knew, the reprisals would have started against supporters of Franco's rebellion.

I'd love to ask Brendan what he means by 'a matter of private conscience.' That they didn't tell their poor mother they were all up to their necks in the Falange? And why? So that they could protect their poor innocent mum and sister from the dangers that they themselves were facing on behalf of National Spain, I suppose. In a pig's ear, Jack Telford!

'Without any trial?' said Dorothea Holden.

'Oh, the Reds never believed in trials. Not for Jesús. Not for Colonel Carrasco. Not for her second son, either. Augusto's only crime seems to have been that he sold copies of the Party's newspaper on the streets. But four days after the murder of Jesús he ended up in Prison at Ondarreta. He's never been seen again.' Shocked gasps.

Señora Emilia spoke again, about her youngest boy, Mario. He had gone off to help Colonel Carrasco and his men, part of a Falange unit that fortified the old Casino. He had died there, cut down by the Reds. She pointed at a set of framed photographs on the wall next to the bead curtain. Her three martyred sons. The oldest looked a lot like Errol Flynn. The youngest barely more than a boy. And next to the photos was the *Medalla de Sufrimientos por la Patria,* awarded to Emilia Pedrón by *El Caudillo* himself.

'Poor Mario,' said Brendan. 'He'd been more afraid for his mother and sister. Insisted that they should hide themselves when the so-called Movement began but nothing happened to *them.* It was the boys. And these two honest women left alone to face the hardship and loneliness of life each and every day. But at least they have the grateful thanks of their country now, safe in the knowledge that the sacrifice of the sons has helped to restore and unite Spain to its former glory. And every time one of the locals, or their neighbours, or tourists like yourselves come to the *estanco,* they are paying their own homage to the grief of these two women.'

There were shared glances of pity and respect between Dorothea and Nora

Hames, between the two nuns, polite applause and, for Jack, the deliberate pressure of Marguerite Weston's breasts against his back.

'Forgive me, Jack,' she whispered, 'for bein' such a cow?'

Jack gave a quiet snort, non-committal, more polite and amiable than he'd intended. He felt her hand touch his backside.

'Are there any questions?' said Brendan Murphy. 'Although I imagine that you'll all be glad to get out into the open again.'

'May I?' said Peter Kettering. 'I imagine that we all feel the deepest respect for the two ladies and I'm sure you'll both thank them on our behalf, Mister Murphy, as well as expressing our condolences in the proper manner.' The guide translated to the faint but appreciative smiles of the ladies in question. 'But would it be possible to ask how they are managing now? In practice, I mean. The *Señora* no longer has the support of her sons. The economy can't be too clever. And there's rationing, I think. How does that affect them? Is there rationing of tobacco, for example?'

'Oh,' said Brendan, 'I think you've got the wrong end of the stick about the economy. Unlike life under the Reds, everybody has work now. You simply need to apply to the Falange for a permit and you can get a job. There is rationing, of course, but at least the State makes sure that everybody has the basics they need to survive. And tobacco isn't one of them, Mister Kettering. There's no rationing of tobacco though it's not always in full supply, as you can see. But the main tobacco areas, including the Canary Islands, have been part of National Spain since the beginning of the *Reconquista*, so there's been no real shortage of smokes on this side of the line. The Reds have to get *their* cigarettes through commie friends in America. *Lucky Strikes*, if you like that sort of thing. But if you want to try some Spanish brands, please feel free.'

Señora Emilia spoke again.

'Right,' said Brendan. 'The *Señora* says that she's also got some special postcards, if you'd like them. With the photos of her sons.'

The woman held up her wares. Postcards indeed, with reproductions of the photographs from the wall, her three sons side by side in sepia immortality and, on the reverse, separating the address section from the other half, an image of the medal received in their memory.

Wish you were here, thought Jack, as the group edged forward for a closer look.

The daughter was also holding up a copy of the local newspaper, open at the page that carried an article announcing the tour group's arrival in San Sebastián. Most of them bought the paper, and Nora Hames promised Julia that she would cut out the piece for their scrap book.

He could not bring himself to buy the postcards but when *Señora* Emilia looked at him expectantly, even Jack felt obliged to make some contribution, so he bought a few packs of *Superiores* at seventy-five *céntimos* for twenty, and many of the others followed suit. But the shop-keeper made sure to check every note, accepting only Burgos money. None of those worthless Republican pesetas.

I'm still not sure how this fits the parable, Jack thought as, amid the parting formalities, they were ushered outside so that they could go for lunch.

Chapter Seven

Monday 19 September 1938

You could feel the storm approaching. The gathering clouds. The increase in humidity. But the carriage horses trotted regardless along the road backing the *Paseo* and the beach. Past the carousel, the clock towers, the yellow and brown trams, the women on laden donkeys, the other carriages, the occasional parked luxury of a Hispano-Suiza or Pescara Eight, the imported Citroëns. And on the promenade itself, the white parasols of starch-skirted nursemaids now being readied to serve as *paraguas*, to protect their baby carriage charges, umbrellas in waiting while, further away, yachts heeled precariously to the veering wind, row boats headed for shore, steam launch engines developed a note of frenzy.

They passed through the tunnel beneath the *Pico del Loro*, that hummock of royal parkland that separated the Playa de la Concha from the Playa de Ondarreta.

'So, Mister Telford,' said Brendan Murphy, 'will there be a re-match tonight? The whole hotel was talking about last night's game. Our Miss Britten is quite the character, isn't she?'

Jack noticed the pursing of Carter-Holt's lips, some annoyance at Julia's name causing her to stare more fixedly at the white-caps forming in the bay.

'What do you think, Miss Carter-Holt?' he said. 'Would you help me to tackle the formidable Miss Hames and Miss Britten? With a doubles team there might *just* be a chance of beating them.'

'I'm afraid I shall have copy to write this evening,' she replied.

'From the visit to the tobacconist's shop?' said Jack. 'More tales of Red Terror?'

She ignored him.

'You don't believe the ladies' stories, Mister Telford?' said Murphy. 'There are plenty who could bear witness, and many more you could speak with.'

'Of course I believed them,' Jack replied. 'Why should I *not* believe them? After all, Mister Murphy, as you have eloquently illustrated, there's hardly been a war in history that hasn't bathed itself in atrocities. And once the dust has settled, some objectivity returned to our historians, sensational journalism taken out of the equation, they usually turn out to have been perpetrated by *both* sides, not just one.'

'I can live with that,' said the guide, 'except for one thing. God cannot be on both sides of a conflict, Mister Telford. And while God's warriors may sometimes commit sins in their ardour or fear, it is the godless who are always guilty of the worst excesses, in this case the Reds.'

'Well, we'll see, I suppose. But so far it seems that all the examples we've been given date from the beginning of the war. And you mention fear, Mister Murphy. Is it not fear that drives atrocity? It is natural enough to *hate* our enemies. Of course it is. How could anybody kill another person unless they had learned to hate them? But when you are afraid of them too, terrified by them rather, isn't *that* when atrocity begins? Scared beyond reason. We call it the Terror always. For you it's the Red Terror. For the Republicans it's the White Terror. But actually the real terror is in the hearts of those who commit the atrocity.'

'Oh, bravo, Mister Telford,' said Carter-Holt. She applauded. 'And where did we learn our lines today? From our friends on the *Daily Worker*?'

'I've said to you already, sir,' Murphy added, 'that I wouldn't deny some things may be wrong on our side too, but the scale of the atrocities committed by the Reds is beyond belief whereas you'll get the chance later to see how humanely National Spain treats its prisoners.'

'I'm sure the visit will be interesting, Mister Murphy,' said Jack. 'And I'm sure that you won't miss the opportunity to remind us that it was the *British* who invented the Concentration Camp.'

'Ah, the Boer War, Mister Telford,' said the guide. 'Sure, now you've stolen my thunder. Speaking of which…'

There was a deep atmospheric rumble away in the distance as they stopped in the small square outside the Monte Igueldo funicular station. Greetings from the uniformed staff and then ushered into the tiered cars that were soon hauling their way up the precarious and thickly wooded slope, passing the down car at mid-point. *Perfect equilibrium*, thought Jack. *The very thing that poor Spain has yet to find.* There was a short visit to the tower, the former lighthouse, views of the panorama below.

Brendan hurried them back to the funicular and they rattled their way downwards as the first large spots of rain smacked against the translucent green leaves.

They managed to climb back aboard the carriages without getting drenched and the canopies helped to keep them reasonably dry until they had retraced their journey to the road tunnel. From this side it was more obvious that the royal parkland dividing the two beaches also accommodated a substantial palace, although it seemed badly neglected, the grounds overgrown but still splashed with yellow oxalis *vinagrillos*, with fiery marigolds, blue hydrangea, purple anemone.

'That's the Miramar Palace up on our right,' shouted Murphy. 'The Royal Family used to spend August here. It's all boarded up just now but don't worry. Today you'll still dine like royalty. Look.'

He pointed to the left where, upon the beach, there was an extraordinary sight that had been hidden from them travelling in the opposite direction. For, at the foot of the *Pico del Loro*, where a private staircase ran down to the sand, there was a rail track, but with an enormous gauge, perhaps twenty feet across. And upon the rails sat a monumental beach house. It possessed something of the style and splendour of the Royal Pavilion at Brighton, though naturally on a smaller scale, but it remained impressive, its arabesque shutters brightly painted, its onion domes striped in green and white.

For today's purposes, the structure had been hauled to the nearer end of the rails but it was obvious that the entire pavilion could, when required, be rolled down to the water's edge, regardless of the state of the tide, so that their Royal Majesties might take a dip in complete privacy within the enclosed lido platforms at the rear.

Inside, the tour group was welcomed by the city's mayor to King Alfonso's private dining room, while a Bishop was on hand, once again, to bless both their endeavours and their food, although neither could stay for the meal itself. The chef was introduced, *Señor* Armendariz Escurra. He had apparently just opened a new restaurant in the town and, yes, this was a positive sign of prosperity returning to San Sebastián. The food was exquisite. Barely a whisper about 'decent English food' or 'too much oil and garlic.' They enjoyed *brochetas* of either fried prawns in a vinaigrette, or succulent kid with peppers and onion. Marinated octopus. Meat balls in tomato and *txakoli*. Lightly battered cod in *romesco* sauce. Grilled vegetables. Baskets of stale bread to mop up the juices.

And it was wonderful. Until the cockroach appeared.

The creature slipped unnoticed past the two young women who had been employed to wait on table, but ran in plain view of Dorothea Holden, who screamed and rose suddenly from her chair, tipping it backwards to the floor. Several of the others jumped to their feet also, by instinct.

'What is it, my sweet one?' said the Professor.

'*Cucurucho!*' cried his wife.

He craned his long neck, finally spotting the object of her fears as it made a rapid circuit on the wall opposite.

'Ah! I think, my dear, you will find the correct word to be *cucaracha*. A *cucurucho* is an ice-cream cone, unless I'm badly...'

'I don't care about the bloody etymology Alfred,' she screamed. 'I *hate* them!'

'Don't worry, Mrs Holden,' said Brendan, and he shouted to one of the waitresses, pointing at the wall.

'What's the matter?' said Marguerite Weston. 'A mouse or somethin'?'

'Beastly cockroach,' replied Carter-Holt, her exaggerated high-class accent slipping into its more natural cadence.

'I never understood,' Julia Britten said to her, 'why the cockroach is held in such opprobrium, Miss Carter-Holt. Did you? It is an easy enough insect to identify, after all. They scuttle quite distinctively. '

Valerie Carter-Holt ignored her.

'Oh, my Good Lord,' said Marguerite. 'Cockroach!' She rose quickly too, her elbow catching Catherine Kettering on the bridge of her nose.

The force of the blow knocked Catherine sideways so that she fell against her husband's lap and Jack noticed with surprise that Peter looked around the table in obvious embarrassment, quickly restoring his wife to her own seat before showing any concern for her injury. Catherine, meanwhile, was clutching at her face with both hands, blood trickling between them and running down her wrists.

'Mrs Kettering's nose is bleeding,' said Nora Hames.

'D'you know,' said Professor Holden, ' I believe that the word *cucurucho* might apply equally to *any* form of cone.'

'Sister,' said Murphy to the younger of the nuns, and gesturing towards Catherine Kettering, 'would you mind?'

Sister María Pereda spoke rapidly to Sister Berthe Schultz who looked stoically towards the injured woman. A lengthy German diatribe followed but no action, and Frances Moorgate left her own place to offer Catherine some assistance.

'I have a St. John's Certificate,' Frances explained. 'From the library, you understand. We are now an official Civil Defence First Aid Post.'

'I read once,' said her husband, 'that you should never step on a cockroach. It's the easiest way to spread their eggs apparently.'

But this cockroach was in little danger of that particular fate. It scuttled lightning-fast from floor to wall with the waitresses in hot pursuit.

Jack set down his napkin, deciding that he should be seen to do something and choosing a role as Frances Moorgate's helper as his best option.

''Ere, Max,' said Marguerite, 'be a good 'un an' swap places. 'Appen I'll get blood on this frock otherwise.'

'Oy, 'ere's one,' Max replied. ''Ow can 'e tell which end of a worm is which?'

Marguerite struck him a vicious backhand to the head.

'I 'aven't got all day,' she yelled. 'Shift yerself!'

'And am I right in thinking, Mister Murphy,' said Professor Holden, 'that the term *cucurucho* might also be applied to those hoods worn by penitents in religious ceremonies?'

Brendan nodded, managed a polite smile. Dorothea gave Alfred a look of sheer contempt.

'Sister Berthe Schultz,' said the younger nun, 'says that only good things come from God's hands. That even the most humble of His creatures has a purpose, no matter how odious or ugly they seem. She says that God never gives us more than we can bear so that we should tolerate all the forms of His creation with love and respect. She says that even the burden of dealing with a humble cockroach shall prepare us for eternity.'

'I was hoping that Sister Berthe Schultz might be able to help with the injury,' said the guide.

'Then I shall ask her for some advice on injuries,' replied Sister María Pereda.

'No need, Sister. But thanks for the offer,' said Brendan. 'It seems that Mrs Moorgate has everything under control.'

And, just then, *Señor* Armendariz Escurra appeared in the doorway from his kitchen to find out why his culinary skills were not being better appreciated, while the cockroach slipped between the waitresses and made straight for the table. More accurately, it made straight for the leg of Julia Britten's chair.

'Oh heavens,' shrieked Dorothea, 'where's the beastly thing gone?'

'It's on 'er seat,' said Marguerite Weston, pointing at Julia. '*You!*' she shouted, as though the woman was deaf as well as blind.

Jack moved around the table.

'Miss Britten,' he said, 'you need to stand a moment.' And he realised that she was trembling as he gripped her elbow and gently lifted her from the chair.

'They give me the heebie-jeebies in truth, Mister Telford,' she whispered as he moved her away. Julia turned and took his hand. 'Would you mind awfully?' And she guided his arm so that he found himself holding her around the waist. Nora Hames had joined them.

'Oh, Jack,' said Nora, a note of adoration in her voice. 'And my poor lamb. She has a real thing about creepy-crawlies, though she won't admit it, will you Julia?'

Señor Armendariz Escurra had advanced towards Julia's recently vacated chair with a piece of paper in his hand, paused briefly and then, in one deft move, he lifted the cushion and caught the *cucaracha* in the paper. Swift and efficient. He bowed once to the guests and, holding the paper up, he marched back to the kitchen.

'He will burn it in the stove, I imagine,' said Albert Moorgate. 'It's the only efficient way to kill cockroaches, you know. That or boiling water. My father knew a thing or two about cockroaches.'

'There, Miss Britten,' Jack said. 'All over now.' Julia smiled and he led her back towards her seat.

'Oh, Jack,' said Nora, 'you are such a good boy. And you must forgive an old woman for being so grumpy yesterday evening. But the sight of that floozy with her arms about you made me *so* cross. Julia says that the trollop threw herself at you.'

'Nora!' Julia Britten whispered. 'That's quite enough.'

'Lord in 'Eaven,' said Marguerite Weston. 'Now isn't *that* sweet?' She gave Julia a look of pure hatred, then turned her furious gaze first on Jack, then finally on Nora Hames. 'An' be you calling *me* a trollop, you old cow?'

Gasps.

'Mrs Weston, please…' said Peter Kettering. Frances seemed to have staunched Catherine's nose-bleed now, though Kettering's wife was still in some distress.

'I think we should all continue with this fine lunch,' cried Dorothea Holden. 'Such a pity to let it go to waste.'

'Well,' said Nora, 'if the cap fits!' She was defiant, ready for the fight.

'Nora, be still now,' Julia chided, as they resumed their seats.

'Ladies,' said Jack, 'I think that the incident with the cockroach has upset *everybody*. As Mrs Holden says, time to put it behind us and finish our meal. Unless, of course, Mrs Kettering needs any further medical attention.'

Catherine shook her head, still holding a serviette to her face. She spent the rest of their time in the pavilion that way, looking often to her husband for comfort but without truly receiving any. Marguerite Weston remained at the table but never quite managed to let go of her exchange with Nora Hames. Julia used all her skills to keep Nora from responding. Max tried on three occasions to complete the worm conundrum but nobody paid any attention. The Holdens squabbled about which of them had the better grasp of Spanish. Frances Moorgate received general acclaim for her prompt action while her husband explained the modern intricacies of Civil Defence. General discussion centred either on the visit to the *estanco*, with Carter-Holt dominating the theme – Red Terror, naturally – or on the group's favourite topic, Spanish food. The garlic-shaded, pepper red and saffron yellow flavours, it seemed, were entirely foreign to the British palette. And, in the midst of this culinary debate, Sister Berthe Schultz made several interventions about injuries to the soul, injuries against morality, injuries against Our Lady of the Holy Light, injuries to feeling, but never a single mention of nasal damage.

'Well, Mister Telford,' said Brendan when everybody else was engaged in his or her own discussion, 'you seem to have restored at least a semblance of order. The best laid schemes, eh?'

But Jack was still thinking about cockroaches.

The rain had been falling steadily throughout lunch, pattering on the pavilion's cupolas, rattling against the windows but it stopped during dessert, some form of flan and a date tart.

'So,' said the guide, 'another surprise for Mister Telford this afternoon. A real treat for all tennis lovers too. We're off to see the Basque national sport. Oh, that reminds me. We've had two requests for Miss Britten. First, will we all get the chance to see a re-play of your match against Mister Telford this evening?'

'If so I'd need somebody to join my doubles team,' said Jack. 'I've been trying to entice Miss Carter-Holt but without success.'

'I'm not very good,' volunteered Frances Moorgate, 'but I'd be willing to give it a try.'

'There, Mister Telford!' Brendan was exultant. 'No backing out now. We'll look forward to it, I'm sure. And the second thing, Miss Britten, is whether you might play piano for us, after the match naturally?'

'I'd be delighted,' said Julia.

'Good,' replied the guide. 'That's settled. Anything we've forgotten, Mrs Holden? No? In that case, when you've all finished, we'll introduce you to the delights of Basque *pelota*. Oh, just a final thing. After the *pelota*, we've arranged a trip to see the camp where the Red prisoners are being held. But we expected some of you might not want to take that part of the tour. If so, just let me know and we can drop you at the Hotel.'

The *Frontón Moderno de San Sebastián* was ten minutes away in the carriages. The storm had cleared although the wind was still high but the streets were filled with well-dressed people taking aperitifs and seeking lunch. The bars and restaurants seemed as full as churches or bullrings might be. Little evidence of deprivation or austerity in *this* part of town. Not for those who could afford the alternatives, the food, the entertainments that the city had to offer.

And the most popular entertainment in these parts was certainly *Pelota Vasca.*

The main playing court, the *frontón* itself, was housed in a palatial arena and the group was led by Brendan Murphy out onto the *cancha*, open to the sky and surrounded on one long side and two short by high walls, while the second long edge was filled with four tiers of galleries for spectators. It was a Monday, so no matches today, but there were half a dozen players out here already, tanned arms and faces contrasting with their brilliantly white shirts and flannels, waiting to give a demonstration and each carrying the curved hand-held basket, the *xistera*, that had made the game so famous.

'A match normally lasts about an hour,' Brendan explained once they were seated. 'But we'll just get a short exhibition game today. Maybe fifteen minutes or so. And then a chance for some of you to try your hand. It's the fastest ball game in the world, they tell me. And we missed two great matches yesterday, sure. Irogoyen was here. They call him the Lion of Navarra. Wonderful. I saw him play a couple of months ago. Ah, here we go.'

One of the red team players had advanced to a serving line, bounced the ball once, caught it on the rise in the curved basket, now firmly attached to his wrist, and brought the *xistera* round in a long, fast, fluid motion, propelling the ball against the front wall so that it hammered back towards the opposing blues. After that, everything became a blur.

'The ball is goatskin,' said the guide, 'smaller than a tennis ball, Miss Britten, but harder than a golf ball. They say that, once it's in play, it travels at not much less than two hundred miles an hour.' Nora Hames was trying valiantly to describe the action for Julia.

'It's a bit more exciting than cricket,' said Nora.

'Oh, I don't know about that, Miss Hames,' said Professor Holden. 'You should have been at the England-Australia Test. Nine hundred and three for seven declared. Remarkable.'

'Did you see Hutton's three hundred and sixty-four, Professor?' asked an awed Albert Moorgate.

It seemed that Holden had, indeed, seen the historic innings but there was no time to seek his further impressions since the *pelota* match was soon over, the red team victorious and now offering the chance for their illustrious guests to sample the game. Jack volunteered for a quick lesson, Peter Kettering too, but the rest were content merely to watch.

They were patiently shown, each in turn, how to grip the basket-work hilt, the ball to be caught with the *xistera* extended straight backwards, horizontal. Three times the ball came at Jack, not particularly fast, but beyond his ability to intercept. But the fourth time he took the *pelota* cleanly, taking it in the curved body of the basket, halting its journey, as he had been taught, by immediately commencing the downward curve of the basket and using the ball's momentum to propel it forwards again. It smacked low against the wall, too low to count, but at least he had hit *something.*

The tour group cheered his beginner's luck but when the two men returned to their companions, it was clear that all was not well.

'Why should 'e never fall in love with a tennis player?' Max was saying, anxiety in his voice.

'Max, I swear if 'e don't shut your trap...!' said Marguerite. 'That stupid cow just 'it me with 'er cane!'

'It was a simple accident, you silly goose,' cried Nora Hames.

'Nora, please just leave it alone,' said Julia Britten. 'I've already apologised to Mrs Weston and no real harm done, I think.'

'No 'arm? Why, I think my ankle's broke. An' who's *she* callin' a goose any'ow?'

'Can I help?' said Jack.

'Oh, Jack!' Marguerite replied. 'My 'ero. Would you be a love and 'ave a look at this ankle?'

'Well, it's Mrs Moorgate who's the St John's Ambulance Volunteer.'

Marguerite gave Frances a look of disdain.

'No,' she said, 'I want *you* to look at it. You got such a nice touch, see.'

Jack looked around to see that the rest were looking at him expectantly, as though it was indeed his duty to conciliate here.

'But perhaps Max...?' he began.

'What's that, me 'ansum?' said Max. Then he looked forlorn. 'Oh, it's because to tennis players, *love* means nothin'.'

Somebody please tell me he's not really this stupid, Jack thought, then he knelt slowly to the spectators' bench on which Marguerite had extended her damaged leg. He was surprised to see that, despite her tendency to overweight, it was a very fine leg, a shapely leg, a leg to match the hourglass waistline. The nylon stocking was somewhat askew where Marguerite had kicked off her footwear, and the ankle *did* seem a little swollen but Jack was doubtful that this could be attributed to Julia Britten's white cane. He straightened the stocking, replaced the shoe.

'There,' he said. 'No damage done. So far as I can tell. But I'm sure that Mrs Moorgate really would be able to give you a better opinion than me.'

'No,' said Marguerite, 'it feels better already. Just get me up, Jack, an' see if you can 'elp me walk a few steps.'

Jack helped her from the bench while Max explained that fish never make good tennis players because they dislike getting too near a net. Marguerite, meanwhile, had put her arm around Jack's hips and was steering him along the walkway, limping theatrically.

'You do *like* me, Jack, don't you?' she said. 'Only I got this real thing for *you*, see.'

'This morning, as I recall, you had a thing for Mister Moorgate. You had your hands all over him when we came back to the carriages after the castle.'

'Oh, was you jealous then?' she giggled. 'I 'oped you'd be jealous, Jack. An' then I got so angry when you 'eld that cow, just because she'd been scared by some old cockroach.'

'You seemed pretty shaken up by it too, as I recall. And Julia Britten is all right. I like her.'

'Better than you like *me*, Jack?'

'We'd better get back. Come on. And walk properly. There's nothing wrong with your bloody ankle.'

'I likes a masterful man, Jack Telford. An' *you* liked my kiss last night, didn't you? I could tell. I could feel you wet against me all the way back to the Hotel an' all. I know what room you're in, Jack. So I *might* pay you a visit, if you're a good boy.'

Jack laughed.

'What about your husband?' he whispered.

'Who? Max? Oh, 'e'd only come to watch. No use for anythin' else, that's for sure.'

'All mended?' called Brendan Murphy, as Jack and Marguerite returned to the main group.

'Yes,' said Jack, setting Marguerite back upon her bench. 'Right as rain, or seems to be.'

'Good,' said the guide. 'And congratulations to both Mister Telford and Mister Kettering for their fine effort down there on the court. But maybe I should ask Mrs Weston whether she feels up to our prison visit? Or does anybody else, for that matter, think it might be too much?'

As it happened, neither Marguerite Weston, nor Julia Britten and Nora Hames wanted to make the visit, and Brendan used his best skills to find a reason for them to travel in separate carriages. He escorted Marguerite in person, leaving the others to spend a final minute watching the resumed practice games on the *frontón*. Valerie was using the time to take a few last shots of the players.

'Have you had the camera long, Miss Carter-Holt?' Julia asked her.

'A few months,' replied the journalist in that haughty accent again.

'I doubt even *you* can break through that icy exterior,' said Jack in Julia's ear.

'Ah,' said the pianist, 'you may be right, Mister Telford. And how did you get on with Mrs Weston? You'll need to keep your door locked tonight, I gather.'

'How did you know?' said Jack.

'Call it intuition,' Julia replied.

'She's jealous of you.'

'Does she have reason to be, Mister Telford? I wasn't so far short of the mark when I called you a *roué*, was I?'

'I never thought of myself as one.'

'Well, congratulations on your rise to fame as a *pelota* star, in any case. The game's just a bit too fast for me to try, I think. Anyway, I was otherwise engaged up here.'

'Really?' said Jack, wondering whether they were still talking about *pelota*. 'With Marguerite Weston, you mean?'

'Gosh, no. An interesting conversation with the mysterious Mrs Kettering.'

'*Is* she mysterious? You must stop talking to me in riddles, Miss Britten. I'm just a simple man, whatever you might think of me. And you've already hinted that nobody in the group is quite what they seem. I think you owe me an explanation.'

'Do you indeed, sir? Well, we'll see. Maybe tomorrow I shall reveal all.'

'I bet you're a member of Miss Christie's fan club,' said Jack.

'I rather prefer Margery Allingham. And Leslie Charteris, as it happens.'

'Is it true that he's half-Chinese?'

'According to the *Daily Mail*,' she whispered.

'Oh well then...'

'And here is Mister Murphy come to collect me, I think,' said Julia. 'At least, if he can tear himself away from Mrs Moorgate.' Jack looked at the guide. *He does seem to always stand very close to her*, he thought. 'I'll wager he'll be there to watch our match tonight, Mister Telford. That's if you really intend to play with her as your partner? Anyway, don't forget. Six on the dot.'

But six o'clock, and an eccentric game of tennis at the Hotel María Cristina, felt as though they belonged to another life, to some other universe when, thirty minutes later, Jack found himself alighting from the carriages at the *Plaza del Chofre*, out on the eastern side of San Sebastián. The bullring, now serving as a Concentration Camp, was enormous, the exterior wall constructed on three levels, each marked by tall arabesque gallery windows where guards patrolled. The gate, an almost complete circle, forty feet high, was flanked by fading posters advertising *corridas* that had taken place here in '35 and '36. Above the gate, another gallery, shark-tooth battlements and twin towers with elongated domes.

The square itself was busy, stalls and awnings set up around the full perimeter of the bullring's outer wall. Brisk business was taking place, a general commotion of gravel-throated voices.

'This is the *Antiguo Coso de El Chofre*,' said Brendan Murphy. 'One of the biggest rings in Spain. The *Chofre* ranks alongside the *Maestranza* in Sevilla. A capacity of thirteen thousand.'

'Spectators or prisoners?' said Jack.

'It would be inhuman to keep so many prisoners here, wouldn't it, Mister Telford? No, the prisoner population varies a bit but generally there are no more than three or four thousand Reds here at one time. It's a shame to see the place used like this, I suppose, but they have to be housed somewhere. And bullrings make very good prisons. In happier days, though, the *Chofre* has seen quite a few celebrities amongst its crowds. Chaplin was here in '31, Mister Weston.'

Max did another quick impression of Chaplin's walk while the iron gate that had seemingly been added as a temporary entrance was opened by a uniformed guard and several army officers marched to meet them. Brendan Murphy snapped to attention, saluting his superiors in the fascist style, right arm raised towards them. The officers responded, then turned to the tour group and offered them the Nazi salute also. The Holdens responded immediately, Carter-Holt likewise. The Ketterings were somewhat slower to reciprocate and so was Max Weston. The

Moorgates too, though they eventually seemed to accept the act as a polite civility. The nuns bobbed an obeisance.

Jack experienced a moment of panic. He wanted very badly to be inspired by those athletes who had refused to give the Nazi salute during the Berlin Olympics but he was dogged instead by the ignominious image of the England soccer team on tour in Europe during May. It seemed that they had initially been reluctant to comply with Hitler's requirement when they had played the first match against Germany but, on instruction from the British Ambassador, they had finally fallen into line, given the salute. They might have romped home to a six-three victory but the photographs of Eddie Hapgood, Stanley Matthews, Len Goulden and the others, all acting like fascist lap-dogs, had sickened him. *Just give them a nod, Jack, and see whether you get away with it.* He did so. The junior officers looked from one to the other while the most senior amongst them, a major, Jack thought, stared him directly in the eye but spoke quickly to Brendan. The guide stood to attention once more.

'My name,' said the officer, in English, 'is *Comandante* Ponce de Buñol. National Spain welcome you to this prison and thank you for the visit. We show you here how National Spain care for prisoners. Stay together please and follow.'

They were led into the bullring's entrance tunnel, turned right into the offices and entertainment rooms beneath the stands and were offered *refrescos* while the *Comandante* presented an endless stream of statistics about numbers of Republicans captured on various fronts during the past year and the problems of dealing with them. The *Chofre*, it seemed, served as something of a holding camp, particularly for those taken during the Ebro campaign in the east, but also as a more permanent home for prisoners from the local Basque provinces.

'Our first task to separate men, women too, forced to fight for the *Rojos*. In Spain we always trying to convert enemies, not punish them. So, many take oath to National Spain. But here is another problem. Many do not want to go back to their own town, their own village. They have food here. Shelter. And those who live in town still held by *comunistas*, they cannot go back.'

Jack could almost see the article before his eyes.

In the Plaza del Chofre prison, on Spain's Riviera coast, there are four thousand Basque prisoners who are treated with such humanity by their fascist captors that they choose to remain, voluntarily of course, within the Concentration Camp as guests of National Spain rather than accept the freedom that is so generously available to them at any time.

'This may seem a trivial question, sir,' said Professor Holden, 'but the *Corrida* is such an important aspect of Spanish culture. Are there no longer bullfights in the town now that this fine edifice is dedicated to alternative usage?'

The *Comandante* looked to Brendan for a translation.

'We use *El Chofre*, sir,' he said, 'because it is the best for our purpose. There is another, the *Plaza Cubierta de Martutene*. Not so fine. But good. There was another also. The *Plaza de Atocha*, though the *anarquistas* burn it.'

The devils! thought Jack. *Is it true, I wonder, that all the best bullfighters are fascists? And why would that be, d'you suppose?*

'And those who will not take the oath, *Comandante*?' said Peter Kettering. 'What happens to them?'

'Those who remain heretic, who will not reform, they go to other prisons. At Burgos. Other places. True prison. Not camps.'

'And is there room for them all?' asked Kettering.

He's doing the arithmetic, thought Jack. *Four thousand, maybe five, in San Sebastián alone. And we're nowhere near the Front here. Presumably similar numbers in the other main towns and cities then. And unless Spanish prisons were remarkably empty before Franco's rebellion, they must either now be grossly overcrowded or the Nationalists must be getting rid of the surplus some other way. Unless they've all recanted, of course.*

'Oh yes, *Señor*,' smiled the *Comandante*. 'Plenty of room. But come, let me show you our recent arrivals.' They were led to a comfortable presidential box that overlooked the sand-filled ring itself. The wooden barrier enclosing the ring was also topped with barbed wire. 'The *anillo*,' explained the *Comandante*, 'is normally use for exercise. But today, for process to new prisoners.'

Across the diameter of the ring stood a body of men, two deep, perhaps a hundred in total. Their uniforms were ragged, hardly uniform at all such was the variety of clothing, and many had no shoes. Most were bare-headed, weary, lost and defeated.

'All taken on the Ebro, *Comandante*?' said Carter-Holt.

'Yes, *Señorita*. And we have problem. For there are many internationals fighting there. *Comunistas*, of course. Sent here by the Americans. By Russia.'

'You have evidence that the Russians have an army here now, I assume, *Comandante*?' asked Dorothea.

'Oh, but of course!'

You bloody liar, Jack thought. *You've been trying to produce evidence of a Russian army in Spain since '36. If there'd been one, you would have been parading them all over the front pages. All you've been able to turn up is the occasional tank driver or technician.*

'And are there any Russians amongst these captives?' Dorothea said.

The *Comandante* looked doubtful.

'We think some Americans. Maybe few British. We have to find out. To keep separate. We think the *Rojos* will make decision to send home all internationals soon. So we keep them in other places. Ready. For *intercambio*.' He looked to Brendan Murphy.

'Prisoner exchange,' said the guide.

'Yes. Exchange,' nodded the *Comandante*.

Down in the ring, the prisoners had just been searched, presumably not for the first time since there was little evidence that they possessed anything. A book, a letter here, a photograph there. An order barked by the officer in charge of proceedings, a fat little man with a moustache, and the whole ragged line shuffled forward. The officer looked enraged, the *Comandante* clicked his tongue, shook his head. Another order, and Jack heard the word *Americanos*. Nobody in the line moved.

Jack smiled. *They're trying to sort out the International Brigade members from the*

Spanish. That first order must have been for the Spaniards to step forward. But they all moved. And now he's asked the Americans to step forward but everybody's stood still. What is it? Solidarity? Or do they know something that the Comandante *hasn't shared with us? And these Nationalists aren't very bright if they can't tell most of the internationals at a glance.* He looked around him at the prisoners in their barbed wire enclosures, layer upon layer of them, their other activities suspended as they crowded, silent, to watch a familiar spectacle unfold.

The officer walked to the end of the line, surrounded by heavily armed guards. He pointed at the first prisoner.

'*¿Cómo se llama?*' he shouted in the man's face.

The prisoner garbled some invented Spanish name in the worst accent Jack had ever heard and was hauled out of the line. The next few seemed to easily satisfy the officer's interrogation but the fifth was a tall sandy-haired man whose Spanish, to Jack's surprise, sounded perfect.

'*¿Y dónde vive usted?*' asked the officer. *And where do you live?*

The response was seemingly fluent. So there was another question. Then consultation with a list held by a subordinate. And yet a further question. Until, finally, the prisoner smiled, threw up his hands, and was likewise removed from the line.

'How did they catch him out?' whispered Jack to Brendan Murphy.

'They asked him where he was born and then for the name of the most important town in his Province. He was bloody good. But they *all* fail the final question.'

'Which is?' said Jack.

'Who is the patron saint of *your* village, Mister Telford? It's the one thing that every true Spaniard would know, whether they're Catholic *or* Communist.'

They completed the visit an hour later and were escorted from *El Chofre* with all the usual formalities.

'And what's Mikel doing with himself today?' asked Jack, while the group members were getting themselves back into the carriages. They had the same smug, self-satisfied attitude, he thought, that he had seen displayed following press prison visits at home, as though the simple act of entering and leaving a place of incarceration conferred some obvious superiority on those free to do so. *Not just that either. You visit people in prison and it confirms that the inmates are, indeed, criminals. It's subliminal.*

'He has some maintenance to do on the bus,' replied Brendan. 'The cooler reservoirs. Checking the oil and tyres.'

Jack heard a noise in the distance, faint but distinct.

'Was that...?' he began, although as he glanced around the group's faces, it was clear that nobody else had heard. Likewise, trade in the *Plaza* continued without interruption or note. Only Brendan Murphy seemed to have picked up the sound. He grimaced, almost apologetically, Jack thought.

But when it came again, a more prolonged burst, he had no doubt at all. Machine gun fire out in the green and pleasant hills of San Sebastián.

Chapter Eight

Tuesday 20 September 1938

Julia Britten's head had hit the second-floor corridor carpet long before her torso and limbs finally came to rest on that same level.

Jack had been eating breakfast, alone at first and pretending to study the day's published itinerary. It seemed to him that living in luxury at the María Cristina Hotel not only served to distance them from the horrors of the battlefields but also physically to prevent him thinking logically about this problem. He did not doubt that Valerie Carter-Holt would write anything she chose, fictional or otherwise, about the alleged Red Terror simply by repeating the lines that Brendan Murphy so carefully rehearsed for them. But what should *he* write? Would anybody be swayed by the possibility that he may have heard machine gun fire after the internationals had been separated and taken away? It was the worst sort of speculative journalism, surely. In addition, of course, there was the possible danger. He well remembered the story of Arthur Koestler, accredited by the *News Chronicle* and summarily sentenced to death for his anti-Nationalist stance when he was inadvertently captured by Franco's forces. Koestler's fame may have narrowly saved him, making him a suitable candidate for high-profile prisoner exchange, but Jack Telford would enjoy no such protection.

'Might we join you, Mister Telford?' Frances Moorgate had asked.

'Yes, of course. I'm sorry. I was miles away.'

'Still contemplating last night's unlucky defeat, I imagine, old fellow,' said a jovial Bertie. Mister Moorgate had held the chair for Frances, patting her sable chiffon shoulder as she pulled herself towards the table. 'I'm afraid that Frances hasn't played for some time and...Well, the standard of Miss Britten's game is quite extraordinary.'

Jack noticed that Mrs Moorgate's perfume seemed just a touch stronger today, her cheeks displaying a positive hint of colour through the pale powder.

'Entirely my own fault,' said Jack. 'Your wife played some excellent shots but I, too, made the mistake of under-estimating not only Miss Britten but, more importantly, the skills of the formidable Nora Hames.'

Jack had seen Nora crossing the dining room towards them, and had made his comment just loudly enough that Nora would hear it, take it for the compliment that he intended. But he noticed just too late that the old lady was flustered.

'Good morning, Jack,' Nora had said. 'Were you talking about me? I'm just a little distracted, I'm afraid. I can't find Julia anywhere. She said she had to speak with someone but that was an hour ago. I checked in all the lounges and out on the terrace but there's no sign of her. Have you seen her at all?'

'No, I'm sorry, Miss Hames. Did she not say who it was she was due to meet?'

'Not at all. Just like my lamb to be so mysterious.'

'She'll be fine, I'm sure,' said Jack. 'Why don't you sit with us and we can hold a post-mortem on last night's game. You gave us quite a thrashing.'

The scream was distinct but distant.

'My goodness,' said Albert Moorgate. 'Whatever could *that* have been?'

All heads in the dining room turned for a moment, the rumble of conversation, the clatter of crockery, coming to a short-lived hush before resuming again.

Jack and his companions shook their heads, puzzled but unconcerned.

'And not just the tennis, Miss Hames,' said Frances, 'but there she was, barely a half-hour later, performing that piano recital for us. Astonishing.'

'Ah, here come the Ketterings,' said Albert Moorgate. 'I say, what was all that screaming about?'

'Good morning,' said Peter. 'No idea, I'm afraid, but there seems to be some sort of kerfuffle going on. D'you think somebody might have been murdered?'

'You've not read enough crime novels, Mister Kettering,' said Frances. 'The body is always discovered during dinner, never at breakfast.'

'They might do things differently over here,' said Kettering. 'Anyway, we must find a table. It's getting quite busy. What time do we move off?'

'Nine-thirty,' Nora replied. 'Which reminds me. I must finish packing. It's so difficult though unless I know what Julia wants to wear today. I shall have another look for her outside and then I'll just have to get on with it, I suppose. You *will* hurry her along if you see her, Jack, won't you?'

'Yes, of course. I'll just finish breakfast and then come and help you find her if she's not turned up. There's Mrs Holden, look. The fount of all knowledge. She's bound to have seen Miss Britten on her travels.'

Dorothea Holden stood in the dining room doorway, looking drawn, distraught. She finally spotted them and made her way over to the table as Nora Hames was standing to leave.

'Oh, Miss Hames,' she said. 'Please don't go just yet. I have some news. Or, at least, I think I do. It's all a bit vague, I'm afraid. But it seems that there's been an accident. The Manager appears to think that Miss Britten may be involved.'

'Accident?' said Nora. 'I bet the silly girl has fallen again. I'd better go and see.'

'No, Miss Hames. The Manager has asked that we should all wait in the dining room. Until…' Dorothea looked imploringly at Jack over Nora's mop of white hair. There was fear in the eyes of the indomitable Mrs Holden.

'Miss Hames,' said Jack. 'Nora. I think we should take Mrs Holden's advice. Stay here for a moment and I'll go and find out what's happening.'

Without waiting for Nora's response he dropped his napkin on the plate, moved around the table, felt Dorothea Holden's touch on his elbow.

'Mister Telford,' she whispered, 'the Manager has sent for the police. The Guardia Civil.'

'The police?' cried Nora Hames. 'Whatever for? I must go to her *now*.'

Jack tried to restrain her.

'Nora, wait!' he said.

'Let go of me this instant. Whoever do you think you *are*, Mister Telford? To be ordering me about. Let me go at once.'

She pulled herself free from Jack's grip, turned and almost ran from the dining room, but was halted once again, this time by Brendan Murphy. Behind him, two local policemen, not the *Civiles*, moved into position to guard the doors.

'What the hell's going on?' said Jack, as Brendan steered a struggling Nora Hames back towards him.

'Miss Hames,' Brendan said, 'you must listen. There's been a terrible accident and, sure, I have some *very* bad news.'

'No,' said Nora. 'I don't want to hear.'

'I know,' said the guide, 'and I wish that I could give this job to somebody else but it seems that Miss Britten has had an accident. A fatal one I'm afraid.'

'Fatal?' said Nora. The others gasped, expressed words of disbelief, as Nora's legs buckled beneath her and she slid to the floor at Brendan Murphy's feet.

'The Manager has sealed off the area and sent for the authorities,' said Brendan. There's really nothing else that we can do.' He crouched down to cradle Nora's head while Frances Moorgate fetched a glass of water. The guide called to one of the waiters, shouted an instruction so that, seconds later, the man returned with some smelling salts.

The next fifteen minutes were spent reviving Nora Hames, consoling her, receiving offers of cognac, tea perhaps, from the staff, and repeating the limited information available in turn to the Westons, to Carter-Holt, and to Sisters María Pereda and Berthe Schultz – who immediately took up station, kneeling at the edge of the group and offering prayers for the dead.

Finally, a Guardia arrived, spoke brusquely to Brendan Murphy.

'Miss Hames,' said the guide, 'there is a Lieutenant here in charge of the investigation. He needs to interview you. In the Manager's office.'

'Investigation?' Nora replied, her voice dull, distant.

'Yes. Just routine, sure. But he needs to speak with you. I'll have to come too. The Lieutenant speaks no English, it seems. And perhaps…?' Murphy looked at Jack.

'I'd be happy to come as well,' Jack confirmed.

He was *Teniente* Enrique Álvaro Turbides of the Guardia Civil Public Order and Prevention Service. A large man, deeply tanned, his eyes just too cold, his lips just too wide, his nose hooked, his black moustache slick with sweat, his cigar smouldering, his watch expensive, American, and consulted with impatient frequency.

The *Teniente* gave Jack and Nora a cursory glance, spoke briefly to the Hotel Manager standing in the corner at a semblance of attention, then made a short speech for Brendan Murphy's benefit.

'The Lieutenant...' began the guide.

'¡Teniente, por favor!' said the officer.

Brendan Murphy acknowledged his mistake.

'The *Teniente*,' he continued, stressing the title, 'has been asked to express condolences on behalf of National Spain at the loss of such a noted musician,' Nora Hames released a racking sob.

'So my little girl *is*...?' whispered Nora.

'I'm afraid so, Miss Hames,' said Brendan.

'But how? I don't understand.'

The guide translated for the Lieutenant. Another speech.

'The *Teniente* says that this appears to be an unfortunate accident. Miss Britten was seemingly trapped by the lift and killed. But he does not wish to be pressed further at this stage. He must investigate. He asks you to understand that his presence here signifies only that Miss Britten was a foreign national on a state-sponsored tour. Otherwise he would simply have sent a Guardia, a Sergeant perhaps, to check the facts. But, in the circumstances...'

In the circumstances, thought Jack, *his superiors have ordered him to get off his backside and limit any damage.*

'Trapped by the lift?' said Nora. 'But...'

Teniente Enrique Álvaro Turbides spoke again, nodding without expression in Jack's direction.

'The *Teniente* also says,' said Brendan, 'that he will need somebody to identify Miss Britten.'

'So it might *not* be Julia?' Nora cried. 'It *can't* have been Julia. She wouldn't have used the lift. Not alone.'

'I'm afraid that that there's no doubt about it, Miss Hames. But the authorities...'

'Perfectly understandable,' said Jack. 'And perhaps if Miss Hames would allow me...'

'Certainly not!' said Nora. 'I want to see her.' She began to cry again.

'It would be best to take up Mister Telford's offer,' said the guide. 'I'm sure there'll be plenty of opportunity for you to see Miss Britten later.'

There was a knock at the door, the *Teniente* calling on the Manager to open it. An army officer entered, carrying a tripod, a large camera, and at his side was a Guardia with a set of immaculately pressed overalls, a pair of cotton gloves, draped over his arm.

No chance that the Teniente *is going to risk getting his uniform dirty then*, thought Jack.

Behind the Guardia came a third man, an engineer Jack realised from the cantilever toolbox that he carried.

The Lieutenant spoke again.

'The *Teniente* says that he must now supervise the investigation. He will send for you when he is ready and, meanwhile, he has summoned a doctor to provide some medical attention for Miss Hames.'

Being dismissed, Jack escorted a bewildered, lost and lonely Nora back to the dining room where an update had to be given for the rest of the group. He sensed that they had been in some deep discussion, abruptly brought to a halt with Nora's return.

They'll be wondering how long this will go on, he thought. *How long their cosy trip will be delayed. Whether they will ever get further than San Sebastián. Selfish bastards!*

'Poor Miss Hames,' said Frances Moorgate to Jack, following him as he stepped away to light a badly-needed *Capstan.* 'And poor *you!* Having to identify the body. How very distressing. I don't suppose, Jack…I don't suppose that you would consider taking me with you?'

'Whatever for?' said Jack.

'Oh,' she said, 'just so that you don't have to do it alone.'

But Jack made sure that he was indeed alone when they called him an hour later to perform his duty.

The second-floor corridor was in the south wing, but it looked exactly like those on Jack's own side of the Hotel. The section around the paternoster had been cordoned by the use of the Hotel's tall laundry trolleys, sheets suspended between, and inside this makeshift bivouac lay a forlorn bundle on a stretcher, covered entirely by blankets, her only company provided by the Guardia Civil Lieutenant, one of his men and, of course, Brendan Murphy.

The elevator itself had been stopped, naturally, with the floor of the right-hand upward platform just above corridor level and not yet cleaned, so that Jack was immediately sickened by the sight of blood in two distinct but mostly coagulated rivulets down the front visible edge of the platform itself, with more swatches of gore – but surprisingly few to Jack's eyes – appearing as dark stains on the carpet, and already attracting noisome flies. Some form of chalk had been used to mark a circle on the floor here while, on the floor of the paternoster platform, there was another outline, roughly etched in white to show the former position of the victim's legs, pointing towards the back of the lift. There was a smell too, though Jack could not define it. But it made him think, illogically, of butterflies.

Teniente Enrique Álvaro Turbides had succeeded in keeping his overalls clean, though the finger-tips of his gloves were stained with blood. He held out each hand in turn for the Guardia to remove them, never once taking his eyes from Jack. He was saying something. Slow. Bored. That deep, guttural Spanish.

'The *Teniente* thanks you for coming up,' said Murphy. 'He asks whether you're ready, sure?'

'As ready as I ever will be, I suppose.' Jack felt his stomach churn, his head become light.

The guide relayed his consent and the Guardia was ordered forward. He knelt, took the edges of the blanket and looked up at Jack for a sign that he should proceed. Jack nodded, and the man peeled the blanket back carefully, slowly, revealing Julia

Britten's face down to her chin. The head was tilted curiously, as though the pianist was somehow trying to turn towards him, the straight hair now seeming even thinner, more lank. There was some discolouration on her right cheek and the eyes were rolled up under half-closed lids to reveal more than was natural of the whites while the mouth was open, Julia's lips now a shade of pale blue. But it *was* Julia.

Jack nodded again and the Guardia began to stand, to replace the blanket. But as he did so, Jack caught just one quick sight of the previously concealed part of Julia Britten's head below the chin. He took a step backwards, repelled, looking up at Brendan Murphy, then at the *Teniente*, who remained staring at him.

'What in the name of God...?' said Jack.

'You need to confirm the identification first, Mister Telford,' said Brendan.

'Well, of course it's Julia Britten,' Jack replied, angry now. 'But what the hell happened to her?'

The guide spoke at some length with the *Teniente* who, in turn, finally shrugged and gave permission for Brendan to speak.

'The *Teniente* stresses that his investigation is far from complete but he believes that, from his initial inspection, Miss Britten was travelling alone in the lift. It is possible that she fell as the paternoster travelled past the second floor and, when she fell...Well, her head must have been over the edge of the platform. It is certain, Mister Telford, that as the elevator travelled upwards, it severed the head from her body.'

'Oh, Sweet Jesus,' said Jack, steadying himself against the wall.

'A guest staying on this floor discovered Miss Britten's head here, Mister Telford. But her body was still travelling on the paternoster.'

'But Nora Hames is right,' Jack protested. 'There's no way that Miss Britten would have been using the lift alone. She never understood why elevator buttons aren't marked for blind people to use.'

'Well, she *was* in the lift. There's no doubt about it. And she can't have been with anybody else or they wouldn't have left her like this, would they?'

'And there's so little blood. How...?'

'The *Teniente* has inspected the lift shaft, Mister Telford. You must believe me. All the evidence shows that he is correct. The cleaners are already at work on the floors above.' Jack had a momentary vision of the way it might have been, tried to put the vision away, looked up to see a splatter of blood around the upper edge of the opening. 'She would have died instantly, Mister Telford.'

'I still don't understand. If her body was down here...'

'Miss Britten was going up, Mister Telford. The accident happened as the *Teniente* has described. But the paternoster kept going round. We don't know how many times. Not precisely. Three, four times maybe. Then one lady came out here. She screamed. Panic. But another guest, on the floor below, saw the body on the paternoster. By the time she found the emergency button, it had travelled up here again to the second floor. It's just coincidence, Mister Telford.'

Just coincidence that poor Julia's body ended up reunited with her head. Or almost.

'So what now, *Teniente*?' said Jack, addressing himself directly to the Guardia officer.

The Lieutenant's man was helping his superior out of the overalls.

'Now,' said Brendan Murphy, 'Miss Britten must be taken to the mortuary at the José Antonio Hospital. It may have been an accident but it was still a violent death and, obviously, one with a certain profile. So a judge, a *juez de instrucción*...'

'A coroner?'

'More or less. Anyway, the judge must decide whether an autopsy is necessary. If so, one of the hospital doctors will carry out the procedure.' The Lieutenant spoke again. Brendan nodded. 'And the *Teniente* must then submit a report to Burgos. After that...Well, we'll see.'

'Nora Hames will want to see the body,' said Jack. 'And then what?'

'All in good time, Mister Telford. For now it might be best if you say as little as possible about what you've seen here. The *Teniente* hopes that he can rely on your discretion. He needs to interview some of us, myself, Miss Hames. You too. The whole group, I suppose. But I don't think he'll take long.'

Jack returned to the dining room. A doctor had arrived, a small and dapper man with spats, a top hat, and though he had examined Nora Hames, he refused to provide any medication until after she had spoken with the *Civiles*. He seemed to know as well as Jack that such an interview was imminent and he promised to wait until afterwards to make sure that the old lady was properly treated. Jack quietly confirmed Nora's worst fears and she broke down once more, particularly when he told her that she could not see the body herself until much later. But she apologised to Jack for her rudeness towards him earlier. He held her for a while.

Time passed slowly until Brendan Murphy appeared again. He enquired politely enough whether Miss Hames felt able to speak with the Lieutenant and, yes, of course, Mister Telford could still accompany her. He had already been interviewed himself, he explained. Just standard questions.

Standard? Jack wondered.

Banal might have been a better word. At what time had Miss Hames last seen Julia Britten? Around quarter past seven, it seemed, though Nora could not be precise to the minute. And where was Miss Britten going? She had not said. Merely that she needed to speak with somebody. Was it usual, given her condition, for Miss Britten to go unattended in this way? Well, it was hardly a 'condition' and, yes, once she had orientated herself to a new environment, she would frequently go 'unattended.'

'Is the Lieutenant implying some criticism?' Nora added.

'You have to understand, Miss Hames,' said Brendan, 'that the *Teniente* did not know Miss Britten in the same way that you did. He has to ask.'

'Then he would do better to ask more pertinent questions,' Nora retorted. 'For example, why would my poor lamb have been in the lift at all when she *always* made a point of avoiding them? Or why does he not find out where Mrs Weston was at the time of dear Julia's death?'

'Miss Hames,' said Jack. 'Nora. It can't help to make accusations like that.'

'Oh, I might have known *you'd* side with that jezebel!'

'It's not a matter of sides. Really, it isn't. But there's no reason…'

Brendan Murphy had been interpreting the exchange for the Lieutenant, whose tone now became abrupt as he checked his watch once more.

'The *Teniente* says that he has no more questions,' said Brendan. 'Except to check whether you're certain about the time when Miss Britten left you. You said seven-fifteen, or thereabouts?'

'Yes,' said Nora. 'I'm certain of it. But is he not going to follow up my concerns?'

'The *Teniente* will interview everybody, Miss Hames. But meanwhile he suggests that you go back to the doctor. I'm to deliver him a note confirming that he may now administer a mild sedative. You need to get some sleep.'

She protested, naturally, but cooperated reasonably with Jack as he took her back to the dining room, found the medical gentleman and then helped Nora to the first-floor south wing room where the doctor gave her some pills. The old fellow even agreed to sit with her while Jack went to fetch his book, but *The Hobbit* did little to distract him as he took up a silent vigil at her bedside while Nora Hames fell into a troubled, mumbling, drug-inspired sleep. Jack must have dozed himself, chin on chest and jerking in his chair when a gentle knock at the door roused him. It was Dorothea Holden, come to summon him for a group meeting with the Lieutenant. He took a last look at Nora, decided that she would sleep for some time to come, and joined Mrs Holden in the corridor.

'Myself and the Professor have been interviewed already,' she explained, 'but rather for background reasons, I think. Though poor Mrs Weston has faced some strange questions it seems. Did Miss Hames make any accusations against her, do you know?'

'Not that I'm aware,' Jack lied.

The Hotel Manager had now designated one of the lounge rooms, on this same side of the terrace, for the group's use, and *Teniente* Enrique Álvaro Turbides was waiting impatiently to begin when Jack and Mrs Holden finally appeared.

'It was so kind of them to make this room available to us, don't you think, Mister Telford?' said Dorothea as they took their seats.

Oh very! thought Jack. *Keeps us out of sight while they get the Hotel cleaned up again.* But he was surprised to note that it was still only eleven o' clock.

'The *Teniente*,' said Brendan, beginning the now familiar litany once more, 'just has a couple of extra questions.' The Lieutenant spoke. 'First, did anybody except Miss Hames see Miss Britten this morning?' There was a long pause.

'It seems not,' said Valerie Carter-Holt. 'But is the *Teniente* in a position to tell us more about this terrible accident yet? A fault with the lift, surely? And there are such terrible rumours.'

She's forgotten to put on the snooty accent again, thought Jack.

'The engineer confirms,' said Brendan, 'that the elevator's in perfect working order. It's been regularly maintained and never given any trouble. Those old paternosters will go on running forever, sure. And this is a *very* good hotel, Miss Carter-Holt.'

'And is it true, Mister Murphy,' said Frances Moorgate, 'that Miss Britten was... Well, decapitated?' The others coughed, gasped, generally shifted uncomfortably.

The guide relayed the question.

'Yes,' he said. 'The *Teniente* confirms that detail. But he needs to know if anybody is aware of Miss Britten's intended movements this morning. He believes that Miss Britten died at around eight, although Miss Hames is certain that she left their room three-quarters of an hour earlier. He's trying to fill in the missing time.'

But the group had nothing to add and the Lieutenant seemed happy to release them on the understanding that they remained near the Hotel until he could update them, probably mid-afternoon, promising to let them know once he had heard further from Burgos. After all, *El Caudillo* himself had an interest in this matter.

Only Jack was asked to remain as the others filed out of the lounge.

'The *Teniente* has one or two more questions, Mister Telford,' said Brendan Murphy.

'Questions for me?'

The Lieutenant smiled at him, took a cigar from his shirt pocket, spoke to Murphy in a knowing way.

'He says that you were close to Miss Britten.'

'Close?'

'Yes, close. You were friends, Mister Telford.'

'I met Julia Britten for the first time last Friday. Four days ago. You know that, Mister Murphy. Does the *Teniente* have a specific question?'

The Lieutenant brushed aside Brendan's translation of Jack's comment, used a small cutter to chop the point from his cigar, a clean snip, another smile, another comment.

He understands me just fine, thought Jack.

'The *Teniente* asks whether Miss Britten seemed troubled.'

'Troubled, how? I'm afraid, Mister Murphy, that I don't see where this is taking us.'

'I think,' said Brendan, 'that while the *Teniente* is sure that this was merely an unfortunate accident, he is slightly concerned that, as accidents go, this one is somewhat strange, *difficult* was the word he used.'

'Well, that's usually the way with accidents. By definition they take you by surprise. Or does he think that Miss Britten found the most unlikely option open to her for committing suicide?' Jack almost choked on the word, stared directly into the Lieutenant's dark, cold eyes, and saw his father suddenly reflected there. 'Is he serious?' Jack continued. 'Tell him he'd be better occupied exploring Miss Hames's concerns about why Miss Britten would have chosen to break the habit of a lifetime and use the elevator at all.'

The Lieutenant regarded him a while, lit the cigar, spoke to Brendan.

'The *Teniente* says that he is, indeed, exploring all avenues, Mister Telford. His Guardias are interviewing every guest and every member of staff. But this *was* an accident, and there should be no implication to the contrary. You are, apparently, dismissed.'

Jack said nothing but left the room and made his way to the bar. He needed *something*, settled for a whiskey, another *Capstan*. He would be down to the *Superiores* soon.

'Mind if I joins 'e, me old acker?' said Max Weston.

Jack had not even noticed him.

Oh no, he thought. *Just what I need!* But as he turned to face him he saw that the comedian was sporting a real shiner, a black eye that seemed to fit incongruously with his otherwise scrubbed appearance, his Harris Tweed jacket, his flannels. He looked, suddenly, like a small boy polished for Sunday School.

'Where on earth did you get *that*?' said Jack. 'And yes, of course you can join me. Can I get you one?'

Max accepted a whiskey too, while reciting a rambling story about walking into a door. *My God*, thought Jack, *she's thumped him again!* Weston tentatively asked whether he might share a joke, hoping that Mister Telford would not think it inappropriate.

Therapy. But for which of us?

Jack was not sure whether the joke was actually funny or whether he suffered from some delayed reaction, some release from the tension of Julia Britten's macabre death, but the thing made him laugh.

'That's not bad, Max,' he said, 'not bad at all.'

But he could not stay around for another and, having confirmed that the group was due to meet again at three, he slipped out of the Hotel, deciding to pass up on the buffet lunch that was being arranged for them, back in the private lounge. Instead, he wandered the streets near the bridge, picked up the *ABC*, bought a cup of something passing for coffee, a slice of almond cake, ate it guiltily as, outside, two bare-footed urchins stared at him ravenously through the glass.

Jack scanned the newspaper, concentrating on the words in an effort to drive out visions of Julia's disembodied head. *War kills all manner of innocents*, he thought.

And here was the update on the Sudeten crisis. The Czechs, so far as he could tell, had decided to accept recommendations from the French and British Governments – although there seemed to be no details about the proposals themselves. All the same, Chamberlain was apparently planning a second visit to the Führer and compromise seemed to be the order of the day. *So we'll give the fascists a free hand again*, he thought. *We did nothing to stop the Japanese invading Manchuria. Or the Italians in Abyssinia. Or the Germans in Austria. Or Franco here in Spain. Now poor bloody Czechoslovakia.*

He thought about Julia. Her intelligence. Her music. Her tennis. Her humour.

Jack glanced back through the window. The hungry children had gone, replaced now by the ghost of his father again, his arm protectively around Julia

Britten's shoulders. His father whispered in Julia's ear and they each smiled at Jack. He finished the coffee, paid his bill and returned to the Hotel. At three he made his way back to the lounge for the group meeting. Nora Hames was already there, Catherine Kettering sitting next to her, holding the older woman's hands.

'Ah, Mister Telford,' said Dorothea Holden, 'we wondered where you'd gone. I was just explaining that the Lieutenant has sent his apologies but also word that a medical examination of poor Miss Britten will take place on Thursday. He stresses once again that this is simply routine, that arrangements have then been made for…' she paused, 'Miss Britten's remains…to be shipped back to England on Friday. A vessel sailing from Bilbao. The British Consulate is being informed. Miss Hames will accompany the coffin, naturally.'

'She can't travel alone,' said Jack. 'Would you like me to come with you, Miss Hames?'

'That won't be possible, Mister Telford,' said Brendan Murphy. 'The *Teniente* was only able to secure one ticket for the passage, I'm afraid.'

'I'm sure that something could be arranged.'

'No, Jack,' said Nora. 'It's quite alright. I think you'd be more help here.'

'Here?' said Jack. 'Surely we can't go on with this? Not now.'

'As it happens, Mister Telford,' said the guide, 'we strongly recommend that the tour should continue. We can make some slight changes to the itinerary.'

'It's what my poor lamb would have wanted,' said Nora.

'There is apparently an excellent medical officer on the ship,' said Dorothea Holden, 'who will care for all of Miss Hames's needs.'

'Of course,' said Brendan, 'if Mister Telford chooses not to continue, we could always make arrangements for him to be escorted back to Hendaye. We should regret it, sure, but it's understandable. Anybody else too, I suppose.'

But nobody else seemed interested in the offer and Jack, looking at Nora Hames, knew that he too was destined to remain with the group.

'Are you sure that you can manage this voyage on Friday?' he asked.

'I need to get my sweet girl home as soon as possible. Her parents are both dead now but she has a sister. I will try to arrange a telegram later. And I need you to do something for me, dear Jack.'

'Anything, Nora. What is it?'

'Well, you might think that I'm a silly old goose but it really gets my goat the way these people turn everybody who's died in this dreadful war into a martyr. You won't let them do that to my lovely Julia, will you, Jack?'

'Not if I can help it.'

'There's a second thing too. Mister Murphy was saying, before you arrived, that General Franco's office will release an official press statement.'

Jack shook his head, though he was hardly surprised.

'I'll try to make sure they don't say anything stupid. But can you tell me something, Nora? Julia made a comment to me about people on the tour not being what they seem. Do you know what she meant?'

'No,' said Nora. 'I'm sorry, Jack. But she had a bee in her bonnet about *something.* It's why she went off so early this morning. She wouldn't tell me where she was going though. And I know this much. That Julia would never have got in that lift alone. *Never,* Jack.'

'I know.'

'Will you look after something for me?'

'What is it?'

Nora reached under her chair, took out a large book, similar to a photograph album.

'This,' she said. 'My darling's scrap book. I can't bear to look at it. Not yet.'

'You want me to look after it?' said Jack. 'Maybe I could write a piece about Julia.'

'Would you, Jack? You're such a good boy!' Take good care of it though. And bring it safely back to England with you.'

Jack took the book.

'Now what?' he said.

'Now?' said Nora. 'Now I have to pack poor Julia's things. Her blouses. Her skirts. Her powder and lipstick.' Jack had a vision of the old lady, touching each item, each possession, with all the reverence that only the most faithful of retainers, the best of friends, could muster. And, as she did so, Julia Britten would live again. Just briefly. 'And I have one very last favour to ask.' Nora wiped a tear from her cheek. 'I don't know how to convince you, Jack Telford, but I'm certain that Julia's death was no accident. So you must stay, dear boy. Stay and find out who killed my poor lamb!'

Chapter Nine

Wednesday 21 September 1938

The image of Nora Hames's tiny and tearful figure, with its halo of snow-white hair, the linen handkerchief, remained with Jack throughout the morning.

They had each taken their leave of her on the steps of the María Cristina Hotel before climbing aboard the bus, the vehicle now seeming strangely spacious, a welcome and familiar friend after their confinement. There was some confusion about whether they should continue to follow Dorothea Holden's rotational seating plan and, if so, what should happen to the seats previously occupied by Julia Britten and her friend? Jack left them to the debate, chose to settle himself upon the dickie between the *Coors Beer* travel coolers so that he could keep the old lady in sight for as long as possible.

But the image unnerved him. It was that frizzy perm, he thought. Some Disney association with the year's cinematic sensation. Celluloid visions of Julia in a glass coffin, mourned by her faithful, diminutive and failed companion. Julia biting the forbidden fruit. A hooded figure holding out the poisoned apple, the scent of it alone enough to entice the blind pianist towards the waiting jaws of a voracious paternoster elevator.

Can the old lady have been right? he thought. *Murdered?*

They turned a corner and Nora Hames disappeared, the idea seeming preposterous almost as soon as she was no longer visible. *Out of sight...*

Meanwhile, Brendan Murphy was outlining an audacious plan at Dorothea's request. It was difficult, she knew, but if they were going to proceed then a plan was essential. Murphy apologised too, then reminded them that the original intention for the previous day was to visit Eibar, then Durango and Amorebieta before reaching their overnight accommodation, the Palacio Urgoiti in Galdakao, a total journey of just over one hundred kilometres and a full day. Then, this morning, they would have driven back to Amorebieta and taken a detour north to visit Guernica.

'The town's become almost the high point of these tours,' said Brendan. '*Señores* Bolín and de Armas Gourié are both keen that visitors should see for themselves...' Mention of Laureano de Armas Gourié reminded Albert Moorgate that the fellow had promised to join them again in San Sebastián. 'I'm sure we'll meet him again in due course, sir,' Brendan continued. 'But, as I say, the Department is keen for us to see what really happened at Guernica, rather than all the Red propaganda.'

Jack felt his anger rising. *Red propaganda?* he thought. *George Steer's eye-witness account for* The Times? But he kept the thought in check. Plenty of time when they reached poor Guernica itself.

'Well,' said Dorothea, 'I'm sure that none of us should wish to miss it. Can we change the itinerary perhaps?'

'Already arranged, sure,' said Brendan. 'If you're all agreeable, that is. But it makes for a difficult day. We'd follow the route as planned. Drive to Eibar. That's about sixty-five kilometres but the road's not easy. It takes at least three hours, sometimes longer. But we could stop there for some early lunch.'

'Oh, early lunch would be such a relief,' said Albert Moorgate.

'We'll maybe have to settle for something light but there's a decent enough place to eat there. Then we can drive straight through Durango and Amorebieta. Instead of stopping for too long I can just point out some of the main areas of interest. But I've wired ahead to make sure we can get a drink. That means we can still visit Guernica by late afternoon. See the sights, some more refreshments, then on to Galdakao in time for dinner.'

'Sounds like it'll be bed-time when we gets to the hotel,' complained Marguerite Weston. 'Late dinner. Again! An' more o' this Spanish stuff, I suppose.'

'But at least it will put us back on track,' said Dorothea. 'Sounds like an excellent plan, Mister Murphy.'

Yes, thought Jack. *Excellent. Not a mention of Julia Britten. Not a thought for Guernica's thousand civilian dead. But at least the food's all sorted and the bloody trip's back on schedule.*

On schedule and on the rutted road for Eibar, Jack surrendered the dickie to Brendan Murphy while the others arranged themselves in their new seats. He was astonished at the scenery. Luxurious, verdant forest, spread across volcanic peaks. Hilltop villages, crumbling railway embankments, and the apartments of Elgoibar overhanging the river. The ruined church. The gorge. The white water.

'So, Mister Telford,' said the guide, 'we're all a bit quiet this morning. Only to be expected, sure.'

'There are so many twists and turns. I think everybody's concentrating on keeping in one piece.'

'The road, you mean?'

'Do I?' said Jack. 'Yes, I suppose so.'

'And you spent the evening with Miss Hames, I think?'

'Bless her, I'm not sure she realised I was there. Not really. I didn't stay long. Then went back to my room and tried to read.'

'You skipped supper then?'

'Didn't everybody?' said Jack. 'I don't imagine many of us had an appetite.'

He had sat with Nora's scrap book but found himself unable to get past the first few pages. Nora's name and address inside the cover. Several grainy photographs of Julia's infant years. Romford 1894. Romford 1895. Perched on top of a cushion-covered piano stool, aged three and four. The bewildered, sightless five year old, no longer smiling for the camera lens. Small child entering the Guildhall School of Music, a newspaper cutting to mark the event. Enter the youthful Nora Hames, guiding Julia's slender hands over pages of New York Point. *Not everybody is what they seem.* And he had re-lived his own recollections of Miss Britten, infuriating himself on each of the frequent occasions when these settled themselves on the altercations between Julia and Marguerite Weston, at Irún, at San Sebastián.

Conversations elsewhere on the bus seemed stilted, even Max having little to say for himself until, after almost three hours that rattled their insides incessantly, they ran down into Eibar itself. Murphy pointed out the ruins of houses, one hundred of them, he said, burned by Red arsonists. Yet Jack could see little evidence of fire damage, just heaps of rubble between those taller buildings still standing, particularly in the upper sections of the town away to the left.

They stopped at a *bodega* where they were obviously expected, its walls exhaling the soured breath of fermenting wine and oak casks, its beams dripping with a hundred golden hams. The group did no more than pick at the food, with the exception of Marguerite and Sister Berthe Schultz, both of whom seemed determined to compensate for the others' lack of appreciation and Sister María Pereda explaining her colleague's beliefs about the virtues and obligations of hospitality.

'Brendan's superiors are likely to charge him with brutality if they see the shiners that you and Max are both sporting,' said Jack to Catherine as he joined the Ketterings' table.

'Do you think that it might afford me some celebrity, Mister Telford, if I can boast that both myself and Mister Weston were each brutalised on broadly the same day by broadly the same person? And it was certainly *not* our guide!' Jack smirked at her, cast a glance across the room towards Marguerite. 'Anyway, Mister Telford,' Catherine continued, 'we haven't had a chance to say how sorry we were about Miss Britten. An awful thing.'

'I keep having to remind everybody that I only knew Julia as long as the rest of the group. But thanks. And how are you two getting along anyway?'

'What do you mean?' said Peter Kettering, as though there was some trickery behind the question.

'Your brother,' Jack replied. 'I thought you were hoping to discover a bit more about his service here. As well as collecting the medal from Franco, of course.'

'You're not exactly a sympathiser of General Franco, are you, Mister Telford?' said Catherine.

'No, that's true. But it doesn't stop me sympathising with those who lost loved ones to war, Mrs Kettering, regardless of which side they were on. Your husband's loss must have touched you deeply as well.'

She looked up at him, fixed him with a penetrating glare, then returned to her food without answering.

'*My* loss?' said Kettering. There was something clumsy about the stress he put on the thing. 'My brother was a revolutionary in his own way too, Mister Telford. He was very active in the union. Believed it was his duty as a Catholic. To stand beside his fellows and so on. But he believed in revolutionary change. He held strongly to the view that industrial revolution brought more progress for humanity in the eighteenth century than had been achieved in the previous thousand years. And that social revolution in the nineteenth had brought five times as much advance as the century before.'

'Change is certainly happening fast,' said Jack. 'But what next? It feels to me that all the progress we've made in the past two hundred years will be wiped out by these wars we keep fighting. Isn't that what history will say about the twentieth century? That we were the generations who squandered the chance for peace and prosperity?'

'My brother believed that from the evils of war has sprung the New Age of Mankind, Mister Telford. The Age of National Socialism, of course.'

'And you agree with that?' said Jack.

Kettering looked around, furtively.

'Between you and me, Mister Telford,' he whispered, 'I think that it's all tommyrot. You mustn't quote me, mind. It was Donald's belief, not mine. But it would be a blessing to find out something about his time here in Spain.'

Jack decided to stretch his legs and have a smoke before getting back on the bus, found Brendan Murphy talking to Mikel, the driver.

'Mister Murphy,' he said. 'I was wondering about Peter Kettering's brother, Donald. He died fighting with your Foreign Legion, didn't he? Is there any chance of finding out anything about his service record? The Ketterings don't seem to have had much luck tracking it down.'

Well, that's your good deed done for the day, Jack, he thought, as the guide agreed to help if he could, although he warned that it would not be easy. Jack's self-congratulation did not last long, however, for he realised that he had forgotten to ask Murphy about the press release that would apparently be issued from Franco's office about Julia's death. *I must remember to collar him afterwards, see if there's any way I can influence the damned thing.*

The road climbed out of Eibar towards Durango, marked by a succession of wooden barns, granaries raised on stone pillars, distant granite ridges marching across the southern horizon. But it was an easier run, and twenty minutes later they were approaching Durango, turning off to cross the train tracks and stop outside the Basilica, its three-sectioned tower crowned with pinnacles and fine tracery, its roof webbed with crude scaffolding, a dozen workmen still dedicated to the repairs.

'Well,' said Brendan Murphy, 'you have to imagine that it's the end of March last year. Our offensive has cut off the Reds' supply line to the French border here in the north, but they still hold much of the Basque country, and particularly Bilbao. So General Mola launches a major offensive to take the city. It was necessary to hit some key military objectives first, of course, and those included the road and rail junctions at Durango. Our bombers picked their targets carefully; making sure that there was no loss of innocent life.'

'I met somebody who was here at the time,' said Jack, fingering the note-book that he had taken from his bag.

'During the offensive?' asked the guide.

'A few days after the bombing. When the townspeople were burying their dead. Two hundred of them by then, and the death toll still rising.'

'This would be one of your Communist reporter friends, one imagines?' said Professor Holden.

'Calvinist, as it happens,' Jack replied. 'From Anglesey. He was in Bilbao. An ambulance volunteer.'

'But a journalist all the same?' said Dorothea. 'And running ambulances for the Reds, of course.'

'I think that driving an ambulance in a war zone must be the height of bravery,' said Frances Moorgate. 'The Red Cross should be sacred to all, don't you think? To each side.'

'But he *was* a journalist,' said Jack. 'Yes, you're right. He wrote for the *North Wales Observer* and some Welsh language papers. He's with the *Western Mail* now, I think. All very Left-wing, as you know.'

'And not here on the day in question, Mister Telford,' said Brendan. He called on Mikel to stop the bus. 'So I can assure you that only military targets were attacked that day. Yet when the town fell to General Mola's forces, four weeks later, they found that Anarchists had set fire to the town as well. They'd locked up priests and nuns. Shot them. Burned the churches. Or worse. This one they'd turned into a brothel. There used to be some sacred relics here. Mummified remains of the Count and Countess of Durango. The Reds did unspeakable things to them, then set fire to the remains.'

There were gasps. How could anyone abuse the dead in this way?

'My Calvinist friend says that he spoke to some of the nuns who survived,' said Jack. He flipped open the note-book. 'He says that we should visit the Santa Susanna chapel. The bodies of fourteen nuns were taken from the ruins there on the afternoon of the bombing. They'd all been crushed by falling masonry.'

Sisters María Pereda and Berthe Schultz whispered to each other, shaking their heads in disbelief.

'Churches and convents must be easily distinguishable from the air,' said Albert Moorgate. 'I'm not RC, as you know, but I can't believe that General Franco's men would bomb religious institutions, Mister Telford. It's a preposterous notion.'

'Well,' said Jack. 'Not General Franco's men precisely. Eye-witnesses clearly identified these as Junkers heavy bombers. Some Italian machines too. No, Mister Moorgate, this was the first defenceless target in the world to be attacked by Hitler's new Luftwaffe. Not the last, of course, as we'll see when we get to Guernica and Bilbao, I suspect.'

'Ah, the Hun!' said Moorgate. 'I suppose that's different.'

'Oh, how the Left loves to perpetuate a myth,' said Valerie Carter-Holt. 'Is it not possible, Mister Murphy, to stop at one of the churches and interview some people ourselves?'

'Yes,' said Jack. 'Why not start with the Church of Santa María de Uribarri?

Ask the priest what happened to his predecessor? His name was Padre Morilla, apparently. Killed when German bombs came through the roof while he was celebrating Mass. Died along with a score of his parishioners. It's an enormous place, according to my notes. The biggest building for miles. Easy to spot from the air, I imagine. Huge ornate tower, they say.'

An angry Brendan Murphy told the driver to carry on. Mikel asked a question, received a curt response.

'No, Mikel. Amorebieta. *¡Adelante!* We've no time, I'm afraid. But the Church of Santa María still stands, Mister Telford. Its roof too. The Kurutziaga Cross just outside. It's a famous landmark. And I imagine that your friend couldn't explain away the loss of San Pedro de Tabira's mummies, sure?'

He's right, thought Jack. *Actually, I don't remember John mentioning mummies at all. He seemed more occupied with the recently dead for some strange reason.*

They drove further along the main street in almost complete silence, life continuing amongst the peculiar mixture of intact half-timbered houses and the shattered ghosts of others, tall façades with nothing to support them, the interiors destroyed. And suddenly, there before them was another church, its roof gone, an enormous cloistered area at its front, all a mess of tumbled beams.

'Is that...?' Jack began.

'Santa María de Uribarri,' said Mikel, proudly, though Brendan Murphy said nothing at all. The church was, indeed, very large.

Faces turned up towards the bus as it passed, children on their way home from school. Dinner time. But they were faces without emotion, similar to those that John Williams Hughes had shown Jack at the Bristol fund-raising lecture, except that *those* snaps had been taken in Old Colwyn, Basque children all refugees in North Wales.

'Sister Berthe Schultz,' said the younger nun from the seat across the aisle, 'say that *El Caudillo* would not permit the killing of those who have taken Holy Orders, *Señor.* Sister Berthe Schultz say that you have been deceived by the serpent. But I have told her that you are a good man.'

'Accidents happen, I suppose,' said Jack, looking out of the window again. 'Is this a different river, Mister Murphy?'

'The Oka,' said the guide, but offered no further information.

Oh dear, I've upset him. Now he's sulking.

'Speakin' of accidents,' said Max, who had taken the empty seat behind Jack, 'I knows this farmer. 'E goes to the doctor with a bad back. You 'ad any accidents lately? asks the doctor. No, nothin', says the farmer. Ah, says the doctor, but workin' on the farm can be a bit dangerous, can't it? Too true, me old acker, says the farmer. Why, last week I got kicked by the 'orse, butted by the goat and bit by the dog. An' you don't call *them* accidents? says the doctor. Bless 'e, no, says the farmer. Them buggers done it on purpose.'

I need a smoke, thought Jack, but he turned to Max in the hope that he might avert the craving.

'Tell me about this Mexican thing, Max,' he said. 'Where do you get all your jokes? And how will you make them fit the Mexico plot?'

'You're going to Mexico, Mister Weston?' said Carter-Holt, now sitting opposite Max. She seemed genuinely interested.

'Ooh ah!' said Max. 'Marguerite's a-went an' sorted this contract see. New film, like. *Mexican Max* 'e's called. An' I write most o' the jokes, Jack. Most o' the script, in fact. So it's off to the Hotel Playa for Max Weston, me 'ansums. Ensenada. What d'you think about that, Miss Carter-Holt?'

'Intriguing,' said Valerie. 'If you go through Mexico City, you can pass on Mister Telford's regards to Comrade Trotsky. I'm sure they have much in common. As revolutionaries, of course.'

Very clever, thought Jack, recalling last year's interview with the exiled Trotsky by Kingsley Martin for the New Statesman. *Is he still living with Diego Rivera? Red Terror. White terror.*

'Oh, I don't 'old with politics,' said Max. 'I leave all that to Mrs Weston. Marguerite's good at all that negotiatin' stuff.'

But the comedian's brow furrowed.

Jack Dempsey. Poor Max!

They arrived at Amorebieta just after two-thirty.

'We've made good progress,' called Brendan Murphy. 'Time for refreshments, sure.'

Time, too, for the bus to make a rapid circuit of the town. Less damage here than at Durango and Eibar, it seemed, but a team of forced labourers – prisoners of war, apparently – working on the shattered shell of an old church. Burned, inevitably, by the Reds in '36, said Brendan. Then through the Plaza del Calvario to see the building now serving as a women's prison, all the inmates having been sentenced to death for acts of sedition, arson, murder but, thanks to the compassion of *El Caudillo,* now serving commuted sentences.

They arrived at the Town Hall with nobody to greet them. In the distance, an accordion played. But, otherwise, the entire place seemed deserted, its red and yellow flag hanging limp from the balcony. It was *siesta* time, naturally, though this had made no difference so far to any of the tour's various arrangements. In Amorebieta, however, it looked as though they were not expected after all. Brendan hammered on the venerable oak of the *ayuntamiento* doors until a guard appeared. There was a brief argument and the man ran off at Murphy's insistence, buttoning his tunic in the process.

'A problem, Mister Murphy?' said Dorothea Holden as the other passengers alighted, some joining Jack for a smoke.

'He says that the Mayor thinks we cancelled the visit,' explained the guide. 'Some mix-up, sure. I do apologise but we'll try to get it sorted out. We could always...'

But there was no need for an alternative plan, for the guard was already returning, followed by a small man, dark moustache and oiled hair, who pulled a suit jacket over his blue shirt, assisted by a flustered wife, three older children dispatched to various buildings of the square. Fascist salutes were exchanged. An angry Brendan Murphy initially berated the Mayor until the fellow recalled his position and responded indignantly. The guide's turn to look cowed.

'That put 'e in 'is place,' said Max. 'Took 'e down a peg or two, same as that Miss Britten.'

'She didn't suffer fools gladly,' said Jack, wondering what might have caused Julia to have words with the Irishman.

He watched, amused, as the Town Hall was opened properly, as trestle tables began to appear, as jugs and glasses were fetched, as the guests were ushered inside, as other dignitaries arrived. There was a hurried speech, welcomes extended, apologies given and, finally, the fruit *refrescos* available, diluted with iced water.

'Are they safe to drink, d'you think?' whispered Albert Moorgate.

'Beggars can't be choosers, I'm afraid,' said Jack. 'But I'm sure they'll be fine.'

Questions were invited.

'I have one,' called Carter-Holt, note-pad at the ready.

Brendan whispered something to the Mayor, who smiled.

'*¿Por favor?*' he said.

'Mister Murphy was explaining,' she continued, 'that the women in the prison here have all committed capital crimes but had their sentences commuted by General Franco. Is that correct, *Señor*?' Translation. Indeed, that was the case. 'Then could the Alcalde give us some idea of the precise crimes committed by these women? They are all Reds, I assume?' More translation.

'The Mayor,' said Brendan Murphy, 'is explaining that these women have been detained in various parts of the liberated territory. Some are saboteurs. Some are paid spies. Some are part of the Anarchist militias. Arsonists, for the most part.'

'And are any of them local women? From Amorebieta?' said Carter-Holt.

'Just one, according to the Mayor.'

'Then could he give us some details of her crimes? You said that the Reds burned the church, for example.'

The guide conveyed her question. The Mayor replied, at some length. Murphy queried the response. The Mayor repeated, indignant, his voice raised, hands stressing the point.

'He says,' Murphy began, 'that this woman was well-known as a member of the Socialist Youth, then later part of the Communist Youth. But he says that the evidence against her was confused. There were accusations of arson but other witnesses, all suspects themselves, gave her an alibi. Yet there was one crime that she could not deny. A murder, he says. In cold blood.'

'And the victim?' said Valerie, scribbling furiously. Murphy looked at her, then at the ceiling.

'The Mayor alleges…' he said, '…that it was his cat.'

Jack had to escape, turned and retreated hastily from the Town Hall.

How bloody priceless! Max Weston couldn't have done better. It would be funny if it wasn't so tragic. Some poor woman locked up in that shit-hole on the basis that she may have killed the Mayor's cat and we're supposed to be impressed by Franco's benevolence in saving her from execution.

He fumbled for one of his last precious *Capstans*, lit the thing and saw Mikel jump down from the bus, a copy of *ABC* in his hand.

'Mikel!' he shouted, and walked quickly towards the driver. *He almost jumped out of his skin. What's he got to be so edgy about?* 'Is that today's?' He pointed at the paper. '*¿Hoy?*'

'*Ah, sí Señor,*' and he offered the newspaper to Jack before imitating the process of urinating and pointing towards one of the side streets.

Jack sat on the lower step of the tour bus.

Pages six to ten carried details of the Sudeten crisis. Tomorrow, said the headline, Chamberlain would be going to Godesberg for a further chat with Herr Hitler.

Jack took it slowly. The Czech Government, he thought, trying to delay matters. England and France warning the Czech Government that they should accept the British plan which, declared the newspaper, would bring lasting peace to Europe.

He barely noticed Brendan Murphy's return.

'Sorry to disturb you,' said the guide. 'For once, I had to escape as well.' Jack snorted. Words failed him. 'Mind if I take a look, sure?' Jack handed over the pages. 'Ah! Chamberlain's going to take his plan to the Führer, even though he's not got the Czechs on board yet. Brave man! And you must have been practising your *Castellano,* Mister Telford?'

'I just look for words that are familiar.'

'Is that so, sure? And where do you stand now on the issue? With the French Socialists? Blum says here that he has sanctified his whole life to the pursuit of peace. That another European war has certainly been averted. But the circumstances cause him to be divided between cowardly relief and shame.'

'Nobody should feel shame about seeking peace,' said Jack.

'There are plenty in Chamberlain's own Party who don't share that sentiment, Mister Telford.'

'Tory war-mongers shedding crocodile tears for Czechoslovakia? They're the very same crowd that wish we had a Hitler of our own. No, what troubles me is whether Chamberlain's plan will avoid war – or cause it.'

'You can't seriously believe that Herr Hitler wants war with Europe, sure? He has enough problems sorting out his own country. Riddled with Reds, Jews, Freemasons, Atheists – the same as Spain. Russia is his problem. Not France, even though they have something of the same infection. But England? Well, Socialists remain a quaint eccentricity amongst the English, do they not? William Morris and Utopia. Tea-drinking. The village green. Cricket. Annoying, Mister Telford – but always tolerable and occasionally entertaining.'

'There's a piece about the International Brigades on the Ebro,' said Jack, deciding that a change of subject might help. 'Didn't you say that they were going to be disbanded.'

'No announcement yet, but it's imminent, I understand. Where's Mikel been, by the way? He's supposed to stay with the bus.'

'He needed to relieve himself. Put me in charge.'

'You might have run off with the vehicle and left us all stranded here,' said Murphy.

'If I knew how to drive, I might have been tempted!'

The others were filing out of the Town Hall now. The guide had words with Mikel, and Jack settled himself back in his seat for the final leg to Guernica.

This should be interesting, he thought.

The engine shuddered into life and a cloud of smoke rose across Jack's window. It cleared slowly as Mikel put the bus in first gear and there, on the corner of a narrow street, half-hidden in the shadows, leaned a man with hands thrust deep into trouser pockets. He wore a striped suit, a shirt with no collar. The man's chin and cheeks were heavily stubbled, the face familiar, fixing Jack with a stare as insolent as the one he had last seen in Irún.

Chapter Ten

Wednesday 21 September 1938

In July, the previous year, Jack had been sitting outside the Café de Flore on the corner of Saint-Germain and Saint Benoit, sipping a *noisette* with Canadian art critic, Angela Alexander. Their subject, of course, had been Guernica. The painting *and* the town. The mural had turned this already controversial Paris Exposition into a hotbed of propaganda, with Franco's supporters slamming Picasso's work as shameless nonsense, while friends of the Republic drew comfort from the spotlight it had shone on civilian bombings.

'You think they'll ever do that to London, Jack?'

'Why should *you* care? You can easily head back to Toronto.'

'London's my home now. But the thought of it being bombed! Or Paris. Jesus, Jack! They wouldn't…'

What price would we pay, Jack had wondered, *to stop Paris being turned to rubble?*

'It hits home when you think about it that way, doesn't it? You still think the Spanish are wrong to have filled their Pavilion with those images? Instead of glorifying the wonders of technology?'

'I simply remarked that people don't want to be reminded of dead children when they visit a World's Fair. I never said that they *shouldn't* be reminded about them.'

'We both seem to have the same problem with editorial control then. The *Globe* turns your art column into an attack on the Popular Front. The *Mirror* turns my piece into another call for re-armament.'

'And how, pray, did they manage *that*, Jack?'

'Oh, with all the fluid ease that only the *Mirror*'s editorial team can muster. I was here on the first day, pushed my way through the crowds to get a good look from the Trocadéro. Somebody had said that the new palace was the best place to see the grounds. And they were right. You've seen it, Angela. My God, what a sight!'

The esplanade had provided an unbroken view of the Eiffel Tower, away across the Seine. But framing the very icon of Paris had been, to the left, the German Pavilion and, to the right, that of Stalin's Russia. In some bizarre twist of imagery, each of them dominated and subdued Gustave Eiffel's structure.

'But no Spanish Pavilion,' Angela had said. 'Not then.'

'In May? No, you could hardly blame them. They'd got a war to fight and win! And they were only seven weeks late with their own opening, when all's said and done.'

'It's not the late opening, Jack. It's more the way they've been tucked away in a corner of the grounds where nobody can find them. If it hadn't been for Picasso raising all the Guernica news again, I doubt whether anybody would have found the place.'

'People have short memories.'

Short memories indeed. George Steer had filed his article for *The Times* about the Guernica bombing on the twenty-seventh of April. It had caused outrage, so much outrage that the May Day rally here in Paris, just a few days later, attracted well over a million people, the word *Guernica* on everybody's lips, a name that nobody had even heard before. And amongst the marchers was Pablo Picasso, living then in the city but charged by the Popular Front Government with producing a masterpiece for display in the Spanish Pavilion, due to open shortly. It was said that the artist almost ran back to his studio, knowing at last exactly what he wanted to create from the many disparate ideas on which he had already been working.

'He may have been inspired, Jack, but I still think that if you're going to create a political painting, you need to be very clear about your message.'

'What? Good guys in white cowboy hats? Franco in…?'

'That's not what I mean. I told you this morning!' He had met her in the Pavilion itself, leaning against the circular railing that fenced off the gallery's central exhibits, natural light flooding through the ceiling panels to illuminate Picasso's oil on canvas. Grey, black and white, eleven feet tall and almost twenty-six feet wide. 'The problem,' Angela had explained, 'is that Spanish artists use the bull and the horse in many ways to represent various elements of their culture. Picasso's used them in different ways on occasions too. I think this makes it difficult for people. And the Republic needs its symbolism to be crystal clear just now.'

'How very Stalinist of you, Miss Alexander. But at least it's upset the Germans. They say that it could have been painted by a four year-old. Do we know where it goes next?'

'A tour of the Scandinavian capitals, apparently. After the Exposition closes in November. Then on to London, I think.'

Yes, London, thought Jack as the yellow tour bus wound along the final section of road north from Amorebieta to the very town whose massacre had provided Picasso's inspiration. *How strange! To be in the place itself just a year later. And the picture due to go on display in London on the thirtieth. Nine days' time. Will I get back to see it, I wonder?*

Jack's article for the *Mirror,* on that second visit to the Paris Exposition, had never seen the light of day. He had thought it important to cover other aspects of the Pavilion apart from just the Picasso. Jennings had been apologetic, but the article needed to concentrate on *Guernica*. How else could they make the editorial point? So the painting had been reproduced, the imagery explained. Many of the original photos from the bombing shown again, the town used – perfectly reasonably – as evidence of Germany's air superiority. Yet the message, to Jack's mind, was over-simplified. Dangerous. Dramatic increase demanded in spending on the Royal Air Force. Prepare for war. *Always bloody war!*

Jack had resigned in protest, having failed to persuade them that war might be unnecessary if a system of proper sanctions could be applied. Still, he very much admired the paper's subsequent attacks beginning this August on Neville Chamberlain and his policy of appeasement. The result had been a series of articles by Churchill that had appeared in the *Daily Mirror* during the past month. In one article Churchill warned that the *'unaccountable delay, whoever is to blame for it, in concluding an all-in alliance between Britain, France and Russia, increases the danger of a wrong decision by Herr Hitler.'* Churchill carefully did not argue for the alliance to necessarily wage war on Germany but, rather, that its very existence, its economic might, would have stemmed the Führer's ambitions.

He reached into the brown leather weekend bag. Greaves of London, a rare luxury. *J.T.* stamped on the front and a pair of leather retaining straps. There were two canvas compartments inside so the bag would expand considerably but Jack kept only his essentials inside. His note-books. Nora Hames's scrap book. Jack's own collection of clippings and papers, including the George Steer article from last year. His Hugo's *Spanish Grammar.* And a prized but neglected copy of Richard Geoghegan's *Doctor Esperanto's International Language.*

'So, Mister Telford,' said Valerie Carter-Holt from just behind him and across the aisle, 'shall we have to endure another Marxist rant when we arrive?'

Jack gazed out of the window. The coarsely cobbled road wound steeply through thick woodland, following a railway track. There were timber mills, logging yards. He looked upwards.

'Approaching Guernica like this,' he replied, 'we're probably following the same valleys that the Luftwaffe used for navigation purposes. To find their target. Except that *they* came in from the north, I think. From the estuary.'

'You see? You really can't help yourself. Despite all the Nationalist Government has said on the matter, all those who've been here and seen the damage first-hand…'

But she fell silent along with the others as the valley finally opened out before them, the narrower confines of steep woodland turning to rolling hills, rich pasture, the scattered *caserios* and the sprawling corpse of Guernica town. For Goya's ghastly man-eating ogre had been here before them, stamping a path through everything that must have stood to the right of the road, his work underpinned by Brendan Murphy's litany.

'This is where the *frontón* ball courts used to be.' Or the convent, the town hall, the garage, the churches, the school, the hospital, the Liceo cinema, the *Palacio de Alegría*, the market.

Oh yes, thought Jack, *it had been a Monday, hadn't it? Market Day.* And the destruction seemed worse to Jack simply because, on either side of the giant's ruinous route, everything seemed normal, untouched. Rubble, a few sparse walls, the occasional house, along this three hundred yard width of wasteland, running away to the north-east. Most of the fallen buildings had been cleared, bulldozed into bomb craters, it seemed, paved over. But some craters still existed, and many walls were pock-marked with bullet holes. Yet, to their left, on higher ground, fine old buildings still remained. And above them, overlooking the town from a distance, was Lumo's Church of San Pedro. To the right, on the other side of the desolation, a spread of industrial buildings.

'What's that large factory, Mister Murphy?' asked Albert Moorgate.

'The Astra plant,' said the guide.

'Astra? What's that?'

'Pistols,' Murphy replied. 'The best in Spain. They make different models. Like this one.' He pulled his own automatic from its holster. Blackened steel, menacing and murderous. 'The 1921 is a classic. *Señor* Unceta owns the place. The factory was moved here by his father about twenty years ago. Rufino Unceta left the company for a while in '36. Refused to work for the Reds. But he was persuaded to come back. It's thanks to him...'

'It was thoughtful of the Reds to leave it intact when they'd spent so much time burning houses,' murmured Jack.

'I think we've all seen the photographs, Telford,' said Alfred Holden. 'Bombs *level* buildings. They don't leave the walls standing and the interiors burned to a cinder. That's the work of Asturian *dinamiteros*. The work of Anarchist militiamen, the town's so-called defenders.'

They were passing people on the road now. Dark-skinned. Rough and wrinkled faces. Black berets. Simple print frocks. More than a few invalids. Crutches. And a smell still wafted from the ruined parts of Guernica. Shit and stale food. *Who said that?* thought Jack. *That the predominant stench of war wasn't smoke or blood. It was shit and stale food?*

Nobody on the bus had spoken for quite some time, except Brendan Murphy, whose list of the now vanished facilities seemed endless. Jack glanced at each of his fellow-travellers, finally at Valerie Carter-Holt, the only one of the party fixed upon the surviving buildings rather than the wreckage. Her hand, he noticed, rested on the Agfa Box Forty-Four that sat on the empty seat alongside her. The back of the casing faced him. The advertisement for Agfa film, in German. *How bloody appropriate!* But something struck him as odd, too, though he could not quite define the detail. He was thinking about aerial bombardment. Somebody had calculated that more explosives were used on Guernica than had been dropped by planes over the entire course of the Great War.

'You're quite right, Professor,' he said. 'High explosives don't damage buildings in that way. But incendiary bombs do!'

'I didn't expect it to be like this,' said Max Weston as the bus finished its circuit, climbing to the highest point, the south-western edge of town. 'On my life, I didn't!'

They had arrived back at the neo-classical buildings Jack had seen as they entered Guernica. The structures seemed strangely at odds with the images he remembered from the Gaumont British News. Immediately to their left was the side of a significant municipal palace, maybe a hundred years old, pale ochre stone, Romanesque. And a short way along, steps led up through iron gates to a courtyard. The whole place was protected today, it seemed, to extremes. For there was a considerable military presence. Regular Nationalist Army uniforms mingling with those of the Guardia Civil and the red berets of Carlist *Requetés*, a cordon across the approach.

'Must 'ave known you was coming, Jack,' shouted Marguerite Weston.

'Just a minute,' said Brendan Murphy. 'I'll see what's going on.'

'Where are we?' asked Albert Moorgate. 'Town Hall?'

'I think you'll find, Mister Moorgate,' said Professor Holden, 'that the Reds burned the Town Hall along with the rest of Guernica. We saw the place, didn't we? No, this is the *Casa de Juntas*. The ancient meeting place for representatives from each of the seven Basque Provinces. This has been the seat of Government for the Basques since time immemorial, as they say. A sacred place.'

'Even for Anarchists, it seems,' muttered Jack. The area around them appeared largely untouched. Houses and a school behind them still standing, the long white walls of a convent or similar religious house at an oblique angle on the further side of the courtyard.

'The Basques are a proud people,' said Dorothea. 'Why, Pliny described the Vascones as having a history and culture far older than any other in Europe.'

'It was Strabo, my dear,' her husband interrupted.

'Yes, well,' she continued. 'They were certainly here long before the old kingdoms of Castile, Aragón and so forth. It's for *that* reason that the Kings of Spain used to come here, to the very tree that stands to this day…'

'Not the tree that stands here *now*, sweet one. The *original* oak.'

'Yes, Alfred. Quite so. To the Tree of Guernica. Where they were required to swear an oath upholding the right to Basque independence. Not only to uphold those rights, but to defend them as the *Señores de Vizcaya*. Not as Kings, mind. Only as the *Lords* of Biscay.'

Not just Spain's Kings either, thought Jack. *Her democratically elected leaders too. Aguirre in '36. Coming here to accept his duties as first President,* Lehendakari, *of the Basque Government. A marriage of convenience. Basque Catholic support for the Republic in exchange for their own autonomy.*

'Romantic nonsense, of course,' said the Professor. 'Should have been dealt with centuries ago. Mistake to encourage them, really!'

'Better late than never, I suppose,' said Albert Moorgate, peering over his spectacles. 'General Franco is making sure that they play the same part in National Spain as everybody else, I assume?'

'But that's such a shame,' said Frances. 'There should be more room in the world for individuality, don't you think?'

Brendan Murphy clambered back aboard the bus.

'Apologies, ladies and gentlemen,' he said. 'There's a meeting taking place in the Chamber. We weren't informed, I'm afraid. But we can go inside through the rear entrance hall for now. Meet a few people and then carry on with the rest of the visit.'

'And the presence of the military?' asked Peter Kettering.

'A Government Representative here, sure,' Murphy replied. 'From Burgos. Should be interesting.'

He led them through the gate and up small steps. Then through a passage and into the central section of the building, large skylights forming most of the roof. The group was stopped twice while papers were checked, the tourists inspected.

The spacious room was packed with people, some of them military, many dark-suited officials, others wearing the blue shirts which often, Jack had noted, marked the civilian Falange members. But it was one of the bureaucrats who approached Brendan Murphy. Long-tailed coat and starched wing collar. Explanations were exchanged, introductions made.

'This gentleman is *Señor* Javier. Currently working as Archivist for the Casa de Juntas. He was expecting us tomorrow, so the news of our changed itinerary obviously didn't get through.' The functionary spoke again. 'And there's a bit of a problem, sure, because they've had a last-minute visit by one of the Government Ministers. From Burgos. But they can offer us some refreshments at least. He says that most of the people we were due to meet tomorrow are here anyway. So if we'll give him a few minutes…' They were joined by another man, horse-faced, blue shirted. 'Ah, this is *Señor* Esquerro. He heads the local branch of the Falange Española de las JONS.' Brendan shook hands warmly with the newcomer, who then offered a fascist salute to the party. There was the normal mixed response.

Under the guidance of Esquerro and the Archivist, they were taken to a table with an assortment of wines and fruit drinks. *Señor* Javier instructed two waiters to look after them and took his leave. Jack decided to accept a cup of white wine, *txakoli*, though he would have given anything for some water at that moment. He suspected that the others felt the same, although Marguerite Weston knocked back the strong local fermentation readily enough. A few settled for the fruit *refrescos* however and, glasses in hand, they were led through the noisy throng to a display table set in the centre of the room. It contained an impressive wooden model, a representation of the town, beautifully detailed.

'Let me guess,' said Dorothea. 'An artist's impression of the *new* Guernica?'

Esquerro smiled with appreciation, spoke at length.

'*Señor* Esquerro,' said Brendan, 'says that the Architecture Section of the Falange has designed the plan. And today they've had the chance to unveil it for Minister Benjumea. He's responsible for the National Department of Devastated Regions. Not the best job title in the world, sure, but very important, you'll all agree?'

He looked pointedly at Jack, obviously expecting some response, but Jack himself was preoccupied with the model, a new town hall, the arcades of a central avenue which must, he calculated, cut through the middle of that wasteland they had so recently seen.

'Oh, look!' said Catherine Kettering. 'This is where we are now. How clever.'

'You like?' said a well-dressed gentleman, standing in a group just behind her. He was perhaps in his mid-forties, dark-haired. Handsome, thought Jack.

'Yes, very much,' said Catherine. 'It's such a shame. What's happened to the town, I mean.'

The man nodded.

'Of course,' he replied. His English was good, heavily accented. 'And then there is all the problem that you cannot see. That we must include in our plan. For water supply. For drainage. Total cost, an estimated one point five billion *pesetas*. But some parts remain.' He gestured around the room. 'The *Casa de Juntas*. *Gernikako Arbola*. The Tree. Though I should not speak in *Euskera*. It is forbidden now.' He smiled, pointed at other parts of the model. 'The Convent of Santa Clara. The Church of Santa María.'

Señor Esquerro spoke to the man, then to Brendan Murphy. Murphy seemed impressed.

'Ladies and gentlemen,' he said. 'Please allow me to introduce *Señor* Unceta, the Director of the weapons factory that we passed earlier.'

'Ah,' said Albert Moorgate, 'the Astra fellow. Delighted, sir. Delighted. Your father started the business, I understand?'

'Yes,' replied Unceta. 'He died four years ago. I thank God that he did not live to see what happened to his town. He was born in Eibar, but Guernica was always his home.'

'Damned Anarchists, eh?' said Professor Holden.

Unceta looked at Brendan Murphy, then at Esquerro. He smiled again.

'Yes,' he said. 'Damned Anarchists.'

'You must have been here when they burned the town then?' queried Peter Kettering.

'*Señor* Unceta is a hero,' said Murphy. 'The Reds had instructed him over and over again to dismantle his equipment. To move his stocks. Ship them to Bilbao so that they wouldn't fall into the hands of our forces. But he kept stalling them. The factory was still intact when the town was liberated.'

Jack's head was spinning.

'Wait,' he said. 'Now just wait. I apologise, *Señor* Unceta. But you're telling us that the *Reds*, as we keep referring to them, set fire to their own town. Burned it almost to the ground so that it wouldn't fall into Franco's hands. But they didn't bother to take out the weapons factory? The very factory that they wanted dismantling?'

'A lot of local jobs depend on the factory, Mister…?'

'Telford, sir,' said Jack. 'You must forgive me. But I don't believe for one moment that Guernica was destroyed by Republicans. The version of events that makes sense is the one promoted by George Steer. That the town was bombed by Franco's Condor Legion. The Luftwaffe, basically. And they would have been very careful to miss your factory, *Señor* Unceta. Wouldn't they?'

They had attracted attention. A Guardia sergeant and a cadaverous army officer.

'These gentlemen will persuade you, sure,' said Murphy, 'that there is a far more plausible version. This is Sergeant Amezaga, who's going to escort us for the rest of the visit. And Captain Ignacio Rosalles.'

'*Capitán* Rosalles,' said Carter-Holt, 'is a Press Officer for *El Caudillo*, I believe?' She stepped forward, offering her hand to Rosalles, while Brendan Murphy offered an explanation. 'So thank Heaven that we can dispose of this nonsense, once and for all. Mister Murphy, would you ask the *Capitán* to explain why George Steer's report is such a red herring?'

'Red herring,' laughed Max. 'That's a good 'un!'

Murphy seemed happy to act as go-between in the exchange that followed.

'First,' he said, 'the Captain confirms that our planes didn't even fly on the days in question. It was too cloudy. He has copies of the official weather reports.'

'But Steer,' Jack replied, 'says that on the same afternoon, and just a few miles from here, he was machine gunned by German planes. And he wasn't alone. He had Monks from the *Daily Express* with him. Corman from *Le Soir.* And one of Miss Carter-Holt's own colleagues from Reuters, Christopher Holme.'

'I can assure you that Holme is a less than reliable witness,' said Carter-Holt. 'And an isolated aircraft, probably lost, is hardly evidence of this aerial *armada* that Steer described.'

'And then,' said Murphy, 'Mister Steer admits that he didn't arrive until two o'clock the following morning. So he didn't actually *see* this alleged bombing. Whereas the eminent Max Massot was here a few days later and found clear evidence of gasoline and dynamite being used to destroy the buildings.'

'Oh,' said Jack. I've read Massot's stuff. Holburn too. Botto. Dourec. Sandri. I've read them all. Not a single consistent story. They all contradict each other. The only thing that binds them is their unquestioning support for Franco.'

'Captain Rosalles,' Brendan Murphy continued, 'says that there are many other inconsistencies in Steer's story. Like his claim that there were seven thousand inhabitants. Nonsense, of course. Only four thousand. And all here waiting for us when the town was liberated. You'd assume, Mister Telford, that they would have fled if they'd thought it was *our* side responsible for the destruction?'

But Jack recalled Steer's description of the refugees. Thousands, he had said, taking the long road from Guernica to Bilbao with their old ox-carts. And the carts piled high with those possessions that could be saved. Thousands. But still only a fraction of the estimated half-million who were said to now be crossing and re-crossing Spain seeking safe haven. Anywhere.

'Well,' he said, 'I suppose the truth is that none of us was here. Oh, with one exception, of course. *You* were here, *Señor* Unceta. That's right, isn't it?'

Unceta looked at Jack and smiled. 'Yes, Mister Telford, I was here.' He raised his wine glass in a mock salute, bowed to the group. 'Ladies and gentlemen,' he said, 'you must forgive me. Please enjoy the rest of your visit.'

'A timely reminder,' said Murphy, as Unceta pushed his way into the gathering. 'Sergeant Amezaga suggests that we should move on. To look at some of the reconstruction work in which National Spain is engaged. Back to the bus, I think?'

'An interesting debate, Mister Telford,' said Peter Kettering as they left the *Casa de Juntas*. 'Will we ever establish which version is correct, d'you think?'

'Hopefully by the end of today,' Jack replied, with as much optimism as he could muster. His head was spinning and he felt even more as though he was experiencing some Lewis Carroll hallucination.

'But you was very manful in there, Jack my dear,' murmured Marguerite Weston, gripping his arm. 'Very manful indeed.'

The bus, now also carrying the sergeant and captain, followed the road back down through a couple of re-surfaced streets, though empty of buildings, to the circular *plaza* outside the gutted train station.

Jack took a final look at the *Times* article, written by George Steer, that he always carried in his case. But he also looked at the clipping attached to it. A cutting from the *Daily Worker* which he prized. At least until now. It was the almost equally familiar piece by Elizabeth Wilkinson.

Yesterday, she had written, *at about 1.30 pm I arrived in Guernica, the ancient capital of the Basque country. It was a peaceful town, with no factories, no munition works and no troops stationed there. Peasant women and children were going quietly about the streets. Then at four o'clock the rebels began a brutal bombardment which continued without stopping until seven in the evening. More than fifty German planes rained bombs on the town and machine gunned the streets incessantly. The surrounding villages were similarly bombarded. The rebel planes even machine gunned the flocks in the fields. At eleven o'clock at night the whole town was in flames, not a single house standing.*

He could not have used it, of course. Quoting the *Daily Worker* amongst this lot would receive the same response as one of Max Weston's quips. But there was something else. He had always favoured Wilkinson's account since it seemed to come, genuinely, from an eye-witness. Yet could she really not have known about the Unceta factory? Its significance? If so, it was appalling journalistic negligence. It was, after all, no more than a hundred yards away from them, back along the tracks. One of the most prominent buildings in Guernica. Steer *had* mentioned the plant, though had seemingly failed to make enough of the implication. That the Republicans, if they had really been about the business of scorched earth, would surely have started with the weapons factory.

As they had seemingly attacked the rail network. For here, at the station, the reconstruction work was far beyond cosmetic. Armed guards stood watching scores of prisoners occupied with shifting rubble, patching and painting the exterior shell, preparing timbers for a new roof. There was an explanation from Press Officer Rosalles. Red captives were held at the Seminary of the Augustinian Brothers and utilised, along with local labour, to clear the town for rebuilding.

'The station took quite a beating then?' asked Peter Kettering.

'Yes. Look at all the evidence of burning around the doors and windows,' said Brendan Murphy.

Max Weston leaned close to Jack.

'It looks, me old acker, like they're fillin' bullet holes, not dynamite damage.'

Jack nodded as their guide led the party north, to the bridge which spanned a green and sluggish Oca River. They were maybe three hundred yards from the former town centre. Murphy explained that this was the very bridge over which the *Gudariak*, the Basque Republican troops, had retreated in the face of General Mola's advance, heading west towards Bilbao, leaving poor Guernica in ruins behind them.

'The bridge too, one assumes?' said Professor Holden. 'It has been repaired since the liberation?'

'We think they may have tried to blow it,' said Murphy. 'But no, we found it mercifully intact.'

Jack looked around him. The rubble stretched away both behind them and ahead on the far side of the Oca. But he could see now that a second swathe of destruction ran from right to left.

Christ in Heaven, he thought, *The place was bombed alright. Franco carved the Sign of the Cross on Guernica, and he used German bombers to engrave it. This was their damned strategic target. But they missed it. How? The weather, maybe? But what about the incendiaries? If your target is the bridge, why carry incendiaries? Because, Jack, they had a secondary target. To teach the Basques a lesson. What had Brendan said earlier in the week? 'Of all the traitors in Spain, the Basque Nationalists are the worst. Because they, professing themselves to be good Catholics, conspired with the atheists – yes, ladies and gentlemen, atheists – to set up their own independent state.' And if this was a religious lesson for the Basques, who gave the orders for it? Franco? Mola?*

Across the bridge, in the next *barrio*, some of the original buildings remained. Badly damaged but many still standing. And, in one of them, an old couple had erected a temporary roof, an old tarpaulin, to keep out the weather while, today, they were struggling to replace a window frame, previously covered by a metal sheet. The house stood alone in a surrounding sea of bricks. The Basques stopped work, stood looking at the group. Jack stared back. He pointed at the damage. Then up at the sky.

'*¿Aviones?*' he asked, to the surprise of those around him. Aeroplanes?

'Mister Telford,' said Murphy. 'Please!'

The old man had turned his gaze towards the skeletal Captain Rosalles and the Guardia sergeant. He spat.

'*Ikastaroa!*' said the man. '*Alemaniako. Italiarreki.*'

'He's a Red,' said Murphy.

'*¡Habla cristiano!*' shouted the Guardia sergeant. *Speak Christian.* But Rosalles admonished him, furious.

The last thing they'd want, thought Jack, *would be a translation. Either into English or Spanish.*

'*Alemaniako!*' repeated the old man. *Germans*, Jack understood. '*Faxista!*' The woman pulled her husband back into the dwelling, while the sergeant's hand went first to his gun, then to his note-book.

Christ, they'll be back for him. And he knows it!

'Perhaps a good time to return, Mister Murphy,' said Dorothea Holden. 'Do you think?'

So they headed back to the *Casa de Juntas*, Jack noticing more *Civiles* conducting searches of houses. *Searching for what?* he wondered. *Weapons? Or books?* He had heard that Basque books were regularly burned.

This time, they walked around to the main entrance, but Brendan stopped them so that they could admire the new oak, planted to replace the original Tree of Guernica that had died a century before. It stood fenced, protected, in front of a smaller building, columns along its façade.

'The old tree is at the back of this temple,' said Brendan. 'We'll see it shortly.'

They passed through the main doors and into the *Sala de Juntas* itself. It was impressive. But Jack had little interest in the lengthy histories which Press Officer Rosalles was reciting. He was thinking, strangely, of Chamberlain. For the first time it occurred to him that the Prime Minister might *just* have had a vision of Guernica in his head during his discussions with Hitler. *I wonder*, he thought. *Is it possible? That he sees Portsmouth, Canterbury, London even, bombed instead of these Spanish towns? That it's this vision which drives appeasement?*

They were led through the central chamber once more, then into the drawing room formerly used by the President, the windows of which looked out onto a rotunda of circular pillars, perhaps twenty feet in height, that now enclosed the stump of the original oak.

'Well,' said Brendan Murphy, 'Captain Rosalles has arranged a photographer. A group picture, maybe. At the tree, sure. But the new one.'

Outside, most of the other troops had gone but there were three soldiers left, each of them wearing the uniform of the Carlists. *Requetés*. Red berets. A woman too. She called herself Juana, and she spoke in halting English at the instigation of Captain Rosalles, helped by Murphy whenever it proved necessary.

Guernica was a beloved town, she explained. Sacred. Like Tordesillas or Santillana.

'Sister Berthe Schultz,' said Sister María Pereda, 'say that this poor town perish like the Lamb of God, sacrificed to save the soul of Spain. She say that Carlist women are like the Mother of Our Lord. Especially those who are from Guernica itself. She ask if you are from this place?'

Yes, she was from the town.

'And were you here when it was destroyed?' asked Peter Kettering.

Of course. But she could not speak about it. It was too terrible. And afterwards. The cleaning after those pigs.

'You mean the Reds?' said the Professor.

No, she laughed. The *Moros*. Yes, the *Moros*. The Moroccan troops in Franco's service. They were amongst the regiments that liberated the town. Stationed in the Church of Santa María. They defiled it, she said.

Another irony of this war, thought Jack. *That Franco has spent so much time building the image that this was a second* Reconquista. *A chance for Spain to live again its Christian Crusade, liberating the country from the heathens who had occupied the Peninsula for so many centuries. Yet, on this occasion, Franco could not have succeeded in the insurrection without his reliance on the Muslim troops from the Army of Africa. Those tens of thousands of Moroccans from the Rif mountains whose savagery had done so much to spread fear within the Republic.*

'So you would consider yourself Basque too, Juana?' said Carter-Holt. 'Even though you are a Carlist?'

'But of course,' she told them. A Basque who remained true to her Faith. And not just Juana herself, it seemed. The first troops to liberate the town were apparently from the Fourth Navarra Brigade. Basques, every one of them. They protected the Sacred Tree from those who wanted to destroy it, she claimed.

'From the Reds?' repeated Alfred Holden, more insistent now.

Juana laughed again. 'No, not from the Reds. From our own. Who thought only that all Basques were on the Reds' *side.*'

Of course, Jack thought. *There would have been an open revolt among Franco's Navarrese regiments if the Tree of Guernica had been damaged. So the bombing raid aimed for the bridge, but with orders to avoid both the Unceta factory* and *the tree. It makes sense now.*

'Time for the photo, I think,' said Dorothea.

So they gathered around the tree. The new tree. The *Requetés* with their rifles and uniforms. Juana, with her Crucifix and smiles. The tourists. The guide. The *Civiles* sergeant. The Press Officer from Burgos.

But not Jack. And, to his surprise, not Carter-Holt either.

'I'll hold your camera if you like,' he offered.

'No,' she said. 'No need.'

'Then let me use it to take a photo of you with the group.'

'I said no.'

And then it occurred to him. The advert in German on the back. For the Agfa film. Had she not said that she bought the camera in London? So why would a camera designed for the English market have an advert in German? Curious, but…

'Well, back to the bus, ladies and gentlemen?' Murphy was saying, as a couple of army lieutenants came sauntering out of the *Casa de Juntas*. There was back-slapping.

'English!' said one of them, suffering from too much wine. 'Friends!' And he insisted on accompanying them back to the bus.

It was a ragged procession. Mikel was waiting for them, as usual, smoking a cigarette. Jack felt like one too. Offered one of the *Superiores* to the lieutenant.

He accepted, though he had taken something of a shine to Max Weston.

'I know you!' said the officer.

'I'm Max Weston, me 'ansum,' replied Max, obviously hoping that his catchphrase would aid the lieutenant's memory. But the man only shook his head, gestured towards the ruins.

'What you think?' he said.

'I think it was bombed,' whispered Max. He made whistling noises, falling movements with his fingers, imitated explosions.

'*¡Por supuesto!*' said the soldier. Of course. 'Full of *Rojos*. We bomb. And bomb. And bomb.' He laughed. 'Like Alicante. Bilbao. Madrid. *Bueno*, why not?'

The lieutenant slapped Max on the back one last time, strutted off up the road.

'Oy,' said Max when they caught up with the group. 'That army bloke just told me they *did* bomb the town!'

Brendan Murphy translated for Captain Rosalles, who responded at length.

'The Captain says that you must have misunderstood, Mister Weston. Anyway, he thanks you all for coming to see Guernica. For listening to the truth, rather than all the lies which, sadly, the English press has done so much to spread around the world. He hopes that you will come back to Guernica when the war is finally over. He says that it will not be long and, on the very day that peace finally comes, the *Generalísimo* has sworn that work will commence on a new Town Hall. At a cost of half a million pesetas. And, on the day that the Town Hall is opened, the people will show their appreciation by officially declaring *El Caudillo* an Adopted Son of Guernica!'

Chapter Eleven

Wednesday 21 September 1938

Decent guidebooks paid scant regard to Galdakao. Emerald hills loomed around the rustic backwater. Yet it sat, twelve kilometres beyond Amorebieta, on the only viable route between Zornotza and Arratia. Men came and went from its three small factories, while others hacked at the rough farmland. The local quarry that had once been noted for its export of stone to the Americas now slumbered except on rare occasions. A bandstand in the dusty *plaza* stood empty but women gathered here with wooden wash-boards to beat wet clothing at the *lavadero*, that section of rocks along the passing stream that served as a laundry. A procession of other women passed by, each of these balancing a precarious cargo on her head. A basket of bread or vegetables. A pitcher of water taken from those filling in the fountain. Men with gypsy *bandanas* tied like skull-caps beneath their hats. A bare-foot girl with a milk churn. Fat-bellied pigs grubbing in the dirt. Children playing spinning top *trompo*. Another world.

They were gathered at table in the baronial hall of the Urgoiti Palace, being entertained by the man now serving as Mayor, *Señor* Ibarreche. It all changed with the war, though, he explained. The village had sat right on the Reds' Ring of Iron. The defences that they had built around Bilbao. The engineer, Goicoechea. God preserve him for betraying their plans to us! Well, Galdakao was strategically crucial. So bombed? Yes, of course they were bombed.

'Were many of the villagers killed, Mister Murphy?' asked Catherine Kettering.

'The town records show thirty-two killed over the two weeks of the attack,' said Brendan. 'Mostly the fault of the Reds. There were shelters, but badly built. Completely inadequate.'

'And much fighting when the town was liberated?' said Professor Holden.

'No, not really. The First Navarra Brigade arrived ahead of the main force. But no resistance, I think. They were able to move on pretty quickly. Across the bridge at Torrezabal, then occupied the Arteta Hermitage as well as the Upo Ridge. We might get a chance to look at them tomorrow.'

Jack excused himself early, climbed the badly lit stair to his room on the third floor. He switched on the flickering table lamp, wrote a while, the ink flowing free in the absence of a typewriter. A piece that would please Sid Elliott. The real story of Spain's Civil War. The struggle of peasants, miners, factory workers to shake off the chains of church and land-owner alike. A people's revolution. And here, in the Basque lands, a struggle *within* that struggle. Not for democracy alone but for independence.

He read it through one more time. Too flowery, he thought. Too romantic. And he set it aside, picked up *The Hobbit*. But sleep *and* the plot each eluded him. So he slipped from under the sheet, sat on the edge of the bed in his pyjamas and smoked the very last *Capstan*.

Jack thought about Julia Britten. About his father. Morbid, midnight imaginings. Apt for the *Palacio Urgoiti*. Then Nora Hames. That last vision of her standing outside the Hotel María Cristina. *'I don't know how to convince you, Jack Telford, but I'm certain that Julia's death was no accident. So you must stay, dear boy. Stay and find out who killed my poor lamb!'* He reached for Nora's scrap-book, turned again to the sepia snaps of them both together, Julia still a young girl. The next pages were full of cuttings, one from the *Standard*, one from the *Express*, several from the *Eastern Evening News*. Julia at eleven. Her concert debut, according to the caption. Mozart. Beecham conducting. A copy of the programme. Then an article from *The Times*, an announcement really. The results of their contest for young musicians, first prize going to Miss Julia Britten of Romford. Two years of private tuition with Sir Edward Whiting. More photographs. Another clipping from the *Evening News*. Local girl wins scholarship to continue her studies at the Royal Academy of Music. Another programme. St John's in Smith Square. The Haydn Piano Concerto in D. Bach's Concerto Number Seven in G Minor. A photo of Julia receiving a bouquet, and the ribbon from her hair carefully attached to the page.

He put the book away, his mind flitting to visions of Valerie Carter-Holt and the camera. The advert in German. But was it so unusual for English shops to stock models manufactured for the German home market? He supposed not. And at that precise moment, a knock on the door. Gentle but persistent.

He switched on the light again, crossed the room, put his ear to the door, holding the brass knob.

'Who is it?' he said in a half-whisper.

'Who d'you *want* it to be, Jack Telford?' said Marguerite Weston, trying to turn the handle from the outside.

Damn the woman!

'Marguerite, it's late. I was asleep.'

'Bloody liar. Now let me in. I be cold and somebody'll 'ear!'

He opened the door a crack. There was little light in the corridor but Marguerite Weston seemed to be wearing a dressing gown. She was leaning against the door jamb, one hand clutching her robe while, at the same time, holding a bottle of wine.

'What d'you want?' hissed Jack.

'What the bloody 'ell d'you *think* I want? Let me in, Jack, my dear.' She raised her voice with the last few words and, against his better judgement, he grabbed her arm, pulled her inside, closing the door behind her. She was heavily scented. Some flower that he could not properly name. Sickly sweet but seductive. And it just about masked the essence of alcohol that clung to her breath. She threw her arms around his neck, still gripping the bottle, stood on the tips of her toes, pressing against him, kissing him, the lipstick sleek against his mouth, her tongue flicking against his own. He felt himself harden at the same time as he pushed her to arm's length.

'This really isn't a good idea,' he said. 'And what in God's name have you done with Max?'

'Oh, never you mind about 'im.'

She looked to find a dresser where she could set down the wine, then turned, slipped the gown from her shoulders. She was wearing an apricot chemise. Rayon, he thought, as she embraced him again. She pressed her mouth to his lips, wider this time, more insistent. She found his hand, pulled it against her full breast, spreading his fingers, running them along a silky seam to find her nipple pressing tight inside the fabric. Then slid his hand down her side, past the broad hips to the embroidered hem of the chemise, helping him to lift it so that he could feel the panties beneath.

He pushed her away for a second time, though it was a less convincing rejection than the first.

'I mean it,' he said. 'I like Max and this isn't right!'

'Managing Max Weston's like looking after a bloody child,' said Marguerite, turning towards the wine bottle. 'You got no glasses, Jack?' She scrutinised the room but could not see any. 'Never mind, eh?' She put the bottle to her lips, took a swig, then held the neck against her groin, leaning back against the door. 'And you're not going to let *that* go to waste.' She admired his erection, still uncomfortably evident within his pyjama bottoms. 'No *real* man would.'

'Honestly, Marguerite. I mean it. You're very attractive but...'

'What?' she said. 'You're goin' to tell me how flattered you be? Well, you'll not get away from me this time, Jack Telford. I made my mind up, see?'

She drank some more wine, set down the bottle, came at him quickly, reaching for the drawstring bow of his pyjamas, spinning him around so that she was sitting on the edge of the bed.

'Marguerite...'

'Oh, let your girlie look at Jack's big dragon,' she said, with simpering stupidity.

He stepped back, his arousal subsiding at last.

'I mean it, Marguerite. I think you'd better go. Come on, I'll see you back to your room.'

'I bet you still be thinking about that blind bitch.' She continued to simper but there was a cruel edge to the words. 'Well, I 'ad somethin' to say to *that* one before she went an' got 'erself killed. Silly cow.'

'What do you mean?'

'Oh, nothin'. Come on, Jack. You knows you want to.' Marguerite lay back on the bed, spread her legs and lifted the hem of the chemise, stretching tight the silky apricot of the matching panties. The thighs plump and pink. A terrible temptation.

'When did you speak to Julia Britten? After the concert? The night before she died?' He was trying to rack his brains, recalling what had happened that evening.

'No, in the mornin'. When she come offerin' her bloody apologies. Stupid woman. Oh please, Jack, I need somethin'. You knows what I needs, Jack.'

'Did you tell anybody you spoke with Julia that morning?'

'I *might* 'ave done.' Marguerite sat up. 'Wouldn't *you* like to know though. I could tell 'e, Jack Telford. If you was a good boy an' all.'

'Marguerite, just tell me anyway.'

'No. Shan't!' She threw herself back down on the bed. 'Bring the wine, Jack. An' come 'ere to your girl.'

Jack walked to the dresser, picked up the half-empty wine bottle, carried it to the bedside table where he set it down. Marguerite Weston turned her languid eyes to him, smiled, lifted a hand to twist a mousey curl of her hair between thumb and fingers. He opened the table drawer, fished out a packet of Spanish cigarettes, his lighter. Marguerite's eyes were closed, her lips slightly parted, wet. He crossed the room again.

'Goodnight, Mrs Weston,' he said, opening the door and glancing back at the woman spread-eagled on his bed. She was looking at him as he left. But not *seeing* him, Jack thought. For her other hand was now thrust down inside the panties and she was, quite literally, in a world of her own.

He made his way through the silent Parador, pausing outside the door that he thought belonged to the Westons. There was an indistinct noise within. *Whimpering?* thought Jack. It sounded like, but he could not be sure.

The entrance hall was empty, dark and shadowed by the ancient furniture. The yard was empty too except for a couple of goats that skittered away when he opened the front door. Jack stood for a moment, lit one of the *Superiores,* then wandered across to the front gate, set within the property's perimeter wall of rough stone, matching the walls of the palace itself. Beyond the gate was a pillar, with a great iron rooster at its top. A twin column stood on the opposite side of the narrow dirt road, though without a matching cockerel. But hanging from *that* pillar was a hefty length of chain.

'Toll-booth,' said a voice from the pitch blackness. Jack swore he must have jumped a foot off the ground.

'Christ, Brendan.' he said. 'Don't you ever sleep? You frightened me half to death.'

'You don't seem to be sleeping too well yourself, Mister Telford, sure. What was it? Bad dreams?

'Something like that. And what did you say?'

'Toll-booth. You were looking at the chain. They used to close the road here, then charge people to go through. Same as a toll-road back home.'

'And is this what you do. Brendan? You stay up all night, waiting out here on the off-chance that one of us might want a snippet of information about the local highways system?'

'Now that would be foolish, would it not? No, sometimes my old ailments keep me awake. And then I prefer to be outside. I like this place too. It's a fine old house, sure.'

'Yes,' said Jack, 'it is. You want a smoke?'

'That's kind, but no thanks. The Palace belongs to an important family. They've been Mayors of Bilbao, or sat on the General Assembly here, for generations. Just like your English landed gentry, eh?'

'You don't like the English, Brendan, do you? But that can't be the reason you ended up out here?'

'Not on your life. I wanted to be a pilot.'

'Pardon?'

'I was a mechanic back in Sligo. Studied aircraft mechanics. Then in '36 O'Duffy started recruiting for the Irish Bandera. The parish priest used to tell us stories from the pulpit every week. Nuns raped. That sort of thing. He said it was the duty of all good Catholics to support General Franco. So I got in touch with O'Duffy. Told him I'd enlist so long as I could serve out here as a pilot.'

'And he agreed?'

'Too true. The next thing, I was on board the *Ardeola* and bound for Lisbon.'

'On a steamer full of fascists.'

'Nah, that's not fair, sure. A good half of us were just believers. Wanting to protect the Faith. That sort of thing. But the rest? Yeah, they were hard-core. Especially the officers.'

'And I bet you never saw much flying either.'

Murphy snorted.

'Bloody *none*,' he said. 'We end up in Badajoz. Then Cáceres. We get our uniforms. Black shirt. Sam Browne belt. Black overseas cap with red piping and tassel. Any old trousers. Boots if we were lucky. Then guard duty. It seemed like forever.'

'Guarding Republican prisoners?'

'Sure, you'll not like the details, Mister Telford.'

'Tell me anyway.'

'Well, it wasn't exactly *guarding* them. It was mostly supervising their execution.'

'How many, Brendan?'

'We used to watch them digging their own graves. If you got up early enough you could see fifty shot in a day.'

'And you still believed you were doing this for religious freedom?'

'I believe it *now*, Mister Telford. It might sound like a *cliché* but we were fighting a war.'

'Surely...'

'Surely *nothing*, Mister Telford. It was a testing ground for us. Two months later we transferred into the Legion. As the Sixteenth Bandera. *La Bandera Irlandesa del Tercio*. When we left Cáceres, people hung the Irish Tricolour from their windows. Good people, Mister Telford. We travelled for days. Hardly any food.

Strafed by Red planes all the time. We ended up on the Jarama Front. At a place called Ciempozuelos. You've heard of it?'

'No.'

'Oh, it's very famous, Mister Telford. The first time we came under fire. Only it was from our own side. Some unit from the Canary Islands. Useless feckers! We took the place, all the same. But it was a town of the dead by then. Not a soul left alive. There must have been a thousand Reds there. Bodies left unburied. Or half-covered in mud.'

'When was this?'

'It would have been February last year. Yes, February. '37.'

'You buried them?'

'We couldn't. We had to dig in straight away. The Reds had started shelling our position. Every time we took a hit, it threw up the bodies. We literally had them raining down on us. It wasn't pretty, Mister Telford. Then the Reds got the train running.'

'Train?'

'An armoured train. There was a rail track just a few hundred yards away. So they'd run this bloody train backwards and forwards, spraying machine gun fire on us. Hour after hour. Eventually, we'd lost so many men they had to pull us out of the front line. By then we were really split in two. Those of us who still believed in the *Reconquista*. And those who'd just become mindless thugs. And that was when O'Duffy's Adjutant ran off with the brigade's wages. After that, things started to fall apart quick. I came down with this bloody illness too.'

'What is it?'

'They don't really know. Some form of Vasculitis. I spent a few spells in hospital. But that was worse than being at the Front. Most of the patients were drunks or deserters. There was an officer in the next bed. He was from the same Canary Islands unit that had fired on us at Ciempozuelos. We got into a fight. He hit me. I hit him back. I ended up in the can. The worst filthy hole I've ever been in. I was still there in June when the rest of the brigade decided they'd had enough. So they sailed back to Dublin. Left me to rot.'

'I remember,' said Jack. 'O'Duffy thought he was sailing home to fame and glory, didn't he? And hardly a soul there to see them.'

'That pleases you, I suppose, Mister Telford?'

'Well, it does give me a certain amount of smug satisfaction, yes. I don't like fascists, Brendan. They're an evil breed.'

'We were fighting for a new world order, Mister Telford. For all the things I was taught to believe in, sure. The funny thing is that I had to prove it over and over again to the Secret Police. They were obviously glad to see the back of O'Duffy too. They'd decided that I wasn't a good Nationalist. Good Nationalists don't strike their superiors. But, in the end, they let me go back to the Front. With the Legion.'

'You didn't want to go home yourself?'

'This *is* my home now, Mister Telford. Every time we liberated a town from the Reds, I felt more like I belonged. Can you understand that? In every town there were people in prison for no reason. The Reds just thought that they were too respectable. Most of the people *hated* the Reds. Hated what they'd done to the churches. Over and over they'd tell me that the stories told by Reds about their priests were lies. Yet the clergy were murdered, persecuted. To be fair, I never came across any stories of raped nuns though.'

'I've spoken to International Brigade members who told me a different story altogether. Good Catholics on *their* side too. Taking Mass before battles. Priests respected. Towns taken by the Nationalists and people shot just because they voted a certain way in the '36 Elections. Why should they be wrong and you be right, Brendan?'

'Maybe there is no reason. Like I say, this is war. Or perhaps it's just something about the Spanish themselves, Mister Telford. They have a terrible tendency for anarchy, sure. All I can tell you is that my Spanish was good. They opened their hearts to me. Which reminds me, your own Spanish is a lot better than you'd admitted, isn't it?'

'What do you mean?'

'The old couple. At Guernica. Asking that Red about the *aviones*. Very clever.'

'Not really clever. I get the feeling that the *Civiles* will have picked him up by now. They'll shoot him, won't they?'

'*Your* fault if they do, Mister Telford. You should learn to leave well alone.'

'There are some things that it's impossible to ignore. Like all that bollocks about the Reds being to blame for shoddy air-raid shelters when the deaths were *actually* caused by German bombing. And, by the way, you surely don't *truly* believe that Guernica wasn't bombed, Brendan? Despite all the evidence. Just between you and me, now?'

Murphy sighed.

'Do you believe in God, Mister Telford?'

The question was abrupt, unexpected.

'Honestly?' said Jack. 'Well, I'm not sure, I suppose. But I don't think so. No, not really.'

'No, I didn't think so. It's a matter of faith, isn't it? There's a whole new breed of so-called scientists out there, trying to tell people that there's no *evidence* for God. But I *know* there's a God, Mister Telford. I don't care about bloody evidence. It's the same with Franco. There are few people in the world today who've done as much to protect my Church, sure. So if Franco assures me that Guernica wasn't bombed, that's good enough for me.'

'It's no wonder you got the job,' said Jack. 'But I still don't understand how you got from the Front Line to *this*.'

'Like most things. Fate or fortune. Maybe the hand of God, eh?' Brendan crossed himself. 'But mostly it was an observant Commander for once. They'd sent a bulletin and he'd bothered to read it. So this April I was sent to Burgos. For an interview with the new State Tourist Department. I thought it was a joke but that's where I met *Señor* de Armas Gourié. He offered me the job as a trainee guide. It was some interrogation. Loyalty to Franco. The *Reconquista*. Spanish geography. Extent of my *Castellano*. Test to be passed in all of them. Twenty of us to start but I was the only foreigner. Fifteen of us got through. New uniform. That's about all there is. This is my third tour.'

'And the most eventful?'

'I'll have some explaining to do when I get back to Burgos. Poor Miss Britten.'

'Never mind. You should score some points for having to deal with *me*.'

'*You*, Mister Telford?' Brendan Murphy laughed. 'You're no trouble, sure. But you *do* need to be careful. Life is cheap out here. By the way, that thing you asked me. About Mister Kettering's brother. They tell me there's a telegraph office in the village. I'll wire tomorrow. See what I can find out.'

'Bilbao tomorrow?'

'Yes, the Iron Ring and then down into the city. Not my favourite part of the tour but, still, it's on the itinerary.' He was silent for a moment, and Jack wondered whether he should seize the moment, return to his room. Find out whether Marguerite Weston had gone. But the guide continued. 'I was wondering,' he said, 'whether you might do me a small favour in return, Mister Telford.'

'What is it?' asked Jack, instantly on guard.

'Oh, it's a small thing. A stupid thing. No, it doesn't matter.'

'You've pricked my curiosity now. What do you want, Mister Murphy?'

'Well, it's the Moorgates, sure. Can you tell me anything about them, Mister Telford?'

'Not much. I met them on the way down here for the first time. Albert Moorgate went out of his way to look after me. In his fashion, at least. He's a banker. His wife is a librarian.'

'Ah,' said Brendan. 'A librarian, is she? You'd never have guessed, sure.'

So, it's Frances that he's interested in. I might have known. All those little courtesies he's shown her. The shared confidences.

'She has a style all of her own, does she not?' said Jack.

'To be sure.'

'And so much younger than her husband. Do you have some particular interest in Mrs Moorgate perhaps?'

'Of course not,' said Brendan. 'Call it professional curiosity. But what about you, Mister Telford? They gave me a bit of a briefing before the tour started. Fill in the gaps for me. Fair exchange, eh? You've had *my* life story. And you don't seem in a great hurry to go back to your room.'

'No. Well, not much to tell. Nothing so colourful as your own tale. Father killed in Flanders.' It was only a modest lie, he decided. 'He'd been a banker too, as it happens. Same as Moorgate. My mother's still alive. And a sister, back in Worcester. I went to Grammar School there, then off to university in Manchester. They were good years. I edited the college magazine. Then became part of the Esperanto Movement.'

'Ah, the languages,' said Brendan. 'Might have known you'd be an Esperanto man. It's another Red affliction, isn't it?'

'It just seemed like a sensible alternative to all that élitism. Everybody thinks they're more special than everybody else. That's a *human* affliction, Mister Murphy. The French think they're better than the English. The English think they're better than the Spanish. Catholics think they're better than Protestants. Moslems think they're better than Christians. Christians think they're more special than the Jews. And I'm no Communist. But you don't need to be a Communist to know that we'll never make this world any better unless we find better ways to work together. And a common language wouldn't be a bad place to start.'

'I thought the British Empire had already decided that *English* was the world's common language. Anyway, you picked up Spanish there too.'

'I was surprised how much Spanish was used as the basis for Esperanto. But history was my first love. And my Professor encouraged me to think about becoming a foreign correspondent. That was *my* crusade, Mister Murphy.' Jack lit another cigarette. 'Peace through Truth. I went on to get a London University Diploma. It was the only formal qualification at that time for a newspaper job. You were supposed to learn journalism the hard way. So I did that too. Freelance work for *The Observer.* They sent me to Germany in '33 to cover Hitler's rise to power. I made a great friend there. Another English journalist. He was killed in China, three years ago. Stupid bloody waste. By then I was working for the *Mirror.* Then *Reynold's News*. That's about it, really.'

'And they sent you on the tour? Peculiar bloody job you've got, Mister Telford, if you don't mind me saying so.'

Jack laughed.

'I was thinking exactly the same about half an hour ago,' he said. 'But you mentioned Julia Britten's death a while back. Can I ask you something? Did Mrs Weston mention anything to you about speaking with Julia on the morning that she died?'

'She didn't need to mention it,' replied Brendan Murphy. 'I was there. Or rather, I was passing the room. I didn't see the Westons as it happened. Miss Britten was coming away from there. And in some distress. She wasn't very specific. Just said that she was going upstairs.'

'You didn't take her back to her own room then?'

'No. She wouldn't let me. Said the staircase would be fine. That's where I left her.'

'I didn't know,' said Jack. 'You never mentioned it when we were being interviewed.'

'When *you* were being interviewed Mister Telford. Remember? I was only there as your interpreter. Though I suspect now that I probably wasn't needed. Anyway, I told all this to the *Teniente*. He'll be catching up with us on Friday night, by the way. There was a message from him earlier. They'll have completed the autopsy by then and, hopefully, Miss Hames will be safely on her way back to England.'

Chapter Twelve

Thursday 22 September 1938

The ceiling of the concrete bunker was barely high enough for them to stand inside, taking turns to peer through the slit, imagining the Maxim machine gun which had so recently been sited here, covering the wooded slope which rose towards them from the valley below.

'There, on the other side,' said Brendan Murphy. He pointed at the white church across the valley to the south-east. 'That's where the First Navarra Brigade took position after they freed Galdakao. Spread out along that ridge. Can you picture them, ladies and gentlemen? Coming up the hillside here to take this emplacement?'

They had left the bus almost a quarter-mile away and followed a winding path up into this labyrinth of tunnels and trenches.

'That's the harbour at Bilbao, I assume?' said Carter-Holt. The outer breakwater was just visible in the distance, a crooked finger appearing from behind some rugged mountainous ground away to the north-west and pointing out to sea.

'Indeed,' said Brendan. 'And, in a way, that's where the battle for Bilbao really started. We'd been bombarding the defences for quite a while. And then the engineer who'd designed them brought us the plans.'

'Ah, the gentleman so highly praised by the Mayor of Galdakao,' said Holden.

'Yes,' said Murphy. 'And it soon became clear that there were serious weaknesses in the Reds' defences. So we hammered them. Bombardments targeted on every vulnerable spot. Their so-called Iron Ring wasn't the salvation they thought it would be.'

Jack recalled the article by Elizabeth Wilkinson for the *Daily Worker.* It would have been some weeks before the final assault on the Iron Ring. King George's coronation day, following the abdication of brother Edward. The twelfth of May.

Hitler is celebrating Coronation Day with the biggest air-raid and bombardment on Bilbao since the offensive began. Already the Nazi pilots have dropped thirty big explosive bombs and hundreds of incendiary bombs on the city. They dropped them when you in England were laughing and shouting. As I write, the sirens signalling a raid are sounding again. I cannot tell what will happen.

'Are you hot, Mister Telford?' asked Frances Moorgate. And he *was* hot. The sun…

'I was telling Mister Telford only last night,' said Brendan, 'that he should take better care of himself.'

'Yes, you really should wear a hat, you know,' said Frances.

But it was lack of sleep that affected him so badly. When he had returned to his room, Marguerite was no longer there. And she had not appeared for breakfast either. Max had joined them though, but said barely a word. His tousled brown hair limp. His bruised eye turning to jaundice yellow. His normally cheerful round face defeated. His clothes in disarray. *He must have had to get himself ready today*, thought Jack. In fact, he had entirely ignored Jack, looking for all the world like a whipped puppy.

'Anyway,' Brendan continued, 'on the thirteenth, the Reds' military council decided to fight for the city. Imagine, putting all those civilian lives at risk!'

'There was no evacuation?' said Jack.

'Well yes,' said Murphy. 'Of sorts. Lots of the children were put on board foreign ships. Taken to France, Russia, England.'

'I remember,' whispered Jack.

'But an honourable surrender would have been the correct thing, don't you think?' said Dorothea.

'Indeed, ma'am,' said the guide, with obviously feigned sorrow. 'Such an unnecessary loss of life. The Basques committing themselves to a futile defence. But by then there were four separate columns breaking through their lines. And famously, of course, Franco's *fifth* column, those in Bilbao who were faithful to National Spain, rose up to attack Aguirre's Reds in the streets. Between that and our bombardment, the crusade was sure to succeed. They say that on the Seventeenth of June alone, we dropped twenty thousand shells on the city.'

'A statistic to be proud of, Mister Murphy?' said Peter Kettering.

'It was war, Mister Kettering. God is on our side, after all. And the fact that we possessed twenty thousand shells proved that the *Generalísimo* is invincible.'

'So invincible that the Popular Front is still fighting,' said Jack.

'Simply a matter of time, Mister Telford. And if Negrín cared for his people, he would have ended the thing by now. Aguirre saw the writing on the wall though, I think. He made sure that all the prisoners held in Bilbao were set free, sent back across the lines. The Anarchists, ladies and gentlemen, were about to slaughter them, it seems. Nine hundred of them. Aguirre also refused to destroy the factories. Not the bridges though. You know the story by now. The Reds do like to destroy their bridges, sure.'

'And were there reprisals?' said Frances Moorgate. 'After the city fell?'

'Oh no, ma'am,' said Murphy. 'In fact, General Franco would only allow a limited number of troops to enter the city.'

'To avoid a repeat of Málaga?' asked Jack.

'Well, the Málaga thing has been a bit exaggerated, sure.'

'Sister Berthe Schultz say that Our Heavenly Father must have sent the Germans to help the people of National Spain.' Sister María Pereda had assumed an air of pious devotion. 'That He sent them on the wings of avenging angels to smite the heathen in his lair.'

'Oh, the Germans are well rewarded for their work, Sister,' said Jack. 'Isn't it true, Mister Murphy, that Franco immediately signed over two-thirds of all Basque mining and steel production to Herr Hitler?'

'Well, there's no such thing as a free lunch, Mister Telford,' said Albert Moorgate. 'It seems a perfectly fair price to pay.'

'You might not think so,' Jack replied, 'when the Germans are using those same resources to bomb *your* bank, *your* home.'

'Oh, a little melodramatic, don't you think?' smiled Moorgate, looking around the group for endorsement.

'And did yourself and Sister Berthe Shultz,' Jack said to the younger nun, 'not question why a supposedly Catholic Movement like Franco's should have inflicted such punishment on the most Catholic community in all Spain?'

Sister María Pereda spoke quickly to her companion.

'She say that the Basques turned their face against God when they side with the Communist heretics. She say that His Holiness in Rome has relayed the Word of Our Lord when he officially recognise the government of General Franco. When he made it a sin for Spaniards to support the godless Republic. When he named all the priests and nuns killed in this conflict as martyrs.'

'But only those supposedly killed by the Republic,' said Jack. 'Not the sixteen Basque priests killed by fascist firing squads in October '36. Or the five hundred who've been driven into exile by Franco's forces.'

'I'm afraid that's another Red fable, Mister Telford,' said Brendan. 'But back to the bus, I think. Let's go and look at the city.'

Jack set aside his frustration once again. It seemed not to matter how many times he raised well documented events, Murphy was trained to simply deny them. And the rest of this bunch accepted the denials without question. But he decided to distract himself by sitting next to Max for the journey down into Bilbao, although the big man tried hard to press himself against the window, doing his best to avoid any physical contact and staring resolutely at the scenery.

'You not speaking, Max?' whispered Jack. 'Have I upset you?'

Nothing.

'Max, is this about last night?'

Weston's left shoulder gave the merest twitch.

'Nothing happened, Max. I wasn't there.'

The comedian's head turned slightly so that Max could see him from the corner of his left eye. Then he looked away again.

'I mean it, Max. I like you. We're friends, aren't we?'

Christ, what am I saying? thought Jack. *I'm not even sure why I'm trying so hard. I don't want Max Weston coming after me, for one thing. He's a big lad, when all's said and done, regardless of how he lets Marguerite treat him. But apart from that...*

'She went to your room,' Max spat at him.

'But I've told you, I wasn't there. Ask Brendan. I was with him in the yard, having a smoke.'

'If 'er wasn't in your room, then where *was* she?'

'What did she say?'

'Nothin'. She never tells me nothin'. Just that she were goin' to 'ave some fun. I knows what *that* means. But if she wasn't in *your* room…'

Oh God, now he's going to start suspecting somebody else.

'Marguerite *was* in my room, Max. But I wasn't there with her. I think she'd had a few too many. She was in the corridor, going down for another bottle of wine, I think. So I let her in and then went outside. I must have been chatting with Mister Murphy for an hour and when I came back, she was gone.'

'You tellin' I the truth, me old acker?'

'Yes, Max. The truth, the whole truth and nothing but the truth.'

'Oy, Jack, that reminds me. 'Ow many lawyers does it take to change a light bulb?'

'I've no idea, Max. How many?'

'Such number as may be deemed necessary to perform the stated task in a timely and efficient manner within the strictures of the following agreement: Whereas the party of the first part, also known as The Lawyer, and the party of the second part, also known as The Light Bulb, do hereby and forthwith agree to a transaction wherein the party of the second part, the Light Bulb, shall be removed from the current position…Well, it goes on a bit after that.'

'Very good, Max.'

'Be you really my friend, Jack?'

'Yes, of course. But tell me about Marguerite. How did you meet her?'

'I was workin' the music 'alls in '23 an' Marguerite was on the same billin'. With 'er sisters. They called themselves *"The Three Roses"*. A dancin' act. We was married next year. 'Er family was none too 'appy though. They was a bit well-to-do.'

'Which explains her hatred of cockroaches, I suppose?' Max smiled.

'Well, anyways, we worked the boards together for about seven years. I kept thinkin' we'd 'ave children but it ain't never 'appened. I 'ad this manager, see, but somethin' went on. I don't know what. But Marguerite got rid o' him, started doin' the job 'erself. Good at it too, Jack. She got me into the movin' pictures. *Ang about, me 'ansum,* first. And then *Madcap Max*.' He looked around, furtively. 'Hey Jack, 'ow much d'you think they paid I?'

'Max, it's none of my business.'

'Thirty thousand for the first 'un. Thirty-*five* for the second. Marguerite looks after it for me. She says the next one will pay even more. I'd be lost without 'er, Jack.'

'Yes,' said Jack, 'I know.'

The bus had skirted an industrial area, then passed some rising ground topped by an enormous church and, finally, a suburb of houses, terracotta, pale grey, deep red, light ochre. They might have seemed drab in another light but in the late morning sunshine they were dramatic. There was no commentary from Brendan Murphy, however. He seemed preoccupied with paperwork, put it away as they reached another *plaza* and funicular station among the apartment blocks at the foot of Mount Artxanda.

'Apologies, ladies and gentlemen,' he said. 'We'll be going back to look at all those sights again later. But first, let's get a bird's eye view of Bilbao.'

The guide produced a letter for the ticket office before they were ushered into the upward sloping open carriages for the rack rail ride to the summit. The incline was steep, longer than the one they had taken in San Sebastián, the city opening below them as they rose through the trees.

'The funicular's been here for over twenty years,' shouted Brendan. 'It was damaged during the siege and only re-opened a couple of months ago. Perfectly safe.' As if on cue, the carriages juddered to a temporary halt before continuing, through the passing place that allowed the downward progress of the descending cars. 'Well, I *think* so anyway!'

There was a small park and viewing point at the top, from which they could see beneath them, to the south, the Basque capital in all its glory, the river looping through its centre. The factory areas, the foundries, belching clouds of smoke and soot that drifted across the scene but, at its heart, parks and gardens seemed plentiful: orderly green patches punctuating the more sombre urban sprawl. Old town to the left. The modern city to the front and centre. *El Ensanche*, Brendan called it. The enlargement.

'It's more hilly than I'd imagined,' said Frances Moorgate. 'For a city, I mean.'

'Yes,' said Brendan. 'The company that runs the funicular also operates lifts joining one part of the city to another. Six or seven, if I remember correctly.'

Jack thought about Julia Britten again, but forced himself to focus on the panorama. From here, the course of the River Nervión could be traced northwards, through more smog-veiled industry, to the ship yards.

Then the descent, sharing their tiered benches with a party of seemingly irrepressible schoolchildren. Jack wondered how they were faring under the new regime. He was at least pleased to see them boisterous.

And soon they were on the bus again, following the river around its curve, for lunch and reception at Bilbao's City Hall on the Paseo Campo Volatín, according to the blue-tiled street sign. Yet nothing could have prepared them for the opulent interior with its grand staircases and collection of priceless art.

'This is just a sample of the heritage stolen by the Reds from all over Spain and stored here,' said Murphy. 'Presumably to be shipped off to Moscow at some stage. These are amongst the most valuable religious artefacts in the world. So many that we'll need a special museum to house them all.'

And they were even less prepared for the Arab Salon in which they were received. Jack had seen examples of Mudéjar already, of course, that mock-Moorish style that had once been so much admired, but this room dated only from the turn of the century.

Down the centre ran a venerable table around which the tour group was dispersed among the normal array of local dignitaries, business leaders and members of the clergy. At its head, the Mayor greeted them with a welcoming speech in excellent English, applauded by straight-arm salutes and cries of *¡Arriba España!* There was a blessing from Bishop Javier Lauzurica, the text of which Jack could not follow. There were speeches too from the Military Governor. From the Civil Governor also, a man called Larroza. And from their old friend, Captain Rosalles, the Press Officer from Burgos, here with a photographer to capture the moment in the same way that they had previously captured Bilbao itself.

The meal was lengthy. Blood sausage in red pepper sauce. Local clams with asparagus cream and garlic. Cod with mushrooms, mustard and Iberian ham in a fiery sauce. Cod cheeks and tripe in red pepper, followed by grilled squid with potatoes and onion. Hake with melon and tomato led the way to a final dish of lightly grilled beef in spicy tomato and wine. The dessert was grilled bread which had been soaked in honey and served with eucalyptus ice cream.

'This is very good,' said Jack, almost to himself. He pointed a fork towards his plate and made the appropriate sounds of appreciation for the benefit of the Military Governor who sat beside him but spoke not a word of English.

'*Torrijas*,' said the Governor, and then rambled into a lengthy lecture that Jack could not understand. Jack nodded and smiled whenever he felt it was appropriate to do so, trying to judge the thing from the fellow's expressions. But it was not easy. Too many distractions since, at these closing stages of the meal, the Spaniards around the table had resumed a series of loud discussions, deep rasping voices and cigar smoke. Garlic. Onions.

'Political differences?' Jack shouted to Brendan Murphy, seated a couple of places to his left and on the opposite side.

'Not on your life, Mister Telford,' he laughed. 'A lengthy debate about the quality of the wine. Have you not noticed that the more Spaniards are gathered in one place, the happier they become? Even here. Even now. It's the real tragedy, is it not? There can seldom have been a people less suited but more prone to war.'

'And what do you think about our fine hall, sir?' said the Mayor. Jack realised that the question was aimed at him.

'Elegant,' said Jack. 'It always intrigues me that, having spent so long chasing the Moors from Spain, the country should then show such admiration for the art of its oldest enemies.'

'You think it is impossible to admire one's enemies, Mister Telford?' said the Mayor. 'If you do not admire or respect them, you will never defeat them. This is a replica of the Hall of Ambassadors at the Alhambra. It was there that Colón received his commission from Ferdinand and Isabella. To search for the New World.'

'Your English is perfect, *Señor*,' said Jack, cursing the banal comment even as he spoke it. It was the worst of clichés. The Mayor, José Lequerica, acknowledged the compliment with a slight gesture of his head.

'I won a scholarship to continue my studies at your London School of

Economics,' he said. 'After I had earned my doctorate at the University of Madrid.'

'But you are originally from Bilbao?'

'Yes, I studied first at the Deusto.'

'Deusto?'

'A private institution operated by the Jesuit Brothers. One of the best universities in Spain.' The man was in his late-forties, Jack imagined. He was cursed with jowls, protruding ears, a receding hairline and a beak-like nose, barely large enough to support his spectacles. 'You may see it later, perhaps.'

'And your thesis?'

'My doctoral thesis? *Georges Eugène Sorel – the Theorist of Revolutionary Socialism*.'

'I always had difficulty deciding whether to place him with the abstract thinkers or the social reformers,' said Jack.

'Bravo, Mister Telford,' Lequerica applauded. 'Though he was, of course, a mixture of both. However, as a mere observer of workers' organisations rather than a revolutionary practitioner, it is safer to place him amongst the abstract thinkers. Am I not correct?'

'I bow to your superior knowledge, *Señor*. But Sorel must have been a strange choice of subject? A supporter of Marx. Then a revisionist. And what did Jaurès call him? The metaphysician of syndicalism? Finally a Leninist. Didn't he grate against your own beliefs?'

'A shallow analysis, I fear. Sorel's views on the true nature of syndicalism, the mobilisation of extra-parliamentary action amongst workers, has been the most significant force in shaping the development of National Socialism across Europe. In Mussolini's Italy. Hitler's Germany. And here, too. I had great respect for Maura. He inspired me to enter politics, Mister Telford. But my own brand of politics became a dangerous pursuit during the years leading up to the *Reconquista*. I spent some of them in Paris until the *Generalísimo* called me back to join the State Technical Board and then to take office as Mayor of Bilbao. An honour, you will agree?'

'Bilbao is a great city, from what I've seen. But I have to confess that I have never understood the nature of parties like the Falange Española. All of the fascist parties throughout Europe, in fact. You use the word socialism liberally enough. But wherever, as here in Spain, there has been a genuine movement of the people to kick off whatever shackles happen to bind them, you repress and attack it. Even where you may have initially provoked it.'

'You know very well, I think, Mister Telford, that such workers' movements are frequently hijacked, as the Americans say, by Anarchists, by Freemasons, by Jews. Here, they tried to use syndicalism as a means to break down National Spain, to destroy our Faith. They had to be destroyed. It was a simple matter of survival.'

Jack recalled that Sydney Elliott had once said to him, *'The social revolution is global in one sense only: that politicians who travel either to the extreme Left or the extreme Right will inevitably meet and meld in the Land of the Despot.'* He smiled at Lequerica, who had all the rationality of Alice's White Rabbit, and glanced around the table.

The staccato chatter reminded him of the machine guns that he had heard at *El Chofre*. And Max was entertaining some minor representatives with a repertoire of jokes that they could not possibly understand but which they seemed to find irresistibly amusing.

The Mayor interrupted them. It was almost time for his illustrious guests to leave and it was only fitting that they should do so in appropriate fashion. Just a short step south from the Town Hall to the place where Mikel was waiting with the bus but, *en route*, stood the Kiosko del Arenal, a bandstand set into modest parkland. There, the trumpets, horns and trombones of the Foreign Legionary garrison regaled them with slow and quick marches. *Novios de la Muerte. La Canción del Legionario. Tercios Heróicos.*

'Max,' said Jack, 'I meant to ask you. Brendan tells me that Julia Britten came to your room on the morning she died.'

'Oh ah! She came a-knockin' on the door. Said she'd come to apologise, like. But Marguerite weren't 'avin' none of it. Told that blind 'un where to go an' no mistake.'

'Apologise for what, Max?'

'Just said 'er knew how she'd upset Marguerite a couple o' times and wanted things to be straight between 'em. That kind o' thing.'

'And what time was this?'

'I don't rightly remember, me 'ansum. Early though. Seven maybe. Seven-fifteen.'

'She just left?'

'Poor thing got right upset. Ran off cryin', I think. Marguerite's got a wicked tongue when she chooses. But don't tell 'er I says so.'

'I won't. But Julia ran off alone?'

'That 'er did,' said Max. 'But Brendan, 'e were in the corridor. The last I saw, they was goin' off together. But she were givin' 'im a right tellin' off for somethin' or other.'

There were final farewells at the bandstand, *Señor* Lequerica making a point of coming to find Jack.

'Well, Mister Telford,' he said. 'You will write something positive about us, I hope?'

'Do you really care what I write in *Reynold's News*, *Señor*? Anyway, I would find it hard to write anything positive about those who rose in rebellion against a democratically elected Government.'

'And you think it would have been different if the Right had won the '36 elections? You think the Reds would have accepted the outcome? They had already promised to fight against anybody they did not favour.'

'Then you might have had legitimacy on *your* side, *Señor*, and I should not have been supporting *them*,' said Jack. It was pompous nonsense, of course. Lequerica laughed.

'Ah, you English!' he said. 'Legitimacy! What do you know of legitimacy in your comfortable little island? You all think this war started two years ago. But it didn't, Mister Telford. It began in 1812. With the Constitution of Cádiz. Write *that* in your paper, my friend.'

'Maybe I will,' Jack replied, and followed Max Weston onto the bus.

The tour took them around the rest of the old city, the *Casco Viejo.* They stopped near the theatre, on the Arenal, at the old quay, still lined with barges, small boats running up and down the river, so that Brendan could lead them along the narrow streets around Calle Bidebarrieta. There was an elegant public library, tall houses with ornate windowed balconies, women chatting loudly to each other from windows high above the alleys, *pintxos* bars, the smell of spices, black tobacco, the ubiquitous scorched olive oil, woodsmoke and soap. A knife-sharpener summoned customers with a shrill flute. A fish vendor sold her wares from a barrow and scales. Jack found a bookstall but, with little time to browse, he picked up a children's' comic, paid twenty-five *céntimos* for it. Not quite the *Beano*, as it turned out, but a copy of *Flechas y Pelayos*, weekly adventure stories published by the Falange so that youngsters of the new Spain could be properly raised on tales of Carlist courage, Communist cowardice. And, as a reminder of the war, when they reached the Arenal once more, they were in time to see a squadron of Nationalist light tanks pass by, each one bedecked with a dozen laughing *señoritas*, all of them dressed to kill, lipstick-daubed.

They rejoined the bus, crossed the river, with the green and yellow façade of the Santander to Bilbao Railway terminus to their left, then followed a wide avenue into the *Ensanche*, into modern Bilbao.

This could be Paris, thought Jack, as the bus ran along the tree-lined boulevard. *The river. The style of those apartments.* He could picture himself living there, determined that he should return in happier days. *But I'm not sure I like all this modern neo-classical stuff.*

The silver slime trails of sluggish trams crossed and inter-crossed around a *plaza*, past the Banco de Vizcaya, while their own yellow Dodge swung right in a line of cars to catch a glimpse of the Albia Gardens. There were still bomb-sites here, the occasional blackened shell with no interior, or half-ruins where, conversely, the shock of shelling seemed to have scoured away layers of the city's industrial grime. Red and yellow flags of National Spain. The red and black of the Falange. Ladies with fans held high above their heads to shade them from the afternoon sun. The contrast of modern frocks and hairstyles against traditional black dresses and *mantillas*. And large numbers of invalids amongst the men, of course, that Jack had noticed almost everywhere but who seemed generally invisible to the others. So, back on the Gran Vía Don Diego López de Haro they admired the Palacio Foral, grey and formidable and, at the Plaza Moyúa, they did indeed get to see Lequerica's old university, the Deusto. Then, at the very end of the Gran Vía, or perhaps more properly at its beginning, the fifty foot column of the Sacred Heart.

'And now,' said Murphy, 'our last stop of the day before we head back to Galdakao. The Hotel Carlton.'

'Another coffee break, Mister Murphy?' said Dorothea Holden.

'No,' said her husband. 'The Carlton, my dear. Let me see. Did the so-called Basque Government not hole up there towards the end?'

The hotel stood on one of the segments across from the Deusto, filling another intersection of the Plaza Moyúa, the *plaza elíptica*. They spent some time inside, admiring the twenty year-old architecture masquerading as Ancient Rome, the furnishings, the photographic display. Images of Basque President Aguirre at his writing desk, the captions condemning him for leading astray loyal Spaniards of Vizcaya. Members of the Basque Parliament, condemned as traitors, rewards offered for information on the whereabouts of named individuals. Nationalist troops hauling down the Basque flag, the *Ikurriña*, banned now by Franco. Victorious Legionnaires on the steps of the Carlton. And anecdotes too. King Alfonso had stayed here, it seemed. In better days, as Murphy put it. Hemingway too, sneered the guide. Ten years ago or more.

'He's a great writer,' said Jack. He remembered seeing the man. Strong as an ox. Exactly the opposite of what he had expected from an author of such erudite beauty.

'You admire him, Mister Telford?'

'Yes, I do.'

'The man is a buffoon, though. How can you admire a man who's so frequently proved to be wrong? He fills American newspapers with nonsense about the *Generalísimo* being doomed to defeat and out of luck. He makes films with phoney footage supposed to prove that we murder civilians.' Jack guiltily recalled the old man in Guernica. 'He stands up at the American Writers' Congress and boasts that *El Caudillo* is being fought to a standstill at Bilbao. Why, we liberated the city just one week later, Mister Telford.'

'But he *did* say that you'd never take Madrid,' said Jack. 'And you haven't.'

I hope to God that Hemingway was right on that one, he thought. *And his view that there won't now be a war in Europe? Please let that be true too.*

'Like I say, sir. Just a matter of time,' said Murphy. 'As soon as we break them on the Ebro they'll have nowhere left to run.'

Nobody seemed particularly interested, however, the group apparently suffering from collective fatigue today. So the return journey to Galdakao and the Palacio Urgoiti was conducted in almost total silence, several of them dozing in their seats. And there was little appetite, either, in the Palace dining room that night. Marguerite Weston was still in her room, the others picked at their supper, then retired one by one to their beds. Inevitably, there were finally only Jack and Brendan Murphy left.

'It always seems to hit the group about this stage in the tour,' said Brendan. 'Not you though, eh, Mister Telford? You've got the stamina, sure. An early night for me too, I think. But just before I go, maybe a couple of things that'll interest you.'

'You picked up a newspaper?'

'I haven't, I'm afraid. We'll try to make sure we get one tomorrow. But I had a look at Mikel's *Gaceta*, sure enough. Just more speculation about the talks between Hitler and your man. No, it wasn't that. I went down to the telegraph office while you were all getting spruced up for dinner. There were two wires waiting for me. Here's the first.'

Brendan had scribbled a translation, in pencil, above each line of Spanish text.

'The press release,' said Jack.

'So it is, Mister Telford. The *Generalísimo*'s office will circulate it tomorrow and he wouldn't have thanked you for any editorial comments now, would he? Anyway, you can study it at your leisure. But this one's interesting.' He held up another telegram.

'What is it?'

'You asked me to find out a bit more on Mister Kettering's brother.'

'And you've got something back?'

'Indeed I have! It seems that Donald Kettering served with the Fifth Bandera of the Legion. That'd make sense, sure. And his service record shows that he died here at Bilbao on the twelfth of June. Last year, of course. An act of outstanding heroism, it says. He was a platoon commander. That's such a rare honour for a non-Spaniard. Which explains why his family is invited to receive the *Medalla de Sufrimientos por la Patria*. He was several times wounded in the street fighting, but stayed at his duty till a mortar bomb broke his jaw and killed him. But here's the odd thing.'

'Odd?'

'Yes. It seems that they sent the invitation to his wife.'

'Not *that* odd. Presumably the wife nominated Peter Kettering to collect on her behalf. Maybe she thought it would be too stressful to come in person.'

'That's not what I meant, Mister Telford. What's odd is the coincidence. Mind, it may be no more than just that.'

'What coincidence?'

'That Donald Kettering's wife, or rather his widow, is apparently *also* called Catherine.'

Chapter Thirteen

Friday 23 September 1938

Jack Telford sat in the shade of a eucalyptus near the toll-gate pillar watching the courtyard of the Urgoiti Palace. The tethered goats bleated miserably and a starved cat rubbed itself against the outer wall. It was particularly interested in the antics of Mikel Iruko Domínguez as he tried to load luggage onto the roof-rack.

Mikel had already dropped two of the cases and been forced to retrieve them, idly brushing away the dust with his sleeve. But, as Jack lit the second of this morning's *Superiores*, the driver fumbled a third case. Down it went, and Mikel cursed. He looked towards the Parador, checking that he had not been observed and perhaps also hoping that some assistance might arrive. Yet he also squinted towards the road, this way and that. *What's he looking for?* Jack wondered. He had been doing so on each of the previous occasions that a trunk had fallen, distraction making him clumsy. *And I've seen him like this before. What the hell is he expecting to see? Well, at least my own case is safely stowed. It's just to be hoped that those others contained nothing fragile.*

The tourists began to leave the Palace, filing out towards the bus, Dorothea Holden producing a list to remind everybody of the seats they had occupied during the previous days.

'Well, I thinks I should stay in the front,' complained Marguerite Weston. 'Mister Telford agrees with me, I'm sure.' She smiled at Jack. 'Ain't that so, my dear?'

'I'm not sure that I have a view on the matter, Mrs Weston. Perhaps you could sit with your husband?' His suggestion was met with a snort of derision.

'Well, we need to stick to our plan,' said Dorothea. 'Which means that myself and Alfred will move across to your old seat, Mrs Weston, and the Moorgates should advance so that they are behind the driver.'

'In the circumstances,' said Albert Moorgate, 'we think that the Ketterings should occupy our seats in the front today. Frances and myself are happy to take their place.'

Peter Kettering smiled weakly, mouthed thanks. The couple were both dressed in funereal attire, and the others stood aside, allowing them aboard first.

Jack had decided to absent himself at breakfast when Brendan had taken the Ketterings aside to share his news, before announcing that with the group's approval, they would make a short non-scheduled diversion from their planned route.

As it happened, it took only twenty minutes for the bus to arrive in the Derio district and come to a halt outside the principal entrance to that spread of cathedralesque columns, archways and carvings that formed the exterior walls of Bilbao's largest cemetery, a veritable city of the dead, the *Vista Alegre*. Jack wondered how they could possibly have arrived at the name. It was a dark joke, surely? Perhaps some local significance that escaped him? But no, their guide assured them, the place genuinely *was* called 'Happy Outlook.'

They continued in silence, Brendan Murphy and the Ketterings leading the cortège to a recently engraved plaque commemorating those killed in the Larrinaga gaol and local prison ships during the early part of '37.

'More martyrs of the *Reconquista*?' asked the Professor.

'Yes, sir. Butchered by the Reds. In retaliation for the bombardment of Bilbao, it seems.'

But, for once, Murphy did not labour the point. Instead, he took them to a farther corner where several dozen white crosses stood in military ranks, none of them blessed with a name, only a simple number. The guide took from his pocket the telegram which he had shown to Jack the night before.

'Which one, Mister Murphy?' said Peter Kettering.

'This one,' Murphy replied, standing aside to let the Ketterings come closer.

Peter looked away into the distance, biting his lip, holding Catherine who wept. Heart-wrenching sobs. She was inconsolable.

She must have been uncommonly fond of her brother-in-law, thought Jack, catching Brendan Murphy's eye.

'It is so sad,' whispered Sister María Pereda. 'Sacrifice of life for the cause of Our Lord. The brother of *Señor* Kettering must have been a very special man. I expect that he is now with Miss Britten, looking down. You think so?'

'Perhaps,' said Jack. 'But not together, I don't suppose. Miss Britten never knew him, after all.'

'In Heaven that does not matter. Miss Britten was here with us. Part of our group. And she must have known this poor *mártir* through her conversations with his family. His brother. His brother's wife. It is enough. After that, the Holy Father or Our Lady will make the introductions...How do you say it? Official? No, formal. He make formal introduction.'

She smiled, pleased with her grasp of English, Jack assumed.

'I'm not sure that Miss Britten really spent that much time with Peter or Catherine either, so far as I recall.'

'Oh, I think they must have been great friends,' said the nun. 'Miss Britten and *Señora* Kettering, I mean. I saw them in such deep conversation.'

'Really?' said Jack, but absently. For he was watching the others in the group. Marguerite fuming with impatience, prodding Max and murmuring angrily in his ear. The Holdens and Valerie Carter-Holt, heads bowed in silent prayer. Albert

Moorgate running his finger uneasily around the collar of his shirt, uncomfortable in these very Catholic surroundings. Frances, looking with adoration at some statuary away in the distance. Sister Berthe Schultz just to Jack's left and fingering her rosary.

'Yes,' said Sister María Pereda. 'On the night before poor Miss Britten died so horribly, for example.'

'She *did*?' Jack was suddenly interested again.

'Yes. You would not remember. After Miss Britten played piano for us. You went to bed early, I think. But Miss Britten and *Señora* Kettering went off to a corner together. A profound discussion, I could tell.'

'Could you hear what they were talking about?' asked Jack, suddenly realising that he knew the answer before the question was even out. The nun looked shocked.

'*Señor!*' she quietly scolded him. 'After all that I have taught you about the sin of curiosity!' Jack raised his hands in surrender.

'Alright,' he said. 'I should have remembered. But how long did this profound discussion take?'

The nun thought for a moment. She whispered with Sister Berthe Schultz. *What's she doing?* wondered Jack. *Checking the facts? Or asking whether it might be another mortal sin to divulge them?*

'Fifteen minutes,' she said, at last. 'We both remember because, just afterwards, Miss Britten had her fight with the Professor.'

'On the same night?' Jack asked, astonished. *How did I manage to miss all this?*

'Of course. But you will not ask me what they argued about, will you?'

'I wouldn't dream of it, Sister María Pereda.' *But I'll make it my business to find out!*

Jack had plenty of time to think about it during the two hours that it took them to leave Bilbao behind, skirting through the western suburbs, polluted with poverty, makeshift shelters, flattened petrol can walls, corrugated roofing.

'If it's not an insensitive question,' said Alfred Holden, there must be literally hundreds of burial sites like the one in *Vista Alegre*. All those fallen heroes. Will there be a memorial arranged for them? Instead of simply numbers on crosses, I mean.'

'Sometimes, Professor,' Brendan replied, 'our fallen haven't even the comfort of a cross. Just common graves. It isn't always easy to know exactly who fell in which place. But *El Caudillo* has promised that when the Crusade is finally over, there will be a monument to rival the most magnificent of the country's holy sites. A fitting tribute to those who have fallen for God and Spain.'

'It's a bit premature to be thinking about monuments, isn't it?' said Jack. 'And what about those who are dying on the Republican side? Many of *them* think they're giving their lives for God and Spain too.'

'If they are true believers, Mister Telford, but simply misled, then I'm sure that space will be found for them too.'

And who will build it, I wonder? thought Jack. *An army of slave labour drawn from the ranks of a defeated Republican Army? Will they create a tribute to God from the foundations of a concentration camp? Like some modern Pyramid of Giza? Is that how the people's revolution ends? A hundred years of Civil War to bring them back to where they started? In feudal servitude?*

He took Murphy's telegram from his pocket, the one containing Franco's press release.

War Route of the North, it was headlined in Brendan's pencil translation.

The General Management of the National Tourism Service regrets to announce the recent death of renowned English concert pianist, Miss Julia Britten, whilst on holiday at the resort of San Sebastián. Miss Britten was due to join one of the successful War Route tours before performing in a private audience for Generalísimo Franco at Santiago de Compostela. Miss Britten died of natural causes as a result of a congenital illness.

The rest of the article, Brendan had scribbled, gave dates and itineraries for tours during the coming month.

Would Julia have seen the funny side of this? Jack wondered, reading the contents for the third time, then testing the limits of his own Spanish against the original text in the hope that Brendan might have missed something. But his efforts revealed nothing fresh. Nothing to relieve or excuse the distorted version of events.

'So, ladies and gentlemen,' called Brendan from the back of the bus. 'Here we are in Cantabria.'

In Castro Urdiales they were served passable coffee at an elegant seaside restaurant. Slender fingers of toasted bread too, topped with tomato, anchovy and olive oil.

They enjoyed a thirty minute stroll around the former Roman port, the medieval old town, the Church of Santa María de la Asunción. But the main object of their halt seemed to be the twelfth century Castle of Santa Ana and its more modern lighthouse.

'The castle was built by the Templars,' Brendan announced. 'The *Generalísimo* is a great admirer. You'll all know about the Templars, sure? Wherever men carry the Cross into battle against the heathen, that's where you'll find the Knights Templar. Great warriors like *El Cid*. Or Don Pelayo. And now, General Francisco Franco.'

Frances Moorgate turned to look at the guide, her dark purple lips parting in a smile of sheer infatuation. He winked his eye in return, a gesture not lost on husband Albert, who removed his hat, wiping sweat from the headband with his handkerchief, his facial expression one of profound irritation.

'They were all Papists, my dear,' Jack heard his angry whisper. 'Every one of them!'

Another hour took them along a cliff-top route, reefs offshore to their right, then inland over some salt marsh near Nocina, the bridge across the silted estuary at Oriñon and a steep valley to hit the coast again at Laredo, almost deserted, narrow cobbled streets, the town virtually closed at this early afternoon hour. Their guide pointed to a few modest factories, to labourers in the fields hauling weighted, stone-studded boards to clear rocks from the soil, the revival of the work ethic, the green shoots of an emerging economy.

They ate sardines for lunch at a hotel overlooking *La Salvé*, Laredo's exquisitely curving beach and looking across to the port of Santoña, just the other side of the estuary, the bulk of Monte Buceiro dominating the bay. The Mayor joined them, inevitably, along with the usual coterie of fascist followers, and delivered a speech about this Capital of Spain's Emerald Coast. Murphy's translation made it sound positively Shakespearian.

'And this is a good point,' said the guide, 'at which to rejoin the tale of our *Reconquista*. It's August. Just over a year ago. Bilbao has fallen to General Dávila, and the Reds have fallen back westwards towards this section of the coast. The Battle of Santander has begun. Our own forces are advancing in two huge columns, one from Bilbao, the other from the south. And the Basque separatists who make up such a large part of the Red army have quite simply had enough. After all, most of the land which they claimed as Basque territory is now held by National Spain. Some of their battalions are holding the Santoña peninsula over there. But it's a lost cause. So they decide to surrender. The Basque leaders arrange a meeting with two of our Colonels, Farina and di Carlo...'

'Italians?' said Jack.

'Yes, Italians,' said Brendan.

'And you say these were Basque leaders. But not President Aguirre, I assume?'

'No, not Aguirre. A senior representative though. Juan de Ajuriaguerra. Anyway, he agrees a surrender. Only for his Basques, of course. As part of the deal, Colonel Farina, without any authority, has agreed that there will be immunity for those who have laid down their arms. And these Basque traitors are free to go! British merchant ships put into Santoña and start to load them up by the thousand. As refugees. Can you imagine, ladies and gentlemen? Naturally, as soon as the *Generalísimo* heard of this, he ordered the so-called Santoña Pact to be ripped up. He forced the British to unload their cargoes and the prison of El Dueso, just across the bay, was soon filled with twenty-two thousand of them. If they thought they could escape the justice of National Spain, they were badly mistaken.'

'But they were treated as Prisoners of War, surely?' said Peter Kettering.

'They were treated as traitors, Mister Kettering. But I understand that half of them have already served their sentences and are now freed.'

'And the other half?' said Jack.

'Still serving their time, of course.'

'Eleven thousand of them?'

'Yes, Mister Telford. Eleven thousand traitors.'

Jack wondered how many of them were still alive. Shuddered at the thought.

'And those that have been released?' asked Professor Holden. 'They have been rehabilitated back into normal society, I hope?'

'More than that,' smiled Brendan. 'Most of them had such an Epiphany that they agreed to enlist in our own ranks. They went on to fight with distinction in Asturias and beyond. Mikel, the driver, he's one of them.'

The Mayor had been listening to the exchange with interest, pulling on a cigar, frequently wanting to know what was being said, some of his companions also pushing forward, pressing a large sack into his hands. Finally, he opened the thing, unfurling a tattered standard. He spread his arms wide, let the folds drop. The fringed trim, once golden yellow, was now caked with mud, attached only by a few threads to the banner's fabric. Faded red ground, a green cross of Saint Andrew, embroidered script on a central white lozenge.

'Taken at Santoña?' asked the Professor.

Brendan nodded but said nothing. *He's a soldier too,* thought Jack. *He'll be proud of these spoils. These battlefield souvenirs. Because nothing so glorifies the deeds of the victor than a display of its enemy's standards. But he'll feel the loss too, won't he? The ignominy that those* Gudaris *who bore it into battle must have felt at its fall. How betrayed.*

They left the restaurant to fascist salutes, to inquisitive inspection by Laredo's citizens, just beginning to emerge from post-siesta hibernation.

'I meant to ask you about Mikel,' said Jack to the guide. 'Is he worried about something? He often looks a bit distracted. As though he thinks he's being followed. Is he alright, do you think?'

'Mikel?' laughed Brendan. 'Yes. And he'll feel more relaxed here in Cantabria. Back in Vizcaya he always imagines that some Basque fanatic is going to bump him off for coming across to our side. But I can always have him replaced, Mister Telford, if you think he's not paying proper attention to his duties. I noticed one or two of the trunks look a bit the worse for wear.'

'No, no. Nothing like that. He's a good driver. But *does* he have anything to worry about then?'

'Well, there've been a few killings here and there. Always *some* lunatic that still thinks they've got a cause, sure.'

'The Basques could take lessons from the Irish on lost causes, I guess,' said Jack.

'Now you *are* on thin ice, Mister Telford.' The humour had drained from Brendan's face.

'Maybe. But one more question?'

'Go on.'

'It's not about Basques. I was talking with Max Weston about Julia Britten.'

'Miss Britten?' Murphy looked crestfallen. 'I can't help feeling guilty about her. I couldn't have done anything...'

'But your bosses in Burgos might not see it that way? And Franco's press release is a disgrace.'

'You expected anything else? Is that what you wanted to ask me about?'

'No. Max says that when you escorted Julia away from their room on the morning she died, she seemed angry with you.'

'I'm amazed that Max Weston should have noticed. But yes. I offered to take her back to her room. She refused. Well, refused is probably a polite way of putting it, sure. She put me in my place, Mister Telford. Said she had somebody else to see. She made me leave her at the stairs.'

'At the stairs? Not the paternoster?'

'You think I would leave her unattended at a paternoster lift?'

It was early evening before the yellow bus pulled out of Laredo for the final forty kilometres to Santander. They crossed the estuary of the Asón by the Colindres girder bridge, pleased to note that it had not been destroyed by Red arsonists, one of Murphy's apparent obsessions in life.

In years to come, thought Jack, *I wonder whether travellers will cross this modest viaduct in peace, glance north to this picturesque little setting, marvel at how quaint it looks. And never have an inkling about the tragedy of poor Santoña.*

But then they were away from the coast to cross the headland formed by the Cabo de Ajo and the Cabo Quejo. The climb was marked by Mikel's steady scrutiny of the bonnet-mounted thermometer, its needle swinging clockwise until, with precocious inevitability, the pressure valve popped, a cloud of steam enveloped them, and the lower gears were forced to engage in a battle of wills between driver and stick shift. The vapour, infused with the essence of grease and hot oil, pervaded everybody and everything within the bus until, finally, the motor rebelled. At first, Jack imagined that they had struck a mine. The explosion caused several of the women to scream.

'*¡Joder!*' yelled Mikel.

'Oh, my goodness,' shouted Albert. 'Is that the cylinder head?'

Brendan Murphy bellowed a question to the driver above the *bang, bang, bang* from the engine compartment.

'He says it's the head gasket,' Murphy advised them. 'He'll pull up wherever he can.'

'To carry out repairs?' said Dorothea.

'Unlikely,' said Albert Moorgate. 'He's more likely to simply take out the sparking plug from the offending cylinder. Ease the compression, you see? Stop some of that infernal racket and make things a bit easier.'

'He says he's got a spare gasket,' Brendan informed them. 'He can fit it once we've stopped in Santander.'

So they limped to the highest ground, the landscape opening before them, rolling hills in front, mountain ridges far to the south. Eucalyptus trees, dense masses of them, almost as far as the eye could see.

'Almost as green as Ireland,' shouted Brendan above the engine's din.

'So much forest,' muttered Jack, as the Eucalyptus marched in mighty battalions across the landscape.

They took their first sight of the wide *Ría Cubas* at El Astillero. Brendan Murphy instructed Mikel to stop at the roadside. They were all heartily glad to escape the noise and smell, to stretch their legs.

'Well, there she is, ladies and gentlemen. Santander. Like I said earlier, the Red army retreated here, forced back slowly by our columns from the south and, after the Basques surrendered at Santoña, along this north coast too. On the twenty-fourth of August, they ordered a retreat westwards towards Asturias. They abandoned the city and we were just too late to cut them off. But we still took seventeen thousand of them as prisoners.'

'And what happened to them, Mister Murphy?' said Jack.

'Oh, sent to prison, sure. We had to convert the Bullring in Santander.'

'You got seventeen thousand people in a bullring?' Jack was incredulous.

'Well, a lot of them were found guilty of serious crimes, of course. Arson. And worse. You'll see when we do the tour later.'

'So they were executed?'

'The guilty ones, yes.'

'How many?'

'I wasn't here in person, Mister Telford. Anyway, that was just about the end of the Reds' Army of the North. Almost, but not quite. At the start of the Battle for Santander, they had twelve brigades. They escaped with just six battalions. The Basque brigades were pretty well wiped out. And the Reds from Asturias, who'd put in twenty-seven battalions, got away with only fourteen. Sixty thousand Republican troops had been wiped off the map. The War in the North was all but won. And our tale is almost told. But we'd best not keep the *charabanc* waiting. The old girl needs a touch of Mikel's loving care.'

The tour group's arrival in Santander assumed, for most of the passengers, almost a carnival atmosphere to match that which Franco's victorious columns must have felt a year earlier. There were still several days of the trip left, but there seemed to be a general sense that the toughest part was over. The bus to be repaired, of course. One or two more battlefields to mop up. But after that would come the golf, the hunt for elusive *chamois*, the beaches, and celebrations at Santiago de Compostela, marred only slightly by Miss Britten's demise.

They checked into Santander's Hotel Real, where Jack was delighted to find himself in a room overlooking the bay and the open sea. It was a contemporary building, of great style, opened twenty years previously, standing next to the modernist Pardo house on the Paseo Pérez Galdós. He was even more delighted, however, to find a copy of *The Times* in his room. It was yesterday's, naturally, but still...

He devoured it, cover to cover.

The Sudeten Crisis, naturally, dominated once again. Chamberlain was due to meet Hitler, of course, but the fresh news was that the Czechoslovakian Government had finally, reluctantly, agreed to accept the Anglo-French proposal for the German-speaking areas to be annexed to Germany. *The Times* warned, however, that this concession was almost sure to cause both Poland *and* Hungary to want their own slices of the Czech cake.

Czechoslovakia, cried the paper, *is faced with the loss in the near future of Western Bohemia, Northern Bohemia, German Silesia, Polish Silesia, and the Hungarian Parts in the south.*

But, between the lines, Jack could sense a change in editorial style. A worrying thing, akin to panic. Just *too* much coverage of the Air Raid Precautions debate.

What's happened while I've been away? he thought. *I have this nightmare that I'll go back and not recognise the place.*

And yet he understood it. He had been *here*, had he not? In this place where Britain's possible tomorrow was already happening. So Jack Telford had every reason to be paranoid about lack of preparation, about the threat to peace. But how had the damned thing managed to convey itself to all those millions back home?

He unpacked, tossed *The Times* and *The Hobbit* together on the bed, cleaned his teeth with the newfangled nylon bristle brush that he had bought in London, then took a lift down to reception so that he could join the early evening tour of the city.

The hotel had arranged for a local bus company to collect them, taking the group down to the promenade, past extravagant private villas, the religious college, then turning north to follow the line of the fabled Sardinero beaches, past the Grand Casino to the Piquio Gardens. The Cathedral next. Then across to a cluster of Government buildings, entered the courtyard of the Finance Ministry. There was a plaque on the wall.

'It was unveiled only recently,' said the guide. 'In memory of José Calvo Sotelo. Murdered by Red assassins in Madrid, July '36.'

Brendan knew, as did Jack, that they would all have some knowledge of Calvo Sotelo, Leader of the Right-wing Opposition Parties after the Republican Popular Front won the elections. His story had filled the front pages at home for days on end. It had been his murder, after all, according to the *Caudillo* himself, that had inspired Franco to act.

'He was killed the day after his own thugs assassinated that lieutenant of the Assault Guards, wasn't he?' said Jack. 'And after he'd threatened mayhem against the Socialists during his speeches in the Cortes.'

'Well, Mister Telford, the so-called Government of the Day found no evidence of that claim. Indeed, they found no evidence of *anything*. Including any indication of who had killed such a senior politician.' Brendan gestured towards the plaque. 'Had they done so, there might have been no need for the *Reconquista*.'

'The insurrection, you mean,' shouted Jack. He knew he was out of control, his heart thumping and his voice tremulous. 'Why can't we recognise it for what it *is*? This was no bloody *Reconquista*. It was a military coup. A treasonous uprising against the elected Government. Does it not occur to *any* of you people that, without the coup, we wouldn't be having to do all this? Trying to work out who's telling the truth about who killed who? Who bombed what? All those thousands of poor sodding lives lost?'

'Oh,' said Alfred Holden, 'I think *we* all know the truth, my boy. It's you who seems to be having difficulty understanding. And I *do* wish that you'd refrain from swearing in front of my wife. It's *so* uncouth.'

Jack walked out onto the street, shakily lit one of the *Superiores*, unsure how much more of this nonsense he could stand, waiting for his racing pulse to regularise again. But he tagged along behind them as they headed for the courtesy bus once more.

'You got a whippin' there, Jack my lad,' said Marguerite, who had fallen back to join him, linking his arm. 'An' all you deserve too, naughty boy. Leavin' your girl like that the other night. Good job for you I'm a forgivin' soul.'

'And what exactly do I need to be forgiven for?'

'You know full well! An' I tells you *this*, Jack Telford. Next time I comes a-callin', you'd best be ready for me. Know what I mean?'

She pinched his backside, waddled forward to catch up with the Ketterings while Valerie Carter-Holt slowed a little, obviously wanting him to join her.

'Was that supposed to be a display of moral indignation, Mister Telford?' she said. 'Hardly professional, d'you think?'

'I find it difficult when the dead are used in such large numbers to re-write history. Not that you'd care, of course, but how can you challenge anything when it's always the dead that they use as symbols?' Jack instantly regretted his acerbic tone, softened to a gentler manner. 'It's like a sacred text. Mystical. You might know in your heart that it's mumbo-jumbo but you can't disprove it. And the more you try, the more ignorance spreads amongst the believers.'

'And what is it that you find so hard to believe? That Nationalist deaths have been the price paid for Spain's future? How could I *not* care? This damned war nearly cost me *my* life too. I've covered a great deal of it, Mister Telford. If it's any consolation to you, I can tell you this. That the Republic broke down because there were simply too many competing interests within the Popular Front. Just too many. But break down it certainly did! Everything that happened afterwards is a consequence of that breakdown. Quite how you *interpret* those consequences depends on which side you choose to take.'

'But the facts...'

'The facts are always written by the winning side. Don't you know that? Of course you do. You're a journalist, Mister Telford. And a good one, I think. Because you care. Yet you must recognise that it sometimes takes many years before the actual winner in a contest becomes clear. Things are not always what they seem at the moment we perceive them, Mister Telford.'

Jack pondered her words as he dressed for dinner and made his way down to the partitioned section of the dining room reserved for the tour group and its guests. They were the first civil words that he had properly exchanged with Carter-Holt. And he had enjoyed the experience, been flattered and excited by her recognition of his journalistic quality. He watched her now as she mingled with their companions for the evening. She smiled often in the company of strangers, he noticed, a beacon that flashed brilliance amongst the sombre suits, the clerical greys and, tonight, the military uniforms. A group of army officers seemed entranced by her dark hair, the thickly arching brows, the brown eyes. But which army? Not Spaniards, that was clear. Italians, Jack concluded. They seemed to be admiring the medal with its ladies' ribbon, pinned to Valerie's red lapel. Admiring it just a little too closely for Jack's liking.

He had expected his presence to cause some awkwardness tonight after his earlier outburst. But not a bit of it. In fact, Brendan Murphy seemed to make a particular point of gathering him into the small party for which he was working the room and making introductions. The Ketterings were included, and so were the Westons, though Jack kept as far away from Marguerite as he possibly could. So they shook hands with the President of the Santander Provincial Council, with the Bishop of Santander, with more leading members of the local Falange, with several business leaders, and with a prominent landowner. The ubiquitous Captain Rosalles, of course, and his press team. And the Italians, already in the added company of Dorothea Holden and her husband.

'Am I supposed to acknowledge that these fellows are Italian or not, Mister Murphy?' whispered Jack. 'Or are you going to tell me that they're not really here? That they're another figment of my imagination?'

'Difficult, Mister Telford. They're apparently here because the Provincial Council has decided to name one of the town squares in their honour. To recognise the role their troops played in liberating Santander. The *plaza* near the Casino, apparently. The weekend papers will be full of it, sure.'

'And there's really no difference,' said Dorothea, 'between General Franco's assistance from the Italians and the Popular Front's use of the Russians.'

'Except that the Russian army isn't here, Mrs Holden,' Jack replied. 'It would have made its presence felt by now otherwise, don't you think? Whereas there are whole brigades of Italians here, despite the Non-Intervention Pact. Most of the German Luftwaffe too.'

'The Germans have a perfectly legitimate role here, Telford,' snarled the Professor.

'Well, the founding member of the Anglo-German Fellowship would say that, I suppose,' Jack smiled.

'We had *quite* enough of that from Miss Britten, thank you very much,' said Dorothea. 'Oh!' She put her fingers to her lips. 'How indiscreet.'

The army officers were looking on in amusement, seeking an explanation but receiving none. Carter-Holt made some polite excuse in apparently impeccable Italian and they, in turn, insisted on sitting near the group when everybody was finally placed at table.

There was a blessing from the Bishop and a speech. He was round-faced, full-lipped, bespectacled. He had been imprisoned by the Reds at the start of the *Reconquista*, he said, but freed just a year ago so that he was able to return and resume his duties. Many of Santander's priests had not been so lucky, however, and the visitors were invited to join him in prayer as he recited their martyred names.

Dinner featured fried squid *rabas*. Whitebait with fresh shellfish. A wonderful stew of meat, chickpeas and cabbage. Fistfuls of bread.

'You still think,' said Brendan, 'there's any question about whether the Reds killed priests, Mister Telford? And in large numbers. You think the Bishop is lying? He'd worked with all those men.'

'No, I don't think he's lying. And there's never an excuse for killing innocent people, Mister Murphy. But how can so many ordinary people build up such rage against the Church unless they believed it was guilty of great injustice against them? The promise of Heaven held out to them so they would meekly accept feudal slavery in *this* world? What sort of abuses must they have thought they were avenging? Who was it said that in Spain even atheists are Catholic? So what *drove* the Spanish to such acts? And this is always about whether I, Jack Telford, am going to deny the so-called evidence you keep presenting to us. But what about *you*, Mister Murphy? Are *you* really going to deny that your Nationalist friends have murdered at *least* as many Left-wingers in the name of God? Simply because they belong to this political party or that? Voted one way or another? This war is a madness. An infectious disease. And infection kills all manner of innocents, my friend.'

They were served dessert. Small *quesada* cheesecakes. Sponge *sobaos pasiegos*. Puff pastry *corbatas*. And decent coffee, of course, served as the clouds of cigarette and cigar smoke thickened. While, just a few hundred miles south, thought Jack, Madrid was still being bombed into oblivion by Franco's liberators. Madrid, where there was no power, no fuel for the coming winter, no food. Black-marketeering too, they said, on an epidemic scale.

Late guests. Two of them. *Teniente* Enrique Álvaro Turbides of the Guardia Civil Public Order and Prevention Service. Even larger than Jack remembered, even more tanned. His thick lips salivated over the pastries, sipped at the coffee that clung to his moustache, his eyes remaining ice-cold above the eagle's nose while he surveyed each of the travellers in turn. He lit a cigar, spoke quietly to Brendan, nodded towards his companion.

'The *Teniente*,' said Murphy, 'suggests that we adjourn to a room which he has arranged for our use. No rush, of course.'

No, no rush. Although Jack noticed the frequency with which the Lieutenant looked at his watch while the meal was concluded and farewells exchanged. But it was not the Lieutenant that opened the session when they had later re-assembled.

'Ladies and gentlemen,' said the second stranger, in perfect Oxbridge English, 'I hope that you might forgive any failure on my part to introduce myself earlier. So difficult at these things, you understand.' His dinner jacket was immaculate, his hair carefully pomaded in the style of an older generation. He snapped open a gold cigarette case, removed a Du Maurier, began to slip the case back into his pocket, then thought better of it. 'Ah, please,' he said, 'pass them around, why don't you? I imagine some of you must be down to the native varieties by now. Anyway, to business. My name is Fielding. Vice-Consul in San Sebastián. Remiss of me to be away while you were in town, especially...Well, there we are!'

'You have news of Miss Hames, Mister Fielding?' said Catherine Kettering.

'Miss Hames? Yes, indeed. I saw her safely aboard one of our destroyers at Bilbao earlier today. Dear lady. And the mortal remains of poor Miss Britten too. Condolences, of course. Naturally.'

'How *was* Miss Hames?' asked Jack.

'Well, how should one put it? Distressed. A little. But irrepressible. Stoical.

Very…British. A day of drama for our countrymen here in Spain today, one way or the other.'

'*Which* countrymen?' said Dorothea Holden.

'Oh, one shouldn't speak of it. Present company and so on.'

'If you've news, Mister Fielding,' said Brendan Murphy, 'I'm sure one would like to share it.' The sarcasm was entirely lost on the Vice-Consul.

'Ah,' said Fielding. 'Well, it came over the wire while I was in Bilbao. News from the Ebro Front. The Republican Fifteenth International Brigade fell back across the Ebro last night. That's the Brigade which includes the British Battalion, of course.'

'Communist scum,' snarled Alfred Holden. 'Don't deserve to be classed as British.'

'British citizens, sir,' replied Fielding, testily. 'Some question about the legality of them being here but that will resolve itself as well now, seemingly.'

'How so, Mister Fielding?' It was Peter Kettering.

'They're to be withdrawn, I gather. Negrín has made the announcement at last. The rest of the Internationals were moved back from the combat zones two days ago. Now that the Americans and British volunteers have joined them, they can all be repatriated. And we diplomats can sleep soundly in our beds knowing that the Non-Intervention Pact is finally being observed.'

Was it irony? Jack wondered. Madrid still being bombed by the Luftwaffe. And their own group had just left a room full of fascist Italian officers, their battalions still serving within Franco's army, yet…

'And is that what brings you to Santander, Mister Fielding?' asked Dorothea Holden. 'The repatriation?'

Fielding coughed, stubbed out his Du Maurier. He stared around the room until his gaze, Jack thought, fell on Carter-Holt. Their eyes met. A mere instant, but Jack was convinced that something had passed between them.

'No, good lady. No. More immediate business to attend, I'm afraid. It concerns your own party. And Miss Britten, as it happens.'

'I don't understand you, Vice-Consul,' said Dorothea. 'You said that Miss Britten's remains are safely aboard one of our ships.'

'Indeed, ma'am. But it's rather delicate. You see, ladies and gentlemen, that the *Teniente* here arranged an autopsy yesterday. As a result of which he now seems to think…Well, it's damnably difficult, but I'm afraid I must ask you all to surrender your passports. To me, of course.'

There was uproar. They were British, when all was said and done. And what strange notion, pray, had this impertinent fellow got into his head. Outrageous. The very idea. And what about the Sisters of Our Lady of the Holy Light? Surely…

But Mister Fielding had a note from the Swiss Attaché, authorising him to collect the nuns' passports too. They would be carefully looked after, of course. So they all complied, a forlorn queue, waiting to hand the simple symbol of their sovereign rights to His Majesty's representative. It was almost as if King George the Sixth himself was confiscating the things. They were collectively sullied by the act. Yet it was not the King, nor even Telford's father – though Jack felt his ghostly presence here too – standing at Harold Fielding's elbow.

'And are we going to find out exactly what the autopsy concluded?' said Jack as he reached the table.

'Do you know,' Fielding replied, 'that you're the only one to ask, Mister…?' He flipped open Jack's passport. 'Ah, Mister Telford. Of course. *Reynold's News*, is it not? We never miss an edition at the Consulate. And Miss Hames sends her particular regards. Sent a message, of sorts. Says not to forget. That mean anything? But the autopsy. Not sure that one is allowed to say, really. But it seems that they found some strange marks upon the poor lady's back. Marks of a shoe, they think. Well, to be precise, a woman's fashion heel!'

Chapter Fourteen

Saturday 24 September 1938

For the second time in a week, Jack was convinced that the tour would not be permitted to proceed. But, no, they were told. Not so. *Teniente* Enrique Álvaro Turbides simply had some routine enquiries to make. The conclusions of such autopsies were notoriously prone to re-evaluation. Probably nothing.

The ladies were all required, naturally, to display their shoes. The nuns, obviously, possessed only laced walking pumps. No heels at all. Whilst the others, Dorothea Holden, Valerie Carter-Holt, Catherine Kettering, Frances Moorgate and Marguerite Weston, each shared a similar range. Walking pumps too, of course. Flat soles for daytime wear, the bus journeys and informality, Gillies for Dorothea, the rest with Mary Jane straps. And for dress, dinner or hotel, a bewildering array of fashions and colours, price ranges too, but all sharing a similar style of heel. The Louis, the Tango, the Curve. Marguerite alone possessed a pair of the platforms so favoured by Joan Blondell. The rest were pure Bette Davis, Carole Lombard, Greta Garbo, Ginger Rogers. Shoes of the stars!

Marguerite, to nobody's surprise, won the contest so far as quantity was concerned. Carter-Holt seemed to possess the most admired, a pair of original Ferragamo's. Frances had the most astonishing choice in colours. Catherine exhibited conservative elegance. And Dorothea...Well, Dorothea had the only pair of Gillies. But they all shared this common feature. That any one of the women would have preferred to stand naked before the whole of Santander rather than allow the entirety of their footwear collections to be made public in this unseemly and singular circumstance. It was worse by far than having to surrender their passports. And what on earth did it establish? One heel was exactly like any other, after all.

Yet the *Teniente* lavished lascivious attention on each pair. He ran his fingers carefully along the leather, peered closely at the stitchings, sniffed imperiously at the uppers with that aquiline nose until, finally, Vice-Consul Fielding suggested that the travellers should be allowed their breakfast and get on the road for the next section of the journey. After all, they needed to be in Covadonga by nightfall.

'I thinks 'e's just got a thing about women's shoes,' said Marguerite when they were outside. 'Dirty ol' bugger!'

But Jack could not be so certain. He had dismissed Nora Hames's belief that there might be something suspicious about Julia's death almost as soon as the old lady was left behind. And, if he were honest, he had initially been merely amused by Harold Fielding's message from her that he 'should not forget.' Yet he could not now reconcile that the Guardia Civil, hardly renowned for troubling themselves with trivia, should remain so interested in the case unless there was some smoke. At least the *hint* of a fire. True, the tour was high profile, important to the *Generalísimo* himself. He would not want any avoidable international embarrassment – to which his downright dishonest press release bore witness.

Fielding, however, had been less than forthcoming with his own views, so why mention the shoe heel? If there was, indeed, suspicious bruising on Julia's back, surely there could have been a dozen accidental causes. And what made this particular marking so distinctive? He had not spent any time reporting criminal news and had never been a huge follower of detective fiction. So he felt wholly ineligible to judge. Then again, what might such bruising signify? That Julia had been kicked? Trodden upon? It made no sense.

But, with the bus now fully repaired, they ran through the industrial zones, the unremarkable farming lands west of Santander. *Well,* Jack thought, *there'll be no golf today, anyhow. No fly-fishing either.* For the rain was coming down without remission from a firmly constructed emplacement of low cloud, concrete-grey and forbidding. And he had no hat, of course. He would doubtless pay for that omission later, when they stopped.

It was Mikel who came to his rescue when they arrived at Santillana del Mar. The bus, it seemed, had a small luggage compartment on one side, nowhere near large enough to hold the group's collective cases, but sufficient to stow spare parts, a few day bags, emergency supplies, a couple of extra batteries, and an assortment of antique umbrellas. Santander was thirty kilometres behind them so it was time for coffee, dodging the steady drizzle, to reach a bar past the Convent of the Poor Clares and the Palacio del Peredo at the southern end of the village's main street. Raincoats were shaken and hung to dry wherever there was space.

'We're not going to see much if this keeps up, sure,' apologised Brendan, peering through the misted window. 'And the ladies just need to take care on these cobbles. Shame though. Santillana's always been an important stopping point along the *Camino de Santiago*. And, of course, there'd *be* no *Camino de Santiago* if it was left to the Reds. Our Lady be praised for General Franco, eh? All those pilgrims. Tens of thousands every year. Even when the fighting was going on.'

All heading for Santiago, thought Jack. To the place where the remains of Saint James had been found. By a shepherd led there with a celestial guide. *Compostela.* The Field of the Star. *But it's hard to suppress the British too,* Jack realised, *when they have a thirst for travel.*

'And rain, after all,' as Albert Moorgate said, 'is the Englishman's natural environment. Something that Johnny Foreigner will never understand.'

'This bloke, 'e says to me,' said Max, 'tell me, 'ansum, 'ow does 'e find the weather down 'ere. Easy, says I. Just steps outside an' there it be!'

So the raincoats were donned once more, brollies were raised, handbags and purses clutched tight. They took shelter wherever they could, dodging cattle and milk churns, while Brendan guided them skilfully along the cobbled thoroughfare into the Plaza Mayor, with its baronial manor houses, the barracks of the Guardia Civil, the *casonas* for which the village was so famous. *And no wonder,* thought Jack. *This place doesn't look like it's been touched since the Middle Ages. Doesn't seem like it would be any more cheerful without the rain, either.*

'Hey, Max,' called Jack, 'how far have we come since Santander?'

'I dunno,' replied Max. 'How far?'

'About a thousand years.' *And it's true,* thought Jack. *In Spain you calculate the distance between city and country village not in miles but in centuries.*

The Town Hall displayed the same antiquity. The neighbouring *Torre de Don Borja* too. Fourteenth century, according to Brendan. Then scurrying onwards, watched suspiciously from every open window by a charcoal-shaded crone, around a bend to join another street of ancient dwellings, each displaying its own stone carved coat-of-arms, its balcony of bright geraniums, its wood smoke scent upon the air, its goats' cheese pungency, its cider press. Shelter again beneath the pantile-covered roof of a trough, where a conduit brought water to the place. The chance for a quick cigarette. And then a dash back towards the bus, pausing only to admire one further palace, stopping at an *estanco* so that Brendan could pick up the *ABC*, today sporting another front page portrait of Mussolini, this time at a march-past of the Italian army in Trieste.

'Any more news of Chamberlain?' called Albert Moorgate from the front of the bus, since Dorothea had insisted on returning to the original rotation as it would have been had they not made yesterday's quite proper concession to the Ketterings.

Brendan thumbed through the damp pages.

'There's a piece on page three about the British Ambassador's meeting with Herr Goebbels in Berlin.' The Sisters of Our Lady of the Holy Light smiled appreciatively. Brendan held up pages four and five. 'Photos of shops and houses in the Sudetenland,' he said, 'where the owners have painted swastikas to show they support German annexation. Ah, here we go. Page seven. Chamberlain completes his discussions with Hitler and returns to London today. Poland and Hungary insist on reclaiming their old territories. Russia threatens Poland because the Poles have been moving troops to the Czech border.'

'Just an excuse,' said Alfred Holden. 'The Soviet Union pulling strings behind the scenes. Red attempt to start an Imperialistic War.'

Strange turn of phrase, thought Jack, *for a paid-up member of the British Union of Fascists.*

'I'm sure you're right, Professor,' said Brendan.

Their stop at Altamira was another disappointment.

Brendan had spent some time whetting their appetites. The British knew little of the treasures here, he had explained. Most people knew about the cave paintings of Southern France, but these were on a much grander scale. The Sistine Chapel of

Prehistoric Art, he quoted. But the caves were closed today. The rain, said a crusty old woman. Too dangerous. She allowed them only to visit a decaying house, serving as a museum. Old sepia photographs of the gentleman and his daughter who had made the discoveries. Blurred images of bison and horses. Some prints of sketched reproductions.

Back on the road again, the bus paused at Comillas. There was a hill overlooking the harbour and the statue of some local notable who had made his fortune in Cuba. To Jack there was nothing remarkable about the modernist sculpture, but it transpired that the statue itself had originally been adorned with beautifully rendered bronze angels, allegories for the old Spanish Colonies, and these had been torn down by the Reds to make ammunition. It was another sacrilege, of course, and caused Valerie Carter-Holt to write furiously when their journey resumed, past the gothic ruins and frowning seminary. She was in front of him, her scent probing his senses, Max Weston sitting behind.

'Have you managed to file much copy while we've been here?' Jack enquired.

'Of course,' she replied.

'Anything interesting?'

'To whom?'

'Your editor at Reuters, I suppose. Is the Agency likely to place any of your stuff?'

'My *stuff*, as you call it, *always* gets placed, Mister Telford. At least, whenever I get the chance to finish it. Was there something particular…? Ah, I see. A few words of consolation yesterday evening and you assume we are friends. We are *not*, Mister Telford, and I think that we never *shall* be. Now, do you mind?'

'You did well there, me 'ansum,' whispered Max. 'I thinks she likes you!'

But Jack felt genuinely rebuffed, his enquiry intended to be taken seriously and, yes, he *had* been encouraged by the previous night's exchange.

The bus passed through a picturesque valley, the road lined with chestnut trees, past wetlands, withies and wading birds, then dropped down to a view that even the rain could only moderately spoil. There was a broad estuary, more properly two bays, or *rías*, separated by a headland, topped by a dramatic castle and church. And to reach the headland, a bridge. Stone. More than two dozen arches, Jack calculated. It reminded him of pictures that he had seen of Conway. *La Puente de la Maza*, explained Brendan. Fifteenth century. Reconstructed in the eighteenth and, in its time, one of the wonders of Spain. It was magnificent. The old quarter of San Vicente de la Barquera ahead of them, palms along the waterfront, the dramatic Picos de Europa in the background.

Yet still it rained, darkening the stone bastion that guarded the Santander Gate of the town's neglected walls. And it hammered on the pantiles of the ancient Palacio del Corro, now serving as the *Ayuntamiento,* where the travellers were served lunch, having completed the final dash to this destination on foot. Raincoats and umbrellas again.

'But all this rain. It's not how I imagined it,' said Peter Kettering. 'I was thinking of dusty streets. Sleepy men in *sombreros*.'

'That's Mexico, dear boy,' said Albert Moorgate. 'Nothing sleepy about Jack Spaniard. Not really. He gives the impression of being a bit slow. Starts work early enough. It's the *siesta* thing that we misinterpret.'

'I'd always thought that siesta was only in Southern Spain,' said Jack. 'Or maybe in the north during summer. But the entire country closes like a clam at one-thirty prompt, doesn't it?'

'It's their culture, Mister Telford. Culture, sir. They return to work after siesta at five. Work until late in the evening. Eat at ten. Chat 'til midnight. Stroll until two. Then get up again at six-thirty to do the market. Start all over again.'

'*Pick yerself up, dust yerself off...*' Max began to sing. 'Oy, Marguerite. We could do Fred and Ginger in *Mexican Max*. What d'you think?'

But Marguerite was too busy with her meal to worry about Kern, Astaire *or* Rogers. Jack marvelled at her propensity for food consumption. Also at the Holdens' ability to absorb such large quantities of wine with no visible effects. Apart, that is, from the Professor's tendency to call him 'Telford' on such occasions.

'And how are *you* doing now?' Jack said quietly to Kettering. 'It must have been a bit of a shock. Finding out about your brother just when we were in Bilbao itself.'

'Frightful,' said Peter Kettering. He turned to his wife. 'Mister Telford was just asking about Donald. It was quite a shock. Never expected to actually find the place where he's buried. Might enquire whether we can have the poor boy shipped home.'

'You'd have to consult the family, I suppose?' said Jack.

'Family, Mister Telford?'

'Oh, I'm sorry. It's just that Brendan mentioned there may be a widow...'

Catherine Kettering's fork clattered to her plate. She pressed a napkin to her lips.

'Yes, culture,' Albert Moorgate continued. 'When they're not shooting each other, these must be amongst the most considerate and thoughtful people I've ever met.'

'It doesn't stop them shouting at each other under my hotel bedroom window at one in the morning though,' said Jack, pleased to leave the Ketterings to themselves again. *I shouldn't have raised the bloody thing*, he thought. *None of my business.*

'Ah, that's the Anarchist in them all,' Albert continued. 'Anarchism comes easily to Jack Spaniard. He is a fellow who lives on the street, as they say. He couldn't really conceive of anybody being in bed at such an early hour, Mister Telford. You mustn't take it personally.'

'Damned strange business about the shoes though, eh?' said Alfred Holden.

'This morning?' replied Moorgate. 'Yes, your wife seems quite distressed by the whole thing, Professor. Feels as though she's under suspicion, eh?'

'She's not the only one,' said Frances, in righteous indignation. 'That policeman can't possibly imagine...'

On the tree-lined patio outside, the rain was easing, some inquisitive sparrows venturing out to discover whether there might be any morsels discarded from the table. A hoopoe too. Jack had never seen one before but it was unmistakeable. Barred wings. Orange-brown fan on its intelligent head. Slender beak poking at the soil.

He thought about the bird long after they were settled once more on the bus, mackintoshes, slickers, trench coats and Brendan's *poncho* draped wherever there was space, the interior beginning to steam with that unique odour which Jack remembered from early-morning journeys with London Transport. He had always associated it with the smell of wet dogs.

They climbed out of San Vicente to follow the sweep of the Ría de Tina Menor, then on to Unquera, hugging the meandering stream. At Pesués they headed inland, past Val de San Vicente following the Deba River until they reached Panes, turning right and rattling towards the sharp, almost volcanic peaks ahead of them.

'Welcome to Asturias, ladies and gentlemen,' said Brendan. 'This is the Province where National Spain brought the war in the north to a close.'

Jack had been thinking about Asturias a lot, as it happened. He delved in his day bag for his note-book, flicked it open. *I wonder...*

'I'd never thought about this before,' he said, just loud enough for the guide to hear, 'but I suppose it's also the place where it all began, too.'

'What was that, Mister Telford?' said Brendan.

'Nothing,' said Jack. 'Merely thinking out loud.'

'No, but it's a good point. Would you like to elaborate, sure?'

Jack shook his head.

'Not really,' he said. 'It was probably just nonsense.'

'Oh, allow *me*,' said Alfred Holden. He was excited. 'How wonderful that it should be Telford, of all people, who reminded us.'

Still under the influence then, I see, thought Jack.

'You seem to have the floor, so to speak, Professor,' said Murphy, the other travellers turning in the seats to listen. They had to hold on tight though, for the road was narrow and twisting, crossing the Deba many times where it tumbled down its path from the distant peaks to the sea.

'With pleasure, my dear sir,' said Holden. He smoothed his toothbrush moustache, smiled widely at his audience. 'But where to begin? Ah, of course. Mister Telford is fond of reminding us about the so-called victory of the Left in '36. But what about the elections three years earlier? A clear win for the Centre-Right as political commentators might put it. The CEDA Coalition, was it not, Mister Murphy?'

'Indeed it was, Professor,' agreed the guide.

They look pretty pleased with themselves to be on this ground, thought Jack.

'But did Mister Telford's democratically-minded socialists accept the outcome?'

'There was a General Strike, wasn't there?' said Peter Kettering.

'Indeed there was,' said Dorothea Holden. 'The following year, I think. Though, as I recall, it fell apart quite quickly.'

'It fell apart, my dear, everywhere except Catalonia and *here*. Mainly here. In Asturias. Isn't that so?'

'In part,' said Brendan, 'you could say that it was Asturias that sparked it. There'd been a big conference of the CEDA Coalition in Covadonga, where we're heading now. That would have been September '34, I guess.'

'I've never even 'eard o' this Covey-dangey place,' said Marguerite, looking bored with the subject already.

'Covadonga, ma'am,' said Brendan. 'Most people outside Spain won't know about it. But for many Spaniards, it's the heart and soul of the country. Not Madrid. Nor even Santiago de Compostela. And that's despite Santiago being the resting place of Spain's patron saint. A holy place. But maybe we should save Covadonga's story until we get there. For now, it's enough to know that the Coalition met there *because* it's such a symbolic shrine. What would it be like? The English Tory Party holding its annual conference at Canterbury, maybe. Or in Westminster Abbey.'

'And the Left didn't like *that*, I assume?' said Professor Holden.

'No. They organised a huge demonstration. It's not the easiest place to reach, as you'll see later. But the unions put thousands of their agitators on the streets. Caused mayhem. Disrupted the conference. At least, until the *Civiles* arrived. It was a short-lived victory though, because a month later the General Strike started. Here in Asturias it was the miners mainly. Nobody really knows how many were involved. A hundred thousand, maybe. And all of them armed.'

'Armed by *whom*, I wonder?' sneered the Professor. *Smug bastard*, thought Jack.

'Well, Mister Telford?' said Murphy. 'Shall you tell them, or shall I?'

'I wouldn't dream of depriving you, Mister Murphy,' Jack smiled. Brendan Murphy smiled too, but there was uncertainty in his eyes. *He thinks this is too easy*, thought Jack.

'It was those so-called moderates in the Socialist Party, of course,' said Brendan. 'They arranged for a ship-load of rifles to be landed. Though the miners brought their own dynamite along too, of course. It all began on the fourth of October, when they occupied several towns. They attacked Civil Guard barracks and other targets. On the fifth, they occupied Turón, south of Oviedo. Forced their way into a school and captured nine priests there. A few days later, they shot them all.'

The Sisters of Our Lady of the Holy Light prayed fervently.

'So what was their excuse for killing priests in '34, I wonder,' said Dorothea. 'They could hardly blame the *Reconquista* before it even started, I suppose?'

'I don't know, ma'am,' said Brendan. 'What I *can* tell you is that, all told, thirty-seven priests were killed during the Asturias Rising. And fifty-eight churches were attacked. The work of Communists, ma'am. Atheists. Reds. Probably Jews and Freemasons, too. But you see now what I've been trying to explain? They were already here, sure. Corrupting the very soul of Spain.'

'And how long did this all go on?' said Valerie Carter-Holt. 'All this Red mayhem?'

'Two weeks,' Brendan replied. 'And then…Oh, hang on. What's this all about?'

They had been travelling along a narrow mountain pass. Mikel wrestled the gears around one horseshoe bend after another, watching the thermometer closely again too, where the road rose from the end of the pass. But now he slowed almost to a stop. It was still raining but, through the windscreen, they could see a man in the road, waving a large red flag at them.

How symbolic, thought Jack, but he saw that Brendan's hand moved, almost involuntarily, to the holster attached to the Sam Browne belt that he habitually wore over his black dress uniform shirt. *He looks pale today too. He always seems a bit nervous when he's obviously not feeling up to scratch.*

The guide shouted to the driver and the bus halted. Brendan went forward, opened the door. There was a discussion with the Flag Man, then a heated argument, shouted against the weather, and it was a clearly exasperated Brendan Murphy who eventually closed the door again, a full five minutes later.

'Bad news, I'm afraid. There's a bridge just ahead. It's been…Well, damaged recently. They've had a team out to fix it but they can't work in this rain. And they don't want the bus to use it. They say there was a sign back at the turning. But Mikel didn't see it. We *could* go back. Head to Covadonga along the coast. But there's no way that we could get there tonight. It's too far.'

'And the alternative?' said Catherine Kettering. It was the first time she had spoken since lunch and Jack felt guilty all over again.

'The man says,' Brendan spoke slowly, 'that the bus might not be a problem if it's empty and we take it slowly. But that means everybody has to get off again. Only *this* time it's sheeting down!'

The debate lasted for some time. Most were reluctantly willing to risk the rain once more, although Albert Moorgate did not now seem quite so affable about this being the Englishman's natural environment. Marguerite was difficult, naturally. Surely, she argued, it couldn't make any difference if just *one* person stayed on the bus besides Mikel. Max, on the other hand, prattled happily about ducks and puddles until, eventually, some drenched Asturian farmer came hammering on the side of the vehicle, disclaiming loudly that he was stuck behind them with a cart full of something or other.

'Well, I suppose that settles it,' cried Dorothea and grabbing a still damp slicker, she climbed from the bus like a true leader of men.

The rest followed, Marguerite being cajoled into action by Albert Moorgate's soothing words and prophylactic umbrella. The Flag Man led them across, keeping them away from the sheer drop to their left, while Brendan stayed at the back of the bus, pulling up the hood of his *poncho*, and Jack joined him, holding the collar of his gabardine closed and sheltering beneath a black brolly with one of its spokes broken.

'Want company?' he shouted. The guide shrugged.

'Why did you open up the Asturian Miners thing?' asked Brendan. 'You must know where it's going.'

'It's part of the story, isn't it? You'd have got around to it sooner or later. But what's all this about damage to the bridge? Damaged how?'

The farmer behind them was trying to pacify his oxen while still yelling obscenities at the yellow bus. Brendan shouted something back, lifted the hem of the *poncho* so that he could pat the pistol at his side. The farmer hushed a little, but not much.

'Bloody Asturians,' muttered Brendan. 'And the bridge? I don't know. Not really. But from what I gathered...Promise you won't tell the others?'

'Of course.'

'There's apparently been some more bandit activity in the area.'

'Bandits?' Jack was incredulous. 'The bandits that don't exist?'

Mikel started to edge the bus forward towards the bridge. Brendan and Jack followed. The ox cart behind them.

'Bandits,' Brendan repeated. 'Outlaws. Fugitives from justice.'

'Ah,' said Jack. 'Guerrilla fighters? I'd heard that some of them have taken to the mountains. But here?'

'Don't glorify the feckers, Mister Telford. Most of them are criminals. Priest-killers and the like. Too frightened to face the music for their sins. Plenty of places for them to hide in the mountains. But we won't rest until we've rooted them all out. Every single one of them.'

'Are they a danger?'

'Not unless you happen to be daft enough to get caught standing on a bridge when the buggers blow one, sure. Apart from that it's all cowardly killings in the dark. The *Civiles* are their targets mostly. But we always get them. Always.'

'The *Civiles*,' said Jack. 'Yes.' He thought of *Teniente* Álvaro Enrique Turbides. The shoe-sniffer.

The passengers dribbled back aboard the bus, Brendan at the rear and waiting only long enough to offer a fascist salute to the farmer. The farmer, for his part, returned the honour by rubbing his hands together briskly, then holding them out in front of him to show that they were clean, untainted by Murphy's presence.

It was wild, daunting, remote. And wet. But by the time they reached Canales, heading through upland pastures, then dropped down towards Benia, the rain had at least begun to ease, though the cloud was still low.

'You never finished your story, Mister Murphy,' Jack said to him. 'About the Asturian miners.'

Brendan examined him again, suspiciously.

'I did not, did I?' said Murphy. 'Well, that will never do now.'

'The Government sent in the troops, one imagines?' said Alfred Holden.

'They did, sir. But not before the strikers had occupied most of the major towns. Oviedo. La Felguera. They set up Revolutionary Committees everywhere, to take over control from the Town Councils. They set up courts so they could put class traitors on trial. That's how most of the priests ended up shot. Two weeks of sheer anarchy. And who, ladies and gentlemen, do you think the Coalition Government sent in to sort out the mess?'

'Oh, Brendan,' said Jack. 'You *are* a tease! Go on. You know you're dying to tell us.'

'It was none other than General Francisco Franco. Flown over with two *banderas* of the Legion and two *tabors* of Moroccan *regulares*.'

'It would have been excellent practice for him,' Jack laughed. 'He must have spent the next two years just *itching* to do it all over again. But on a bigger scale.'

'You could be right, Mister Telford,' said Brendan. 'You see, it allowed the General to see the scale of the Red menace that faced Spain. He's spoken about it often. That it was the Asturias Revolt which first caused him to see clearly the path upon which God had set him.'

'And what happened when the troops arrived, Mister Murphy?' It was Catherine Kettering again.

'There was a great deal of fighting, naturally. At least, at first. General Franco lost over two hundred men trying to put the Rising down.'

'And the miners?' asked Albert Moorgate.

'They were badly led. They lost quite a lot, I think. Not sure of the numbers.'

'Civilian casualties?' said Jack.

'The priests, you mean?'

'I was thinking more about people in the towns and villages. Journalists, maybe.'

Jack could see awareness dawning upon Brendan Murphy's features. Valerie Carter-Holt swivelled in her seat towards him.

'You mean Sirval?' she said. There was a hint of a smile upon her lips. 'How clever of you, Mister Telford.' Jack nestled himself deep within the folds of her admiration.

'What's this?' said Alfred Holden. 'Another Commie reporter?'

'Hardly,' Jack replied. For once, he felt excited. As though, on *this* occasion, he might *just* have the upper hand. 'Will you tell them, or shall I?' he said to her. 'Or perhaps we should ask Mister Murphy to elaborate. He is the official guide, after all.'

It was Murphy's turn to shake his head.

'No, it's fine, Mister Telford. As *you* might say, it's probably just nonsense. Please continue, sir. Give us the benefit of your knowledge.'

'It needs some independence, I think,' said Jack. 'Miss Carter-Holt, would you do the honours?'

Even Marguerite and Max Weston seem eager for this snippet, he thought, as the Reuters correspondent collected her thoughts.

'Well,' she began. 'Luis de Sirval was a Madrid journalist working for *La Libertad*. As you'd assume, it's a liberal newspaper, Republican but pretty much middle-of-the-road in political terms. After the first week of the Asturias Rebellion,

Oviedo was *packed* with journalists, including several foreign correspondents. Most of them stayed throughout General Franco's heroic suppression of the miners and his army's subsequent occupation of the territory. Sirval wasn't his real name, by the way. Just his pen-name.'

'You don't need to do this, Miss Carter-Holt,' said Professor Holden. 'Not just to pacify Mister Telford, my dear. I'm sure that the rest of us aren't *really* interested.'

'Oy, you speak for yourself!' said Marguerite.

'In any case,' said Valerie, 'on this occasion, Mister Telford's sources are impeccable. I was almost going to say unimpeachable. As, indeed, they proved to be. Did they not, Jack?' Jack nodded, trying desperately hard not to now feel smug himself. 'So,' Carter-Holt continued, 'Sirval started to file reports but usually backed up by others. He relied heavily on witnesses that you'd have to say were impartial. It was Sirval who first provided any real evidence about the scale of the death-count. And, yes, he carefully listed all the priests who were killed. But also the two thousand miners who were apparently shot by the troops. The twenty thousand put in prison. And then detailed accounts of those in prison who were tortured. Horrific and corroborated stories of the systematic violation of women in the towns and villages occupied particularly by the Moroccans. Of course, the reports all stopped when Sirval himself was arrested. And shot.' There were gasps from most of the group.

'He was shot, Miss Carter-Holt,' said Brendan, 'because he attacked one of the Legion's officers. The lieutenant in question acted out of self-defence.'

'And how do we know that there was any truth in all this?' said Dorothea Holden. 'He was just a puppet of the Republic. Wasn't he?'

'I think I should let Mister Telford pick up the story now,' said Carter-Holt. 'He seems to have quite a scoop with this one.'

'Well, there are one or two things that help us here,' said Jack. He was careful to hold the gaze of each passenger in turn. Those that would look at him, at least, and whenever he did not need to refer to his note-book. 'First, there was a Court of Enquiry held in Oviedo the following August. This was '35, remember, so the tribunal had no axe to grind. They looked at all the witness and medical evidence. The fact, for instance, that the lieutenant responsible for the shooting… You recall? The one who fired in self-defence? It seems he found it necessary to put seven bullets into one unarmed prisoner. Anyway, the Court of Enquiry found unanimously that Sirval had been shot in an extra-judicial killing. The second thing to remember is that the findings were reported in fine detail not by the Republican press but, on this occasion, by the Right-wing *ABC*.' Jack reached over and took Brendan's copy of today's edition from the back seat. He brandished it like a captured banner. 'Third,' he continued, 'the same story was picked up by *The Times* a few days later. Through a Reuters correspondent, I think, Miss Carter-Holt?' Valerie nodded. 'And you know what? There has never been an official denial ever since. Even *El Caudillo*'s famous Press Department has never bothered to retract or re-write the story.'

'Which proves what, exactly, Telford?' said the Professor.

'Well to yourself, Professor, probably nothing. But to me, and to every other intelligent person on this bus, it probably proves, first, that Franco deserved the nickname which he was given after the General Strike was over. *The Butcher of Asturias*. Second, it probably goes some way towards explaining the way that ordinary men and women behaved when they knew that he was back from the Canary Islands again with the same killers and rapists in July '36. His own insurrection this time. The panic, the fear, the ferocity.'

'And third?' said Carter-Holt.

'Third? Well, if there *is* a third thing, it's likely to be a balance of probabilities issue, rather than proof as such. But all these details that Brendan's been feeding us, the Holy Crusaders of Franco against the Red Heretics and Murderers of the Republic, it's tripe, isn't it? Go on, Brendan, admit it. Just put the script away for a minute.'

But he did not, of course. Brendan had snatched back his copy of the *ABC* and was studying it intently. The Holdens were silent too. And the two nuns. Whilst the others whispered quietly to each other as the bus trundled through claustrophobic Corao and then, just before Cangas, swung left, climbing up an even narrower rock-strewn road. It was liable to subsidence too, apparently, just wide enough to allow the yellow Chrysler to pass a warning sign at the roadside. Jack stared hard at the thing.

¡Peligro! it said. Danger.

Chapter Fifteen

Saturday 24 September 1938

Covadonga presented Jack with the most dramatic setting that he could ever have imagined. The approach road was, indeed, treacherous, rising steadily by a series of bends through a ravine, the broken bed of a disused railway on one side, and a series of raging rapids on the other into which the surface had, at regular intervals, collapsed. It was less than ten kilometres but took them thirty minutes to negotiate, through several villages, with Mikel stopping frequently, leaning out of the open driver's window to gauge whether or not he could continue. There were, in fact, two separate occasions when he decided that it was impossible to go any further but, upon independent examination, Brendan over-ruled him both times despite the driver's ever more obvious trepidation. There was even a moment when the front wheels seemed to slip sideways towards an abyss, causing no amount of panic amongst the passengers. But Jack thought this was due more to careless clumsiness than any real peril. In any case, Murphy scolded the driver, where exactly would they turn around, even if they wanted to?

Then, finally, the road widened. They stopped by an inn, the Fonda de Covadonga, a traditionally solid stone structure. Beyond the inn, and beyond an old engine shed, the road curved to the left, near a scattering of farm buildings. High above these, from thickly wooded slopes, the lofty twin towers of a rose-pink Basilica rose into the cloud. Incongruous for such a remote place. But, even here, Mikel seemed nervous, window open once more, gazing up and down the road.

'Remarkable!' said Albert Moorgate from the front seat.

'We'll get a closer look in a minute,' said Brendan. They had traversed the train tracks on a crossing some distance back, and these now ran on the left, through an abandoned station. A wagon rotted in a siding, surrounded by weeds. 'We're going to turn off for the hotel just past the bend there,' he continued. 'If you watch out, you'll see that the road goes on. In fact, about twelve kilometres further on it comes to one of the most beautiful locations in the area. Lake Enol and Lake Ercina. Fabulous. If we've got time, and the road's not too bad, we might try and get there tomorrow. You'll like it, sure. The *Generalísimo* used to come here for his holidays when he was a boy. It's his favourite haunt, they say.'

Franco's answer to the Berghof, thought Jack. Hitler's getaway in the mountains of Bavaria. A Spanish *Berchtesgaden*.

Half a mile further up, they turned right, crossed a bridge, climbed again past a scatter of dwellings, a limestone cliff-face ahead of them, a cave in its centre, water cascading into a pool below, a long flight of steps leading up to the cavern. The nuns pointed, excited.

'The Holy Cave itself,' said Brendan, but their view was cut short as the bus swung around to stop outside the Gran Hotel Pelayo. It was a long building, three storeys high, and it had seen better days. To their right, a huge area had been sculpted into a sunken parkland of oak, poplar and pine. At its farther side, a buttressed wall rose up to a higher plateau, and upon this upper level stood the Basilica. The road on which they were parked pointed straight towards the wall, as if placed there by an artist who wished his vanishing point to draw the onlooker's eye towards the magnificence of the cathedral which, quite simply, dominated everything else.

The rain had finally stopped and, from the hotel, a reception committee emerged. The Manager, the priests, the servants, the water and the wine.

Jack wandered around the small lobby while Brendan translated the welcomes, the apologies. For the hotel had been badly ravaged by the Reds, apparently, during their occupation. One half of the building was currently closed. For renovation work, of course. But it would not be allowed to inconvenience their stay. No, this was a fine establishment, the very best.

The walls displayed photographs of former guests, though Jack recognised none of them. Except Franco, naturally.

'Time to freshen up, do you think, Mister Murphy?' called Dorothea Holden.

The luggage was passing behind her in elephantine procession from bus to stairs and elevator, though there was now no sign of Mikel at all. The work of unloading seemed to have been delegated entirely to the hotel porters.

'Indeed, ma'am. And shall we meet again in, say, an hour? Looks like it might turn into a fine evening. So we could have a stroll before dinner.'

In his room, Jack wondered whether he should unpack. They were only here for one night again. Tomorrow they would be away to Gijón. Or was it Oviedo? Or both? But so many of his clothes were becoming badly creased. He could always ask the hotel to provide a maid for the ironing, he supposed. But later, maybe.

He woke with a start, no recollection of laying down, let alone falling asleep. *How long?* he wondered. *Dammit!*

More than an hour, that was sure, he realised, looking at his watch.

So it was a crumpled Jack Telford who returned to the lobby where Murphy was already lecturing the group.

'Mister Telford,' said Dorothea, 'you *do* make a habit of being late for these things! Lucky we sent Miss Carter-Holt back for her camera. According to Mister Murphy, she would not want to miss the photographic opportunities this evening.'

Do I make a habit of it? thought Jack. *Just the one time in Fuenterrabía, wasn't it?*

'You've not missed much,' said Brendan. 'Maybe just a quick recap. I was explaining that, back in the early part of the Eighth Century, the Moors had swept across almost the whole of Spain, crossed the Pyrenees and would have taken

France as well if they'd not been turned back at the Battle of Toulouse. Their defeat put some fire in the bellies of the Christians here in Asturias too, and they revolted against their Muslim masters. The Asturians were led by a man called Pelagius. Pelayo in Spanish. The Moors arrived near Covadonga to put down the rebellion. But Pelayo had set a trap for them, hiding his soldiers up on the heights around the valley. The *big* thing, though, was that Pelayo was visited in the cave we saw by Our Lady on the night before the battle. She promised him a victory. And a victory he got! The Moors were slaughtered. Their leaders killed. Pelayo became the first King of Asturias and he set up his capital at Cangas de Onís, close to here, as you know. Since Asturias was the first part of the Peninsula to be properly free of the Moors, Cangas can rightly claim to be the birthplace of the Spanish monarchy. This was certainly where the original *Reconquista* began. And El Caudillo was so inspired by tales of Pelayo as a young man, maybe you could say the *second* one started here too.'

'Did the Moors ever return?' asked Dorothea, just as Valerie made her *own* reappearance, camera now in hand. 'Here to Covadonga, I mean.'

'Well, not for some time,' Brendan laughed. 'It's a bit of an irony, I suppose. But last October, when we were advancing towards Oviedo, it was our Moroccan *regulares* that drove the Reds out of Covadonga.'

'What a romantic ending to the story!' said Dorothea.

Romantic? thought Jack. *They were presumably the same* regulares *who'd raped the miners' wives and mothers back in '34.*

They wore coats again since, while it was now dry, the rain had left a chill wind behind it. And, uniquely, Mikel had decided to join them. So the enlarged group followed Brendan up the steps which took them to the plateau and the Basilica de Santa María la Real. They passed a group of prisoners going in the opposite direction, guarded by three *Civiles.*

'They're using the old Pilgrims' Hostal as a temporary prison,' said the guide. 'And the cells at the Guardia barracks. While these Red scum put right some of the harm they did. Can you imagine *anybody* wanting to damage a work of art like this? Even atheists?' He stopped in front of the church. 'Neo-Romanesque, they tell me. Modern. It might look old but it was only completed thirty-seven years ago. It took them just twenty-four years to build. Quite a feat. All local stone and marble.'

They admired the delicacy of its twin spires, the decorative architecture of the front elevation, the gargoyles, the columns, the intricate design of the capitals, the statuary. Inside, cool evening light poured through the stained-glass to illuminate arched aisles, three naves, towering pillars whose roseate tones were now turned to fiery red. Plainsong in the depths, the occasional clatter of gratings. The sickly smell of incense. Albert Moorgate seemed even less comfortable than usual amid the Popish idolatry. And it was no wonder, since a corpulent priest with heavy wet lips reading scripture to himself kept them constantly under surveillance from a confessional. The few worshippers seemed frozen in adoration, barely human, mummified in their pews. Frances, however, hung on Brendan's every word. Yet it seemed a heresy to even breathe in the place, let alone speak.

It feels like it's crushing me, thought Jack. The atmosphere was overpowering, oppressive.

He wandered down one of the aisles so that he was near the Ketterings when they rose to catch up with the group.

'Look,' he said, his voice echoing embarrassingly around the temple He changed to the barest audible tone that he could manage. 'About lunch. I just wanted to apologise. When I mentioned your brother's family...'

'No need to apologise, old boy,' said Peter. 'It's still a bit raw, that's all. For both of us. Catherine was very fond of Peter too. Just a bit of a shock when you mentioned him again.'

Catherine managed a half-smile.

'Yes,' she said. 'A shock.'

'But I had a specific question to ask,' said Jack. 'You see, Sister María Pereda told me that you had a long discussion with Julia Britten on the night before...well, on the evening that she played piano for the group.'

'With me?' replied Peter Kettering.

'No, actually. She said that it was just Julia and *Mrs* Kettering.'

'That could well be,' said Catherine. 'I spoke with Miss Britten several times. I don't really understand...'

'I only wondered if you'd mind telling me what it was about.'

'I don't see,' replied Catherine, carefully annunciating each syllable, 'that this is any more relevant than an examination of my shoes, Mister Telford. Except, of course, that the Lieutenant at least had the authority of his office to pursue whatever strange line of investigation he thinks necessary. You, however, if you'll allow me to say so...'

She refused to say anything further and Jack, suddenly self-conscious, moved towards the exit. *Damn the woman! Dismissed me like a stupid schoolboy.*

Outside, the group gathered on the long esplanade to gaze at a small obelisk, surmounted by an intricate stone cross.

'It's a replica of the Victory Cross that they keep in the Cathedral of Oviedo,' said Brendan. 'The original wooden cross was carried into battle by Pelayo. Then, later, they encased the wood in gold, added gems and the like.'

Crows wheeled in the sky above, calling raucously to each other in deep-throated Spanish masculine voices, climbing high amongst the tall pines that clung to every crag and slope of the valley walls that enclosed them, a thin mist or remnant of smoke curling among the trees themselves. On the slope above the wide path that led towards the end of the esplanade and another limestone cliff-face, stood a further monument. Two stone pillars and a cross-piece supported an enormous bell, twelve feet in height and a gift from some wealthy Italian Count to the town following his pilgrimage here. Below and ahead of the bell was a tunnel leading into the rock, iron gates open at the entrance, a priest there to welcome them, though Brendan declined his offer to accompany the party.

'*Gracias*,' said the guide. '*Pero no, gracias, Padre*.'

'*El Caudillo* must have come here frequently, I suppose,' said Dorothea Holden.

'Every year, ma'am. And they say that, when he had to choose a codename, to be broadcast, or spread by word of mouth, launching the new *Reconquista*, he chose the word *Covadonga*. It means *Deep Cave*, by the way. In case you were wondering.' He turned to Mikel, spoke some harsh words to the driver, who shook his head.

Asking whether he'd not prefer to go back to the hotel as likely as not, thought Jack. *No wonder either. He's been on hot pins since we set out.*

They passed through the iron gates into the tunnel. It was crudely hacked into the limestone and perhaps wide enough for three people to walk abreast. Water dripped from the arched roof at times but the floor was at least tolerably level, smoothed that way by countless numbers of pilgrims, their way lit at regular intervals by oil lamps or, more commonly, by banks of votive candles.

'How far Mister Murphy?' asked Professor Holden. His voice echoed in the confines of the passage.

'The tunnel?' said Brendan. 'Just a couple of minutes. The alternative is to climb the steps up from the pool below the cave. There's more than a hundred of them, I think. I decided this was the best option for this evening. You can try the steps tomorrow morning if you like. Good bit of exercise.'

'I can see light at the end,' shouted Max, and Jack decided he could not be the only one unsure whether Weston intended this to be jocose.

'I don't think I'll be climbin' no steps,' murmured Marguerite. She had managed to manoeuvre herself alongside Jack. She pretended to stumble, grabbed his arm for support. 'I 'ad another sort of exercise in mind for tonight, Jack. What d'you say, me 'ansum?'

'It's not a good idea,' Jack replied in the best whisper the tunnel would permit.

'I could look after you, Jack, so I could. Look after you good, I means. Nice clothes. 'Olidays an' all.'

'What? With Max Weston's money?'

'It's *my* bloody money,' she replied. 'You don't seriously think 'e'd be capable of makin' any without my brains be'ind 'im?'

'Max had a decent career before you met, as I recall.'

'Workin' the Music Halls for buttons? 'E'd be there still if it weren't for me. I'm talkin' *big* money, Jack my love. You'd never 'ave to work again. Never.'

The prospect of eternity with Marguerite Weston suddenly made all the alternatives at once attractive. He was, after all, now thirty. Unattached and likely to remain so. He had his mother, of course. And his sister. Yet they seemed more like formal appendages than a source of comfort or affection. Like his clothes, in a wardrobe somewhere to be taken out and worn when the occasion demanded, then put away again. Out of sight until needed once more. It was his duty, of course, to see them from time to time. But it was a schedule. Written in his diary for every second Thursday in the month. Whenever he was home, of course. And apart from this sparse family life, what else? Oh, he had his work, of course. And journalism had taken him to Germany, to Paris, now to this strange part of Spain. But would he ever grow beyond *Reynold's News*? He doubted it, somehow. He was too modest for the profession, in all truth. Too reserved. Career development in the newspaper required something that Jack did not quite possess. So he had no attachments. An empty vessel, as he saw himself. But would he want Marguerite Weston to fill the vessel for him? No. Definitely not. He carefully disentangled himself from her arm and side-stepped behind the Moorgates. They had come to a viewing point, where a small side passage led to an opening in the rock.

'Be careful,' said Brendan. 'That railing isn't very secure.'

So they took turns at edging towards the cave mouth while, behind them, a group of women visitors passed along the main tunnel, making their way out. They were all talking at the same time, a musical Spanish chatter that reverberated around the passage. *Birds in an aviary*, thought Jack.

'Is there time for a smoke?' he asked.

'Need to be quick, Mister Telford,' Brendan replied. 'They'll be closing soon. Wouldn't want to spend the night in here, sure. And it's only about fifty yards to the *Cueva de la Santina* now.'

Jack took out the packet of *Superiores* anyway.

'Do you have one of those to spare, Mister Telford?' It was Carter-Holt, camera slung from her shoulder. 'Thank goodness Franco had control of the Canary Isles,' she said. 'Otherwise we might not even have these beastly things to smoke.'

'They're not so bad. I must be getting used to them. But down to my last packet of these too, now. Must buy some more tomorrow.'

'Oh! Well if you'd rather not share…'

'No,' said Jack. 'I didn't mean that at all. And I'd be delighted to share my fags with you. After all, you *did* give me some unexpected support with the Sirval thing.'

'A modicum of objectivity is essential in our line of work, don't you think? Not *too* much though. And what a view, Mister Telford. Breathtaking. The cliffs over there look close enough to touch, do they not?'

'It's the late evening light, I guess. And you *could* call me Jack.'

'And have you call *me* Valerie? Or Val? How banal, Mister Telford. No, I don't think so. But thanks for the cigarette.'

She flicked the half-smoked stub away, heedless of its destination.

Jack followed her back into the main tunnel, through two sets of large wooden doors that had each been knocked from their hinges, and past an open gateway leading down to a balcony, while they themselves climbed eight steps into the actual Holy Cave of Covadonga. They passed through another gateway, narrower than that by which they had entered the tunnel itself but similarly protected by a pair of rusting gates. There were a few other pilgrims here, being ushered diplomatically towards this exit by an elderly priest, but they were clearly reluctant to leave, a difficult flock whose more unruly members kept turning back for a final look at this or that. The *canónigo*, for his part, seemed anxious to carry away the bag of coins he clutched, while he locked a large walnut chest which advertised masses at a range of prices.

To his left, Jack could see the way by which this group had evidently arrived, the flight of stairs that led steeply down from the balcony to the side of a pool, far below. There was a sign here, once screwed to the wall but now set upon the ground. The intention of the Spanish was clear. *Out of respect for the Holy Virgin, please do not talk, nor spit, nor write upon the walls.* And if he leaned out far enough over yet another insecure fence, he could see where a thin spout of water reached the pool itself from somewhere beneath the floor of the cave in which they were standing. To his left was a stone tower, seemingly built into the cliff-face, and the roof-tops of buildings. Directly ahead was the Basilica. And, to the right, the narrow pass up which they had travelled on the bus.

It was crowded in here, however, for there were others in the narrow cave apart from themselves, a scattering of wooden chairs and the recalcitrant pilgrims. Some prisoners too, under the watchful supervision of a Guardia corporal armed with a rifle. There were four of them, and they seemed to be scraping painted political slogans from the moist rock face of the cavern, where ferns sprouted from every available crevice. The prisoners wore ordinary workmen's clothes, including the one woman amongst them, but all sported a crude red star stitched to the back of their tattered smock shirts. Some large straw bags with long carrying handles were stacked nearby. *To hold whatever tools they're allowed to use, I guess*, thought Jack. *Working late though, poor buggers. Those others we passed must have finished a good half-hour ago.*

The Guardia had his back to the tourists, sparing them barely a glance as they squeezed past behind. But Brendan still went to speak with him. A professional courtesy.

'The Corporal tells us to stay away from his charges,' said the guide, 'but says that we have nothing to fear from them. Just keep your distance, ladies and gentlemen. And *whatever* you do, please don't get between the Corporal and his prisoners.'

He led them carefully past the labour gang to a recess containing a tomb. White marble. Jack thought instantly of Colonel Telford's headstone, back in San Sebastián. *One hundred years of civil war.*

'Don Pelayo's final resting place?' asked Dorothea. 'Is it truly?'

'The one and only,' said Brendan. 'Delightful, isn't it? The King's son brought Pelayo's body here, laid his father and mother side by side in this very sarcophagus. In the same place that Our Lady had appeared on the eve of battle.'

It was a simple stone coffin, set lengthways into an archway, an ancient inscription, a few flowers and candles. But the Sisters of Our Lady of the Holy Light had moved on. To an altar further along the wall of the cave, in a deeper recess. They knelt carefully upon the marble floor, heads bowed, and the group seemed collectively bound to follow their example, standing with heads uncovered, all silence except for the scraping of the prisoners' implements. Jack looked at the captives, wondered at their lack of restraints, but caught one of the three men staring back at him, defiance in his gaze.

'I expected…' Catherine Kettering began.

'What?' said Brendan. 'That there'd actually be a *Virgen de Covadonga*? An effigy? Oh, there *was*, Mrs Kettering! But you'd better ask *them* what happened to her.' He jerked his thumb towards the prisoners. 'This is all we've got left.'

The altar was covered in flowers, of course. It was decorated with a simple wooden cross, more candles. But in the place where the holy statuette would once have stood, there was now simply a framed photograph of the Virgin. It had been hand-coloured but not particularly well. The skirts of Our Lady's robe were pale green, the elaborate crown and halo not gilded but a faded yellow.

'Where is the original?' said Alfred Holden. 'Have we any idea?'

'None,' Brendan replied. 'She simply disappeared during the Reds' chaos.'

'Scandalous,' said Dorothea. 'One cannot really credit such a thing. Don't you agree, Mister Murphy?'

'Anybody capable of *this*…' Brendan indicated another sepia picture. 'This is Father Poveda. He was once a Canon at the Basilica. He did a great deal to organise pilgrimages here at one time. He was shot by the Reds in Madrid. In '36. The local people consider him to be something of a saint.'

Jack found another tomb, just to the right of the altar, down a couple of steps and apparently belonging to Alfonso the First and his wife, Hermesinda. Then he drifted back past the nuns to the furthest extremity of the grotto, where an old sanctuary, a small chapel perhaps, had been built against the rocks. But it was crumbling, its half-roof almost collapsed. He poked his head through the door but the smell was unpleasant.

'Anything in here?' Jack asked.

'Not any more, Mister Telford,' said Brendan. 'And just watch your head there. It's not very safe.'

Jack shook a wooden lintel. Dust and mortar fell from the edge of the doorway.

MIkel was behind him, he realised, trying to look inside the shelter. So Jack made room for him, stepping to one side. As he did so, he turned around. The old priest seemed finally to have snapped at enough pilgrims' heels to now have them heading in a single group towards the gates, his arms spread, Christ-like, to prevent those at the back escaping him yet again. And, as the last of them disappeared into the tunnel, the cleric called politely but firmly to Brendan also, producing a set of keys from his pocket and, still holding his bag of coins, went down to close the outer gate at the head of the staircase. The priest waved to somebody below, and two tiny bats twisted and turned about his head.

'That's it, ladies and gentlemen,' said the guide. 'Time to go. And dinner awaits. The best that the Gran Hotel Pelayo has to offer, so I'm told.'

Strange bloke, that Brendan, thought Jack. *I* should *dislike him intensely. His bigotry. His unquestioning acceptance of anything Franco's stooges put in his head.*

I probably would *dislike him if I met him anywhere else. But here…*

The priest climbed patiently back up to the inner gates, one of them held open. A clear invitation for them to leave. And the Corporal of *Civiles* was standing near him. Jack saw him speak to Brendan, a half-snarled outburst of Spanish.

That's a bit officious, thought Jack. *The old priest was making a perfectly reasonable job of clearing us out by himself.*

But the priest seemed puzzled, looked at the Corporal with a frown. And Brendan had also evidently been surprised by whatever was said to him.

Sister María Pereda was still praying in front of the altar but she turned also, looked at the tableau, whispered to Sister Berthe Schultz who got to her feet and moved towards the gate. She said something to the priest. *In German?* Jack wondered. *No, Latin, of course.*

The scraping had stopped. There was a moment of complete silence apart from the echoing crows out in the valley.

Then Mikel tried to push past Jack, coming out of the sanctuary, buttoning his flies.

The driver halted, hands still at his crotch. He was looking at the Corporal, disbelief on his face. So Jack looked too. Past the uniform this time. To the coarse, peasant's face. The heavily stubbled chin and cheeks.

It's him! thought Jack. *The man from Irún again. But what's he doing…?*

The Corporal spoke again, louder this time, so that Brendan looked around at his tourists, then glanced down at his own holster.

'*¡No!*' said the Corporal. And he levelled the muzzle of his rifle towards Brendan's chest.

His prisoners were suddenly that no more. One of the men stepped forward, behind Brendan, slipped open the holster's flap, removed the pistol and brought it down hard on the guide's head.

Brendan slumped to the ground, while the other prisoners dived for the basket-weave bags, threw out some cloths and oddments, produced their own weapons. Two heavy revolvers and, for the woman, a submachine gun, a stubby perforated barrel. With a crack that echoed violently around the cave, she pressed a box-type magazine into the wooden stock.

Somebody screamed. Catherine Kettering perhaps. No, it was Carter-Holt. She seemed totally distraught about Murphy. And Marguerite Weston swore. A foul profanity as, for the first time in probably many years, Jack imagined, she moved close to her husband for protection.

There was a moment when all was still. Frozen.

It's a dream, thought Jack. *I've over-slept. I'll be late for Brendan's chat.*

But then the old priest broke free from the inertia. His keys dropped to the floor and everybody turned towards him as he looked wildly towards the tunnel.

No, thought Jack. *Don't!*

The priest pivoted around the bar of the gate, took one step down, two. He dropped the bag. Coins scattered about his feet. The woman fiddled with the submachine gun's bolt, paced forward, fired. The weapon kicked in her hands, the muzzle swinging as though it had a life of its own. Each barking, automatic eruption battered their senses in that confined space. Hands covered ears. Nostrils recoiled at the harsh cordite stench of it all. Jack shook his head, peered through the drift of smoke. He saw that the priest was sprawled down the length of the bottom stairs. He was perfectly still. And near him, sleeping peacefully against the iron grille, sat Sister Berthe Schultz, a bouquet of blood-red roses scattered across her black habit.

Chapter Sixteen

Saturday 24 September 1938

Cries and curses chased the ghost of gunfire and its finally fading echoes from the grotto. Revolvers pointed wildly in every direction, forcing the tourists to lower their heads, to cover their vulnerability. A useless reaction.

The men's anger ran in no obvious direction. They simply bellowed at their captives. And the captives, in turn, remained for the most part fearfully silent – although Marguerite Weston had whimpered incessantly, while Catherine kept repeating, 'I knew it! I knew it!' Valerie Carter-Holt still pressed them to do something for the guide. But Jack had the vivid impression that the three men also raged against something external. Perhaps whatever fate, whatever sense of injustice, drew them here. Though it was not anger alone, he saw. *They're feverish too. Their blood is up. Battle frenzy or whatever you call it.* Yet, however it was named, he prayed fervently that they would stop waving those damned guns about.

Only the fellow in the Guardia uniform seemed immune from mindless fury. His own was full of purpose, direction. First, towards the three *pistoleros*.

'*¡Tranquilo!*' he shouted. '*¡Joder, tranquilo!*' Then an instruction, following which Jack and the rest of the group were corralled towards the side of the altar, forced to sit. Hands on heads. Children at school again. A new lesson in life to be learned. Together. All except Sister María Pereda who remained at her fallen colleague's side, stroking the older nun's lifeless fingers, praying to Our Lady for the merest modicum of Her Holy Light to be shed upon this devout servant.

The second target of the Guardia's acerbic tongue, meanwhile, was the woman with the submachine gun. She had gone almost immediately to the priest's corpse, kicked it once or twice, then turned with a dismissive smile. She even looked as though she expected praise for the deed, but all she received was snarling disdain, fast and fluid, though Jack understood not a word. The woman tried to defend herself, though it only made the verbal assault on her more severe. This was a man who would brook no argument. And, when it was done, the Guardia issued her with two short orders.

In response, the woman moved to Sister María Pereda, took her roughly by the arm and dragged her, protesting, across the cave to join the remaining members of the ill-fated tour group. Then the woman took up position in front of them, the weapon moving, menacing, from one to another while her three male comrades, relieved of their previous duty and some of the tension too, finally put away the revolvers and Brendan Murphy's automatic.

The machine gun's muzzle leered at Jack, pupil-black and cruel, each time the woman turned in his direction. He expected at any moment that it would once again begin to spit fire and death.

The three men moved to the gate, collected the dead priest's keys, and were about to haul his body into the tunnel when a new commotion broke out below. The inhabitants of Covadonga had finally realised that something was amiss. That, yes, it was indeed small arms fire they had heard from the Holy Cave. And they had come out to investigate, the sounds of agitated voices swelling as the crowd grew, out of Jack's sight, but somewhere down beyond the pool.

The Guardia held his rifle out, barrel towards the sky, gripped tightly and squeezed the trigger. The explosion was even louder than those of the submachine gun, more clipped, but it rebounded in the same way, and it served perfectly well to scatter the spectators. There were sounds of panic for a few moments, then nothing but Marguerite's sobbing, the illusion that it was her endless tears which fed the waters below. The man yelled into the near-silence.

'Oh, Heaven defend us,' said Dorothea. 'He says something about English people from the Hotel. That he will kill us all if…Well, I didn't catch the rest.'

'I think we can guess the rest, my dear,' whispered the Professor. 'I suggest we all sit quietly. No sudden moves, eh?'

The Guardia rattled the rifle's bolt, ejecting the spent shell, pressing another into the breech. And he nodded to the three men. They continued with their task, removing the priest with no more care than they would have lavished on a sack of rubbish, came back moments later to collect Sister Berthe Schultz. Jack glanced at Sister María Pereda who was now staring towards the photograph of the *Virgen de Covadonga*. The others remained rigid, hands still on their heads, fear etched on their averted faces.

When he turned again towards the Guardia, Jack saw that the man had placed the rifle's butt on the ground, the muzzle resting against his hip while he unbuttoned the uniform jacket. The movements were clumsy, his fingers replicating in action the disgust which showed on the fellow's features. With the last button undone, he struggled free of the khaki jacket, tossed it towards Brendan's prone body with disdain. Jack could not be sure whether the guide was dead or merely unconscious but, as he watched, the man also removed the distinctive three-cornered hat, skimmed it towards Brendan Murphy's back, then spat after it. Whether the sputum was intended for the uniform, for Brendan, or for both, Jack could not discern.

The three companions now returned, carrying unlit oil lamps, locking the iron grille. The man with the rifle spoke to one of them who came forward, crouching, revolver trained also on Brendan's recumbent form as he checked for signs of life. He looked up, nodded once, edged backwards as the rifleman, the group's leader, Jack was convinced, let his gaze wander to the railings at the cave's edge. There was another order, rope fetched from the basket-weave bags, and Brendan Murphy was tied to the rails, groaning slightly as the ropes were fastened so that he sat, arms spread-eagled, crucified in a sitting position against the railings of the *Cueva de la Santina.*

The leader looked pleased with their handiwork, stood back a couple of paces. *He's satisfying himself,* thought Jack, *that anybody trying to snipe from below is likely to hit Brendan in the process. At least, on that side. A sacrificial lamb. A human barricade.* And not just from below, it seemed, for the man also checked the possible lines of sight from the back of the Basilica and other points.

Jack was shocked to realise that no more than five minutes had elapsed since the attack had begun. Five minutes before and the world had seemed very different indeed.

There were more orders, and the men returned to their bags. The contents were laid upon the floor. More rope. Another revolver, which the leader pushed into the waistband of his uniform trousers. Belts and magazines of ammunition. Small cooking pot. Ladle. Bundle of clothes. Blanket roll. A wineskin, or something similar. Tied paper parcel. Another package, but wrapped in sheepskin. Some tools, hammer and cold chisels. Reels of tape. Roll of thin wire. Flat wooden box, treated with great reverence. A taller box, with a small lock on the front, lid at the top, and a shoulder strap. And sticks of dynamite. A great deal of dynamite. Everything was carried to the walnut chest so recently locked by the priest, the lock smashed, their goods stowed within. Everything but the small wooden box.

The three men set to work under the expert guidance of their leader. He traversed the cave from end to end. Not searching, for he had obviously enjoyed plenty of opportunity to survey the place earlier, but leading them from one location to another, four in total, fissures or holes in the rock, where they began to tape sticks of explosive together, several to each bundle, before wedging them firmly in place.

'Do they mean...?' whispered Peter Kettering.

'I don't believe that it's intended for us particularly,' said Carter-Holt. But she was distracted, had not seemed focused since Brendan Murphy was struck down. 'I imagine that the grotto itself is as much a captive as we are. But you can't threaten rock with a machine gun.'

'I just 'opes they knows what they's about,' said Max Weston. Then he added. 'Curly, Larry and Moe, I means.'

Curly, Larry and...?

'Mister Weston,' hissed Dorothea. 'It's hardly the time...Oh, yes. I see what you mean. Jolly good.'

Peter Kettering suppressed a snort of laughter. It burst from him like some repressed outpouring of his anxiety. The woman took a step backwards, levelled the gun at him, turned to see what had amused him. Jack did likewise, looked at the three men properly for the first time. One of them was almost bald, only a thin wisp of receding hairline remaining. The second was thin-featured, tightly curled chestnut hair. And the third looked as though his black mop had been crudely cut with a pudding bowl. The Three Stooges. Jack smiled. *Trust Max!* he thought.

'What do you think they want?' said Alfred Holden, also in a whisper. It seemed the right way to communicate. Not to attract excessive attention.

'We seem to be hostages of war,' said Carter-Holt. 'It's something in which the Reds have a certain expertise. That and their dynamite, of course.'

'Just do as they say, old chap,' said Albert Moorgate. 'The best way, you know.'

'Well it ain't fair,' wailed Marguerite. 'What we done to *them*, eh?'

'I wouldn't take it personally, Mrs Weston,' said Carter-Holt. 'We are no more than bargaining chips, I think.'

'Mrs Weston is quite right,' said Frances Moorgate. 'We're hardly prisoners of war, after all. And even if we *were*, there are rules about these things, aren't there?'

'I think that, perhaps,' said her husband, 'the rules do not quite apply in Spain.'

The last of the dynamite bundles was carefully placed. Or almost the last. For, when the men had finished inside the cave, they cautiously unlocked the tunnel gate again and one of them disappeared, shock-haired Larry, along with the leader and further taped explosives.

'Are you alright, Sister?' Catherine said quietly to the younger nun.

'Poor Sister Berthe Schultz,' said Dorothea. 'What do you say *now*, Mister Telford. You *still* doubt that the Reds murder priests and nuns?'

'I never doubted it,' said Jack. 'I simply tried to point out that it's a story with two sides. Some fanatics on the Left may kill clerics for political reasons. But fanatics on the Right kill trade union leaders, socialists, those who support the Republic. It's a tragedy that those two people were killed. But it wasn't actually *because* one was a priest and the other a nun.'

'It sounds like you're defending these murderers, Telford,' sneered Professor Holden. 'I don't believe it. I really don't!'

'I'm *not* defending them,' said Jack. But it was weak. He was exhausted. The fear, he assumed. And he was fighting an urge to think about the killing of Sister Berthe Schultz. It was curiosity, after all, that had taken her to the gate, to speak with the old priest. And curiosity, as the good Sister had pointed out…

'I pray for her soul,' said Sister María Pereda, as though she divined his thoughts. 'But I cannot bear to think of her out there. Cold and alone. She should have stayed with the group, I think. But she taught me many things. How will I explain to Herr Alexander?'

The leader and his companion returned from the tunnel. The gate was locked behind them and they went quickly to the wooden box that had been left by the bags. The leader carried the small chest to the first of the wedged dynamite bundles, removed a slender metal cartridge and pressed it carefully into one of the sticks. As the tourists held their breath, he repeated the operation for each other bundle. The gate was unlocked once more but, before going back into the tunnel, the second man was sent to fetch the roll of wire. They checked the tunnel carefully, then slipped out. They were back very quickly, unrolling the wire behind them and securing the gate while, at the railings, Brendan Murphy stirred, groaned.

'What in God's name do they intend?' said Albert Moorgate. His voice shook. 'They've turned the whole place into one enormous bomb. They don't need *us*, surely. Mrs Holden, you speak Spanish. Say something!'

'I think we need to work together on this,' said Carter-Holt. 'Begging for our lives might not be the best thing.'

'Quite right,' said Alfred Holden, though he sounded less than convinced.

'Do you think they want money?' asked Catherine. 'Is it one of those things where they will hold us for ransom?'

'Like the Lindbergh baby?' said Frances Moorgate. It was an unhappy analogy.

'It won't have anything to do with money, Professor,' said Carter-Holt. 'These Reds don't care about money. And you know what happened at the Alcázar? In Toledo?'

Mikel muttered something. In Basque, Jack thought.

'I was born in Toledo,' said Sister María Pereda.

'Heroic,' said Holden. 'Franco's defenders held out against impossible odds. For over a month, wasn't it? But what's that got to do with us?'

Jack remembered the siege. It had begun just a few days after Franco's insurrection. A few hundred *Civiles* had occupied the old fortress palace in Toledo for National Spain and held it, week after week, against one Republican assault after another. The place had no real strategic value, he recalled. It had simply become a symbol. And the Nationalists succeeded in holding it even though, over a month and more, it turned to rubble around them. It had become a favourite item for *Pathé News*, for the papers.

'The Nationalist Commander was Colonel Moscardo,' said Carter-Holt. 'Somehow – I can't remember how – the Republicans managed to capture Moscardo's son. He was sixteen at the time. Luis, I think. The Reds demanded that Moscardo surrender the Alcázar or else they would kill the boy.' She looked towards Brendan Murphy. 'Luis shouted to his father that the Reds really *did* intend to shoot him. The Colonel told him that if they carried out the threat, his son should commend his soul to God and die like a man. Well, that's the way I heard the story, anyway.' But she sounded distraught, as though she was simply presenting a rehearsed script with which she was now bored.

'And what happened?' asked Frances.

'The Reds shot him. Naturally,' said Alfred Holden.

'Yes,' said Carter-Holt. 'They shot the boy. They *kill* hostages.'

Their captors' leader had now worked his way from one explosives location to another, a small pair of pliers crimping stripped wire into each of the blasting caps, the cables secured and run to the tall wooden box. He unlocked it, flipped the lid, exposed a pair of brass terminals and a plunger handle, bared and attached the wiring. He checked everything once more, seemed satisfied with the results.

'Are you saying that we're not actually the targets here, Miss Carter-Holt?' said Jack. His arms were beginning to ache, and the slabbed floor of the cave was cold, despite his trench coat. He shifted, stiffly, wondered how the women were coping. Not well, if Catherine and Marguerite were anything to go by. But Frances seemed stoical enough. And the indomitable Dorothea.

'Quite right, Mister Telford,' said Valerie. 'Faculties all functioning today, I see. No, these Reds will have something they want, I imagine. Their target is actually whoever can deliver it for them. But I don't understand how they got here. And did they plan on us being in the cave? Or is that just an accident? It's damned inconvenient.'

'Inconvenient?' said Jack. 'Funny way to put it. But, yes, I think they've been following us. The boss man was in Irún. He's the bloke that Nora Hames and I saw with Mikel. I'm sure I saw him again at Amorebieta. I *think* it was there, anyway.'

'I remember the Irún incident,' said Dorothea. 'Mister Murphy thought the man was after cigarettes, didn't he? I say,' she whispered even more quietly, 'do you think...?' She jerked her head towards Mikel.

'He looks as miserable as the rest of us,' Jack replied.

And Mikel soon looked even more miserable. The leader of their captors had found his old striped suit jacket amongst the bundle of rags and clothes, put it on, then a bandolier of rifle ammunition over his head, across his chest. His dark hair was greasy, parted in the centre. The fellow smoothed each side, slapped Larry on the back. *Congratulations on a job well done*, thought Jack. He saw the fellow collect Curly and Moe. They came forward, exchanged a few words with the woman, then dragged Mikel to his feet, pulling him away from the group.

'Oh, my goodness!' cried Dorothea. 'What are they doing?'

'Easy, Mrs Holden,' said Albert Moorgate. 'Fortitude, dear lady.'

At the railings, Brendan moaned again.

'Mister Murphy need help,' said Sister María Pereda. 'Shall I speak to the *Jefe*?'

At the word, the leader came forward, pulled the revolver from his waistband, crouched and placed its barrel against Sister María Pereda's forehead. He snarled something at her. The nun looked back at him, held his gaze, perfectly calm. She spoke. The man looked over his shoulder at the guide, then back at the Sister. He laughed, though without humour. Two or three fast words.

'What does he say?' whispered Frances.

'He say, *All in good time*,' said the nun.

'*Jefe*,' said Dorothea. '*Agua? Para...*' She partially lifted her right hand, pointed towards Brendan.

The leader spoke to Sister María Pereda.

'He say, *Why do you have hands on heads*?' she said.

'We thought...' Dorothea began. 'Oh well.' She took her hands tentatively from her head. The rest followed suit, nervous, embarrassed, foolish. 'What are they going to do with Mikel?' The driver was making pleading noises.

There was another exchange.

'The *Jefe* say that Mikel must help. Me too. He want to know who is who.'

'Why doesn't he just ask us?' said Jack.

'Tell the fellow nothing,' whispered Alfred Holden. 'We should insist on being treated as prisoners of war. Name and title only. Nothing more. Don't you think, my dear?'

'Please be quiet,' replied Dorothea. 'I can feel a migraine coming on.'

Somewhere behind them, beyond the mountains which hid the *Cueva de la Santina* from the outside world, the sun was setting. The shadows had lengthened over the cave mouth, down into the valley beyond, the sky darkening quickly. Larry was ordered to light an oil lamp. But carefully, since below there was the sound of military boots on cobbles. *Civiles*, under cover of gathering gloom, taking up position. Sounds of activity, too, at the further end of the tunnel.

'I'm hungry,' Marguerite complained. She had at least stopped sobbing now.

The *Jefe* instructed Mikel and Sister María Pereda to stand alongside him, rifle slung from his shoulder, revolver pointing carelessly at an angle to the ground. He motioned for Max to stand and, as the comedian did so, the chief asked Mikel a question. There was a lengthy response. Jack caught the word '*Caudillo*' a couple of times but little else.

'Mikel tell him,' said the nun without being invited to speak, 'that Mister Weston is funny man. Famous. That he sing and dance too. That he make the movie. That he makes *El Caudillo* laugh. And that Mrs Weston is...Well, that she is his wife.'

I bet that's not all he said, thought Jack, stealing a glance at Marguerite, who was just offering the *Jefe* her best smile possible in the circumstances. The man spoke again, pointing at Catherine Kettering.

'He ask,' said the nun, 'why Mister Weston and Mrs Kettering both have the black eye.' But it was clearly a rhetorical question.

'*¡Basta!*' shouted the *Jefe*. Enough. And Moe frisked the comedian. The chief told Max to sit again, dismissed him as though he was the court jester who had failed to please his master.

It was Peter Kettering's turn. A brief commentary from Mikel, the words *Medalla de Sufrimientos por la Patria* clearly enunciated in the middle. There was a query.

'*No*,' Mikel told the *Jefe*. '*Su hermano*.' His brother. Another search and Kettering rejoined the seated group.

'Does he think we're carrying weapons?' whispered Peter.

Jack shook his head as Albert Moorgate was brought forward, surprised at how short the man now seemed. The banker's shoulders were hunched within his Aquascutum raincoat. Mikel spoke a few words.

'Mikel say him that *Señor* Moorgate is important man in City of London,' said Sister María Pereda.

'Oh, I'd rather he didn't,' protested Moorgate. Jack was unsure whether he meant Mikel or the *Jefe*, for the latter had taken Albert's straw Fedora from his head, exposing the older man's thinning hair, knocking his spectacles askew. The fellow admired the red and blue band, tried the hat himself, sought opinions from his companions. They laughed, admiring his panache, tensions eased somewhat.

Then the *Jefe* stretched out his hand to Moorgate's raincoat, fingered the material, murmured appreciatively.

Albert Moorgate's hat was returned to him, though reluctantly, and the banker sat down. It was Jack's turn. The *guerrillero* they had christened Moe began to search him, discovered nothing of significance. There was a query from the *Jefe*. Mikel replied. Then a further question.

'*Es socialista*,' explained Mikel. He's a socialist.

'What's he asking?' said Jack.

'Oh,' said Professor Holden, 'you'll find yourself amongst friends here, I suppose, Telford.'

'No,' Sister María Pereda interrupted again. 'Mikel tell him that you are a journalist, *Señor* Telford. *El Jefe* ask which fascist *periódico* you write for. Mikel say that your paper support the Republic. So he ask whether you are Marxist then. Mikel say no. Only *socialista*.'

'*¿Y ella?*' said the leader, pointing at Carter-Holt. And her? '*¿Su mujer?*' His woman?

Valerie found it impossible to mask her disgust and Jack found himself wounded by her response despite the gravity of the moment.

'*No*,' Mikel smiled. '*¡Qué va!*' No way. '*Otra periodista*.' Another journalist.

Carter-Holt was required to come and stand near Jack, who gathered that the *Jefe* was asking whether Valerie, too, was a socialist. Mikel laughed. There was a long story, the word '*Teruel*' mentioned several times.

'Sounds like he's getting your life story,' said Jack.

'I can understand Spanish perfectly well, Mister Telford,' whispered Carter-Holt. 'Clearly better than your own inept efforts.' Jack was stung once more. 'Mikel,' she continued, 'seems to have found it necessary to explain my award of the Military Merit Cross by the good General in person.'

The *Jefe* grinned at Valerie. '*¡Joder, fascistas!*' he said, then noticed the camera, demanded to see it. Jack saw her hesitate, put a protective hand to the Agfa's case, then reluctantly raise it towards the Spaniard. He made a point of placing his fingers over hers. She did not flinch. So he took the camera, hefted it in his own hand, made a gesture as though to comment on its weight, then turned it over. There was a question.

'He ask whether you were given this by Herr Hitler. Or Herr Goebbels, perhaps,' said the nun.

'No,' Carter-Holt blanched a little. 'I bought it in London. *Lo compré en Londres*,' she added.

'*Bien*,' smiled the *Jefe*. '*Habla español. Muy bien*.' And he handed back the camera. Then took her handbag, checked it, told one of the men to search through each of the other ladies' purses. Only Dorothea objected, her obstinacy rewarded by having the contents of her lizard-skin clutch scattered across the cave.

There was a question for Jack, as Dorothea tried to pick up her mints tin, card case, lipstick and other possessions.

'He say,' Sister María Pereda began, 'why you travel with all these...*Facciosos*?'

'Fascists?' said Jack, trying to be helpful but clearly upsetting his fellow-captives.

'No,' replied the nun. 'It means...Rebels, I think you say.'

Good question, thought Jack. But it was *The Hobbit* that dominated his attempt to conjure a logical response. Perhaps it was the cavern. Gollum's lair. The riddle. *'What have I got in my pocket?' Why* am *I travelling with these fascists? String or nothing. For Sydney Elliott? For* Reynold's News*? For a father who chose the certainties of death over the random risks of life? For my mother driven so forcefully to pacifism by his suicide? If only I had the Ring.*

'String or nothing,' murmured Jack.

'String?' said Sister María Pereda.

'It doesn't matter,' Jack replied. 'Just tell him that my newspaper sent me.'

'I needs food,' Marguerite complained again, louder this time. *Much* louder. The *guerrilleros* turned to find out what was the matter. 'Max, my love. Tell 'e that I be 'ungry. When we goin' to eat?'

'Oy, *Signore*,' said Max, obediently. 'Chow-chow?' And he mimicked the finger action of pushing food into his mouth.

Mikel translated, though it was largely unnecessary. The *Jefe* spoke quickly to the woman, left her on guard again, and told one of the men to bring the driver. They quietly opened the inner gate, as well as the outer one onto the staircase and the leader crouched down behind Brendan Murphy, who was now beginning to regain consciousness. The *Jefe* shouted something out into the darkness.

'He ask to speak with the man in charge,' said Sister María Pereda. 'Of the *Guardias Civiles*.'

There was silence for a moment, then an answering call from down in the valley. The guerrilla leader responded.

'What's he doing?' asked Dorothea. 'Do you think he plans to let us go?'

'I do not think so,' said the nun. 'He say again he has English friends of Franco here. He say too that he has *dinamita*. Dynamite? If they try to attack, he will destroy the Holy Cave. Kill everybody.' There were gasps from the group. 'But he tell them he has first demand. That he will send out a man. The bus driver. To collect food. He say if anything bad happen, he will shoot one of *El Caudillo*'s friends.'

Another pause, then a reply. The *Jefe* looked pleased, whispered instructions to Mikel, then motioned for him to go down the steps. The driver disappeared from view.

'Oh, thank goodness,' said Marguerite. 'Food at last.'

And poor bloody Mikel having to hump it all the way up however many stairs Brendan said there are, thought Jack. *What was it? A hundred? More?*

'Sister María Pereda,' said Frances Moorgate. 'do you think it might be possible to also ask the *Jefe* whether we could do something for Mister Murphy. He must need attention.'

Yes, Carter-Holt agreed enthusiastically. A capital idea, though nobody else seemed to have thought so earlier. *Me included*, Jack thought, guiltily.

The nun called to the *Jefe*. There was a further dialogue, as a result of which Frances was allowed forward. The obvious choice, a qualified expert in first-aid, after all. She examined Brendan's wound, asked for water, and one of the men went to the small cubby-hole behind the altar where there was a water pipe, a primitive pump for the use of priests taking Mass, and from which he filled the cooking pot. Frances persuaded her husband to donate his handkerchief, used the water to bathe the back of Brendan's head. They spoke together, quietly. Binding the wound was more difficult. Frances had attempted to tear strips from her petticoat, but the task proved impossible. So another handkerchief was volunteered. Peter Kettering this time. And the thin fabric belt from Catherine's raincoat, tightened just enough to hold the dressing in place.

'How many fingers am I holding up?' they heard Frances ask, though they could not make out his answer. But she seemed pleased, smiled.

'What's she doing?' said Dorothea.

'Checking to see whether he has any lasting damage, I think,' said Peter Kettering.

'And what was the last thing you remember saying to us?' Frances said to the guide.

'Sure,' Brendan replied, 'wasn't it something about not getting between the Guardia and his prisoners?'

'Very good,' smiled Frances. 'I think you'll be fine, Mister Murphy.'

'It's a great shame that Mister Murphy did not take more notice of his own advice,' whispered Dorothea, 'before he got us into this mess.'

'You can hardly blame Mister Murphy,' protested Catherine Kettering.

'Who else *should* we blame, Mrs Kettering?' Dorothea hissed. '*Señor* de Armas Gourié did warn me. The fellow has been in prison. Did you know?'

'He served some time,' said Jack, 'for striking a superior officer. One whose men had fired on Murphy's unit.' *Why am I defending him, for God's sake?*

'All the same,' Dorothea continued, 'it was a mistake on my part. I thought it would be useful to have a real English-speaker.'

'But he's Irish, my dear,' murmured the Professor. 'You can never wholly trust them. He could be a Fenian for all we know. He certainly has no liking for the English. He's made that plain. It wouldn't surprise me if he was in league with these bandits.'

'I can't see that they would have hit him so hard if that were the case,' said Jack. 'Or crucified the poor bugger like that.'

'It could just be play-acting,' said Alfred Holden. 'And what about that damned driver. A bit too free with the information. Don't you think? It'll be interesting to see whether he even comes back.'

'Now he *is* a suspicious character,' said Albert Moorgate. 'And Mister Telford's actually *seen* the fellow chatting to these bandits as far back as the border.'

'I don't think it helps if we start apportioning blame,' snapped Valerie Carter-Holt. 'Does it really *matter* how this has happened? And the very *idea* that either Mikel or Mister Murphy might be responsible...'

'Easy for you to say, Miss Carter-Holt,' sneered the Professor. 'We shall see what we shall see. But I need to stretch the old legs.'

There was the sound of somebody labouring up the stairway. The unmistakeable bark of military orders further away. A vehicle starting. And Alfred Holden began to get to his feet.

'Is that a good idea, Professor?' said Albert Moorgate.

The attention of the submachine gunner had been distracted momentarily by the noises behind her but she turned now, back to focus on her duties. So the sight she saw was that of the tall Englishman, the one with a Charlie Chaplin moustache, rising towards her. She started at the perceived threat, not pausing to discover whether or not it was real. She stepped forward, fear and fury mingled on her face, pressed the muzzle hard into Holden's chest, catching his attention in turn. He jumped backwards.

'Get that thing away from me!' he yelled, eyes fixed on the cooling vents of the perforated barrel.

'Easy!' yelled Jack. 'For Christ's sake.' He flinched. *The woman looks half-mad,* he thought. *It wouldn't take much. Why doesn't the silly bugger sit down?* 'Sit down, Holden, why don't you?'

'I need no lectures from the likes of you, Telford!' the Professor shouted back, just as the woman shoved him once more.

'Now, look here,' said Holden. '*¡Puta roja!*'

'*¿Puta roja?*' screamed the woman. Red whore? '*¿Puta roja?*' she repeated, and there followed a spitting, articulate stream of invective as she jabbed him with the gun. Once. Twice. Then she snatched back the small bolt at the weapon's breech, cocking the thing for automatic fire. The Professor was pressed back as far as he could go, against the altar. The photographs and flowers scattered. Glass from a picture frame smashed to tiny shards upon the ground.

Jack found that he was incapable of anything except closing his eyes. Tight. There was shouting. Running feet. The *Jefe's* voice. But no shots. Jack cautiously opened his eyes again. The *guerrilleros'* leader had his hand clamped over the gun's muzzle, but he made no attempt to remove it from Holden's chest. And the *Jefe*'s words were soft, reassuring. He called the woman by name. Not once but many times, until Jack was sure that he had heard correctly. 'Encarna,' said the *Jefe*. 'Encarna.' The woman gradually relaxed, spat in the Professor's face and moved back. Holden wiped at the spittle with his sleeve but the *Jefe* took his own revolver, pushed its barrel into the loose flesh below the Professor's chin, pushed upwards until the Englishman was standing on the very tips of his brogues.

The Spaniard spoke. Slowly. Deliberately.

'The *Jefe* tell your husband,' Sister María Pereda said to an almost hysterical Dorothea, 'that they did not need to ask questions about him. That he is well-known to the Republic. A *fascista* of the front file. No, the first rank. A man who deserves to die.'

Holden's knees buckled but the revolver held him upright as Mikel finally appeared, breathless, at the top of the steps carrying a bundle. Curly and Moe searched him, relieved him of the package, sent the driver back to join the group. Mikel was reluctant, unwilling to put himself so near to the volatile scene before him. The *Jefe* summoned his two henchmen, gave them an instruction, released the Professor to their charge. They heaved their captive towards the iron barrier, his legs pedalling furiously but ineffectively, as though they intended not to stop, to pitch him straight out of the grotto.

'Nooooo!' wailed Holden. His wife screamed. Marguerite too.

But at the last moment they *did* halt, jerked the Professor around, pushed him to the floor until he was sitting along from Brendan Murphy. One kept him at gunpoint, the other went for rope, and they tied him to the upper rail in exactly the same fashion as they had previously done with the guide. And the *Jefe* was not yet finished. There was another order, Frances Moorgate also gripped by the arm, the ladle with which she had been giving water to Brendan Murphy thrown to the ground, herself forcefully dragged back towards Albert.

'I say!' said Moorgate.

The *Jefe* looked at him. What? he seemed to say. You want to join your friend? Albert lowered his head, silent now. Only the *guerrillero* spoke.

'He say the next one to move without permission will die,' whispered the nun. 'And he say that now we starve also.'

'What?' Marguerite began, horrified. But even Marguerite Weston knew enough to say no more than that.

So they settled to their fate, pressed against the cold marble floor of Spain's spiritual birthplace, themselves born again to a new experience, a new stratum of sensations. *Stay calm*, Jack thought. *You can survive this. You can survive.* The long hours of sable stillness were still ahead and only Albert Moorgate's quietly spoken understatement broke the silence.

'Perhaps we should have chosen Guernsey or Sark after all, my dear,' he whispered.

If that had been Max, thought Jack, the chill beginning to attack his bones, his stomach aching, *it would have been a gem. Fancy being upstaged by that straight-laced banker. Still, a honeymoon to remember. Let's hope so, anyway.*

It was almost midnight. There was a distant rumble, difficult to identify at first. But after a few minutes, the noise resolved itself. It was the complaining roar of a truck, gears grinding, taking the bends somewhere far down the valley road. And not one truck. A whole convoy of them, Jack realised, as the narrowed headlights began to slice slender searching beams through the dark.

Chapter Seventeen

Sunday 25 September 1938

Jack Telford thought of all the British heroes who must have looked down upon them that night, the opening hours of Sunday morning, and admired the tour group's morale-raising endeavours. Shackleton, Bligh, Scott. A dozen others were invoked to support them. The repertoire was extensive. *The British Grenadiers. Hearts of Oak. Goodbye, Dolly Grey. Pack Up Your Troubles. It's a Long Way to Tipperary.* But when they moved on to *Abide With Me*, the atmosphere became maudlin, negatively charged.

Max did his best to lighten things again but the stories and jokes only served to make matters worse. And, meanwhile, Mikel had been summoned by the *Jefe* to give a more detailed account of his trip to the enemy camp. Sister María Pereda provided a whispered account of the conversation.

'Mikel say they treat him badly at first. They search him. Ask questions. Then the Manager from the hotel comes to confirm that he is driver. That he works for National Spain. Then Mikel has to tell the *Civiles* about the *banditos*. About the priest. About poor Sister Berthe Schultz. About the *dinamita*. About Mister Murphy. About us. How many. Where we are. Now the *Jefe* asks about the *Civiles*. Mikel tell him where *they* are. How many he has seen. Who is in charge. Only a *teniente*, he says. And the man seem afraid. The *Jefe* ask if he is waiting for orders. Mikel says he think so. From somebody else. From Burgos maybe. The *Jefe* say that from all those *camiones* at midnight, Burgos is now here.'

Both Brendan Murphy and the Professor were suffering badly, cramps causing them severe pain until, finally, the *Jefe* ordered that they should be tied differently. Their arms were released, the blood returning to their benumbed limbs causing them insufferable discomfort. The ropes were shifted, wound about their chests, a series of half-hitches around the upper rail and stanchions, knotted again between their shoulder blades so that they stood no chance of releasing themselves.

At times, the captured tourists dozed, but each only for a few minutes.

Otherwise, they felt the cold, the damp. Their stomachs rebelled against a lack of food. Catherine Kettering had difficulty breathing. Dorothea had pleaded twice with the *guerrilleros* for a fire, a bite to eat, some water. But they were unrelenting. Her husband's insult to the woman, Encarna, had cut deep, Jack thought. For their part, the captors seemed relaxed, taking turns to sleep, to share bread, cheese and *chorizo* from the package that Mikel had brought, to sit on the chairs and clean their weapons, to guard their prisoners, to guard the tunnel gate. The contents of Dorothea's mints tin had long been consumed by the prisoners and their only other joy had come from the last of Jack's *Superiores* after he had sought permission to smoke from the *Jefe*. Naturally, all five of the *guerrilleros* took this as an invitation to help themselves to the packet also, leaving only two cigarettes for the group. And the *Jefe* was clear that neither Professor Holden nor Brendan Murphy should be afforded this comfort. But Jack shared the remnants and everybody else except Albert Moorgate and the Ketterings partook of the weed, including even Sister María Pereda, though the process caused a serious coughing fit.

By three o' clock, Max had exhausted all of his jokes and finally drifted into a troubled sleep.

'Sister,' said Dorothea. 'I wonder whether you might ask the *Jefe* what one is supposed to do about washing one's hands.'

'Washing hands?' replied the nun. 'You need water, *Señora*?'

'I was speaking figuratively, my dear. The bathroom. What if one needs the bathroom? Oh, this is *too* much.'

'The toilet, Sister María Pereda,' said Jack. 'What do we do for toilets in this place?'

Dorothea Holden was too tired and distressed to be embarrassed, and the nun spoke sharply to the *guerrillero*. There was an argument.

'He say that we must use the chapel over there. I have tell him that it is a holy place. But he say not any more. We use chapel. Or nothing.'

'You mean…?' said Dorothea.

'I'm afraid she does,' said Jack. 'We should have talked about this earlier. We don't know how long this is going to last. We must all be in the same boat by now. I've had my own legs crossed for the past hour or more.'

Dorothea looked at him with disgust.

'I hate to admit it, but he's right,' said Carter-Holt.

'I'm already quite desperate,' said Catherine Kettering.

'I think that settles it,' said Jack. 'Sister, can you ask whether we're allowed to move?'

They were indeed, but only under supervision. Yet Dorothea still did not shift from her position.

'Your turn first, I think, Mrs Holden,' said Carter-Holt.

'No, I think I can wait,' said Dorothea. 'Oh, this is just beyond the pale.'

Max was about to comment but Jack stopped him. It was bound to be a bucket joke.

Valerie put her arm around the older woman, whispered in her ear, tried to reassure her.

'Mrs Holden and I will go to the bathroom together,' she said.

'Are you sure…?' Catherine Kettering began.

'It will be fine,' said Carter-Holt. 'I have at least some experience from my time in the war zones. No need to fuss. Really. Come along, Mrs Holden.' It was Dorothea's turn to whisper. 'Oh yes,' Valerie remembered. She mouthed the word 'Paper' to the nun.

Sister María Pereda looked around for a moment, then spoke to Mikel. The driver smiled, reached into his back pocket, pulled out a copy of *La Gaceta del Norte*, ripped off the back page and handed it to Carter-Holt. By the time the two women returned, the nun had made a further request to their captors and another pot of water had been carefully poured for sullied hands. The captives availed themselves of these limited facilities, one after the other, Mikel's precious broadsheet slowly disappearing, each of them escorted to the chapel's damaged door but at least allowed to enter unaccompanied, a second lantern having been lit and hung inside. And with each visit, the stench became worse.

'Could somebody ask…?' groaned the Professor, but received only a kick to his ankles from Encarna by way of response. Sister María Pereda made a short plea on behalf of both men but it was met by a swift rebuke from the *Jefe*.

'I am sorry,' she said. 'He say something like, *They have got themselves into a mess. Now they can sit in it.*'

'How barbaric,' said Dorothea. 'Surely…'

Brendan Murphy was conscious and awake, but he was silent, his head bowed, and Jack gathered that it was too late to worry about the niceties in his particular case. *I imagine he's had to put up with worse though,* Jack thought. *Too proud to complain, as well.*

There was a sudden movement from one of the *guerrilleros*, Moe, who had taken station near the tunnel gate. He hissed a warning to the *Jefe* and, without needing an instruction, Encarna, Curly and Larry came forward to cover the prisoners, gesturing for them to remain silent and still. The *Jefe* himself edged towards the grille, his rifle ready, quietly working the bolt. He knelt there for a moment, listening carefully, then nodded. He gave a soft whistle, attracted Curly's attention, drew his hand across his face. Curly dimmed the oil lamp.

Jack could hear nothing, strained to pick up whatever had alerted Moe, who was now on the other side of the tunnel entrance from the *Jefe*, his back to the rock and Brendan Murphy's automatic pistol in his left hand.

Dorothea was about to speak but Encarna clamped her hand over the woman's mouth. The Professor looked up, peering through the gloom to see what was happening to his wife, and Larry put a revolver to Holden's head.

They all held their breath, Jack thinking of nothing except the dynamite that he had earlier seen the *guerrilleros* take into the tunnel. Surely, if there was any shooting now…?

Seconds went by, each seeming like a minute until, finally, they all heard it. The sound of movement in the tunnel. Just the slightest sound. It might have been a rat. *But rats rarely wear metal-shod boots,* Jack thought. *Though I guess the* Jefe *would say that the Civiles fit that description perfectly.*

Once again, the captives were clearly signalled to keep quiet.

The *Jefe* had eased himself down on the ground, pushed his rifle through the bars without touching them, rested the wooden stock carefully on the horizontal lower frame. Moe followed suit, laying prone beside his commander.

More seconds went by. The *Jefe* pressed the butt into his shoulder, took aim through the sights, though Jack could not imagine he had an actual target. Then he spoke. And so did the guns. The noise was incredible, terrifying. The entire world turned to chaos, order banished. The rifle roared. Then again as the *guerrillero* pumped another bullet into the breech. The pistol fired rapidly, Moe emptying the entire magazine in only a few moments. Cordite again. Smoke. And the smell of oil. Burning oil. They had fired low but Jack still could not believe that they had managed to avoid hitting the dynamite.

The firing stopped.

From the tunnel came a continuous screaming. An attacker severely wounded. And others moaning more softly. There was shouting, but the *Jefe* did not reply. There were cautious footsteps. A voice spoke, echoing in the tunnel. Then again when there was no response. And, finally, when they must have felt secure enough to do so, just the sounds of the dead or wounded being dragged away, groans and complaints, more tortured screeching, the pain of injured animals. And weeping. The noises ebbing into the distance, flowing back again as the military received their casualties out on the esplanade. Lights and truck engines.

Sister María Pereda was praying. Dorothea too. The Ketterings clung to each other. Marguerite Weston was hiding behind Carter-Holt, and Max seemed to be sheltering behind his wife. The Moorgates were both lying prone, their heads covered. Alfred Holden was holding his hands in front of his face.

Jack had felt very little. It was almost a sense of shock, but he found himself staring at Brendan Murphy. The Irishman returned his gaze. He was smiling, but there was a look of deep pain in his eyes. Pain, or fear?

'So you got to see some action after all, Mister Telford, sure,' said the guide. 'Cool as a cucumber. You'd have made a good soldier. Maybe you still will. What do you think, Miss Carter-Holt? Does Mister Telford here have the makings?'

'No,' said Jack. 'Never.'

Murphy laughed, earned some harsh words from the *Jefe*. And the blood of the *guerrilleros* was up again. They joked, nervously. Another skirmish won. More fascists killed. Moe was dispatched to empty Murphy's Sam Browne ammunition pouch. Three more magazines, some loose cartridges.

Jack tried to see his watch. Not even four-thirty yet. He huddled in his coat, shifting around on the rocky ground in the hope of finding a position that might be more comfortable. The rest of the group members were whispering among themselves. Marguerite Weston was sobbing quietly. Alfred Holden wanted water, just a sip, he pleaded. Their captors ignored him. Only one of them had been left on guard – Larry, now holding the submachine gun on his knee, sitting on a chair with his back to Pelayo's tomb, to Jack's left, next to the workmen's' bags. The other four sat, summoned into a tight circle near the tunnel gate, barely visible in the shadows but taking turns to drink from the *bota*, the wineskin, that they had brought with them. They were deep in discussion, an angry debate, with the *Jefe*'s voice dominating, responding to every point put forward by the others and occasionally having to drown them collectively when they all spoke at the same time. But the entire argument was conducted in muffled, conspiratorial tones. Jack had become accustomed to hearing the Spanish converse about even the most innocuous issues at the tops of their voices, as though they might come to blows over the quality of a wine, the texture of a cheese. It could be daunting to hear. Though it was never so fearsome as this measured, careful discourse. They were planning, and it was a private, secretive matter.

He must have slept for a while since, when he woke, the *guerrilleros* had fallen silent and another hushed argument had broken out amongst Jack's own companions. Larry remained on guard, his features hidden in the gloom but Jack imagined that the man might be amused by their obvious bickering. Yet the last thing that Jack himself wanted was to be drawn into yet another fruitless row. He lay motionless, listening.

'I still think you should offer them money,' hissed Professor Holden, from the railings.

'We don't *have* any money, Alfred,' Dorothea replied. 'At least, not here. And they're hardly likely to give us time to fetch it, are they?'

'What about Mister Moorgate then?' whispered her husband. 'What d'you say, old boy? The Westminster would put up the money, wouldn't it? Stand as guarantor, so to speak? We could get a message through somehow, surely.'

'I've already told you, Professor,' said Carter-Holt. 'This isn't about money.'

'In any case,' said Bertie Moorgate, 'you can hardly expect the Bank's customers to put their savings at risk in such a venture.'

'But what about dinner?' moaned Marguerite. 'I was tryin' to get Jack Telford to put in a good word earlier. Wi' them friends of 'is. But 'e weren't 'avin' any. Miserable bugger.'

'Well, what can you expect?' said Dorothea. 'The fellow is little better than a Communist himself. I blame *him* for this.'

'How can you blame *Señor* Telford?' said the nun. 'He has shoe on same foot as all of us.'

'*You* means…' Max began.

'Because,' said Professor Holden, 'if it weren't for the likes of Telford and other bleeding-heart liberals, the Reds would never have had so much support. They would have been defeated a year ago. And we wouldn't be in this mess.'

'Perhaps, Professor,' said Catherine Kettering, 'if we hadn't been so helpful towards General Franco, *he* would have been defeated. The Republic now at peace.'

'Mrs Kettering!' hissed Dorothea. 'After the sacrifice made by your brother-in-law! I must say. But, Mister Murphy, there is *one* thing. We were wondering. About you-know-who.'

'Mister Telford, you mean, ma'am?'

'No, not Telford,' said the Professor. 'The *other* one. Can't say his name or he'll know we're talking about him. The *chauffeur*.' This latter word was barely audible.

My God! thought Jack. *They really are unbelievable. The whole bunch. Most of them, anyway. Before too long, they'll have worked out that Mikel and myself are both part of the same conspiracy. It's the trouble with the English. Bloody class system still alive and kicking. Because I don't share their fascist views, I must be some sort of revolutionary. And Mikel's just a driver, so he's got to be a potential Red too, in their eyes. Mind, I've never found out properly what was going on in Irún.*

'Oh, no,' Murphy replied. 'I don't think you've anything to worry about in that direction, sure.'

'It was just,' said Dorothea, 'that Mister Telford told us he'd seen their leader before. At Irún. You remember? He took Miss Hames back to the bus, saw that fellow and our driver in conversation.'

'The bloke who was bumming the cigarettes, you mean?' said the guide. 'I doubt it. Just Mister Telford's imagination, eh?'

'It certainly looked like Mikel recognised him earlier,' said Catherine. Mikel spoke at the mention of his name. Brendan Murphy said something soothing. 'Oh, I'm sorry,' Catherine continued. 'How silly. Anyway, he looked as though he'd seen a ghost when he spotted him.'

'All the same...' said Brendan.

'Of course,' said the Professor, 'we only have Telford's word for what went on. Perhaps it was him *and* the *chauffeur* having a cosy little chat with the *Jefe*.'

I bloody knew it! thought Jack, tempted now to get up and give Holden the thrashing he deserved.

'Miss Hames was there too, remember?' said Murphy. 'I *do* think this is dangerous talk, Professor. Believe me, you all need to stick together in this.'

'And doesn't the real fault lie with these bandits?' said Carter-Holt. 'I think we should at least *try* to keep things in perspective.'

'Perspective?' protested Peter Kettering. 'Not much chance of that when none of us has had a wink of sleep.'

'Mister Kettering's right, sure,' said Brendan Murphy. 'You need to get some rest. Try, at least.'

'How can one sleep in these conditions?' said Dorothea. 'And, of course, I agree with Mrs Weston. I'm quite sure that Mister Telford *could* use some influence to make things better. He could at least ensure that my husband and yourself were made a little more...Well, comfortable, Mister Murphy.'

'It's good of you to be so concerned, Mrs Holden,' said the guide. 'Very good, sure. I'm amazed that you don't hold *me* responsible for getting you all into this mess.'

'Oh, as if such a thought would even enter one's head!' she said. 'And we still need you to lead us out of here, do we not?'

'You are a saint, ma'am,' said Brendan. 'But I think that botched job by the *Civiles* may mean that we'll all need to be a bit more self-reliant from now on, Mrs Holden.'

Jack drifted back into a fitful sleep, snatches of dreams in which he stood accused of many crimes. He woke with a start, shaken by a sharp noise which, he finally realised, had been his own snoring, so sudden that he could not remember how the dream had ended. The other captives were either asleep or almost so. Except Sister María Pereda and Mikel. The young nun had started to tidy the shrine. The driver was helping her. But she made a ghostly apparition, her dark robes making her form almost invisible, her white coif like a halo, framing just the small disembodied face. She carefully put the photographs back in their places, picked flowers from the floor and arranged them around the picture frames, picked slivers of glass gently from the altar cloth, collected it on her palm, looked for somewhere to set it down again so that it could do no harm. Mikel relieved her of the burden, but not before she had pricked her thumb on a small splinter. There was an intake of breath, and she muttered something in Spanish. '*¡Bendita Madre de Diós!*'

'Should we wake Mrs Moorgate to have a look at that?' whispered Jack.

'Thank you, *Señor*, but there is no need. A warning from Our Lady about the need to remain vigilant. Not to fall into the sin of carelessness.' She picked at the wound, extracted the splinter, sucked at the thumb. 'See? It is done.'

Mikel had returned, pushed the fringe of his hair to one side, out of his eyes. He asked her something and the nun put a hand on his arm, shook her head. The driver went off to sit down, alone.

'He likes you,' said Jack. She smiled.

'He is a good boy. But the others…'

'I heard,' said Jack. 'And thanks for defending *me*, by the way?'

'You were listening? *Ay, Señor.* Have you heard nothing that I say to you? Was it curiosity that drove you? If so, you know that is a sin. A terrible sin. But to listen in secret when others talk about you. It is worse. For it is vanity that makes you listen. You hope to hear good. Conceit, *Señor.* But Our Lady will always make sure that the curious listeners shall only ever hear bad of themselves. And when you hear those bad things? Do you forgive the person that spoke them? No. I think that you have evil thoughts. Another sin.'

'To be honest, I just went back to sleep. But Mikel. Shouldn't we…?'

'I have already asked Mikel this thing. He say me that this *Jefe* approach him in Irún, tell Mikel that they know about him. How he had fought for the Republic, then fight for *El Caudillo.* The man call him a traitor. Ask him for information about the roads we travel. The dates when we arrive at places. But Mikel refuse. And then he say that you come back to the bus with the old English lady.'

'He didn't tell Brendan?'

'No. He say now that he is ashamed. But then, he was frightened. He thought the army would send him back to the front.'

'But these *guerrilleros* are on the side of the Republic too. Aren't they? Mikel could just switch sides again. Join them. Or when they sent him down for the food, he could have run away.'

'Mikel say that after Santoña, the war was already lost for the Basques. For his people. Now, he just want it to end. For the killing to stop.'

'Coming back up here with the food isn't going to help stop the killing.'

'No. He say that he did that for me.'

They both looked at the driver. He was sitting quietly, his wide eyes fixed on Sister María Pereda, a gentle smile on his lips.

'You never told me,' said Jack, 'how you came to be in Switzerland. Did you take your vows there?'

'Yes. My father was the same as *Señor* Moorgate. Your father too, I think. *Un banquero.*' Jack wished that he could speak with her about his father. *Really* speak with her, but the young nun was in full flow. 'He travel to Switzerland many times. I wanted to study medicine. But my mother was very devout. And *Papa*, he believe that Spain was finished. Even ten years ago. More. He used to say that Spain was once the greatest country in the world. He did not like the English, *Señor* Telford. He say that England only become rich by stealing. *Piratas*, he call them. He say that Madrid was centre of the whole world when London just a sewer of *Los Tudor.* He say that London was not even fit to be called a sewer when Córdoba and Granada were filled by water gardens, by public fountains, by beautiful palaces. But now all is change. Even ten years ago, it had all gone. And he knew about the Foundation. From his travel. He approach the Mother Superior at Axenstein, Sister Inge Rolfe. And soon, my father and mother send me there. Six months as Postulant. Then a year as *novicia*. And I learn. But only to keep records. Accounts. *Funcionaria*. Administrator. To speak German. English. French. My first vows. Three years more. Soon I must make petition. Is that correct? So that I can make solemn vows.'

'Your parents must be very proud of you,' said Jack.

'My parents? *Mis padres son muertos, Señor.*'

'Dead? I'm sorry. I hadn't realised. How?'

'At Toledo. Two years ago. A shell hit their house.'

'An artillery shell?' said Jack. 'Whose?'

She looked at him with pity.

'Does it matter?' she said. 'They are with Our Lady now.'

The first promise of light had appeared in the eastern sky, not enough to bring them any ease, but a promise. *For a new day's dawning*, thought Jack, *will lift even the most embattled spirit.* The very fabric of optimism. I have survived the night, it seemed to say, and if I can live to see the sun rise once more…

Their captors had stirred too. It was just after six, and the *Jefe* had gone to crouch near Brendan Murphy, disturbing the guide's fragile slumber and peering down into the valley.

Jack had been wondering about whether the Holdens' criticism might, in fact, be justified. It had gnawed at him. Perhaps he *should* have dared more in order to help everybody else. Or was this itself a conceit? One for which Sister María Pereda would condemn him. But he could at least try, could he not? He owed the Holdens nothing, of course. Nor mad Marguerite neither. But Max was decent enough. The Moorgates too, albeit slightly strange. And the Ketterings, though he knew now, as sure as eggs were eggs, that they were certainly not what they seemed. The answer appeared obvious. But he would wait until a more appropriate time. It was their business, after all. And he *was* merely curious. Unless, that was, there happened to be some connection between the Ketterings' secret, a certain fashion heel, and the death of poor Julia. Yet he thought not. Just curious. Sinfully so. Strangely though, he found that he cared most about the very people who seemed to epitomise those things that he especially abhorred. The young nun. The Irish guide. Carter-Holt. Mikel too, in some way.

He looked to find their guard. Watches had been changed during the past hour and it was Encarna who now had the submachine gun again. Jack used hand signals to indicate that he was stiff, wanted to move around, and the *guerrillera* nodded her consent. He stretched himself, rubbed vigorously at his thighs, got the circulation going again. His pantomime had moved him to the middle of the grotto, away from the rest of the group and close enough to the *Jefe* that he could make himself heard without talking too loudly. It was a slim chance, he thought, but maybe not *too* slim. He rehearsed the words one last time.

'*Ĉu ili atakos ree?*' said Jack, quietly. Will they attack again?

There was a pause, then a snort of laughter.

'*¡Coño!*' said the *Jefe*. '*Vi parolas Esperanton, sinjoro Telford.*' You speak Esperanto. '*Kie vi lernis?*' Where did you learn?

'*Ĉe Universitato,*' Jack replied. '*Prezidanto da la societo.*'

'But not Marxist?'

'No, not Marxist. Will they attack?'

'Yes. They will attack again. If I do nothing.'

The *Jefe's* rapid Esperanto caused Jack to frown in concentration. 'And what will you do?'

'Send a message.'

'Will you ask again for food?'

The *Jefe* looked around at his prisoners, then turned and sat with his back to the rock for a few moments, digging at the floor slabs with the front sight of Brendan's automatic. He smiled, but there was no humour in the thing. Then he shouted to one of his men, Curly. The large man with receding hair. He called to Sister María Pereda too, reverting to Spanish.

'Oh,' cried the nun. 'The *Jefe* say that we can eat. I think Mister Telford has perform a miracle.'

Jack ignored the tributes that he received from all quarters, while Curly fetched the remnants of the *chorizo*, bread and cheese that Mikel had fetched, supplemented by a further parcel of cheese that the *guerrilleros* had brought and saved for themselves.

'You're a man of many talents, sure, Mister Telford,' said Brendan. 'A bit of Spanish. And now Esperanto.'

'I've not got much vocabulary left though,' said Jack. 'I'll have to use it sparingly. What about you, Brendan?'

'And what would a good Catholic boy be doing with a language like that?

All the international brotherhood nonsense, now. Doesn't sound like me, does it, Mister Telford?'

The *Jefe* was standing, shielded by the wall of the cave, looking out into the brightening east.

'*¡Teniente!*' he bellowed. He kept repeating the word until, finally, there was a reply from below.

The captives were all busily breaking their long fast, Dorothea still having enough grace to ensure that the food was distributed evenly from the greased paper on which Curly had set their allotted share. The *guerrilleros* watched them with some amusement, eating their own rations near Pelayo's tomb. Jack chewed slowly on a piece of spicy sausage that Sister María Pereda had brought for him, and they stood together, watching for the *Jefe*'s next move. The fellow had the attention of the *Civiles* now; it sounded as though he was goading them, shouting at the top of his voice so that it echoed around the valley.

'He ask whether they enjoy their little surprise during the night,' said the nun. 'He ask how many of them will not see the sunrise.'

They were joined by Dorothea Holden, nibbling on some cheese.

'Mister Telford,' she said. 'I simply cannot tell you how grateful...My, whatever is he doing?'

'Sending a message, apparently,' said Jack. 'Sounds like it's going to be a long one.'

'Now he remind the *Teniente*,' said Sister María Pereda, 'that he warn them last night not to do stupid thing. He tell them about the *dinamita*. He say he promise to kill Franco's English friends if they did something foolish.'

'But he hasn't, has he?' whispered Dorothea. 'I think that's described as having one's bluff called, is it not?'

'He say that he is honourable man, who keeps his promise. But he will send down somebody with a new message.'

'He intends to send down a strongly worded note, one assumes,' said Dorothea.

But the *Jefe* had called for Curly again, who untied Brendan's ropes, helped him to his feet. The guide staggered momentarily, then held himself upright with the railings to assist him. The leader of the *guerrilleros* spoke to him. The Irishman responded, glanced north as the bells of the Basilica began to call the faithful to prayer. Lauds, Jack thought it must have been.

'I think he ask Mister Murphy if he understand. That he must take the message. He say better than the alternative.'

'And Mister Murphy has agreed, I gather?' asked Dorothea. 'I do hope so. I wonder whether he might ask for some sanitary paper?'

'What did he say?' said Jack. 'I couldn't catch it.'

'I am not sure,' replied the nun. 'It sound like he say that he misses the front. But perhaps...'

Jack found that he could not remember the Esperanto word for food. That he was overtaken by a sense of panic.

'Jefe,' he said. '*La kolbaso.*' The sausage. '*Dankon!*' Thanks. 'But what are you doing?'

'I told you. We send a message. It is important. To show we are strong. We make a promise, we keep a promise. You understand, *sinjoro* Telford?'

Jack realised the significance. He looked at Brendan Murphy.

'Brendan…' he said. But he could think of nothing else to add.

'No, Mister Telford. It's not a problem, sure. I knew when those silly sods attacked last night. Please, just let it go.'

The *Jefe* lifted the automatic. Brendan straightened his uniform, moved uncomfortably in the trousers still damp from earlier in the night. But, to Jack, the man visibly succeeded in rallying his dignity. *My father,* he thought. *Did he summon reserves of courage in the end too? Or was he simply swamped by cowardice?*

'*¿Comprende, fascista?*' said the *guerrillero.*

Brendan nodded.

'Understand?' said Dorothea. 'Understand *what*, Mister Murphy? He hasn't given you any message yet.'

'No, ma'am,' replied Brendan Murphy. 'I *am* the message.'

Chapter Eighteen

Sunday 25 September 1938

The Irishman, Brendan Murphy, died at precisely nine minutes past seven on Sunday morning, the twenty-fifth of September. Jack Telford considered it his duty to note the hour, the circumstance, for future reference. The guide's head jerked to the left, so quickly that Jack could not be sure whether it was the bullet or a broken neck that might most accurately be described as the cause of death. Then Murphy sat against the top of the railing, stood for a moment, arms hanging limp at his sides, and toppled backwards out into the abyss. There was a splash. And silence.

Dorothea Holden screamed.

She screamed, Jack thought, for *all* of them. For their shock and their horror. Another death, twelve hours or so after that of Sister Berthe Schultz. But a second death so very different from the first. He could scarcely believe how quickly he had come to categorise the nun's demise as just another accident.

Dorothea screamed, he saw, for the mess that had spattered across her husband's face as he cowered, heaving against his bonds. 'I'm next,' he cried in fear, as though he expected the *guerrilleros* to physically shift him to the space so recently vacated by the guide.

She screamed and disturbed the first crows of morning, that called back to her across the valley, alarmed, rising as darker angels against the aurora's murk to escape whatever vicious predator might be stalking them.

She screamed for all those emotions that roiled about Jack's brain. The entirely irrational feeling of guilt. That he had somehow provoked Brendan Murphy's death through his fervent desire that he would find some empathy here with his captors. So that here he might discover reason. Structured paragraphs would flow from his pen in neat order to explain the Red Terror, to condemn the White. But those that he had already written, that should be sleeping peacefully in his notebook back at the Gran Hotel Pelayo, suddenly appeared before him and slipped into the chasm. And he knew that, in war, there was simply one truth. The most primal of human instincts. That you identified your mortal enemies, those who would kill *you* without hesitation, and you killed them first. That to be at war, you did not need to be in uniform. And that *this* war, as he had so frequently been reminded, had begun *long* before Franco's insurrection. The rest was just political and philosophical cant, but, all the same, Jack Telford's world became an empty void at that moment. All the good things he had ever known. They all died with Brendan Murphy. And Jack wanted to be anywhere else except here in the *Cueva de la Santina*. Anywhere.

There was a flurry of activity below, more commands, boots on cobbles, raised voices at the pool's edge, the sound of somebody wading in water, the splashing as they recovered Murphy's corpse.

The *Jefe* turned the pistol sideways, examined it, pursed his lips. Not bad, his expression seemed to say. Not bad at all. Then he put the thing in his jacket pocket, quickly looked over the railing, spat and turned to find Jack staring at him.

'*Kial?*' Why? said Jack.

'I told you why, *sinjoro Anglo*.'

'It is not your fault, *Señor* Telford,' said Sister María Pereda.

'Isn't it?' Jack replied. *I wonder. And what was that little act with Carter-Holt? What did he mean by saying I would make a good soldier? Me, a pacifist!*

'No,' said the nun. 'No more than the death of Sister Berthe Schultz was mine.'

Jack looked around the others. A tear had run down Weston's pippin cheeks, his funny farmer's features transformed to a tragic mask. Max was holding Marguerite, whose head was buried in the comedian's shoulder, her mess of curls tumbling across his encircling arm, pieces of bread and cheese dropped at her knees. She complained that her head hurt. It hurt so badly. Frances Moorgate stood in her black slicker, hands clasped to either side of her face, pressed against the long, raven hair, those deep purple nails like a tiara across her brow, eyes shut tight against the horror. Her husband, this new husband, stood a little uselessly to one side, the Fedora clutched before him. The Ketterings knelt, side by side, turned towards the altar. Unable, it seemed, to share the scene. And Mikel Iruko Domínguez wept bitterly, in a rage contained only by Encarna's submachine gun held to his heaving breast, and by Valerie Carter-Holt's restraining hand as she pulled the driver away from danger, soothing him.

Time passed, with little spoken between them. Dorothea was given leave to wipe Brendan's blood and brain from the Professor's face. The *guerrilleros* held another debate, seemingly to decide whether one of the other *rehenes* should take the guide's place at the rail, for they were more cautious now about exposing themselves in the daylight. Fear of snipers, Jack supposed. But, in the end, the *Jefe* seemed to persuade them that it was an unnecessary precaution and they resumed their normal activities. Curly and Larry were stationed at different points to guard the prisoners, Moe and Encarna rested, the *Jefe* checked his wiring and the dynamite. The prisoners sat closer together, joining the Ketterings near the altar.

And then, at around eight, Encarna whistled, pointed down the steps from her vantage point. There were sounds from below and somebody calling up to them. In Spanish. But it was a clipped Oxbridge Spanish. Fluent enough, but surely the voice of the British Vice-Consul from San Sebastián.

The captives seemed to feel a unifying sense of relief, thought Jack. His Britannic Majesty's representative come to save them. There could not have been such joy since Ladysmith, surely. There were no bagpipes in the distance, no *Highland Laddie* to signal the arrival of a kilted column, no jingle of harness to accompany the lancers' swagger, no Coldstream Guards, no Royal Horse Artillery, no Union Jack. But, by God, there *was* Harold Fielding. Surely their ordeal would now soon be over. They tried to rise, to move towards the railings, to savour the moment, but were forced to sit again, to remain silent. Blessed relief though, all the same. At least, for everybody except Sister María Pereda.

'He introduce himself,' she said, Jack and the others eager for every word. 'He say he must check that all British citizens are safe.' She looked crestfallen.

'I'm sure he means you too, my dear,' said Dorothea Holden. 'You're one of us now. Well, almost.'

'The *Jefe* ask him,' the nun continued, 'whether he has come to negotiate. *Señor* Fielding says he does not have that *escrito*...'

'Brief?' said Carter-Holt.

'Yes, brief. But he say him that if the *Jefe* wants to list his demands, he will pass them on. The *Jefe* tell him to come up and they will talk. *Señor* Fielding say that he cannot. That his superiors fear he will also become prisoner. The *Jefe* say that he will only talk face to face. *Señor* Fielding say him that it is too difficult. That a priest has been killed. And a nun. He means Sister Berthe Schultz, I think. That the *Civiles* found their bodies in the tunnel. That some *Civiles* too were killed.' The *guerrilleros* looked at each other with some satisfaction. 'And now the tour guide, he say. An Irish man. He say this make things *complicado*.'

'*¡Falangista maldito!*' muttered Encarna.

'The *Jefe* tell *Señor* Fielding that he has his word. As an honourable man.' The Holdens snorted in concert. 'He say that no harm will come to *Señor* Fielding. That it make sense for Englishman to negotiate for English lives. As a neutral power, he says.'

'Well,' said Peter Kettering, 'he seems to find it all bloody amusing. We *are* a neutral power, aren't we?'

'There seems to be a certain belief on the Republican side that Britain may not be quite so neutral as she appears,' said Carter-Holt. 'According to some of my Reuters colleagues, that is. They claim that, in the early stages, Britain was supplying ammunition to the Nationalists through Gibraltar. That the Royal Navy may have been supplying intelligence to the Germans about Russian arms shipment to the other side. That *El Caudillo* could not have progressed without oil and vital credit from British businesses. That the British Ambassador in Paris was especially helpful in preventing the French from actively supporting the Republic. That the British have turned a blind eye to every infringement of the Non-Intervention Agreement, even when her own shipping was being sunk in the Med by the Italians. Oh, and of course that's not even to mention that it was an English pilot that flew from Croydon to the Canary Islands, collected General Franco and General Mola and took them to Morocco so that they could start the *Reconquista*. Cecil Bebb, wasn't it? The pilot, I mean. And all arranged by your friend, Jerrold, they say, Mrs Holden.'

'Oh, Douglas has a legitimate interest in the issue,' protested Dorothea. 'He edits the *Catholic Review*, you know. But the story is nonsense, of course. Captain Bebb was merely on a pleasure flight. It's all been fully explained.'

'Yes,' said the Professor. 'Even had two young ladies with him.'

'Two young ladies,' said Valerie, 'and a certain Major Hugh Pollard, an intimate of His Majesty's Intelligence Services, according to my sources.'

'My dear girl,' said Dorothea. 'Hardly an intimate. Such conspiracy. Such careless gossip. And from a supporter of the *Generalísimo* too!'

'I was simply trying to explain why these bandits may not have quite as much faith in British neutrality, Mrs Holden. From *their* viewpoint, naturally.'

Jack should have felt pleased at this falling out amongst thieves but he took no satisfaction from the exchange. He felt himself obliged to underline Douglas Jerrold's active membership of the Anglo-German Fellowship, his connections with 'high office' at Government level, but he constrained himself. During his time at the *Mirror*, one of his colleagues had tried to establish a link between the Government and Bebb's De Havilland *Dragon Rapide* trip but, of course, each of the trails proved false, cold. Though one day, perhaps...

Poor Sister María Pereda had pressed on regardless with her commentary.

'I *do* apologise,' Dorothea said to her. 'How rude of us!'

'*¡No pasa nada!*' said the nun. '*Señor* Fielding has agreed to come up. But he will stay outside, he say. For now. On the balcony. But he tell the *Jefe* that if there are any *trampas*...Tricks? Yes. If there are any tricks, that his Government will hunt them down. He is official diplomat, he say. An attack on his person is attack against Britain herself. Against London.'

The *Jefe* did not seem especially troubled by the threat but he waved for the Vice-Consul to climb the stairs and, a few minutes later, the pale linen suit and Panama hat of a sweating Harold Fielding appeared on the other side of the outer gate. He set down a small wooden crate that he was carrying and removed the Panama, mopping his brow, smoothing the pomaded hair.

'Well,' he said, 'it hardly seems appropriate to wish you good morning, ladies and gentlemen. What a pass, eh?'

He craned his neck, holding the bars and peering up obliquely towards them, gazing from one to the other. *What a sight we must look*, thought Jack. *A bit different from our last meeting, I'll bet.* And he tried to see his fellow-captives as Fielding must be seeing them.

'You find us not quite at our best, Mister Fielding,' called Dorothea. She had splashed some water on her face earlier in the morning, then rummaged in her lizard-skin handbag for her compact, yet lacked any enthusiasm to apply the powder. The finger waves which should have lasted a week were becoming merely a straggle of loose strands.

'We weren't expecting visitors so early,' said Frances, crossing her arms to pull her raincoat more tightly closed, wrapping herself in the black fabric as though trying to hide. But the coat had acquired a layer of dust, its sheen vanished. Her dark lipstick had smudged too, showing just a hint of the pale pink beneath.

'Naughty man!' pouted Marguerite. 'You should 'ave given us some notice you was comin'. Shouldn't 'e, girls?' She had assumed something of her normal pose, distanced from Max, yet she looked as though she had somehow come undone. Her flowered print frock seemed to have unpicked itself at the seams. She shifted uncomfortably, adjusting the shoulders, the bust, the waist, the hem. But at least the pin curls were natural, and bounced back into place as she quickly ran fingers through them. Yet within a few moments, she was sobbing again.

Catherine Kettering went to support her. She had run a comb through her own locks so that they were almost straight, lifeless, while Carter-Holt's darker imitation of Joan Crawford had remained remarkably untouched by the night's tribulations. Her Lyle and Scott twinset, however, had definitely seen better days, despite the mackintosh which should have protected its navy wool.

Sister María Pereda, by contrast, seemed as fresh as the new day's blossoming light.

'Ah, Sister,' said Fielding. 'I am so *very* sorry to hear about your colleague. It must have been an awful shock. And then that fiasco during the night. But at least they had the presence of mind to recover poor Sister Berthe before they retreated. The priest too. I will make a full report to the Swiss Attaché, naturally. He will, I am sure, contact your Order straight away. Did she have family, do you know?' Sister María Pereda thought not. 'And then there is Mister Murphy, of course. The authorities in Burgos will do whatever is necessary, but the Consulate will be expected to contact Dublin, naturally. Something of an embarrassment, to be honest.'

'An embarrassment, Mister Fielding?' said Jack. None of the others seemed to have picked up on the remark. But, then, his male companions had sunk into their own forms of despair, as though they, in turn, were embarrassed by the Vice-Consul's presence. The proud cockerels unable to defend their own farmyard, their own brood of hens. Max had sat on the ground, scrubbing at his tear-stained face. Albert stood like a flamingo, trying to polish the uppers of his right shoe against the back of his left trouser leg. Holden's chin had dropped to his chest. Peter Kettering looked lost without Catherine at his side, for she continued to fuss around Marguerite Weston. And Mikel had disappeared into the former chapel.

'My goodness,' said Fielding. 'That's a little ripe, isn't it? No sanitation up here, I suppose. And yes, old man, an embarrassment. De Valera tried to prohibit Irish involvement in the war. Then had to stand by while O'Duffy raised his Blueshirts for Franco. I assume that's how Mister Murphy came to be here, by the way? The whole issue blew up again when Frank Ryan raised the Connolly Column for the Republic. Though there's no doubt that the *Taoiseach*'s real sympathies lie that way too. He's half-Spanish, isn't he? Well, half-Cuban anyway. Then O'Duffy's men turn up back at Dun Laoghaire in shame. There's all the international furore about Ryan's death sentence in Burgos, and De Valera forced to make a stand on the issue. And now he'll have all this publicity when Mister Murphy's body is shipped home, presumably with the Catholic Bishops demanding that he should be classed as a martyr.'

'Damned awkward for him,' said Jack.

'Well, yes,' Fielding replied, then turned to exchange some words with the *guerrillero* leader. 'Ah, fine,' the Vice-Consul continued. 'I brought up a few goodies. Just a few. And the *compañero* here says that I can distribute them. A concession, you see?' he whispered. 'Always good to get the other fellow to make the initial move, don't you think? Need to see which side blinks first, eh? It sets the tone for everything that follows. Now, what have we got?' He lifted the wooden crate he had brought and Curly was allowed to unlock both gates so that he could receive the contents. 'Need to get our priorities right,' he smiled, showing the first item to the *Jefe*. 'Two tins of fifty.' One hundred *Senior Service*. The circular tins, familiar white and blue wrappers, the sailing ship *motif*, the laurel leaves. *Such a simple comfort*, Jack thought. 'All we could muster, I'm afraid,' said Fielding. 'A decent single malt, though. *Glenfiddich* alright? Could only spare one bottle, of course. Two blankets. No food though. Maybe next trip if all goes according to plan.' He winked at them.

'Next trip?' said Dorothea. 'You mean we have to *stay* here, Mister Fielding?'

'I fear so, dear lady. It's a tricky situation, you see. I was just explaining to our Spanish friend exactly *how* tricky it is. These fellows have pulled off some audacious things in the past but this one's a bit new for *all* of us. Foreign nationals, you see? And the position of His Majesty's Government none too clear just now. Shouldn't be telling you this, really, I suppose.'

'And what exactly do you mean by *these fellows*, Mister Fielding? They make a habit of this?' said Peter Kettering.

'But *Señor* de Armas Gourié assured us,' protested Dorothea Holden, 'that the entire region is now under the safe control of National Spain.'

'Gilding the lily just a *bit*, I'm afraid,' said Fielding. 'These are some of the remnants from the Republican Army of the North. They claim that there are a thousand of them hiding out here in the Picos. Anarchists, naturally. This lot call themselves the *Machados*.'

'*Machados*?' queried Jack.

'After the poet,' said Fielding.

The *Jefe* heard the reference, directed a question at the Vice-Consul. There was a discussion.

'Is everything alright, Mister Fielding?' said Dorothea.

'Yes, good lady. But he wants me to take their demands to the authorities. Don't want to upset him. Mustn't chat for too long.'

'But if you leave us here,' she said, 'the *Civiles* won't do anything foolish again, will they?'

'It's not just the *Civiles* now,' said Fielding. 'They were moving troops into Covadonga all night. It's not widely known but there are fifteen *tabores* of Moroccan *Regulares* and eight battalions of infantry in Asturias alone doing nothing but trying to track these fellows down.'

'You sound as though you admire them, Mister Fielding,' said Peter Kettering. 'Do I have to remind you that these bandits are holding us captive?

They've already murdered one priest, one nun and our guide. And Heaven only knows who'll be next.'

'Good gracious, Mister Kettering. This is a case for cool heads.'

'I'm sorry, Mister Fielding,' said Jack. 'But have these *Machados* actually achieved anything notable? I've never heard of them.'

'More than you might have expected, Mister Telford. The Republicans created their Guerrilla Army Corps last October. But Negrín hasn't given them much tangible support. All the same, a bunch of the rascals attacked the Carchuna Fortress down in the south and sprang three hundred Asturian prisoners. There were some Internationals involved. A Finn. A couple of Yanks from the Lincoln Battalion. But down to business, I think. Negotiations to conduct. Pretend that we haven't started yet. But we *have*, of course. *Bien, compañero,*' he said to the *Jefe*.

'Whose side is that fellow *on*?' whispered Alfred Holden, as the Vice-Consul began the negotiating process. Or rather, he leaned on the bars as though it were a gentleman farmer's gate and he was exchanging pleasantries about the suitability of the weather for harvesting this year's crop. But, Jack noticed, whenever the *Jefe*'s eyes were averted, Fielding's would instantly scan the cavern and its surroundings, as though registering the details, the positions taken by the *guerrilleros*, the weapons at their disposal, the location of the captives, the dynamite and its wiring, the detonation system. His eye-lids snapped at each detail, like the shutter on Carter-Holt's Agfa Box Forty-Four. And Jack noticed, too, the way that Vice-Consul Fielding's gaze would stray periodically to Valerie. The way that she would always be ready to catch and return the glance.

There was a pause in the proceedings while Fielding produced his gold cigarette case, passed a *Du Maurier* to Curly for the *Jefe* while the latter gathered the other *Machados* for a short consultation. The captives, of course, remained under careful vigilance throughout.

'I was just explaining,' said the Vice-Consul, 'that the Lieutenant who ordered last night's attack by the *Civiles* is obviously no longer in charge down below. Your old friend *Teniente* Álvaro Enrique Turbides arrived early this morning with me but his duties are restricted to the investigation into Miss Britten's death. More of that anon, by the way. There's a Colonel here now, in charge of the regular troops, but he has orders to wait for a decision from Burgos about overall command, though it looks like that might be the Military Governor. Hard-nosed fellow. They know him, of course.'

'Have they said what they want yet?' said Albert Moorgate.

'Afraid not. They'll get to it in good time, I imagine. Just now, they seem more intent on knowing whether there are any journalists down there. As if the *Caudillo* would allow an independent journalist within a dozen miles of the place, eh? There was never a word about the prison-break at Carchuna in any of the Nationalist press. Can't blame them, really. Funny thing, of course, is that Burgos will be *just* as worried that we have two journalists of our very own being held among the hostages. Ah, here we go again.'

The *Jefe* had returned to the low barrier, though still making sure that he was protected by the grotto wall from any prying eyes down in the valley or around the Basilica.

The discussion continued, back and forth, for some time until Harold Fielding finally slapped the gate, beamed at the *Jefe* and held up his thumb to seal whatever agreement had been reached.

'Good news, Mister Fielding?' said Dorothea.

'Oh, the best, ma'am. Principles established. That's the main thing.'

'Principles?' she repeated.

'Yes, dear lady. Incredibly important. And mustn't rush things along too quickly. D'you follow my drift?' He tapped the side of his nose.

'No, not really.' Dorothea looked lost, tried to tidy her hair. 'I thought that we might have been released by now.'

'It appears,' said Fielding, 'that you might have to be patient for a while longer, Mrs Holden. After all, I have no official status in this thing. I have no problem about conducting the negotiations but it is difficult. I can't really agree *anything* without the say-so from Burgos, but then the *Generalísimo* may just feel slightly constrained by you all being British citizens. Well, with the exception of two people, anyway.' He beamed a smile at Sister María Pereda and at Mikel.

'But *do* you know what they want?' snapped Moorgate.

'Oh, yes,' said Fielding. 'But just a moment!' He turned to speak again with the *Jefe*. The *guerrillero* leader shrugged. 'Protocol, you know. Needed to check whether he had any problem with me sharing the demands. Can never tell whether these fellows speak more English than they let on. Anyway, in a nutshell, he's given me details of three different prisons from which they want people released. Asturians mostly. But they also want Juan de Ajuriaguerra released from the prison at Burgos and brought here. He's the chap that signed the Basque surrender at Santoña. He...'

'Yes, we remember the story, Mister Fielding,' said Dorothea. 'But brought here for what purpose? And what about us?'

'Well, their plan is that Ajuriaguerra comes here, they load him and all of you onto the old yellow bus, then off you go together to the French border. Once across, they wait for word that their other fellows are free and then – well, that's about it. Oh, and they want some news coverage.'

'But that could all take days,' said Catherine Kettering. 'Weeks even.'

'Jumping the gun, Mrs Kettering, I'm afraid,' said Fielding. 'No idea yet whether Burgos will even entertain the idea. Bound to have some views of their own, eh? And will certainly want some proof of good faith, I imagine.'

'What sort of proof?' said Jack.

'No idea, old man. But we'll find out soon enough. Better trot off and deliver the news, don't you think?'

'You mentioned principles, Mister Fielding,' said Dorothea. 'What were they, exactly?'

'Oh, the usual things. All negotiations face to face. Him and me. At the inner gate in future. No abuse of the captives. Yourselves, in this case. Your driver fellow to be used as the messenger if one is needed. To fetch medical assistance should it become necessary. Food, that sort of thing.'

'And...?' Dorothea hesitated.

'Yes, dear lady,' whispered the Vice-Consul. 'Never fear. The best quality that the Gran Hotel Pelayo has to offer. I hope to be back very shortly, but anything else in the meantime?'

'Newspaper,' said Jack. Dorothea looked at him, puzzled. 'To read, I mean. Anything will do. We can always translate.'

'Ah,' said Fielding. 'You don't know then? No, I wouldn't suppose...'

'Know what?' said Alfred Holden.

'Bad news, I'm afraid. Came across the wires yesterday. Talks have broken down between Herr Hitler and the PM. Czechs and Hungarians mobilising their armies. France and Germany too. The Führer simply refuses to say that he won't just take the Sudetenland by force. And he's given us an ultimatum. Negotiations to be successfully completed within a week or else. Strange parallel, don't you think? And what about this rain! Hope it won't get any worse.'

He looked once at his expensive Italian shoes, then was off down the stairs, leaving the captives with the deepest sense of loss. Morning mist rose from the trees, carrying the essence of pine and resin. A thin drizzle fell.

'It reminds me of Argyll,' said Carter-Holt.

But Jack considered the news. What had Fielding meant when he said that the position of the British Government was now less than clear? Had it been affected so quickly by the Sudeten development? Was Chamberlain finally beginning to see, as Churchill had tried to impress upon him, that alliance with the Soviets might be a more worthwhile prospect than appeasement of the Germans? If so, it could well affect the British stance on Spain. It was in their power still to stop the Germans and Italians having such a free hand here. Though too late for the Republic, surely?

The morning passed slowly. Very slowly. Dorothea recalled that it was Sunday again, suggested that they should pray together. For departed souls, that sort of thing. Perhaps a communal hymn. But it was a hasty and unenthusiastic service. There was a sense of abandonment amongst the group far worse than they had felt during the night. Jack put it down to lack of sleep, to the aftermath of Murphy's assassination, but he knew that it was also due to Harold Fielding. They had expected salvation, yet he had gone and they remained. How could this be? Britons were inviolate, surely? Could not be enslaved in this way.

At exactly ten o' clock, as though by prior arrangement, Mikel was sent down to collect food, returned with another parcel fifteen minutes later. More bread and cured meat. And when it was shared out by Encarna, Jack noticed that the Moorgates and Catherine Kettering chose to eat their own rations in company with the *guerrilleros*, that the *Machados* seemed content with their company. They even managed to tease a few words of Spanish from Albert, the first that he had uttered during the whole trip, so that he was clumsily able to explain his time in Barcelona.

Jack took his own portion and sat with them too. Catherine edged sideways, made room for him.

'Peter not joining you?' he said.

'No, apparently not. He thinks we should stay well away from *these people*, as he calls them. But I told him. At least they're feeding us, I said. It's not right, of course. What they did to poor Mister Murphy. But he *was* a soldier, after all.' Her eyes misted, though Jack believed that it was not for Brendan Murphy.

'And where did you meet your husband, Mrs Kettering? If I'm not being too nosey, that is.' She looked at him, bit her lip.

'I was working in Cambridge. My family had fallen on difficult times during the 'Twenties. So I had to give up school. Got a job as a waitress. He'd been educated at Wellington, then came to Trinity, Cambridge. To read for the bar.'

'But I thought that Peter…'

She looked him squarely in the eye.

'Peter isn't my husband, Mister Telford,' she whispered. 'But I think you already know that.'

'Donald?' said Jack, quietly. He remembered Brendan Murphy telling him about the coincidence. That Donald Kettering's wife was *also* called Catherine.

'Yes,' she replied. 'They were both born in Polynesia, you know. Their father was a circuit judge. Donald used to thrill me with stories of giant turtles, native canoes, shark tamers. Saw himself as something of a social revolutionary. And very devout. Deeply religious but an active union man all his life. But the rise of Communism alarmed Donald. Thought it heralded the end of the Catholic Church. We were married in '33. Never truly happy. Donald met somebody else and I met his brother. Peter was quite charming.'

'He still is. *Most* of the time,' said Jack.

'Yes,' she agreed. 'He is. By the time Donald found out about us, the war had just started here. He was deeply shocked, despite his own little sins. But he said he was even more shocked by the atrocities against his Church that were being reported from here. Before I knew it, he'd arranged to come to Spain. He joined a Carlist unit first. That would have been November '36. And then I heard that he'd been transferred to the Spanish Foreign Legion. It was *so* like him. Very *Beau Geste*. And then came the news that he'd died. The telegram. This July a letter from the Nationalist Government. They wanted to award a medal. The invitation and so on. Peter agreed to bring me, Mister Telford. But I'm not sure why I'm here. Not really. The place scares me, if I'm honest. And I can't help feeling that Donald *chose* to die here.'

'You blame yourself?'

She smiled.

'The guilty wife? No, Mister Telford. Peter blames himself, I think. He is more prone to Catholic guilt than me. But I suspect, like you, that it's just the war that's to blame. And General Franco, of course. For starting it, I mean.'

'But you'll accept the medal?'

'It's Donald's medal, Mister Telford. Of course I'll accept it. With as much grace as I can muster. If we ever get out of here, naturally.'

Jack thought for a moment, chewed on a piece of tough smoked ham.

'Do you mind if I ask you something?' he said.

'Julia Britten again? I should have told you last time you asked. But my own little affairs all seemed so much more important then. More private. Now... Anyway, yes, Miss Britten knew about Peter and me. She'd overheard something that I'd said to him. She was very astute, wasn't she? And concerned. It was mostly concern. She thought it might be difficult for me if it came out somehow. Just offered me a sisterly shoulder, really. Dear woman.'

'Yes,' said Jack. *And hardly a reason for murder.*

'I say, Telford,' shouted Albert Moorgate. 'You have a few words of the lingo, don't you? And that other gibberish you speak too. Any chance of explaining a couple of things for me?'

'Of course,' Jack agreed. Bertie was enthusiastically talking about the intricacies of his job. The concept of mortgage. But Frances, he noticed, was somewhere else. Her vacant eyes looked towards that empty section of railing where once had sat a very different man.

It was two hours later when Vice-Consul Harold Fielding finally returned. They brought him up to the inner gate and searched him. There was a long but apparently amicable discussion with the *Jefe* and he, in turn, opened another debate with the rest of the *Machados*.

'Well,' said Fielding, 'so far things couldn't look better. The military managed to patch me through to Burgos, and General Franco's office has confirmed that I should continue to undertake the negotiations. I have a free hand in the matter. Well, almost!'

'Almost?' queried Peter Kettering.

'Yes. Subject to the requirements of the military here on the ground, naturally. And the ultimate sanction of the good General.'

'That's a free hand?' said Jack.

'One could hardly expect anything better, Mister Telford. No, I am extremely happy with the situation.'

'And the *Jefe*'s demands?' said Dorothea. 'They will be met? We will return to the French border, as you suggested?'

'Now *there*, I'm afraid, you will all have to be patient. There are two considerations. First, the officers down below only have provisional authority. To act purely in the case of any unforeseen situation. Thankfully, that will all change when the Military Governor arrives later this evening.'

'And then we shall be on our way to France?' said Kettering.

'Heavens, I shouldn't think so. No, the Military Governor will be charged with making a proper assessment of his own. With analysing the progress made in the negotiations. He'll then have to report to Burgos.'

'Mister Fielding,' said Carter-Holt, 'you must forgive me but these feel like delaying tactics.'

'Dear lady, please,' hissed the Vice-Consul. 'Not so loud, I beg you. Why should you think such a thing?'

'And meanwhile we stay in this filthy place?' said Alfred Holden.

'Well, in your own case, Professor, I am going to insist that you should be untied and allowed to join the others. But, for the time being, I've given these fellows a couple of more difficult things to think about.'

'And those are?' said Jack.

'Well, for one thing, General Franco's office has indeed asked for some proof of good faith. They wouldn't normally bargain in this way, you understand. So Burgos has suggested that some of you might be released as a gesture of goodwill. Or perhaps that the *guerrilleros* should dismantle their explosives. The threat to the shrine seems to weigh very heavily on the *Caudillo*.'

'More heavily than his concern for our safety, presumably,' said Catherine Kettering.

'I'm sure that's not the case, Mrs Kettering,' said Fielding. 'And I've tried to push the former suggestion a bit more. After all, a bus journey all the way back to the border with the whole group of you *and* these *Machados*, plus *Señor* de Ajuriaguerra, even without…Well, you'll take my drift. Ah, it looks like they might have reached a decision. Excuse me, won't you?'

The *Jefe* had returned to the bargaining fence.

'Some of us may be released then,' said Dorothea Holden. 'I suppose we should make some preparations. Decide who deserves to remain behind.'

'Well me an' Max, we 'as to meet General Franco,' insisted Marguerite. 'We can't be gettin' back on no bus.'

'*Most* of us have an appointment with the *Caudillo*, Mrs Weston,' said Peter Kettering. 'We'll need a different set of criteria, I'm afraid.'

'Different *what*?' Marguerite looked confused. Max searched for a joke, was unable to find one.

'My husband is certainly in no fit state to cope with further anxiety,' said Dorothea. 'There should be no question about it.'

'I have to be in Santiago as well,' said Carter-Holt, apparently and unusually suffering anxieties of her own.

'Do you?' said Jack. 'I'd assumed you were only along to cover the group's story for Reuters. Surely the real story is going to be on the bus. So you can leave *me* out of the selection process anyway.'

'How very noble of you, Telford,' sneered the Professor. 'I'm sure you'll feel more at home staying with your Bolshevik friends anyway.'

'I don't *think* they're Bolsheviks, somehow,' Jack replied, as Mikel was summoned over by the *guerrillero* leader.

'Now what can they possibly want with Mikel?' said Frances Moorgate.

Sister María Pereda smiled at them.

'They ask him how many seats are on the bus,' she whispered.

Albert Moorgate, Peter Kettering and Dorothea Holden each began counting heads at the same time.

'Oh dear,' said Dorothea. 'I'd quite forgotten...'

The *Jefe* dismissed Mikel, shook hands with Harold Fielding, and went to join his comrades, while the captives crowded around the gate.

'Well,' said the Vice-Consul. 'Mixed news, I think. Some bad, some good.'

'I think we've already worked out the bad news, Mister Fielding,' said Dorothea. 'There seem to be enough spaces on the bus, now, for all of us that are left, plus the *Jefe* and his friends. Including Ajuriaguerra. That's supposing *El Caudillo* agrees to his release, of course.'

'Indeed, Mrs Holden. You seem to have smoked the thing. But at least they've agreed that your husband should be untied. And they're happy for Mikel to collect some more food. Sunday lunch, eh? Spanish are very strong on it, you understand. And I happen to know that there's an excellent stew being prepared for you down at the hotel. As we speak. Almost wish I could join you, to be honest.'

Jack pictured a barometer hanging on the wall of the cave. But in his mind's eye, this particular instrument measured the atmospheric morale of the captives. And the needle, which the hope of release for at least a few had momentarily swung upwards towards 'Change', had now plummeted again, back to 'Stormy'.

'Is that the sum total of the good news, old boy?' said Bertie Moorgate. 'It seems like only the most marginal progress.'

'Not at all, Mister Moorgate,' Fielding replied. He looked quite offended that his negotiating skills had been questioned. 'No. I told you that there was some good news, did I not? And you recall that I mentioned some proof of good faith? That Burgos might look more favourably on their demands if the *Machados* made some sort of concession?'

The barometer's needle flickered again.

'Yes, Mister Fielding?' said Dorothea.

'Well,' whispered the Vice-Consul, his excitement barely constrained, 'it *seems* as though they know the whereabouts of the Virgin. Of the *Santina* herself. And they may be prepared to divulge their secret.'

The hostages looked at each other in disbelief and even Jack felt a sense of betrayal. But, at his side, the young nun fell to her knees, giving thanks to God for this divine intervention and claiming that she could feel the sacrificed spirit of Sister Berthe Schultz at work in the miracle.

Chapter Nineteen

Sunday 25 September 1938

It was the best stew that Jack had ever tasted. It arrived in an iron pot, a cloth wrapped around the lifting handle so that Mikel could manage it without burning his hands. On his back was a small satchel. Fresh bread. Small ceramic bowls to drink from. And, at Dorothea's request, the hygienic paper. Manufactured in Bilbao. The *motif* of *Papelera Española SA* on each pack, along with the company's symbol: a rampaging elephant. Three packs of four hundred sheets. 'How long might this siege last?' they asked each other as they supped at their *cocido*.

The cook at the Gran Hotel Pelayo had gently fried the garlic and onion, the chopped chorizo, the chunks of ham, then simmered them in a rich stock with cabbage leaves, celery, potato, carrot, chickpeas and coriander. Or was it chilli? Jack was unsure.

Vice-Consul Harold Fielding had left them with a cheery wave of his hand and wished them '*bon appétit*'. They had been angry, but not *so* angry that they forgot to shout their last requests. A newspaper. More cigarettes. A razor. Some firewood. A pack of cards, perhaps. To help them pass the time. But they had no idea when he might return.

Thus time had now become their principal enemy.

I wasted time, and now doth time waste me, thought Jack. What *was* that? Shakespeare, he knew for certain. But *which*? *Richard the Second? Yes, almost certainly.* The image of an abandoned and betrayed monarch alone in his cell, awaiting an uncertain end, filled his head.

'Damn the fellow,' said Albert Moorgate, as he accepted a chunk of bread from the *guerrillero*, Moe, who sat next to him. 'I shall have something to say about Mister Fielding when we get home.'

'I can't get over how agitated he became,' said Catherine Kettering, 'when Valerie...you don't *mind* if I call you Valerie, my dear? When Valerie mentioned the use of delaying tactics.'

'But why would 'e want to 'old things up, like?' said Max.

'Don't be stupid, Maxie,' replied his wife. 'It's like 'e told us. They wants to see 'oo blinks first.'

'Lull these fellows into a false sense of security,' said Professor Holden, free at last from his ropes. 'Let them think they're winning. And then...'

The *Jefe* spoke.

'He want to know what we are talking about,' said Sister María Pereda. The nun replied to him. Several sentences. 'I tell him that nothing can excuse the murders he has committed. But perhaps Our Lady will find it in her heart to forgive them if they allow the *Santina* to be returned, here, to her shrine. I hope that the army does nothing that might prevent this,' she added.

Jack wanted to remind her that this was something of a misrepresentation, that they had not mentioned the Virgin once, that this was therefore a lie. But he let it go.

'I don't think we should criticise Mister Fielding's negotiating tactics,' said Dorothea. 'Not really. It's a difficult job, after all.'

'Oh, I'm not critical of his negotiating style, Mrs Holden,' said Bertie. 'Can't fault him on that score. He has all the classical skills of the diplomat. Never actually says no to anything. Keeps the thing positive. Never even a suggestion that these fellows won't get what they want. No, it's his *loyalty* that I question. Who's he working for, eh? Us, or General Franco?'

'Let them think they're winning, and then *what*, Professor?' said Carter-Holt.

'Well, I suppose,' he said, then fell into a whisper, 'they'll try to *dispose* of them, somehow.'

'And us in the firing line,' cried Moorgate. 'Exactly my point. How dare they!'

'The *Jefe* want to know why everybody so angry,' said Sister María Pereda. 'He say do we not like the *cocido*? If so, he will demand that they bring up the cook and he will shoot him.'

They all looked at the man. His left hand was holding the bandolier of bullets that crossed his chest. Then he lifted it, wiped some residue of stew from his heavy black moustache with the tips of his fingers, scratched at the silver stubble on his cheeks. He gazed from one to the other. Eyes chestnut brown, glistening and darting with light and life. And he laughed. He slapped at his knee and laughed.

'Well, me 'ansums,' said Max, 'He 'ad us that time an' no mistake.' And Max laughed too. A hollow, artificial laugh. But he laughed.

And their combined noise set off the crows once again.

The *Jefe*, pleased with himself, set down his bowl, issued some orders. The tunnel was checked, as they did every thirty minutes. Curly and Larry fetched more water from the pipe, careful now since there was no human barricade any longer to provide them with cover. But when it was done, they swilled water in the bowls, set them on the altar to dry.

'He say that we must work too,' said the nun. 'We have to clean in the chapel.'

'You mean…? said Dorothea.

'Yes. He says that the *mess*…That was not his word, but the mess must be collected together. Paper too. Then all burned. He say that the English are a soft people. Not used to cleaning up their own…mess. He say you must learn.'

'Well, I don't think…' Dorothea began.

'It seems perfectly reasonable, Mrs Holden,' said Peter Kettering. 'We can hardly expect the hotel to arrange room service. And we can't put up with that stench. We'll all die of cholera or some damned thing. No, it's time for one of your famous rosters, I think. Men only this time though, I'd suggest. And that includes your husband.'

'Now look here!' protested the Professor.

'Shut up, Alfred,' said his wife. 'You're giving me a headache again. Oh, now there! I wish we'd remembered to ask Mister Fielding for some aspirin.'

The list was produced on the back of a visiting card, Carter-Holt's, with a pencil that came from the correspondent's handbag. Kettering and Telford would work as one team. Holden and Moorgate as the other. Mikel excused duty on the basis that he was not English, for they had decided to take the *Jefe*'s instruction literally. The work to be carried out each evening. For time might be their enemy but, all the same, one way to defeat this foe may be to accept that their confinement would not now be as short as they had hoped. In this way, Jack rationalised, once you understood the nature of a thing, you could begin to deal with its consequences. Overcome them.

So he and Peter found some pieces of crumbling timber in the old sanctuary, found a place where the floor had apparently been hacked away, pushed and shoved amongst the rubble at half-dried turds and evidence of similar bodily wastes to the best of their ability until the hole was half-filled, then swept pine needles on top, the soiled scraps of Mikel's *Gaceta del Norte*, another sheet ripped and twisted into fire-lighters, then set a match to the entire noxious mess. It was a less than satisfactory exercise but it made them feel as though they had recovered some of their dignity. And it was the *Jefe* that they had to thank. Not the vanishing Vice-Consul. It was the *Jefe* who was restoring order from the chaos.

In fact, they would have burned the rest of Mikel's newspaper too. But Jack had spotted the pages dealing with Czechoslovakia and snatched them from Peter Kettering's hands.

'You still think it matters what happens in the Sudetenland?' Peter asked.

But Jack did not answer him. He came out of the chapel, let everybody know that he was taking a *Senior Service*. It was duly noted by Dorothea Holden, now elected as their Quartermaster. And he went to sit alongside Sister María Pereda.

'Would you mind?' he said to her. So she translated.

'It is like Mister Fielding say,' she said. 'Talking between Herr Hitler and Mister Chamberlain broken down. Everybody massing their armies.'

'Do you see?' said Jack. 'Why would the Führer threaten to take by force what has already been offered to him peacefully? Chamberlain has already promised him everything he wants. It can't be true. He'd have to be genuinely mad.'

'Herr Hitler is a man of peace, *Señor* Telford. How can you doubt it? He is a kind man. He loves children. Young people.'

'Yes,' said Dorothea. 'I can vouch for that.'

But an endorsement from Dorothea Holden…

'Yet *you* could entertain us, Mister Telford,' said Carter-Holt. 'Explain your fluency in Esperanto to us. It *is* a Communist-inspired language, is it not? Russian, anyway.'

'I would have expected a Reuters correspondent to know that those two things are not synonymous,' Jack snapped. 'The inventor may have been Russian, but he intended only that harmony could be most easily fostered between the peoples of the world if there was a common language, sophisticated enough to share complex thought but with a grammar that was sufficiently simple for all to grasp.'

'I read that the word *Esperanto* means *one who hopes*,' said Dorothea. 'Is that correct?'

'We must all have hope, *Señora* Holden,' said the nun. 'And faith, of course. Finally, charity. I learn a little of this language too. In Switzerland. Until Herr Alexander say that it is language of the *Rojos*. But I do not agree with him. Peoples begin to speak Esperanto all over the world. In China. Japan. Australia. France. America. Just imagine. If we could all speak with each other.'

'Still sounds like some totalitarian utopia nonsense to me,' said the Professor.

'Can you *sing* in Esperanto, Mister Telford?' asked Frances Moorgate. She had said little or nothing since Brendan's death.

'I don't sing in *any* language, Mrs Moorgate, I'm afraid.'

'Please, Mister Telford. For *me*,' said Frances.

But she means for Brendan Murphy, he thought, without really understanding why.

'Well, there's this, I suppose,' said Jack. 'And you can all join in. You know it?' He began to hum a tune.

'Oh, it's *Alouette*,' cried Frances.

'It was just in one of the lessons,' said Jack. And he nervously began to sing.

'Esperanto, bela Esperanto, Esperanto, lernu ĝin kun ni...'

Most of the others knew the French version, Sister María Pereda thumping out the song as though she were still in the convent. But a familiar refrain to accompany Jack's own rendition.

'Lernu pri la alfabet', Lernu pri la alfabet'. Alfabet', alfabet'. Alfabet', alfabet'. Oooooh...'

The *Machados* looked on in amusement.

'*Tre bona!*' said the Jefe, also in Esperanto. Very good. And he applauded. The others too. '*Ay, Encarna*,' he said to the woman. '*¿Santa Bárbara Bendita?*' She shook her head '*¡Venga!*' He insisted. She shook her head again, gave him a curt reply, but the men began to beat out a rhythm with the palms of their hands, fast and regular with a louder stress every eight beats or so. They kept it up until, at last, Encarna began to sing. She had a good voice, yet while the rhythmic clapping was rapid, the song was slow, tragic, relentless. But it had a phrase, repeated over and over again throughout the many verses. A dramatic line, full of emotion and fire. *Trailarai larai, trailarai*. So that, one by one, the captives understood when it was coming, sang along for the appropriate lines. All except Alfred Holden.

'Nel pozu María Luisa, Trailarai larai, trailarai...'

It continued, verse after verse, until Encarna finally came to an end. But there was no applause this time. It did not seem appropriate.

'*Ésta es una canción, Inglés*,' said the Jefe. *This* is a song. He stood. So did the other *Machados*, and went about their business.

'Some Commie concoction, I dare say,' sneered the Professor.

'No,' said Sister María Pereda, 'though the miners here in Asturias use it during their revolution. No, it is old. A mining song. Holy Santa Bárbara is their saint. Many die in the mines. So the song is words of a miner. His wife is Maruxina. He sing her. In the María Luisa mine, sixteen have died. Look at me, Maruxina. Look how I am coming home. My shirt is red with the blood of miners, Maruxina. Look how I come home. My head is broken in the blast. Look how I come home. Blessed *Santa Bárbara*, patron saint of miners. Many have died and I am one of them. Look, Maruxina. Look how I am coming home.'

'It is *so* sad,' said Frances Moorgate. And Jack knew that it was not *he* that had sung at Brendan Murphy's wake, but this Spanish *guerrillera*, one of those responsible for the Irishman's death. It was a mad world, and he understood it less and less.

Down in the town itself, life seemed to continue its normal pace. The railing was still considered to be a dangerous location for the cave's occupants, particularly since the buildings in front of the grotto were so close, and it was clear that troops were stationed within. But as their confidence grew, and their situation regularised itself, the captives would occasionally relieve their boredom by laying on the rock floor and edging towards the iron bars, so that they could peer into the valley. Then, during the afternoon, the Basilica bells had rung again. People had promenaded. In the distance, admittedly, along the avenue near the hotel, through the sunken parkland. But they had promenaded, all the same. And when Mikel had arrived with the *cocido*, it was as though the townsfolk had received a signal. For within ten or fifteen minutes, they had gone. The streets cleared. Sunday afternoon's family meal. Then their *siesta*. So the hostages did the same. Some strayed towards the rail, watching the troop movements, but most just dozed. It was not especially warm yet they were too starved of sleep to care very much.

At about four o' clock, Jack woke to see Dorothea Holden and Catherine Kettering in a hushed conversation with Sister María Pereda. He strained to catch the drift.

'She has such a beautiful voice,' Dorothea was saying. 'I can't believe that she is simply a mindless killer.'

'It can't do any harm to ask her,' said Catherine. 'We should at least try to find out how she comes to be here.'

'I cannot,' hissed the nun. 'It is the sin of curiosity.'

'We simply needed you to translate, my dear,' said Dorothea. 'The sin would be all our own. Nothing to do with you.'

'But Sister Berthe Schultz would have told me that the act of helping another to sin is a sin in itself.'

'What if this woman has sins of her own?' said Catherine. 'Terrible sins. But has strayed too far from the paths of righteousness to be able to confess them? Is it not our duty to help her? And we can only help her if we know about them. About her life. It is no more curiosity than hearing confession, surely.'

'We are not ordained to hear confession,' protested the nun. 'It is a heresy to even suggest such a thing!'

So the curiosity of Catherine Kettering and Dorothea Holden about the *guerrillera* went unsatisfied, though it troubled Jack that he, too, did not understand what brought these four men and one woman, these *Machados*, to the mountains. He had made some superficial assumptions, initially based on the obvious. That they were remnants of the Republican Army of the North. Basques, Cantabrians, Asturians. Defeated but having avoided death or capture. Cut off perhaps, and forming small groups like these to keep dealing damage or revenge against Franco's forces. Like the *guerrilla* bands from the Peninsular War that Forester had immortalised in *Death to the French* and *The Gun*. These were as much a part of his inherited images of the country as gipsy dancers, donkeys, *mantillas*, bullfights, *Semana Santa* penitents, the Inquisition's *auto da fe*. The Spanish had invented the concept of *guerrilla*, after all, the 'little war', during their struggle to free themselves from Bonaparte. But the idea that the Republican Government, defending itself against Franco's *coup d'état*, should have established its own Guerrilla Army Corps, as Fielding had told them, had come as a surprise. It seemed too organised. To fly in the very face of some principle or other. It did not fit into any of the patterns that he understood.

'*Pri kio vi pensas, sinjoro Anglo?*' said the *Jefe*. What are you thinking, Mister Englishman?

'*Pri Encarna*,' Jack replied. About Encarna.

He had not seen the *Jefe* approach, but he saw now that the man had been rummaging in the workmen's bags, just along from where Jack had been resting. He had taken out a sheepskin-wrapped bundle, perhaps twelve or fifteen inches long, and he held it on his knee now, squatting with his back to the Pelayo tomb.

'*Tabakon?*' said the Jefe, and Jack got up so that he could fetch them both a *Senior Service*.

'Mrs Holden,' shouted Jack. 'I'm taking two. One for the *Jefe*.'

'Very good, Mister Telford,' she replied. 'We shan't set the *Jefe*'s cigarette against your own ration, never fear.' She was still in conversation with Catherine and Sister María Pereda.

'*Ĉu Encarna plaĉas al vi?*' asked the Jefe, as they lit their smokes. Do you like Encarna? Or, more correctly, thought Jack, Does Encarna please you? *Now how does he mean that?*

'She is very fair,' Jack replied, trying to choose his Esperanto carefully. 'She sings beautifully. But sad. Is she your woman?'

The Jefe *laughed*, almost choked, took the *Senior Service* from his lips and admired it.

'Good tobacco,' he said. Then he became serious again. He led Jack across to the other side of the cave, near the tunnel, to the walnut chest used for the collection of donations from the faithful, now the *guerrilleros'* storage cupboard. He sat upon its lid, invited Jack to do the same. 'Why do you ask about Encarna? For your newspaper?'

'Perhaps. There is much that I do not understand.'

'About the *Machados*?'

'Yes,' said Jack. Then he searched for the word he was looking for. He knew that the Republicans used the word *Movimiento* to describe the Nationalists' rebellion. 'But about the Movement too. And the revolution of the workers.'

'About Encarna?'

'Yes. Encarna too.'

'Why should I tell you all this, Mister English? Will it help me? I do not think so. But I will try. Slowly. I will speak slowly in Esperanto.'

'That is good,' said Jack. 'I will follow. To understand.'

'Then this, Mister English. How old is this Encarna?'

Jack gave the woman a cursory glance. Her long hair was prematurely grey, tied in a bun, eyes afire but skin flaking. It was a trick question, naturally. Jack had been in situations like this before. The reports that he had filed during the Hunger Marches. *How old do you think she is?* somebody would ask about a miner's wife here, an unemployed engineer's mother there. You were supposed to guess an age that was less than she looked but more than you thought was factual. It was a game. *So how old? She looks as though she's forty. Probably thirty.*

'*Tridek kvin*,' said Jack. Thirty-five.

'But really you think she is thirty?'

'Perhaps.'

'She is not yet twenty, Mister English. Her father and brother were miners. Franco came to stop their strike. Four years ago. He came with his *Moros*. The *regulares*. They may be the same as down there. In Covadonga. I do not know. But they came to the village of Encarna. They took the men. They marched them away. Encarna was fifteen. She ran to the officer of the *tabor*. She asked where they took her father and brother. So they took her also. They did damage to her. I do not know the word in Esperanto. In Spanish, *una violación*. You understand?'

'Yes, I understand.'

'Not one time. Many times. Over and over. She never saw her father and brother any more. Two years ago, when the Movement began, the priest in her village said to the people that soon all would be better. That General Franco was coming. To take the country back from the Reds. Encarna shot him. She knew what it meant to say that Franco was coming. She had friends. They all knew what it meant too. So they found all the *fascistas* in the village. Thirty of them. They shot them too.'

Jack could not think of the word for a trial.

'*Ĉu ne jura proceso?*' No legal process?

The *Jefe* laughed.

'This game of legal things. Tribunals. Trials. *Checas*. It is a joke. Each of us is responsible for his own action. If he is guilty, he is guilty. And to put him in prison? Better to shoot him.'

Jack's face betrayed him.

'I am sorry,' he said. 'I was not here. It is hard to imagine.'

'Yes, Mister English. Hard. And last year, when she knew that Franco *was* coming, his army here in Asturias again, she joined the *Machados*. To kill *fascistas*.' He was boastful, but there was also a hint of shame. Jack misread the shame. He was a fool, imagined that it was shame for the killings. Yet he was wrong. 'But we cannot have killed *so* many *fascistas*,' the *Jefe* continued. 'See how many of them are still left? *So* many.'

'And you? You were in the strike? Four years ago?'

'I am not from Asturias, Mister English. I am from the south. A *campesino*.'

'You worked on the land?'

'I was a slave. I try to explain. When we make the Republic…' He stood, drew a circle with his boot in the dust and pine needles, marked off about two-thirds. 'This much of the land was owned by twenty men. Men like the Duke of Alba.'

'He is in London now,' said Jack. 'The representative for Franco. With the British Government.'

'You know how much land he owns? Only as Duke of Alba?'

'No.' Jack saw the *Jefe* think carefully about the numbers.

'Thirty-five thousand *hectáreas*. Thirty-five thousand, Mister English. As big as Andorra.' Jack did a quick calculation. *Ninety-two thousand acres.*

'But he has castles too,' said the *Jefe*. 'In Madrid. Marbella. Segovia. Salamanca. Sevilla. San Sebastián. Alba de Tormes. And then he is also the Duke of Alba de Tormes. Olivares. Huescar. Arjona. And a Count too. Of Lemos. Lerín. Montijo. Also the *Márques*. Of here. There. Everywhere. Imagine all *that* land.'

'And in England,' said Jack, 'he is also the Duke of Berwick.' He spoke the word *Berwick* as closely as he could to a Spanish pronunciation. *Ber-wick*. Don Jacobo FitzJames Stuart y Falcó. What had *The Times* said about him? A surviving member of the exiled Stuart Kings. And Winston Churchill, it seemed, called him cousin.

'But Alba is just one,' continued the *Jefe*. 'One of a select group. These landowners. But much power. In the south, on the *finca* where I worked, the *campesinos* were owned like slaves. There was no legal process for us, Mister English. No rights. They could pay us if only they want to pay us. Evict us when they want. Starve us when they want. We live like animals. We have lived like this for five hundred years. More. And normally the landowners are not even there. They spend their summers in San Sebastián or Biarritz. Their winters in the *Caribe*. *Absentistas*.'

Absentee landowners, thought Jack.

'But the Republic gave land to the *campesinos*,' he said. 'They took it from the *absentistas* and gave it to the *campesinos*. Yes?'

'Yes. The Land Reform. The Republic tried to make changes in one year that have taken the rest of Europe a century and more. I was lucky. I got some land. Thousands of others too. But not enough. And they gave us no seeds. No tools.'

'And when the Movement began?'

'We became *milicianos*. To defend our land.'

'Did you kill *fascistas* too?'

'People were terrified, Mister English. They might not have been in Asturias but they knew what would happen. You know why?'

'Because the *fascistas* had told them?'

'Yes. The *Falangistas.* The man with the *panadería.* The woman in the fruit shop. The local *hidalgos.* All the rich people. They told them what Franco would do to the *campesinos* and their families when he came back. So those who were terrified were driven to act. And some of the young men, excited to hold a gun for the first time. Some stupid *borrachos* too. Somebody who wanted the *panadería* for himself. But mostly those who were terrified, Mister English. They took them all to the bridge. Threw them down into the gorge. It was fear that drove them to kill. Not politics. Not like Franco.'

'And your own priest?'

'Our priest was a good man. Poor. Like us. He tried to stop the killings. We let him live. In the end. But lots of my people asked why it was wrong to send priests and believers early to their heaven. Priests have always kept us quiet that way. Accept this life with humility and obedience, they would say, and God will reward you in the next. Why would they not be happy to be in their heaven sooner rather than later?'

'Those killings...' Jack began. 'I understand what you are telling me. But there are many who believe that stories about the killings, in the newspapers, stopped people from supporting you. In England. In France. Other places.'

The Spaniard laughed.

'It is always *our* fault that the world did not support the Republic, is it not? Why not *your* fault, Mister English? For not being here two years earlier to ask your questions. But what is it you want to understand? Whether I would do it differently?'

'I suppose so. Yes.'

'The clock only moves one way, Mister English. It will not go backwards. Yet if it could, then yes, I would live it differently. Across the river, in the next village, the priest was not good. There were stories. About him. About children. Before, nobody would say anything. But when the *Movimiento* began, he ran away. We would have killed him, Mister English. But he ran away. So we crossed the river. To some lands of the Duke of Alba. We found the place where his family was buried. A *mausoleo.* Tombs of marble and gold. Each tomb was worth more than all the *milicianos* together could earn in a lifetime. We broke them. A *relicario* too. They say it was worth a million *pesetas.* And *la momia...*'

La momia? thought Jack. The mummy?

'*La momia?*' he said. 'Who?'

'The Duchess. She had died in '34 also. Like Encarna's father and brother. But they had no tomb. Not like the *Duquesa.* A fortune spent to preserve her body. A fortune, Mister English.'

'And...?' asked Jack, though he was not sure that he wanted the answer.

'And nothing. We left her there. On the floor. But soon the *fascistas* came. In Granada and Córdoba and Sevilla they came quickly. There were stories. But we did not believe them. Hundreds shot, they said. Then hundreds more. Do you know Córdoba, Mister English?'

'No. They say that it is a beautiful place.'

'Yes, beautiful. But imagine the streets filled with the dead of our people. By then I was with the army. And in my village, that priest came back with them. With the *fascistas*. The priest went from house to house of the *campesinos*. This one a socialist. That one a communist. This one an anarchist. Some who had killed the *Falangistas*, most who had not. Just politics. They shot ninety-eight people. One village. One night. We should have killed that priest when we had the chance. The priest and every *fascista* like him. That is what I would do differently. Kill them early and kill them all.'

'And now?' said Jack.

The *Jefe* grinned.

'*¡Coño!*' he said. 'Now we can only kill a *few* of them. And traitors too.' He partially unwrapped the sheepskin, touched the object inside with reverence. Jack could not see it well, but he could see enough. A telescopic sight. For a hunting rifle. Or perhaps a sniper. 'They will bring Ajuriaguerra here. And Latorre. Then we shall see.'

'Latorre?'

'The Military Governor of Asturias, my friend. Rafael Latorre Roca. He has signed the death warrant of hundreds in the past year. Seen them executed. Thousands more in prison.'

'Is there something about this,' Jack gestured around the grotto. 'that I do not understand?'

'What is there to understand, Mister English. Madrid is still being bombed. The battle on the Ebro is being lost. Cataluña is our last hope. But in Cataluña we have a civil war of our own. Communists kill Trotskyists. Trotskyists kill Anarchists. Anarchists kill Communists. Madrid only survived because the *milicianos*, the International Brigade and Kléber defended it. But now he is in Moscow, held by the Comintern. Durruti killed in Madrid too. But who killed him, Mister English? Andreu Nin murdered there. Tortured to death by our own side. But there are still *fascistas* to kill. You see, Mister English, even now sometimes the Republic needs an executioner.'

'An executioner?' said Jack. 'Or an assassin?'

Chapter Twenty

Sunday 25 September 1938

Harold Fielding did not return until sunset. He called from the bottom of the steps to announce his arrival, then climbed to the outer gate, where Encarna searched him for weapons. He wore the same linen suit and Panama hat but the ascent did not seem to have distressed him so much in the gathering evening chill. Still, he watched nervously as the woman also checked through the satchel that he carried. Then he mounted the final few stairs to stand outside the inner gate while Encarna locked it behind her.

'There!' he cried. 'Done it. I counted them that time. One hundred and one steps exactly. To here. They tell me that true pilgrims climb them on their knees.'

'We didn't expect it to take so long, Mister Fielding,' said Dorothea. It was a terse statement.

'You mean the negotiations, of course, dear lady,' he replied. 'Not the climb, I assume.' He turned to answer the *Jefe*, who had greeted him with a rebuff far more curt than Dorothea Holden's.

Tension had been rising steadily for the past couple of hours, in truth, as the light had begun to fail and the oil lamp was lit once more. There had been some vague sense amongst the captives that they *might* not have to spend another night in the cave but growing anxiety seemed, to Jack, far more evident within the group of *guerrilleros*.

'The *Jefe* say that Señor Fielding may give us the *regalos*, the gifts,' said Sister María Pereda, 'but then tell him what answer from Burgos.'

The *Jefe* had long since committed the telescopic sight and its sheepskin wrapping to the safety of the walnut chest, but he had taken to playing nervously with Brendan's automatic.

'The old man is a bit tetchy this evening, isn't he?' said Fielding. 'Somebody been upsetting him?'

'I rather think,' sneered Bertie Moorgate, 'that *you* have, Mister Fielding. I believe we all expected some response long before this late hour.'

'Oh dear,' said the Vice-Consul. 'Ruffled feathers, I expect. Thought I had been clear though. These things take time. And can't be running up and down a hundred steps just to say *no news yet*, eh? Anyway, just a few trinkets. Soap for the ladies.' He sniffed the small packet appreciatively. 'Mmmm. And a pack of cards. Who was it that wanted these? Ah, Miss Carter-Holt, I believe.' He waited until

Valerie had come over to collect the cards in person. 'That's about it for now. Oh, more tobacco. Only *Lucky Strikes* though. No English newspapers, I'm afraid, Mister Telford. Maybe tomorrow.'

'No razor either?' said Jack, rubbing at his two days of stubble.

'Didn't think I'd get it past her ladyship,' whispered Fielding, with a flick of his head towards Encarna. 'But better get on with the thing, don't you think?' He winked at them, conspiratorially. 'And there'll be more food for Mikel to collect. In an hour or so. Some firewood too, perhaps.' He spoke again to the *Jefe*. There was a brusque reply. 'Ah,' Fielding continued. 'No fires apparently. Sorry about that. Worth a try though, don't you think? Perhaps more blankets then.'

'The fact is, Mister Fielding,' said Catherine Kettering, 'I don't think any of us would have expected the *Jefe* to allow a fire. Not during the night. Any more than you would have expected them to permit a razor. He's not stupid. I trust that you won't underestimate him during your negotiations?'

The Vice-Consul looked around the group, pursed his lips when only three or four returned his gaze, the others all staring at the ground.

'Ah!' he said once more, quite quietly. 'Well, must get on with the business at hand. Take it the good Sister will translate for you as we go along? Excellent. But will share any nuances when we're done, eh?'

It began, as custom now demanded, with the cigarette ritual, the *Jefe* responding positively to Fielding's ebullience by relaxing slightly, though he still seemed impatient, vexed.

'*Señor* Fielding say him that he has good news. That Burgos will accept the return of the *Santina* as a sign of goodwill. But they know that if the *Virgen* has not been destroyed, she must be in hands of the Republic. So they want to know how she can be part of the negotiation. No. How they can bring her back.'

The *Jefe* indicated that the Vice-Consul should continue.

'*Señor* Fielding says that next part is more difficult. That Burgos want the *Machados* to let go four of the *rehenes*, the prisoners. To let go four of us. If they have the *Santina* and four of us, they will bring *Señor* Ajuriaguerra here. Release him to the *Jefe*. General Latorre will arrange it. But not the others that the *Jefe* has named. Burgos tell him that these prisoners will go to Irún. The *Jefe*, his people, Ajuriaguerra and the rest of us, those not released, can then go on the bus to Hendaye. On the other side of the French border. When we are released, sent back across the International Bridge, the Republicans will also be released, crossing bridge from Spain into France. The *Jefe* ask when this will be. *Señor* Fielding say that they can bring Ajuriaguerra *al amanecer*. At daybreak? Tomorrow. They then let go four of us. They drive to the border. They can take food. With one stop for *gasolina* they can be at Hendaye late tomorrow night. And then, *¡ya!*'

'Four of us, do 'e say?' said Marguerite. 'Can go free? You 'ear that, Maxie?'

'Well, I really *can't* stay here any longer,' protested Alfred Holden.

'Alfred!' hissed his wife. 'It is by no means certain that the *Jefe* will agree any of this.'

'Why should he not?' said the Professor. 'The scoundrel is getting everything he wants, isn't he?'

But it was clear that the *Jefe* was far from happy. He raged at Fielding, and Sister María Pereda winced at the tone of the language.

'He ask why *Señor* Fielding insult him. That he trusted him. That he has no intention to let anybody go. Not until Hendaye. He says that Burgos wants a gesture of goodwill. But, he says, where is *his* gesture of goodwill? What concession does Burgos make to *him*? After all, he say, he has all the good cards. He has the Holy Cave. He has the English friends of Franco. He has the *Santina*. The *Jefe* says that if Burgos does not agree, he will have to send them another message. Like the *Falangista*. Like *Señor* Murphy.'

There was a gasp from the captives, especially from Marguerite.

'I don't think 'e means it,' whispered Max. 'Seems a real acker.'

'A real *acker*?' sneered Professor Holden. 'What on earth...?'

'Oh, Alfred,' said Dorothea, '*do* be quiet. I'm perfectly sure that we are in no danger. Not from the *Jefe* at least.'

'Mrs Holden, my dear lady,' called the Vice-Consul. 'If you don't mind the intrusion, this is hardly helpful.'

'Well, I never!' said Dorothea.

'I told you, Mrs Holden,' said Bertie Moorgate. 'Can't tell whose side the fellow is on.'

Fielding returned to face the *Jefe*, the latter enraged, shouting to his comrades, gesticulating towards the Vice-Consul. Harold Fielding did his best to pacify the Spaniard.

'He say to the *Jefe* that he understand the struggle of the *Machados*. That he has sympathy, More than the *Jefe* can know. But he tell him that he has *responsabilidad* also. For his countrymen.' The nun looked crestfallen once again, glanced at Mikel, received a reassuring pat on the shoulder from Dorothea. 'So *Señor* Fielding say him that if anything happens, anything bad, that all those people the *Jefe* wants to be released, they will all die. And many more. Yes, says the *Jefe,* but they are all soldiers. That these are all people who Franco will kill anyway. That they know *los riesgos*. The risks? Yes. He tell *Señor* Fielding that, all the same, if their demands are not met...But *Señor* Fielding tell him that he should not say more. That to make threats at each other is a bad thing. That perhaps they should share some more tobacco. To think about each other's position.'

The *Jefe* merely took another of the Vice-Consul's *Du Mauriers*, returned to the other *guerrilleros*. They had fallen into their own routine, Jack noticed. When they were sharing food, discussion, anything else with their captives, they would do so in a circle, mixed amongst the hostages, normally sitting on the ground. But when they kept their own counsel, or were simply on watch, they would sit on chairs against the sheltering wall of the cave, that which held the gate to the tunnel, with just one of them gripping the submachine gun and slightly away from the rest, at Pelayo's tomb, Jack noticed, and he saw that Fielding was taking careful note also.

'Going splendidly,' beamed the Vice-Consul.

'You think so, Mister Fielding?' said Catherine Kettering. 'You seem to have succeeded only in angering them. Our lives threatened once again.'

'I do not understand,' said Dorothea Holden, 'why the *Caudillo* cannot simply agree to their demands. Does he not realise who we are?'

'General Franco is naturally reluctant to negotiate under such a threat, dear lady. It is perfectly understandable. Why, whatever would happen next? These *guerrilleros* are all over the show. They would be doing this at the drop of a hat. For heaven's sake, there wouldn't be a foreign citizen safe from them anywhere within National Spain. And the Church is livid, naturally. This is Sunday, after all. Masses were scheduled to be held here today. The bishops are kicking up a real stink about this. The local faithful too. But you mustn't fret. *Any* of you.' Fielding sank to a whisper. 'Needed to test the fellow. See how he might react. That kind of thing.'

'Isn't that just a bit dangerous?' asked Jack.

'Well you seem to have spent more time with him than anybody else, Telford,' said Professor Holden. 'Surely he wouldn't shoot such a good friend? All Reds together, eh?'

'Professor,' said the Vice-Consul, 'it is *very* important that everybody keeps a cool head, don't you think? It's helpful if some of you build a good rapport with them. Not *too* good, of course. Wouldn't want any political converts, eh? I am, of course, trying to do the same. You *are* sure that none of them speak English? Good. Then you must understand that only by working on these relationships can we contemplate a satisfactory outcome here.'

'A peaceful settlement?' asked Carter-Holt.

'Yes, of course,' said Fielding. 'A satisfactory one.'

Yes, but satisfactory for whom exactly, Mister Fielding? thought Jack.

'And you expect us to play some part in this?' said Albert Moorgate.

'Was that a serious offer, Mister Moorgate?' replied the Vice-Consul. 'If so then merely a modest part, I think. Good to know a little about these fellows if that may be possible. What makes them tick, that sort of thing. General information. Are they rational? Are they not?'

'Rational?' said Moorgate. 'They have already killed three people in the past twenty-four hours alone. Hardly normal behaviour, Mister Fielding!'

'We can only do our best, dear fellow.' The *Jefe* was back at the railing. 'Ah! Back to business, I think.'

The Basilica bells pealed again and Jack kicked a pine cone across the floor of the grotto. *What's going on?* he thought. *I should speak to somebody about that telescopic sight. But who? Fielding?* It had been troubling him constantly since his discussion with the *Jefe* but he could make no sense of it.

'The *Jefe*,' said Sister María Pereda, 'makes a proposal. He tells *Señor* Fielding that the *Santina* is at the Republicans' Embassy in Paris. *Señor* Fielding can confirm this with a telephone call. If his demands are met the Jefe will give *Señor* Fielding a password. Some sort of code. The Embassy will then release the *Santina* to the

British Embassy. But he will only give the password if the rest of his plan is agreed. And none of us will be released, not until Hendaye. He say if they do not agree tonight, he will send them another message. In the morning. *Señor* Fielding say he will do his best to persuade Burgos.'

The *Jefe* rejoined the other *Machados*, having accepted a final *Du Maurier* for himself, a handful for his comrades.

'Well,' said Fielding. 'Looks like I have yet another climb to make. I've promised that I'll get on to Burgos straight away and then come back with their answer. After I've got the thumbs up from General Latorre, of course. It seems I have a deadline to meet as well. But never fear. We shall have you out of here in a trice, I'm certain. Why, I can already sense the sweet scent of compromise wafting on the evening air.'

'That's very reassuring, Mister Fielding,' said Dorothea. 'But if Burgos says no? What then?'

'A bridge to be crossed in due course, dear lady. I foresee only the most positive of outcomes.' He tapped the side of his nose once more. 'Now, any special request for my next visit?'

Aspirin for Dorothea, of course. Blankets. As many as possible. Then, once the Vice-Consul had begun his descent, they settled to a troubled debate. Alfred Holden and the Westons now hoping that Burgos would hold its ground, that Franco would insist on some of them being released, their assumption being that the *Machados* would be forced to concede if they truly wished to succeed in this banditry. The Moorgates hopeful of early release too but, overall, fearing that a tough stance by Burgos might lead to more reprisals from the *guerrilleros*. The rest either mute on the subject or convinced that it was Burgos that must surely make the concession and, therefore, that they would all soon be heading back to Hendaye. But where would this leave them? The Ketterings and Sister María Pereda seemed genuinely distraught at the prospect of not reaching Santiago. Carter-Holt too, though she said little on the subject, maintaining a sullen aspect that Jack found surprising. Yes, she was haughty. She had a high opinion of herself. She could be irritable in the extreme. But not normally sullen.

Jack noticed that when the opportunity presented itself, she moved away, alone, to sit beneath the oil lamp. The shadows cast by the amber light made her seem younger, the features softer so that, for all her negative attributes, her usually sulphuric attitude towards Jack himself, he found that he could not help feeling protective towards her. The stirrings of desire too, driven by that succubus visitation, back in his hotel bedroom at Jaúreguí. Something to do with the unattainable, he supposed. She had the pack of cards with her that Fielding had brought. It was not a new pack and she glanced about, furtively, Jack thought, before opening it. Why had the Vice-Consul been so careful to pass the thing only to her? he wondered. The others were still deep in their debate, the *Machados* engrossed in their own, Larry now on watch but carelessly. Jack made some pretence at involvement in the discussion but kept Carter-Holt within his peripheral vision until...Yes, he was sure that he had seen it. Valerie's quick check that she was unobserved and then something slipped from the pack and into her shoulder bag. Almost a sleight of hand, she was so fast. And then she began to play with the cards, a game of Baker's Dozen.

'Oh,' she called, all trace of gloom now banished, 'I thought Mister Fielding had brought us a Gipsy Tarot deck. But Spanish. How very elegant.'

Slowly, the others went to see. Sister María Pereda advised them on the unfamiliar suits. The coins and cups, the swords and clubs. Advice was offered on how one might play the game without the presence of red or black. Spanish Patience, of course, offered Marguerite. That was the way she had played it as a child. The foundations built up on the four Kings regardless of any suit.

And out in the darkness, there was the changing twin-stroke music of a motorcycle, gearbox shifting up and down to take the bends and gradients of the valley road. The *Jefe* heard it too, shifted on his walnut chest, craning his neck to stare out into the night. It was clear. There were stars. A waxing moon. Wood smoke on the air again. Wood smoke and the smell of pine.

What goes through that man's mind? wondered Jack. The enigma had been with him all afternoon, since they had chatted together. He wished he had his note-book, wondered how many of the details he would remember when he came to write his article for Sydney Elliott. And he certainly had enough material now. A hundred years of struggle. Luckless *campesinos* against feudal landlords. And he would tell the *Jefe*'s tale. Encarna's too. He could *feel* the euphoria. But Elliott would never print it, of course. He would, Jack supposed, quite properly see it as the worst form of emotional trash. Come to think of it, if he was going to write about the *Jefe*, how would he explain the telescopic sight? Or Julia Britten? He had a momentary vision of Turbides, waiting to arrest his prime suspect at the very moment of their release from captivity. But who? Marguerite, after her various rows with Julia? Dorothea Holden? What had she meant, that she had taken enough of this from Miss Britten? Enough what?

Mikel had gone to collect the food and returned with some local variant of flatbread. And there was wine too. A heavy red sent up in a new pigskin, small wooden cups to share between them. With the wine for company, Jack returned to his private thoughts.

Not everybody is what they seem, Jack. Which reminds me…

Carter-Holt was now alone with her food and another game of Solitaire. She had, as yet, been unable to complete a single one, it seemed.

'What did it say then?' he whispered, edging alongside her.

'Oh, Mister Telford!' she replied. 'Tired of your new friend already? You had *such* a lovely long chat. All in Esperanto too. How very civilised.'

'Don't change the subject. What did it say?'

'Perhaps just a bit more clarity around the question, Mister Telford? Ah, now look what's happened. What *shall* I do with this Three of Coins?'

'I *saw* the way that Fielding made sure it was *you* who received the pack of cards, Miss Carter-Holt. I *saw* the looks that passed between you in Santander. I *saw* you take something out of the box. It was a note of some sort, wasn't it? What did it say?'

'Did you start on the *Glenfiddich* without sharing it amongst the rest of us, Jack? *Whatever* are you babbling about?'

'You called me *Jack*.'

'I did? How remiss. Now I should like to finish my game.'

'But what *is* your game, Miss Carter-Holt? Or are we *both* on first-name terms at last?'

What's it got in its pockets, Jack, my love? Gollum hissed in his ear.

'You must have picked up that line from some cheap detective novel.'

'About the first-name thing?'

'No. The *What* is *your game, Miss Carter-Holt* line. How *have* you survived so long as a journalist, Mister Telford? I really have *no* idea why you should think that anything passed between myself and the Vice-Consul, either by way of looks *or* secret notes. The very idea.' She laughed, shook her head. It caught some of the others' attention, though they soon lost interest again as they tore hungrily at their flatbread.

'Well, there was *something*,' Jack insisted, though he was now beginning to feel foolish about the whole exchange. 'And another thing. That was a pretty little speech you made about why these *Machados* might not trust the British too much. I know all that stuff about Franco being flown from the Canary Islands to Morocco in a British plane. But there *are* no sources to show there was any official involvement, are there?'

'There you go again, Mister Telford. What *do* you think I am? Some private research library. Why on earth should I share anything with *you*? Unless, of course...'

'Unless?'

'Well, fair exchange might be acceptable, I suppose.'

'Exchange of *what*, exactly? Information, you mean?' Though Jack was desperately struggling to imagine what information he might possess that could possibly be of interest to Carter-Holt.

'Well,' she replied. 'You did spend rather a long time with you-know-who. It might help me if I knew...'

'You first!' said Jack. 'I *asked* first, I mean. I'm happy to tell you anything he said but what about Franco's flight to Morocco?' Valerie Carter-Holt smiled. She was trying to set down a Six of Swords but could find nowhere to play it. Jack could see the problem immediately. 'You *do* know, I suppose,' he mused, 'that there is no Seven of Cups in this pack?'

'How observant, Mister Telford,' she said. 'Very well. I feel generous tonight. But fetch me one of those *Senior Service*, will you? Oh no. Actually, I'd prefer one of the *Luckies*.' Jack did as he was told. 'For one thing,' she continued, blowing a stream of cigarette smoke downwards, 'you'll remember that when we were in Santander, Mister Murphy sold us the usual line about Calvo Sotelo's murder being the incident that sparked the *Caudillo*'s rebellion?'

'Yes, of course,' Jack replied. 'But nobody really believes that. You can't just launch a *coup d'état* without a lot of planning.'

'Well, you *can* have a plan prepared for a rainy day and then decide to trigger it because of a particular development, of course. That's always been the argument for what happened here, has it not? And Captain Bebb has always insisted that he just happened to be in the Canary Islands with Major Pollard when Sotelo was killed. That his plane was effectively commandeered by the Nationalist conspirators.'

'And?'

'And I happen to know that the plane was hired, not by Pollard, but by friends of Franco, on the fifth of July '36. It was a full week later that Sotelo was killed.'

'Friends of Franco?' said Jack.

'Yes. Primarily, Luis Bolín. The very man who's now running Franco's Tourism Department. Who arranged these trips, Mister Telford. Except then Bolín was working for *ABC* in London. But all this is small fry, I think. The *real* question is whether the British Government was actively involved.'

'And?'

'And now it's your turn, Mister Telford. Tell me all you can remember about the *Jefe*.'

Jack repeated the earlier conversation, omitting nothing, so far as he could recall, but unsure why this was of any interest to a Reuters correspondent. And particularly one with such pro-Franco sentiments. Yet while he might have detailed the conversation, he certainly omitted any mention of the telescopic sight.

'That's very interesting, Mister Telford. So you think,' she sank to a barely audible whisper, 'that he really *is* ruthless enough to kill more of us? If their demands aren't met?'

'Yes,' said Jack. 'He is.' And it confused him. His profound belief in peace was shaken. He could not conceive how he himself might have responded to the circumstances that the *Jefe* and all those millions of like-minded Spaniards must have faced. How would Jack have reacted in a similar setting?

'And these are Trotskyists, do you think? Or Anarchists?'

'I have to confess,' said Jack, 'that I have never fully understood the difference. At least, not here in Spain.'

'Oh, it's really rather simple, isn't it, Mister Telford? The Trotskyists believe that the only viable alternative to Franco is total workers' control. The Anarchists want workers' control too, of course. But they stand more violently against the symbols of Privilege and the Church.'

'And the Bolsheviks?'

'The true Bolshevik believes that nothing matters more than winning the war, regardless of the political complexion that the country may inherit afterwards. It is inconceivable for the Bolshevik to understand the fascism of the Trotskyist. These *Machados* amongst them perhaps.'

'Fascism?' said Jack. 'How can they be fascists? They devote their entire existence to *killing* fascists!'

Carter-Holt laughed.

'Really, Mister Telford! Those who advocate world revolution rather than single-state Marxism are Trotskyists. Trotskyists oppose true Soviet Bolshevism. Fascists are the natural enemies of Bolshevism. Therefore, Trotskyites are fascists. It's perfectly simple.'

'It's tautological nonsense,' said Jack. 'Anyway, what about the British Government and Franco's flight to Morocco? Were we actively involved or not?'

'Oh, far worse than that, Mister Telford. Major Pollard is a murky figure. Clear links to the Intelligence Services. But whether he's actually employed by them...? Well, who can say? But this much is beyond dispute. That whether our Government actively helped Franco in July '36 may be uncertain. But the British Embassy in Madrid knew at the end of *March* '36 that there would be a *coup d'état*. It doesn't matter how I know. I *know*. The end of March, Mister Telford. And they never said a single word to the Spanish Government. Not a word. If they had done so, the Republic would have had months to prepare. Could probably have prevented it happening. But instead of that, the British settled for the Non-Intervention Agreement which so actively prevented other countries from supporting the Republic. It probably would have been less damaging if we had actually declared war on the Popular Front.'

'Well,' Jack replied, 'you must be very proud of them.'

'Oh, of course,' she said. 'Inordinately proud. How could a true Briton *not* be proud of our Government, Mister Telford?'

'So you'll go on writing that horse-shit about Red atrocities?'

'Well, that rather depends on whether we get out of here at all, doesn't it? And that, Mister Telford, may depend on whether you decide to tell me whatever it is you're still hiding.'

'Hiding? I told you everything that the *Jefe* and I talked about.'

'Don't act the fool, Jack. What about the thing you *didn't* talk about?'

'How...?'

'Just tell me.'

'He's got a telescopic sight. For the rifle.'

'It's a Mosin-Nagant, isn't it? The rifle. I saw plenty of them at Teruel. The question is, what does he intend to do with it?'

'A Mosin-Nagant? Really? I wouldn't know one if I tripped over it. But he said that when Ajuriaguerra and General Latorre get here, we'll see. That's all. He said, *we'll see*. Do you know anything else about Ajuriaguerra?'

'Not much more than Brendan Murphy told us. After Santoña, he was condemned to death by Franco. But his sentence was commuted last October. They say that the Pope intervened directly on his behalf. Because Ajuriaguerra was himself such a prominent Catholic. But it didn't stop Franco having fourteen more of the Basque leaders killed. So Ajuriaguerra organised a hunger strike. He was at El Dueso then, I think. They moved him to Bilbao over the winter. Then to Burgos. He's a real thorn in Franco's side.'

'And in Negrín's side too?' said Jack. 'The Republic must consider him a traitor, surely? The surrender at Santoña?' She shrugged. 'Then what about Latorre?'

'General Latorre? Nothing. Why?'

'I don't know,' said Jack. 'The *Jefe* said something about the Republic needing an executioner.'

'You think we should mention this to Fielding? It could be important. And here he is. Speak of the devil!'

The Vice-Consul was calling again from the steps.

'Perhaps we should just keep this to ourselves,' said Jack. 'For the time being. Until we see how the negotiations are going. Anyway, I'm not sure how we *could* tell him. Unless, of course, your little messaging service is a two-way thing.'

Carter-Holt shook her head, gathered the cards together, while Fielding climbed once more to the inner gate, the outer entrance having been left ajar for him, and was searched once more, this time by Moe.

'Ladies and gentlemen,' he called. 'The bearer of aspirin, blankets and the best of good tidings! I was intending to bring some *Gauloises* but, by tomorrow night, you should be able to buy your own. In France!' Yet if he expected a round of applause, he did not receive one. 'And Miss Carter-Holt. The Spanish deck of cards didn't throw you too much, I hope?'

'Certainly not, Mister Fielding. Once I got the hang of them it was all perfectly simple. Though there seems to be one missing.'

I knew it, thought Jack. *He's passed her a message somehow. But what is it? And why? Reuters correspondent, my backside!*

It was a little before ten o'clock, the stars were obscured now by gathering cloud, thunder somewhere in the distance and an occasional flash of electrical discharge, low in the sky to the north. The Vice-Consul had brought a couple of decent cigars. To celebrate, he said, and the two negotiators each lit one. It was a certain sign that agreement was imminent.

'*Señor* Fielding say him that the past two hours have not been easy. That there has been much worry in Burgos about what will happen next. In case such a thing happen again. He says that there are many with *El Caudillo* who tell him not to negotiate. To take another path. But good sense is prevail at last. So here is *el trato.* The, er...?'

'The deal, I imagine?' offered Dorothea.

'Yes. Deal. He says very well. The *Jefe* must give him password. *Señor* Fielding will telephone to the Spanish Embassy in Paris. Spanish Embassy must send the *Santina* to the *British* Embassy, also in Paris. They telephone to *Señor* Fielding to confirm that the *Virgen* now in safe hands again. The British Embassy will hold the *Santina* for the *Generalísimo.* This will all happen as soon as there is agreement tonight. At the same time, General Latorre will arrange for Juan de Ajuriaguerra to be brought here from Burgos.'

There was a lengthy question from the *Jefe.* The Vice-Consul looked thoughtfully at his cigar.

'What is it?' asked Catherine Kettering. 'A problem?'

'I don't know,' said Sister María Pereda. 'The *Jefe* ask about the others. The other men who must be released. He say that if they are not brought here all together, there is no *pacto,* no deal.'

'I wish I could remember the Spanish,' said the Vice-Consul to himself, just loud enough for them to hear, 'for a ha'p'orth of tar.'

'I don't understand,' said the nun.

'It's perfectly alright, my dear,' said Bertie Moorgate. 'I think we follow his drift.'

'Drift? Well, *Señor* Fielding now tell him that it is a *paquete*. A package. All or nothing. Better perhaps to wait until the *Jefe* hear the whole thing. He say him that, if the *Santina* is with the British Embassy by six in the morning, he will return here and say so. They would then allow Mikel to go down and collect the bus. He will drive to the end of the tunnel and signal with lights. If the *Jefe* is satisfied at that time, General Latorre will send up Juan de Ajuriaguerra.'

Another question from the *Jefe*.

'*Now* what is it?' snarled Professor Holden. 'Has he no concept of a good deal when he sees one?'

'He ask about the *Caudillo* wanting four of us to be let go. He say that he will not negotiate about this. *Señor* Fielding tell him that is why he asked for the *Jefe* to wait until he has finish. He say that General Franco himself has told him he will not demand this. But only if the rest of the Republican prisoners are not let go either. Not until we are safely in Hendaye. When we are at Hendaye, the Republican prisoners will be taken to Irún. At an agreed time we will walk across the bridge, back into Spain, the Republican prisoners will walk across to freedom in France.'

The *Jefe* stood for a moment, scratched at his cheek, turned to consult the other *Machados*.

'You see?' whispered Carter-Holt in Jack's left ear. 'Trotskyists. If they were true Bolsheviks they wouldn't waste so much time on all this chatter.'

Several minutes went by, while the hostages stood nervously silent. Even the Vice-Consul seemed unusually lost for words. But then the *Jefe* returned to the gate.

'Well?' said Frances Moorgate. 'What's the answer?'

'He say *bueno*. He say it is good. But he warns *Señor* Fielding. He say that if there is any problem, any trick, any *decepción*, they will destroy the Holy Cave and everybody inside it. With the *dinamita*.'

A few of them nodded. *How strange*, thought Jack. *Not a murmur from any of us. Not even from the Holdens. As if we all expected such a thing. A perfectly rational caveat in the circumstances. We must all be mad!*

'Well,' said Dorothea, 'it looks like Mister Fielding has done it! Bully for him, I suppose. Oh, now what?' There was a final comment from the *Jefe*. 'Well?' she said. 'What does he say? I couldn't catch it. He has such a strange accent.'

But the nun did not reply. She simply clasped her hands in front of her and smiled sweetly at the assembled hostages.

'The *Jefe*,' said Valerie Carter-Holt, 'has told the Vice-Consul that the password is *Durruti* and that he expects him back here at six tomorrow morning. *En punto*. On the dot. He says that if Mister Fielding is late, they will kill Sister María Pereda.'

Chapter Twenty-One

Monday 26 September 1938

In the morning, the *Jefe* had said, when there was light, they would have a photograph. When they stopped for *gasolina*. They would ask somebody to operate the camera of *Señorita* Carter-Holt.

It was not the first attempt that he had made to break the layer of ice which had frozen relationships between hostage and captor since Mister Fielding's last visit, the hopefully successful conclusion of negotiations. Even the Vice-Consul had tried to assure them that he did not personally take the threat very seriously. That it might even be helpful, in some strange way, so that he could reinforce the continuing urgency of the situation with those to whom he must now report. And soon, of course. There was a deadline to be met. The *Santina* to be recovered.

Then, almost as soon as he was gone, the *Jefe* had opened a stilted dialogue with Dorothea Holden, though much of the exchange was lost in translation.

At perhaps one in the morning, Jack had also been approached. In Esperanto, naturally.

'*Sinjoro Anglo*,' he had said. 'It was important to say this thing. A message for Burgos. But I told you my story. You know I would not kill a priest or a nun unless they deserved to die.'

'*Vi mortigis sinjoron Murphy*,' Jack had replied. You killed Mister Murphy.

'That was different. He was a *Falangista*. All *Falangistas* deserve to die.'

But the *Jefe* had not pursued the point. Not until now.

'I have naturally told him,' said Carter-Holt, 'that he shall *not* use my camera unless our good friend, Sister María Pereda, is there to be part of the photograph with us.'

She had earlier finished the rest of Jack's wine ration in addition to her own. It had mingled in her veins with blood starved of sleep, a dangerous enough concoction in itself. But, once fortified with a shot of the *Glenfiddich* which the group had also decided to share, it made her unusually verbose. Forward even. She had insisted on a blanket of her own. Then begged Jack to allow her the use of his watch, her own having such a tiny face that it was utterly useless in the dark.

'Well he seems unwilling to take no for an answer,' said Dorothea.

'He's a Trotskyist, Mrs Holden,' Valerie replied. 'What else would you expect? But I have told him, twice now, that if he wishes to set the record straight he should speak with Sister María Pereda directly. Rather than attempt these rather foolish stratagems of which he seems so fond.'

But, since Fielding had gone, Sister María Pereda had not moved from the altar. She had been on her knees for the best part of four hours now, Jack calculated. *She must be bitterly cold and completely numb,* he thought. Yet still she prayed. And, not far away, Mikel kept watch over her.

The other captives were engaged in a useless conversation about how strange the return to Irún would be without Brendan, maudlin memories of the care he had lavished on them. His admonitions not to wander off alone. Well, he would never guide them around Gijón now. And is that where they should have been yesterday? Yes, Sunday. And today – later today, naturally – they would have been heading to Oviedo. Frances Moorgate had so wanted to see the beaches and *rías* of Galicia. She had heard that they were stunning. It was certainly meaningless at one level but, Jack realised, it also served a purpose. Some release for the tension that had developed amongst the whole group, himself included, as the night lengthened. It kept him awake. The others too, apparently. For while they had made various attempts to settle, the *Machados* mingled amongst them, to snatch some well-deserved and much-needed sleep, not one of them had so far succeeded. And the dark hours had thus developed a pattern: periods of nervous chatter interspersed with spells of silence. Utter silence.

Shouldn't we all be feeling relieved? he thought. *The prospect of release? So what is it, Jack? Possible that you might actually miss some of these people? Absurd.*

But perhaps not. Now he came to think about it, he had not generally overheard anybody else relishing the prospect of freedom as he might have expected either. With the exception of Marguerite, perhaps, and Alfred Holden, of course.

'Well, I shall certainly be glad to see the back of all this,' said the Professor, his voice slurred by the alcohol.

'I thought that we were going to try the War Route of the South next,' said his wife. 'Seville. Granada. Just imagine.'

'I wouldn't come back to this stinking hole,' shouted Holden, 'until Franco's cleared out every one of these Red…'

The *guerrilleros* glanced at him. Smiled. '*Borracho*,' they whispered.

'Professor,' said Bertie Moorgate, 'I think you've said quite enough.'

'Well,' snarled Holden. 'Then pass me the bloody bottle.'

'It's all gone, I'm afraid,' said Carter-Holt, holding up the empty *Glenfiddich* with a shaking hand. She was hardly more sober than the Professor.

'Perhaps we could try a few hands of whist?' suggested Frances. 'We could bring the oil lamp over.'

'Gin Rummy,' muttered Holden. 'Or Bridge? Maybe these Reds can play Bridge. Ask them, why don't you? Bloody card games. Here, of all places. Yes, we could all go in for a bit of sacrifice. No, *sacrilege*. That's what I meant. Sacrilege. What would the little nun say about *that*, eh?'

But the little nun was still at her prayers, and Mikel maintained his vigil.

'Alfred!' said his wife. 'Could you not try to catch forty winks? You'd feel so much better for it.' And she turned to Jack. 'You must forgive him, Mister Telford. He has been quite beastly to you on more than one occasion. Although, I find, you *are* a somewhat opinionated young man. All the same, one should never forget one's manners. That's what I always say.'

'I'm sure it has sometimes been trying for all of us,' said Jack. 'Never easy when such a disparate group is thrown together like this.'

'That's true,' she said. 'I don't suppose you ever imagined sitting in the Holy Cave of Covadonga at two in the morning chatting with the Treasurer of the Anglo-German Fellowship. Not that one is seeking a political debate on the subject. Just...'

'It is without doubt the most bizarre moment of my life,' Jack laughed. 'But no. Political debate would be quite beyond me at the moment. I can't understand why any intelligent person could support the Germans but let's leave that for another day. The other side of the French border perhaps? I did have one question though. It was about Julia Britten. Do you mind?'

Dorothea was about to respond when Marguerite Weston screamed.

She had leapt to her feet, pointing out into the night.

'Look!' she screeched.

The *guerrilleros* jumped or rolled from their positions, the *Jefe* going for his rifle where it rested against the walnut chest. The other three men drawing their revolvers and lining themselves along the cave wall, forming behind their leader. Encarna took the submachine gun to crouch near the detonator box. Jack scuffled away from it. They all did, sliding on their backsides away towards the old chapel.

'I seen somethin' out there,' Marguerite wailed. 'A face. A white face.'

Encarna had the plunger in her right hand, the wooden box steadied by her left. Her eyes were wide, fanatical. She pulled the handle upwards and Jack could hear the toothed rack of the shaft rattling harmlessly upwards against the gears of the blaster's internal dynamo. But when the plunger was depressed, the fly-wheel spun, the dynamo engaged, then sufficient charge would be generated to blow the detonator caps.

'Jesus Christ!' shouted Jack, and he rolled onto his front, pressed himself into the cold rock, clasped his hands over the back of his head. *Useless*, he thought. *Sodding useless.*

There was shouting. More screaming. The *Jefe* calling. The panic slowly subsiding.

Jack ventured a glance at the others. Each cowered in their own fashion. Except Marguerite who was still standing, apparently rooted to the spot in her fear. And Carter-Holt, who was holding the face of Jack's wrist-watch towards the oil lamp, tapping the thing, shaking her head. She was quite drunk.

'The *Jefe* says that it was probably an owl,' she told them. 'Nothing to worry about.'

'Nothing but this mad woman and her dynamite,' Jack yelled, scrambling to his feet. 'For God's sake, she was just about to blow us all to Hell!'

'*Sinjoro Anglo*,' said the *Jefe*. '*Trankviliĝu!*' Calm down.

'*La eksplodaĵoj*,' Jack replied. '*Ŝi...*' The explosives. She...

But the words would not come. And he wept with frustration. He had genuinely thought that he was going to die. That Encarna was going to destroy them all. Yet when she had not done so, he felt a bizarre sense not only of relief but of gratitude. *Bloody gratitude.*

'Come on, old boy,' said Bertie Moorgate, putting a hand on Jack's shoulder. 'Getting a bit much for all of us, eh?'

The *Jefe* had crossed to where Encarna still held the plunger. He grabbed her arm, dragged her away from the detonator box. She dropped the gun and he shouted at her, furious, slapping the flat of his hand against his own forehead, for emphasis.

'*Hombre, ¡eres una loca!*'

And Encarna shouted back, shaking his grip from her arm, gesticulating towards the prisoners.

'She says that she is not crazy, it's that he is too weak,' muttered Carter-Holt. 'That he has allowed himself to become too close to us.'

'Well,' said Moorgate, 'I suppose the feeling is somewhat mutual, don't you think? And how are *you* now, dear lady?' He put a comforting arm around Marguerite Weston. 'Better now? You gave us quite a start.'

'I thought...'

'Yes, of course,' said Bertie, leading her to sit down as the group gradually settled again. The *guerrilleros* too, though not Encarna who, freeing herself from the *Jefe*, had gone to sit alone, recovering the submachine gun.

'This will be our last night together,' said Frances. 'And we still don't really know each other. Do you think, Miss Carter-Holt, that the *Jefe* would tell us a bit about himself. Or one of the others, perhaps?'

'Oh, you should ask Mister Telford,' said Valerie. 'He's quite the expert.'

'Well I think it's a jolly good idea,' said Dorothea Holden. 'It will help to pass the time.' She spoke to the *Jefe* in broken Spanish. He laughed, spoke to the others, nominated Larry, ruffled the fuzzy hair. Larry refused, naturally. So the *Jefe* told the story for him. A slow translation.

His name, amongst the *Machados*, was Romero. Thirty-four years old. Born in Aragón. Another poor *campesino*, raised by his father on tales of the workers who died resisting conscription during Cataluña's Tragic Week, though Romero had been only five when it happened. So it had been the most natural of things to join the Anarchists' union when he reached the age of fifteen and, later, to become an organiser for them, finding support and members among the farms and *fincas*, the sugar workers and others. He was away from home when the Movement began, returned there as soon as he received the news to find that the *Falangistas*, backed by *Civiles* and a regiment of regulars had overrun the local militia, killed most of them. Romero himself had barely escaped, eventually crossed the Ebro, met up with hundreds of others escaping from the *facciosos*. Once safely back in Republican territory, he joined the Durruti Column, spent months helping other comrades escape the clutches of the Fascists or carrying out sabotage behind the enemy's lines. They burned bridges. Blew rail tracks. Captured seminaries. Raided barracks of the Guardia. And on one occasion, disguised in the uniform of a *Falangista*, Romero had spied to great effect on the Nationalist units within the Teruel salient. So it transpired that Larry – this Romero – and Carter-Holt had both been at Teruel. And when that most ice-bound blizzard of battles was finally lost by the Republic, with the Guerrilla Army Corps now formed, Romero had volunteered for its ranks. He had been deep inside Franco's conquered provinces ever since.

'Anarchist, eh?' said Albert Moorgate. 'Not a Catholic then?'

'Oh, Bertie,' giggled Marguerite, and she struck him on the arm. 'You be a one!'

'And the others?' asked Frances. 'What are *their* stories?'

Carter-Holt translated.

'He says that they each have their own tale to tell,' she said. 'Each one different. He says maybe later. On the bus.'

Frances fumbled for her purse, black and gold embroidery. She fingered the red bakelite ball closure, rummaged inside, found it wanting.

'Are there any cigarettes left?' she asked. Jack reached for one of the *Senior Service* tins, offered the contents to Frances. 'And you, Mister Telford. Your father was a soldier too, didn't you say. Won't you tell us about him?'

'I know very little about him,' said Jack. 'Too little. He fought in France, of course. But he wasn't killed there. He caught some form of influenza. Died afterwards. In hospital at Saint Albans.' *Safe in Saint Albans*, thought Jack. *He could have come home to us. But instead he chose…*

'*Kion vi diras?*' said the *Jefe*. What are you talking about?

'*Mia patro*,' Jack replied. My father. 'I see his ghost sometimes,' he continued, in English. 'In uniform. Watching me.'

The others fell silent. A cold wind stirred the pine needles of the grotto's floor.

'Is he…?' whispered Marguerite, glancing over her shoulder.

'Here?' said Jack. 'No, Mrs Weston. Not tonight.'

'That's a shame,' said Frances.

'Hey now, me 'ansum,' said Max, 'you're givin' me the shivers.'

But Larry, the *guerrillero* Romero, had found something else to interest him. It was Albert Moorgate's Fedora. He admired the hat. The blue and red band. And Bertie, to the surprise of them all, offered it as a gift. Romero tried it for size, received the admiration of his fellows, protested that he could not possibly accept but, finally, set it firmly upon his own head, muttered thanks in pidgin English.

Another silence descended.

And into the silence, Carter-Holt fell to a fitful slumber although, at regular intervals, Jack saw her jerk awake, look about as though she could not remember how she had come there, then examine his watch, holding it close before her eyes or, once again, turning it towards the dim lantern. It was the silence of waiting, the echo of a prison cell for the condemned. The silence of death mask eternity. A concerto score laid on a piano's music stand with no performer at the keyboard. Even the sounds that occasionally shattered the nocturnal hush were themselves muted reminders of a universal void. Nightjars, churring in the trees, then swooping just beyond sight, their wings slapping. Single cry. *Coo-wick. Coo-wick.* The ticking of a clock within an empty room.

Jack could taste the silence. That slightly acrid flavour of a pre-dawn zephyr bringing the promise of a coming downpour. He could smell it too. The muted library musk which Frances Moorgate still carried with her despite the gardenia. Mist and fog. Deep forest resins. Quiet cathedral incense. He remembered those other silences. Those that come with the running of fingers along the coffin of a loved one. Those that had immersed him whenever he swam, the taciturn peace of the pool, the gentle suspension of a tranquil sea.

Silence.

Until it was punctured once more by the roar of new vehicles arriving at Covadonga. *Who?* thought Jack. *Is this it? The convoy from Burgos bringing Juan de Ajuriaguerra?*

Jack slept at last too, dreaming of Carter-Holt as it happened, opening his eyes again only to wonder if he was, in fact, awake. For he found her camera hovering just in front of him. He sat upright, rubbed at his face until the vision cleared.

It was the *Jefe*, crouching between Jack and Valerie. He had picked up the Agfa Box Forty-Four and was turning it over in his hands. He pointed the lens in Jack's direction, his fingers pushed through the small carrying strap.

'*¡A ver!*' he said, and made a clicking noise with his tongue.

'Cheese,' whispered Jack. The *Jefe* looked puzzled. '*Ni diras fromaĝo.*' We say cheese.

'*Fromaĝo? Pro kio?*' Why?

'*Tio funkcias bone en Anglio.*' It works fine in English.

Carter-Holt stirred, saw the *Jefe*, and her face contorted. Anger. Or was it fear?

'No!' she cried. 'Leave that!'

Those who had been asleep were suddenly awake. Those who were already awake turned quickly to see what was happening. The *guerrilleros* tensed. The *Jefe* put up the hand which still held the camera, a mock gesture of defending himself from the onslaught.

'*¡Ay, Señor!*' he laughed.

'Please,' she instructed. 'Please give me the camera.' She put out her own hand, motioned towards the Agfa.

The *Jefe* inclined his head just a little, regarded her, scratched the bristle of his neck with broken, blackened fingernails. He offered her the camera. She snatched for it but it remained trapped by his fingers beneath the strap. He held it there for a moment, the smile disappeared from his face. Then he pulled it back, away from her grasp, slid the fingers free, weighed it in his hand briefly, as he had done once before.

'It won't work in this light,' said Albert Moorgate. 'Not a chance.'

'You needs one o' them flash things,' offered Marguerite, holding up her right hand as though she was, indeed, operating such a unit.

'Now 'ang about me 'ansums,' said Max. 'I got a good 'un this time. What did Snow White sing when she was waitin' for 'er snaps to be developed?' Nobody knew. It was his first joke since...When? Jack could not remember. Max waited. 'Some day my prints will come!' And he began to sing it. They all joined in. Over and over again.

The *Jefe* did not understand a word, looked around the faces of these strange and eccentric folk, passed the camera back to Carter-Holt. Catherine Kettering smiled at him in the gloom, touched his arm, gestured towards Sister María Pereda.

'*Por favor,*' she said.

The *Jefe* watched the nun for a moment. She had not shifted, not for the entire night, while Mikel was now sleeping soundly not too far away.

What must it be now? thought Jack. He looked at his wrist, momentarily forgetting that Carter-Holt still had his watch.

'Almost five-thirty,' said Valerie, without needing to be asked.

The *Jefe* glanced around at his comrades. Larry was asleep against the far wall, Bertie Moorgate's Fedora pulled down over his eyes. Curly and Moe were sharing a cigarette. Only Encarna remained alert, watching her leader as he half-crawled across to the altar, sat down beside the nun. He spoke to her, but too quietly to be overheard.

'We just bought a new camera, we 'ave,' said Max. 'Its shutter speed's so fast it'll take photos o' my missus with 'er mouth closed.'

Marguerite was not amused but the others thought it was a wonderful joke.

'I thought you'd lost your sense of humour, Max,' said Jack. 'Well done, old fellow. It's good to have you back on form again.'

'You mean that, me old acker? I didn't think 'e liked my stuff very much.'

'Well, let's just say it's grown on me. And what now, Max. After we get back to Hendaye. Will you still go on for your meeting with Franco?'

'I don't think I wants to meet 'im, Jack. It were Marguerite's idea in the first place. Somethin' to do wi' that Mexico thing.'

'That might not be very helpful, you know. Mexico is just about the only country apart from Russia that's done anything to support the Republic. They're Franco's enemies.'

'Well then we won't go to see 'im!' said Max. And, Jack thought, he seemed quite determined. At least, by Max Weston's standards.

They were interrupted by Catherine Kettering. She said nothing, but she touched Jack lightly, nodded towards the altar. The *Jefe* was on his knees, head bowed, next to Sister María Pereda. He stayed there for several minutes while that familiar silence settled on the cave once more. The silence of sunflower heads sunk low at season's end. Jack noticed Encarna, shaking her head in disbelief. She spat on the ground. Then a dog howled, somewhere along the valley. A second dog barked in answer, closer to the cave. The nun turned to the *guerrillero*, smiled at him, and he stood, then helped her to stand also. She was barely able to do so. Mikel woke, looked guiltily about him, then got to his feet and took her other arm.

A rising wind began to whistle through the surrounding trees, branches whispering as they brushed one against another.

And Vice-Consul Harold Fielding was back.

'Is anybody awake up there?' he called.

'Yes, all awake, Mister Fielding,' shouted Albert Moorgate, though he was quickly told to be quiet by the *Jefe*.

The *guerrillero* called down in turn.

'He ask whether the *Santina* is safe,' said Sister María Pereda, still rubbing at the front of her thighs through the dark material of her Holy Habit.

'What time is it?' said Dorothea.

'Not quite six,' replied Carter-Holt.

'*Señor* Fielding say he come back early but, yes, the Santina is now at the British Embassy in Paris.' The nun turned to the others. '*¡Bendita Madre de Diós!* She is safe. The *Santina* is safe. Oh, now the *Jefe* tell him that it is good to be early. He say that now he will not have to kill the nun.' The *Jefe* clearly thought that this was hilarious, but Sister María Pereda offered them only the hint of a smile. 'I think it is just *una broma*. A joke?'

'Yes, of course,' said Catherine. 'We told you so all along, didn't we?'

'What about the rest o' the plan though?' said Marguerite. 'Can we go now?'

'*Señor* Fielding tell him that everything is almost ready. That he should send Mikel down in a half-hour. To collect the bus. That *Señor* Fielding will come back to say when it is time. Then the *Jefe* ask if Juan de Ajuriaguerra is here. *Señor* Fielding say yes.'

'Did you get all that, ladies and gentlemen?' shouted the Vice-Consul. 'I certainly hope so. I'll be back just before seven, I think. Seven. Is that clear?'

They were not sure whether they should answer. The *Jefe* was back in conversation with the other *Machados*.

'Yes,' yelled Carter-Holt. 'Loud and clear!'

There were instructions from the *Jefe*.

'He say that we must eat breakfast now,' said Sister María Pereda.

Curly and Moe fetched the last of the cured meat, the cheese, the bread, the wine. Water was carried across from the pump. They ate, but mostly in silence. And as two separate groups now.

'Oy, what's 'appenin'?' said Marguerite. 'We was all gettin' on so well!'

But everybody else understood that things had changed. They were clearing for action, everything stowed away neatly as soon as they had eaten their fill. Weapons checked. The *Jefe* had taken the sheepskin package from the walnut chest and then, closing the lid, he sat down again, picked up the Mosin-Nagant. Jack went to squat alongside.

'*Kion vi faras?*' he said. What are you doing?

'Getting ready,' said the Jefe. He rummaged in the side pocket of his pin-striped jacket, produced a worn tobacco tin, removed from it a length of string with a lead weight on one end, a loop on the other.

'Ready for what?'

'For anything,' the *Jefe* replied. 'We are soldiers, *sinjoro Anglo.* Like your father. Perhaps, one day, like you.'

He took a small patch of cloth from the tin also. It was oiled, already smeared with dirt, and the *Jefe* fixed it through the loop.'

'In San Sebastián,' said Jack. 'At El Chofre. They separate the Spanish from the Internationals. Then take the Internationals away. Later, I thought we heard guns. Do you know what happens?'

The *Jefe* had removed the bolt, turned the rifle towards the oil lamp, peered through the barrel, then dropped the slender weight down through the muzzle until it came out through the breech. He dragged it clear, the string and oiled patch following. He repeated the operation.

'We find them sometimes. The Internationals. In places the *facciosos* have been killing them.'

He looked through the barrel again, put the pull-through back in its tin.

'But why? They were being sent home.'

The *Jefe* removed something else from his pocket. A small metal clip, perhaps six inches long. It looked like a miniature girder, perforated with holes. He replaced the bolt and, with it left open, located the clip in the breech before pressing five bullets down into the magazine.

'In the past,' he said, 'when the Internationals are captured, they have been sent home. Many of them. Often, they come back to Spain. If they are captured a second time, they are shot. It is automatic. Perhaps Franco fears that, this time, they will all come back together. So he shoots them first. Who knows? *Fascistas* do not need a reason to murder. The hate is inside them.' Jack looked over at the Holdens. *Is that true, I wonder?* he thought. *The professor certainly. But Dorothea? She's like Sister María Pereda, isn't she? Just deluded by fascist nonsense.* 'And not just the *fascistas,*' the *Jefe* continued. 'They say that sometimes the Internationals are killed by their own. Deserters, naturally. Some who make crimes. But some also for speaking against Comrade Stalin. Who knows?'

'Like the fighting in Barcelona?' said Jack. 'Between the Anarchists and the Communists?'

The *Jefe* pushed home the bolt, watching to check that a round had been chambered. He turned the handle downwards, then took hold of the knob at the back of the bolt, pulled it rearwards, turned it counter-clockwise.

'There,' he said. 'Safe now. And you, *sinjoro Anglo,* ask too many bad questions.'

The *Jefe* set down the rifle, looked out at the black sky, just showing the first tattered wisps of a paler shade. He called to Mikel, brought him close, gave him instructions, emphasised them by prodding the driver's chest with Brendan Murphy's automatic. And then, it seemed to Jack, he issued the instructions all over again, but more slowly, deliberately. He told Moe to open the gate. Mikel turned to the nun, a foolish grin spread across his face. Then he was gone.

The *guerrilleros* returned to cleaning their weapons, the *Jefe* checking the pistol, the three other men their revolvers, and Encarna the submachine gun.

Sister María Pereda approached. She was still having difficulty walking, so the *Jefe* cleared space on the walnut chest, invited her to sit next to him. Then he unwrapped the sheepskin, removed the telescopic sight, sliding it into place and adjusting a knurled nut on its side.

Jack got to his feet, went back to where the others were huddled in their coats and blankets.

'What's she doing?' whispered Catherine. Jack smiled. *She must imagine she's found a convert*, he thought.

'I ask the *Jefe* why they do this,' said the nun. 'He say that he has already explained to *Señor* Telford. He say that they must prepare.'

'Prepare for what?' said Max.

'He say for treachery,' said the nun.

'Treachery by whom?' said Dorothea. 'Surely he can't suspect Mister Fielding?'

Sister María Pereda smiled.

'The *Jefe* say that his father always told him if the English tell you one thing it is better to believe the opposite.'

The precautionary preparations of the *guerrilleros* continued. Encarna was seen checking the terminals of the blasting box. But, strangely, these activities seemed to lift the spirits of the captives rather than depress them. They reasoned, amongst themselves, that if the *Machados* paid such attention to detail, on the merest offchance that something might go amiss, then all must surely go well.

'Well *my* father always said,' stressed Peter Kettering, 'that if you expect the worst, you will generally be pleasantly surprised by the outcome. Pessimism gives way to pleasure, eh?'

Jack imagined that it must be almost seven and, down below, Fielding had returned.

'Hello the Cave!' he yelled. 'We'll be off quite soon.' Then he called in Spanish.

'*Señor* Fielding say that everything is ready. He ask the *Jefe* if he can come up.'

There was the rumble of an engine, driving up towards the esplanade, the familiar grumbling roar and grinding gears of their Chrysler bus, then lights glimmering through the tunnel.

The *Jefe* peered over the railing, the rifle in his hand. It was still dark but dawn now imminent. He called down to Fielding, then to Curly and Larry. They crossed the cave, extinguished the oil lamp, unlocked the iron gate to the tunnel. But cautiously. They prepared to enter but Larry, Romero the *Machado*, stopped. He turned to Bertie Moorgate, tipped the Fedora to him and, setting it back upon his head, he slipped away with Curly to meet the vehicle.

Everybody else waited until, in the end, the pale linen suit and white Panama of Vice-Consul Harold Fielding appeared on the balcony and, passing through the open outer gate, halted half-way up the final few steps.

Moe went forward to search him.

Fielding looked almost spectral. Jack clutched the back of his own neck, squeezed and kneaded the weary muscles, stretched. The sun had not come up but the clouds showed a lighter grey, ominous, rain threatening. He thought about the Internationals killed at El Chofre. But mostly he thought about the cured meat he had eaten. The scent of it was in his nostrils. And the shit too. From the chapel. The old thought again. *The predominant stench of war isn't smoke or blood. It's shit and stale food.*

Then the bells of the Basilica tolled. The same as the day before, just before Murphy had died.

Carter-Holt looked at Jack's watch.

Moe stretched out towards the linen suit.

Searchlights, the lever switches grinding night to day. Jack was dazzled, caught like the proverbial rabbit.

'Get down!' screamed Carter-Holt. 'All of you. Get down!'

She began to drag Catherine Kettering and Frances Moorgate to the ground. Jack had the distinct impression that Marguerite had been pushed onto her backside, Max beside her, while the Holdens had taken a step towards the altar.

The *guerrilleros* turned towards Carter-Holt, then back to the searchlights, shielding their eyes. And the man wearing Fielding's clothes was silhouetted against the glare, a gun in each hand.

Shots. Four, five, in quick succession.

Moe crashed backwards, the revolver spinning from his trouser belt.

The *Jefe*, too, was hit, slumped back onto the walnut chest. But he gripped the rifle, released the safety and fired at the killer. The man spun backwards towards the outer gate, a briefly dark crucifix against the light, and was gone.

At the same time there was firing from the tunnel. It echoed. Absurdly loud.

The hostages were now mostly on the ground, covering their ears, their eyes. More bursts of fire in the tunnel. Single shots.

And Encarna still held the submachine gun. She looked to the tunnel. Then at the *Jefe*. Then the hostages. Finally at the blasting box, its handle already raised, positioned for use.

There was the clang of metal on metal. Jack thought it was a shot from below, but he saw that it was a grappling iron, hurled up from somewhere beneath them. It missed, fell back, but was followed by a second, which gripped the top of the railing.

The sound of boots scraping on the steps too.

There was smoke in the air. That cordite stench again.

Bertie Moorgate was up, running for the rail. Frances shouted something to him but Jack could not hear what she said. Yet her husband pulled the grappling iron free, hurled it away, immediately staggering back. Back and back, tripping over his new wife and crashing down, blood pumping from his throat, his arms upraised, fingers reaching for something. Jack fell to his knees beside the man, tried to press his hands over the gushing wound.

'What the hell were you trying to do?' Jack screamed at him, as Frances clawed her way towards them. 'What was he thinking?' he shouted to her, then looked frantically around the cave. But there were no answers. No reasons. Not any more.

On the balcony was a soldier in a pale khaki uniform, his head wrapped in a white turban, rifle at the ready. Behind him another, pistol in hand.

Encarna fired, sprayed her enemies with bullets. She howled like a banshee. *'¡Moracos maricones! ¡Moracos de puta!'* They fell away and she ran to the shelter of the cave wall, checked on the *Jefe* who had now slipped to the floor. He was alive. But he looked bad.

The *guerrillera* emptied the rest of her magazine down the steps, though it was impossible to tell whether she had any specific target.

'¡Moracos maricones!' she screamed again.

She ducked down again, ran low back towards Pelayo's tomb.

'¡Moracos de puta!' she said, more softly. She wept. Her hand was on the plunger handle. And there was nothing on this earth that could stop her from pressing it down.

Oh, bugger it all! was Jack Telford's last profound thought.

Chapter Twenty-Two

Monday 26 September 1938

Jack had never believed in miracles and, anyway, the scene now held some quality of the absurd. Encarna still held the plunger and he felt sure that she would have blown them all to Kingdom Come by now had it not been for Sister María Pereda shouting to the *guerrillera*. Something about the Love of God, he thought.

'*¡Me cago en su diós y en la puta madre!*' snarled Encarna through gritted teeth and bitter tears.

But she hesitated, all the same, in the very act of destroying the *Cueva de la Santina*, turned towards the nun. Her tears mingled with mirthless laughter as she saw Brendan Murphy's automatic pistol in Sister María Pereda's shaking hands. Then she heard military boots in the tunnel again, returned to her task, setting down the submachine gun, crouching for better purchase, using both hands to lift the handle a final fraction and…

It was indeed a miracle that the nun was even able to hit her. A miracle, or an intervention of the Holy Light, Jack imagined. But the first shot spun Encarna around, an awful sound as the bullet hacked flesh from her left arm, knocked her over so that she dragged the detonator box onto its side. She tried to press the plunger from this position but it was quite impossible.

Sister María Pereda took two steps across the grotto while Encarna attempted to set the box upright again. Yet the nun was not even looking at her. She was looking upwards, at the roof of the cave, whispering to herself. Or perhaps to Sister Berthe Schultz, thought Jack. Maybe to Our Lady Herself.

The gun spat again, and the ricochet whined away, harmless, from the rock face, but barely missing an astonished Marguerite Weston.

The blasting machine was upright now, Encarna back in position.

The pistol fired. Then fired once more.

The *guerrillera*, having suffered no further harm, grinned at the nun, at the very moment the tunnel gate burst open. Encarna looked into the eyes of a young soldier, steel helmet, dark olive *poncho*. He levelled his rifle towards her. Barely even aimed, fired, the bullet hitting her in the head. It blasted away the rear right side of her jaw and face from the exit wound. And she fell onto the plunger.

Bedlam unleashed as the hostages screamed in collective terror. Yet Jack remained unmoved. He pictured the inner workings. The ratchet engaged as the shaft descended. The dynamo activated. The low voltage charge generated. Circuit completed as the shaft heel hit the base-plate contact. And…

Nothing. Except for the *Jefe*'s feeble, blood-laced cough where he still lay slumped at the walnut chest. Time itself suspended as the captives pondered the possibility of delayed effect. Death still ready to take them by surprise at the very moment when they supposed themselves safe. More soldiers ran through the gateway, weapons trained on the survivors. Moroccan *regulares* on the steps too. But the survivors were focused purely on the potentially fickle mechanics of the blasting box and Jack alone, it seemed, had even noticed the soldiers' arrival.

Was it one of these bastards that killed Bertie? Jack wondered. *Obituary to Albert Moorgate, Esquire. Survived Flanders. Successful bank manager. Killed by Franco's army while on honeymoon at Spain's most holy shrine.*

For Bertie was, indeed, dead. Jack removed Albert's spectacles, closed the eyes, finally lifted his gore-soaked hands from the man's neck, placed them instead on the raven-black hair that spilled across the now stilled heart as Frances pressed her face into Moorgate's chest, crooning softly to her lost husband.

What in Christ's name did you think you were doing? thought Jack. *Why didn't you just leave the blasted grappling iron alone? One more stupid, stupid waste.*

'I couldn't save him,' Frances kept repeating.

No, thought Jack, bitterly. *The Saint John's Certificate probably doesn't cover this.*

He looked around the others as they slowly came to terms with their escape.

Catherine had gone quickly to support Sister María Pereda, holding her tightly as the young nun wept and shook.

Alfred Holden was helping Dorothea to her feet, dusting pine needles from his now piss-stained cavalry twills.

'There, my dear,' he said, though his voice trembled, almost broke. 'It looks like we've won after all, eh?'

The Westons still sat, legs outstretched. Max was sobbing quietly.

'It nearly 'it me, Maxie,' murmured his wife. 'That bullet nearly 'it me.'

Peter Kettering was with the *Jefe*. He was lighting a cigarette for him but the *Machado* was trying to tell him something. Something urgent.

'Please,' shouted Peter. 'I don't understand.'

Carter-Holt got to her feet, shook dust from her hair as she went over to them.

'He's asking for the gun,' she said. She was incredulous, then understood. 'He says that we must not let them take him.'

But nobody made any serious attempt to meet his request. The *Jefe* spoke some more, but Carter-Holt could not understand him and Jack thought that the *guerrillero* stood little chance of truly becoming a captive. He was fading fast.

An officer arrived. A fairly senior officer by the look of him. His first task was to rip the wires from the blaster as he glanced around, ordered a couple of his men to remove Encarna's body. Then two more to remove the *Jefe*. They pulled Peter Kettering roughly out of the way, despite his protestations, and they pushed Carter-Holt aside.

'*¡No!*' shrieked Sister María Pereda and she, in turn, shouldered her small form between the troopers, to kneel at the *Jefe*'s side. She looked up at the officer, crossed herself, yelled at him with biblical anger. The *Jefe* reached up to touch her arm, to still her. He spoke. She responded. She seemed to be pleading with him. He shook his head and she rebuked him. Then she took the rosary from her belt and began to pray. The soldiers looked confused, the officer irate. He allowed the nun to continue for perhaps a minute, then gestured to his men. They lifted Sister María Pereda as gently as they were able while some Moroccans came forward to carry away the *Jefe*, out towards the tunnel.

The *guerrillero* looked across at Jack.

'*Adiaŭ, sinjoro Anglo,*' he said. '*Memoru pri mi!*' Remember me.

'I will,' said Jack, but quietly.

'*Memoru ankaŭ,*' cried the *Jefe*, his voice echoing in the tunnel. 'Remember too. If you do not fight the *fascistas* here, you must surely fight them somewhere else!'

And he was gone.

Sister María Pereda was weeping softly.

'What did he say to you?' said Carter-Holt.

'He tell me that his father say him another thing. Never fight an Englishman at sea, nor a Spaniard on land. He say, not even a Spanish nun. Another joke, I think. He ask me for his gun too. But I cannot. It would be a sin. Though I tell him that I will not insult him by sending to the priest. Anyway, he would not have been to Confess. Or Communion. So he could not receive the...*Extremaunción? Las Exequias?*'

'Last rites?' suggested Valerie.

The nun nodded.

'But I tell him that I can still pray for his soul. On the anniversary of his death. Or to have a Mass offered for him.'

'What did he say?'

'Oh, a very bad thing. But who will pray for me, *Señorita*? The gun...'

'I doubt that you have anything to worry about,' said Carter-Holt. 'Without you, we may all be dead. I wonder, would you tell the officer that we need a doctor?' She looked across at the Moorgates. Sister María Pereda spoke to the officer as requested and he, in turn, walked over, crouched by Albert Moorgate's side. He replied to the nun, then stood, issued more orders to his men. Sister María Pereda hung her head.

'He say that this man does not need a doctor.'

'That's barbaric,' said Catherine Kettering. And, at that moment, Harold Fielding arrived leading a small entourage. He was wearing a tweed jacket, red silk kerchief in the breast pocket.

'Oh, my dear people,' he cried. 'What a dreadful ordeal! And...' He noticed the Moorgates apparently for the first time. 'Good heavens. They didn't tell me. Is he...? Mrs Moorgate, I am so...'

'What?' said Frances, lifting her head for the first time. 'Sorry? *Are* you sorry, Mister Fielding? You treated us like pawns in some game. You were supposed to be looking after our interests, weren't you? And now...'

'Dear lady, you must believe me. It was an impossible situation. General Franco was never going to set Ajuriaguerra free. Nor meet any demands under such duress. They wanted to launch a full attack right at the beginning. It took a great deal of persuasion to prevent them. To try to get you all out safely.'

'Well, it didn't work, Mister Vice-Consul, did it?' sneered Peter Kettering.

'It seems not, Mister Kettering. No indeed. Most unfortunate. My most sincere condolences, Mrs Moorgate. But why has nobody...?' He turned to the officer, indicated the corpse, asked a question. There was a curt response, an even more acerbic riposte from the Vice-Consul, and the officer snapped his heels together, his face set in defiant obedience. At his orders, one soldier fetched a blanket, cautiously lifted Frances and covered her husband's torso and face, while another was dispatched back through the tunnel.

'And did General Franco not think about our safety?' said Dorothea Holden. 'I thought that we were supposed to be guaranteed a safe tour.'

'Can't be too hard on Mister Fielding, my dear,' said the Professor. 'You wouldn't expect the *Caudillo* to make concessions to these Bolsheviks. I think we've come out of it remarkably well. Except, that is...'

Jack watched Alfred Holden's Adam's apple bob as he waved a limp hand towards Moorgate's corpse. He stood, gripped Frances by the arm.

'I'm sorry,' said Jack. 'Truly sorry.' And he turned, took two steps, threw a right hook that caught Holden on the cheek, sending him sprawling back against the altar, scattering the photographs and flowers exactly as he had done two nights before. 'They should have thrown you over the cliff when they had the chance,' Jack spat.

The Professor steadied himself, came back with his fists clenched, gangling, almost comic, until Max Weston threw his arms around him, restraining him.

'Let me go,' shouted Holden. 'Pity it wasn't *you*, Telford! One less bloody Red to pollute the British race.'

'Fascist bastard!' snarled Jack, attempting to launch another punch but himself gripped by Peter Kettering.

If you do not fight the fascistas *here, you must surely fight them somewhere else.* But he suspected that the *Jefe* had not intended his words to be taken quite so literally.

'Gentlemen,' said Fielding. 'It's perfectly obvious to me that everybody must be suffering badly from your ordeal. And none more so than this dear lady, surely?' He took one of Frances Moorgate's hands between his own.

'Jack,' whispered Carter-Holt, 'this isn't helping. Calm down now. Look, here's your watch.' She handed the time-piece back to him.

'Alright,' said Jack. 'Alright. And I apologise, Frances. That was unforgiveable.'

'No, Mister Telford,' said Frances, looking Professor Holden squarely in the eyes. 'No, it was not.'

Holden shook himself free of Max Weston's embrace, straightened himself.

'Bloody peasants,' he muttered, as Dorothea led him towards the tunnel. She gave one backwards glance, pulled a face which seemed to say, *But what can one do?*

A stretcher arrived, and Bertie was lifted onto the thing.

'Plenty of time for recriminations later,' said Harold Fielding. 'Full explanations too, of course. But for now we should try to get you all cleaned up, don't you think?'

'Just one question, Mister Fielding,' said Jack, still nursing his fist. It hurt like hell.

'Of course, dear fellow. What is it?'

'The *Jefe*. Where have they taken him?'

'The bandit? Oh, to the Guardia barracks, I assume. They took another one as well. Wounded, but still alive. At least for now. The fellow with the fuzzy hair. Looked a bit like one of the Stooges, didn't you think?'

Sister María Pereda wanted to tidy the altar one last time, but the others persuaded her that somebody else would look after things, and Catherine took charge of her, led her to join the strange cortège that followed Albert Moorgate's bier from Covadonga's *Cueva de la Santina.*

The army officer arranged for the last of his men to collect the scattered weapons, the *Machados*' accoutrements, and they too joined the procession.

Jack noticed the quiet words exchanged between the Vice-Consul and Carter-Holt as they walked behind the Westons, through the tunnel, out into the light. But he halted just before the tunnel's end, stooped to pick up a crumpled Fedora that had been kicked against the rock wall. He flicked dust from the straw crown, straightened the brim and set it upon his head. He hoped that Frances would not mind. But she simply offered him a crumpled smile when she saw him, while Carter-Holt went so far as to lay her fingers on his arm. Almost tenderly. He turned to her as they waited to board the bus. His face was hard.

'What?' she said.

'You knew,' he whispered. 'All that sodding time. You knew!'

She ignored his comment while, at the front of the queue, Albert Moorgate's stretcher was lifted into the back of a waiting ambulance. Frances went with him.

The Holdens, on the other hand, were ushered onto the yellow bull-nosed Dodge, though the vehicle seemed now to be only a shadow of its former self. Neglected, mud-spattered, the name *Badajoz* along the bonnet barely visible beneath the grime.

'I say,' called the Professor, 'couldn't they find somebody other than a wog to drive us?'

A Moroccan was sitting in the driving seat.

Jack still felt guilty about his earlier actions but mostly because he believed his assault on Holden to have shown disrespect to Frances Moorgate and her grief. But he sincerely wished, at that moment, that he had hit the bloody man again. And again. And again. *So much for the pacifist Jack Telford*, he thought. But he remembered Encarna too. Her story.

'What's happened to Mikel?' said Catherine Kettering.

'Oh, they've taken him for routine questioning,' said Fielding. 'Just to get his account of the story.'

'Good thing too,' said Alfred Holden. 'He was one of them, you know. Turned out he'd been having secret meetings with the bandits as far back as Irún.'

'Alfred!' protested Dorothea. 'That's not true. We all know what happened.'

'*Señor* Fielding,' said Sister María Pereda. She was badly distressed. 'She is correct. Mikel had nothing to do with this.'

Holden snorted.

'Well, it will all sort itself out in due course, I'm sure,' said the Vice-Consul.

They fell into silence, no sooner seated, of course, than the bus had turned, doubled back across the esplanade and down the short stretch of road to the hotel.

'It is such a beautiful country,' said the nun, 'for so much killing.'

The Gran Hotel Pelayo seemed to have been converted into a hospital. There appeared to be nurses everywhere, though in truth there were probably no more than three or four. But they helped to usher the passengers through the entrance lobby, draping fresh blankets around their shoulders. Most of the former hostages accepted their help submissively although Catherine, Jack noticed, shook away the proffered assistance. She was angry, distant even from Peter. *Peter her lover,* thought Jack.

Inside, the place smelled of disinfectant. Carbolic soap. The furniture had been pushed back, making space for several other stretchers on the floor.

'Two *Civiles* wounded on Saturday night,' explained Fielding, 'waiting to be shipped off to hospital. And one from this morning, I assume.'

A medical team was completing their treatment of this soldier, his head almost entirely swathed in bandage, bulging with a wad of lint or cotton wool over his right eye. There was a doctor with them, but he left the wounded man as soon as the group arrived. He spoke to the Vice-Consul, then went from one to another, a rapid visual examination, tilted heads, peered into their eyes. Jack was one of the first to attract his attention. The blood, Jack thought. Questions to Fielding again until the doctor was satisfied that Jack was, after all, unharmed.

'I got a terrible 'ead, Mister Fielding,' whined Marguerite. 'Can 'e give me anythin', d'you think?'

'He says that he would recommend a mild sedative for each of you. Luminal. Derivative of barbituric acid, isn't it?'

'Acid?' said Marguerite. 'Ain't 'e got aspirin, then?'

'Oh dear,' said Dorothea. 'I'm afraid I left the aspirin in the cave. I meant to put them in my bag, but then...'

'I'm sure that the doctor will find you some aspirin, Mrs Weston. But I would recommend that you take the sedative too. It's quite harmless, I assure you. And then a hot bath. The hotel will take care of everything for you.'

'Personally,' said Jack, 'I'd settle for a Scotch.'

'Not a problem, I'm sure, Mister Telford. I'll see what I can do.'

'And what about our clothes?' said Dorothea. 'Do you think they might...?'

'I'm sure that they will do everything in their power to make things shipshape again, Mrs Holden,' Fielding replied.

Oh, the tedious routine of it all, thought Jack, as the questions went on. *Half an hour ago we were all ready to string Fielding up for playing us like fools. And now we treat him like Jesus Christ Almighty because he offers a laundry service.*

But the mood swung again when Frances Moorgate returned, just as they were being returned to their rooms.

'It's an absolute outrage,' she wept. 'They've put poor Bertie in an ice house. I couldn't make them understand. Why is he in an ice house, Mister Fielding? With all those...'

'Gracious!' said the Vice-Consul, taking a clean handkerchief from his pocket and passing it to Frances. 'Some misunderstanding, I'm sure. Would you excuse me? I shall escort this dear lady and find out what on earth is going on. You all need some rest and perhaps we should meet back here at...Well, what time shall we say? At one? Very good. Now, Mrs Moorgate. Let's see if we can get this sorted out.'

He beamed at her, offered his arm and led Frances back through the front door of the Hotel.

Jack's room was exactly as he had left it, though a silk dressing gown had been laid across the bed and his copy of *The Hobbit* had been cleared to a bedside cabinet. He peeled off his trench coat, dumped it by the door, the shirt too. He placed the Fedora on the bed post, unfastened his brogues, removed his socks, his light-weight trousers. And then, wrapping himself in the gown, he took his toilet things from the trunk and padded along to the bathrooms. He found Max Weston there too, in his cotton combinations, a pair of striped garters holding up his socks.

'You wore those in your first picture, didn't you?' said Jack. 'I thought you were just playing it for the laughs.' Max stopped in the middle of lathering his face with shaving soap. His eyes were red, misted.

'What d'you mean, me old acker?'

'The combinations, Max. But it doesn't matter.'

'I thought we was all goin' t' die, Jack.'

'I know.'

'But I liked 'e. That leader. I liked 'em all. Why's it like this, Jack?'

Jack shook his head. He could feel tears welling himself. It was worse when he looked in the mirror. So he skipped the shave, went straight to the bath stalls, soaked in the steaming water, hoping to sweat the memories from every pore.

When he returned to his room, his dirty clothes had gone and there was a tray waiting for him. Whiskey. A jug with ice, another with water. He tried to sleep, convinced that it would not be difficult, particularly after a couple of straight shots. But all that happened was a newsreel that played itself over and over again. Grey-shaded images of the past two days. Monotonous repetition.

The clothes in his case were as badly creased as they had been when he arrived. But they somehow looked even worse now. Still, he sorted them as best he could.

*I would have hung them up on Saturday evening if I'd known how long...*He cursed the stupidity of such trivial consideration. How *could* he have known? And he had to keep reminding himself that it was only thirty-six hours. Surely he must have miscalculated.

He went down early for the meeting, not wanting to reinforce the impression that he was always late for such things. But there was nobody else around. One o' clock came and went. He became convinced that he must have made a mistake. That the time may have been changed. Perhaps while he was in the bath. That they had forgotten to tell him. But at quarter-past they began to arrive. The Ketterings. Then Carter-Holt. Sister María Pereda. Vice-Consul Fielding now accompanied once more by *Teniente* Álvaro Enrique Turbides. The Westons. And, at almost one-thirty, the Holdens. They all had the same problem, it seemed. An inability to meet each other's eyes. Greetings were hushed, almost guilty. *Is this really all of us?* thought Jack. The waiting was painful, and even when the Holdens had finally arrived, Fielding led them to another room but did not seem to know how to begin. He kept glancing at the door as though, perhaps, Sister Berthe Schultz, or Brendan Murphy, or the Moorgates, were simply delayed.

'I assume that Frances won't be joining us?' said Catherine, at last.

'No, indeed,' said the Vice-Consul. 'The saw-bones prescribed a stronger sedative for the poor dear.' Jack felt the inside pocket of his jacket, expecting to find a packet of *Capstan* there. But they had all gone. Of course they had. 'Oh, please...' said Fielding, offering his cigarette case, the *Du Mauriers*. 'Have one of mine. Now, where shall we start?'

'With poor Mister Moorgate perhaps,' said Catherine. 'Did you manage to find what they've done with him?'

'Yes, of course, dear lady. Dreadful. There is an ice house that serves the hotel. For refrigeration purposes, you understand. Cold storage. Some of their foodstuffs. Since there's no hospital in the vicinity, the army thought it advisable...Well, you take my drift, I'm sure.'

'But the poor man has been moved now?' Catherine was becoming impatient, vexed.

'Oh, yes. The local undertaker from Cangas is giving him the best of attention, even as we speak. Mrs Moorgate was not entirely satisfied but I've persuaded her that it is the best we can expect, in the circumstances.'

'The best that we can expect?' said Jack.

'Yes,' said Fielding. 'They intend to lay him out...Is that the correct expression? Yes. In the Basilica.'

'Are you being serious, Mister Fielding?' said Dorothea. 'Mister Moorgate was so...Well...'

'C of E,' said Jack.

'Just a temporary measure,' said the Vice-Consul. 'I fear that he is likely to become something of a martyr for the folk hereabouts.'

'Another photograph for the altar then?' said Peter Kettering.

'Yes, perhaps. Though there seem to be one or two questions about the way in which he met his end.' Fielding turned to say something to the *Teniente.* 'Caught in the cross-fire, we assume?'

'Caught in the act of trying to help those bandits, as it happens,' sneered Professor Holden.

'I don't understand you, Professor,' said the Vice-Consul.

'Started behaving like a madman,' Holden continued. 'Went for the grappling irons. Heaving them back down again. Began to wonder whose side he was on.'

The *Teniente* asked a question. Fielding shook his head.

'*No*,' he said. '*No pasa nada.*' It's nothing. Nothing at all.

'Well, I think the *Teniente* should know,' the Professor said. '*El Señor Moorgate*...'

'Alfred!' snapped Dorothea. 'That is *quite* enough!'

Holden recoiled like a whipped dog.

'Yes,' said Fielding, 'maybe best to keep that little snippet to ourselves. Just for now, eh? But, meanwhile, *Mrs* Moorgate seems relatively content with the arrangement. A bit unorthodox, I know, but...'

'But the fact is, Mister Fielding,' said Peter, 'that Bertie Moorgate wouldn't have been in danger at all if the army hadn't unleashed that attack. There must have been *some* other way to resolve matters, surely?'

'I'm afraid not. I tried several different approaches to present the *Machados*' demands in a more acceptable way. I even suggested some counter-proposals. But Burgos would have none of it.'

'That doesn't really explain,' said Kettering, 'why we weren't warned.'

'Yes,' said Jack. 'Just imagine how bad it might have been if Miss Carter-Holt hadn't had her wits about her and told us all to get down at seven sharp. Why, somebody might have been *seriously* hurt.'

'Sarcasm is unlikely to help Frances Moorgate deal with her loss, Mister Telford,' said Catherine, and Jack lowered his head. 'And what about the *Machados*, Mister Fielding?' she continued. 'Where are they?'

'In the Guardia barracks, as I assumed,' said the Vice-Consul. 'Though the leader...they call him Guadalito, by the way. Did you know? Just an alias, of course. Anyway, he didn't seem to be long for this world.'

'Good riddance to the scum,' hissed Professor Holden. 'Hopefully, they'll make him squeal before he dies though.'

'I think they're more hopeful of gleaning some information from the other one. Code name Romero, apparently.'

Jack thought about the Fedora.

'Well, we can't just leave them there,' said Catherine. 'Surely?' The foolishness of the question dawned on her. She blushed.

'Like I said,' Fielding smiled sympathetically, 'a difficult time. And, when you're ready, perhaps we could move on?'

'Yes,' said Dorothea. 'What *does* happen next, Mister Fielding? And why is the

Teniente here. Not to trouble us with more nonsense about shoes, surely?'

'Well, I just wants to get 'ome,' said Marguerite. 'Me and Maxie both, Don't we, Maxie?' Max Weston nodded.

'One thing at a time, eh, Mrs Weston? So far as the *Teniente* is concerned, he is merely here to wish you goodbye. He has decided to close the case on Miss Britten. An unfortunate accident, after all, he has concluded.' Fielding spoke to the Lieutenant, and the Lieutenant addressed the meeting. 'There!' said the Vice-Consul when the Spaniard had finished. 'All done.' But not quite, apparently, for the Lieutenant handed Fielding a paper bag, made a further brusque comment. 'Ah,' said the Vice-Consul. 'Your passports.' He sorted through the contents, returning documents to the relevant survivors, discreetly retaining the rest. 'And he says that he is instructed to offer you condolences from his superiors. Hardly the best of holidays, he says.'

'Gosh, no,' said Jack. 'Like going off to Barbados and finding that your hotel isn't quite finished. Or coming all the way to Covadonga and finding repairs in progress. Is *that* what he means?'

Max Weston sniggered. The *Teniente* asked for an explanation and Fielding fobbed him off once again.

'Well, anyway,' said the Vice-Consul. 'The *Teniente* will be stepping out of your life but I'm afraid we're not quite done with the Spanish military just yet.'

'Why ever not, Mister Fielding?' said Dorothea. 'You are surely not going to tell us that we'll be wanted for questioning about the hostage situation?'

'It's understandable, in the circumstances, dear lady. But they promise not to detain you longer than necessary. They say that it will take no more than five or ten minutes each. The Military Governor himself wants to meet you, it seems. So you will remain near the hotel precincts, will you not? Good. And then afterwards... Well, decisions to be made, I suppose.'

'Decisions?' said Jack.

'Yes. It seems that the *Generalísimo* is rather assuming that some of you may want to go on to Santiago. To meet him there. The presentation of the medal on behalf of your brother, Mister Kettering. That sort of thing. And Miss Carter-Holt, of course. General Franco has already received reports of your gallant actions in helping to protect your countrymen and women, my dear. Another medal for yourself too, unless I'm much mistaken.'

'Well I wants to go 'ome,' whimpered Marguerite. 'I can't stay in this place another day.'

'I think myself and Alfred have had enough, too, Mister Fielding,' said Dorothea. 'We can always come back another time.'

'Yes,' said her husband, 'when every last Red has been put in the ground!'

'Mrs Moorgate,' said the Vice-Consul, 'will naturally be returning to England with her late husband. As soon as we can make the arrangements. For Mister Murphy too, naturally. I'm afraid it's becoming rather a regular thing.'

'I have a question, *Señor*,' said Sister María Pereda.

'Yes, Sister. Of course. If I can help.'

'Can you tell me about the *Santina, Señor*? Is it true that she is now with the British in Paris?'

'Why, yes!' beamed Fielding. 'I should have said so, should I not? I'm told, Sister, that your *Santina* will be returned to Covadonga very shortly.'

'Then, *Señor,* I should like to continue. To Santiago. To meet *El Caudillo.*'

'Are you quite sure, Sister?' said Fielding. 'Perhaps I should have mentioned that the Swiss Attaché has been in touch too. Your Order has apparently agreed that Sister Berthe Schultz should be buried here, along with the priest who was killed. There will be a Special Mass said for them this Sunday.'

'Then I shall go to Santiago but return here for the weekend, *Señor.*'

'Capital!' said the Vice-Consul. 'So, where does that leave us? Just yourself, Mister Telford. On to Santiago, or back to Blighty?'

'Well,' said Jack. 'I can't really think of any reason to stay. The *Santina* to be returned to Covadonga, you say? Feels like mission accomplished, doesn't it? Yes, back to England for me, I think. So long as I don't have to travel with the Professor, of course. Would it be a foolish question, I wonder, if I asked how this whole fiasco will be reported in the British press?'

'Ah!' said Fielding. 'No, not foolish at all. Press release being issued from Burgos in the next hour, I understand. Usual thing. Reds on the rampage. Innocent Brits taken hostage. Total disregard for innocent lives. Valiant action on the part of National Spain's armed forces. Mister Moorgate sadly killed by the bandits before he could be freed. General Franco to intensify the campaign to rid his country of these outlaw elements. War Routes of the North to continue with nothing more to fear.'

They dispersed in silence, waiting now to be summoned for their formal debriefing.

'You must be very proud of yourself,' muttered Jack as he passed Carter-Holt.

'No, not particularly so, Mister Telford. But perhaps I will be, when I reach Santiago.' Jack walked away. 'No, wait,' she said to him. He had rarely seen her so hesitant. Almost vulnerable. 'I wonder whether I might ask *you* something?'

'Oh, *anything!*' Jack replied, but he felt like slapping the woman. Slapping her and, at the same time, holding her close to him.

'It's just that I was wondering. Whether you might change your mind, Mister Telford? And come along with me on the rest of the journey?'

Chapter Twenty-Three

Monday 26 September 1938

I must be mad to even think about it, Jack mused as he waited outside the same room an hour later. *Why me?* She had offered him no further explanation. Simply a *take it or leave it* gesture as she left him. And he found that he could not leave it. Did not really want to. Relished the thought of spending time with her, infuriating as she might be.

He had picked up a copy of *ABC* from the front desk. It was yesterday's. But when he carefully asked one of the receptionists whether there was a copy of today's paper, he was sure that the fellow had replied to the effect that there *was* no newspaper today. So Jack flicked through the Sunday edition. There was a full front-page picture of Runciman, in Czechoslovakia as Chamberlain's special envoy, trying to soothe the justified fears of President Beneš. So he turned the pages, hoping to find the associated leader articles. But it was not easy. There were advertisements, for sherry, for stomach medicines. News of Bulgaria's King Boris on holiday in Paris. The blessing and presentation of new banners to the Falange in Santoña. Lengthy celebrations of the advances made under Franco by his New Spain. Kint's victory in the World Cycling Championships. And photographs of Max Factor, surrounded by this year's Miss America contestants, a tribute to his career and recent death.

No more mention of the Sudeten crisis until page seven. Hitler's thanks to Chamberlain for his continued mediation. Hitler's ultimatum to the Czechs, giving them six days to agree annexation of the Sudetenland to Germany. Renewed optimism in England, according to *ABC*, about the prospects for peace.

The door opened. Vice-Consul Fielding thanked the Holdens for their cooperation. They walked past Jack without a word.

Inside the room, the weapons and equipment of the *Machados* were displayed on several tables. Dark metal menace. There was a strong smell of oil, bitter, mechanical, that he had not noticed while they were in the cave. A design on the blasting machine too. A small skull and crossed bones stencilled in faded white on the back, the word *Peligro* underneath.

Jack was offered a seat.

He was in eminent company, apparently. Colonel Balguarde from the Guardia Civil, a senior investigator. Sixty perhaps. Cruelly sharp features. A civilian note-taker at his side. A second civilian, with the well-fed tones of a tenor. *Señor* Caballero, Civil Governor of Asturias. And the Military Governor too, General

Rafael Latorre Roca, a small man with a matching moustache, his army greatcoat draped around his shoulders. According to the *Jefe*, this was the man who had ordered the execution of so many since he had assumed his office a year earlier.

'So why are we here?' said Jack as soon as the introductions were completed.

'They want to know about the bandit leader,' Fielding replied.

'Not bandits, Mister Fielding. Surely not. The *Machados*. Didn't you tell us so? Part of the Republic's Guerrilla Army Corps. I won't play charades with these gentlemen, Mister Fielding.'

'No, Mister Telford. Naturally not.' He paused to offer some explanation to the Guardia Colonel. 'They called him *Guadalito*, as I may have mentioned. A *nom de guerre*, you understand. Real name, Eduardo Pinchón.' Fielding removed an information sheet from a manila file, slid it across the table. At the top of the page was a photograph of the *Jefe*. Not a recent picture. 'They'd like to know what he wanted.'

'Wasn't it *you* who did the negotiations, Mister Fielding? You must know what he wanted much better than me.'

'I think these gentlemen are seeking the inside story, so to speak. Professor Holden says that you spoke with Pinchón at great length. In Esperanto. I was very impressed, Mister Fielding.' The Colonel of *Civiles* asked a question. 'Ah. He wants to know where you learned your Esperanto.'

'Does he want to study it too? It would save him needing an interpreter. Just imagine how useful it would be when he's interrogating Internationals.'

'He asks whether you're a Communist.'

'Is the Pope a Catholic?' replied Jack.

'You *are* a Communist then, Mister Telford?'

'What happens if I say *yes*, Mister Vice-Consul?'

'You're amongst friends here, Mister Telford. These gentlemen have recently rescued you from ruthless killers. I don't believe they would expect gratitude but a little co-operation might help us along here.'

Jack laughed.

'Co-operation? We spent thirty-six hours labouring under the illusion that our Government's representatives and Franco's government in Burgos were negotiating our safe release. And all the time you were plotting another killing spree. You and Miss Carter-bloody-Holt.'

'Mister Telford, I can barely imagine the emotions that you must be suffering just now but all they want to know is why this *Guadalito* needed a sniper's rifle with a telescopic sight. That one. There on the table. You see it?'

'I see it.'

'And...?'

'I don't know,' Jack sighed. 'He said something about when Juan de Ajuriaguerra arrived, and your General Latorre.' He nodded his head towards the old soldier. 'And he said, *we'll see*.'

'Nothing else?'

'No.' *You see, Mister English, even now sometimes the Republic needs an executioner.* 'Nothing else.'

Fielding translated.

'They want to know why Pinchón, this *Guadalito,* should bother telling you his life story?'

'I was curious. It helped pass the time.'

'And did he confess to killing anybody else? Any priests, for example?'

'No. Quite the opposite.'

Jack remembered the *Jefe*'s story. *Our priest was a good man. Poor. Like us. He tried to stop the killings. We let him live.*

'But he *did* kill the priest and nun in the cave?'

'It wasn't him.'

'He was the *Jefe*, was he not, Mister Telford? He was in charge. He holds the rank of Captain, did you know? In the Machado Brigade.' Fielding turned to the others. '*No sabe nada*,' he said. He knows nothing. Colonel Balguarde put another question. 'He wants you to tell them about the driver. Mikel. The Professor says that Mikel met Pinchón in Irún?'

'That's nonsense. The man approached Mikel, called him a traitor, asked him for information about the route we were taking. But Mikel refused.'

'And how do you know this?'

'He told the nun. Sister María Pereda.'

'But not your guide? Not Mister Murphy?'

'Apparently he told her that he was ashamed. That he was frightened. It seems he thought that the army would send him back to the Front.'

Fielding relayed the response to the Colonel, the Civil Governor and the General. Latorre laughed, spoke sharply to the Vice-Consul.

'He says that this driver is not so stupid. For a Basque, he says. It seems, Mister Telford, that this Mikel has already been sent to rejoin his regiment.'

'They can't! He didn't do anything.'

'The Professor says that *you* met Pinchón in Irún too. You see, Mister Telford, they are extremely worried about all this.'

'I didn't even speak to the man. I was with Nora Hames. If anything, I think we scared him off. And, to be honest, Mister Fielding, I'm not really inclined to answer any more of this nonsense. Aren't you supposed to be looking after my interests?'

'You'll never know, Mister Telford. You'll *really* never know.' General Latorre had risen from the table, huddled within the greatcoat and walked around to stand behind Jack's chair. He lit a cigar, whispered to the Vice-Consul. 'He asks whether anybody else can confirm that you didn't speak with Pinchón, in Irún?'

'Nora Hames, of course. And Mikel, naturally.'

'How convenient. You see the problem? You understand where this might lead, Mister Telford?'

Jack understood very well. Arthur Koestler was not the only foreign journalist to have crossed the Nationalists and been jailed for their stance. Jailed or worse.

And, in Jack's case, he had already realised that there was no collateral which could save his neck.

'I'm telling you the truth, Mister Fielding. Professor Holden is a fool.'

Fielding considered for a moment.

'Yes,' he said. 'I know he is.' He spoke to the Spaniards. The Colonel passed some more file pages to Jack's side of the table. General Latorre tapped each of them in turn with the butt of his cigar, leaning across Jack as he did so. More snapshots. 'So what about these, Mister Telford? Encarnación Bodella. Luís Belarmino, also known as *El Pescador*.' Moe. 'Or this one. Jordi Camillo. They call him *Puente*.' It was Curly. 'And finally, Alfonso Toxo. *El Romero*.' Larry.

'What do you want to know?'

'Who killed the priest and the nun?'

Jack tapped Encarna's picture. She was already dead, after all.

'And Pinchón himself shot your guide?'

'Yes.'

'And this Toxo character,' Fielding pointed to Larry's sheet. 'Professor Holden says that Mister Moorgate befriended him. That they became close. How did Mister Moorgate die? They want you to confirm that he was not shot by Nationalists, Mister Telford. It's very important. Better if he was hit in the cross-fire? You can't be sure, after all.'

Jack considered for a moment. 'Yes,' he said. 'Cross-fire.' He thought again about Moorgate. He still had no idea what had driven Bertie to act that way with the grappling irons. Just one more thing to haunt him. Had he thought that he might somehow prevent the inevitable? Had his new-found empathy with Romero turned his head?

'Good, Mister Telford. Good. Now tell us about Miss Carter-Holt. They're anxious to provide a positive report to the *Caudillo*.'

'Well, no problem there. None at all. Miss Carter-Holt definitely saved the day. But, d'you know, Mister Fielding, that you brought the poor lady a defective pack of cards?'

Fielding coughed, spoke at length to the Colonel. The General nodded, seemed pleased, took his seat again.

'Thank you, Mister Fielding. That's very helpful.' The Colonel interrupted him. Fielding seemed confused. 'Ah, he's asking whether there's anything you can tell us about the weapons.'

Jack glanced at the tables.

'I don't understand.'

The Colonel spoke again.

'Oh, I apologise, Mister Telford. I'd forgotten. Professor Holden reminded us that one of the guns is missing. Mister Murphy's automatic pistol. Any idea where it went?'

'None at all. Wasn't it their men who collected the weapons?'

'Yes. Quite so. You're sure you don't know?'

'Yes, I'm sure. Now, is it my turn for a question?'

Fielding looked towards the General.

'What is it?' he said.

'The blasting box,' said Jack. 'What went wrong? Why didn't it work?'

'Are you feeling guilty that you survived, Mister Telford? It's a common enough emotion, so they say.' The Vice-Consul spoke to Colonel Balguarde. The response was lengthy.

'Well?' said Jack.

'The Colonel says that the detonator failed for the same reason that the *Generalísimo* is winning this war. His material is better, both the quality and the quantity. And, of course, they've had some considerable help from friends abroad.'

'Italy and Germany?'

'Great Britain too, Mister Telford. We shouldn't be too modest about these things.'

'What about the blasting machine?'

'A length of faulty wiring, apparently.'

Jack nodded.

'The *Jefe*. What's happened to him?'

'Dead, Mister Telford.'

'And the other man. *Romero*?'

'Almost.'

'Then I suppose we're all finished here,' said Jack.

'I suppose so, Mister Telford.' The Colonel spoke. The General nodded. The Civil Governor too. 'The Colonel thanks you on behalf of National Spain. For all your assistance. He hopes that you will have a safe journey back to the border. And he looks forward to joining you and the others for dinner.'

'Dinner?' said Jack. 'Are they serious?'

'I'm afraid so, Mister Telford. I don't think they expect everybody to attend, in the circumstances, but it would be good if you could be there.'

'Well,' Jack replied. 'Perhaps. But there is just *one* thing.'

'Tell me, Mister Telford.'

'I've changed my mind. I'm not going back to the border. I'd like to go on to Santiago.'

Fielding looked surprised, then alarmed. He stole a glance at the General.

'That may not be such a good idea,' he said. 'I rather think that they would prefer you to leave the country as soon as possible.'

'Then you'd better persuade them otherwise, Mister Vice-Consul. After all, it *is* your friend, Miss Carter-Holt who's asked me to accompany her.'

The dinner was a strange affair and, as it happened, only Frances Moorgate, for perfectly understandable reasons, absented herself from the gathering.

It was almost fourteen hours since their release and they had all had the chance to bathe, to shave, to use a civilised toilet, in most cases to sleep, and to dress themselves in the best attire that their limited luggage might allow. Dorothea had suggested that they should all meet at nine so that they could enter the dining room *en masse*.

She thought it better that way and Jack, though he had initially scoffed at the idea, had been surprised to find himself increasingly agitated, needing the group's company as the hour approached, pleased that she had made the necessary arrangements. He had no particular desire to spend time with some of the individuals, naturally, but he now saw the group as an eccentric collective to which he had unwittingly become a part.

He had packed a white smoking jacket, a dickie bow, hoping to save them for the journey's end but this, he realised, was that very event, the breaking of this disparate company.

'Oh,' cried Catherine Kettering. 'How very Fred Astaire. So elegant.'

But elegant was one word that Jack would never apply to himself. His nose too pinched, he always thought. Chin too severe. Ears just too large.

'Looks more like Groucho Marx t' me,' said Max Weston, and he slapped Jack on the back as though they were friends reunited after a lengthy separation.

Night at the Opera, thought Jack. *How appropriate.*

'You mean Karl Marx, surely?' Alfred Holden guffawed.

'Shall we go in?' said Dorothea. And she led them through the corridors to the fine dining room of the Gran Hotel Pelayo.

There were nine guests to match the nine tourists, though they were no longer simply *that*, Jack realised. They had themselves become a living embodiment of the War Route in the North. The next trip – and, yes, there would certainly *be* a next trip – would arrive at the *Cueva de la Santina* in Covadonga to be shown the *Santina* herself, restored to the shrine thanks to the sacrifice of three more martyrs for National Spain. The Irish Guide. The English Banker. The Swiss Nun. Their photos would join the others lined along the altar.

So the guests, six men, three women, scraped back their chairs. They stood. They applauded. They offered fascist salutes, right arms, rigid fingers, straight, outstretched. But there was this change at least, Jack noticed. For the only response they now received, the only salute returned, was from Alfred Holden. Dorothea managed a self-conscious smile, but the others simply averted their eyes, exchanged embarrassed glances, lowered their heads.

He recognised recent acquaintances amongst these guests who were also their hosts. General Latorre Roca. Colonel Balguarde and a lady that Jack could only adequately describe as 'painted'. The Civil Governor, *Señor* Caballero, with a woman too drab to be anything but his wife. A man that he did not know, dressed in the civilian uniform blue shirt of the Falange, an attractive female at his side, tiny and with Moorish features. Two older associates. The Burgos Press Officer, Captain Rosalles. And the architect of the War Route tours, Laureano de Armas Gourié.

At the foot of the table, neither host, guest nor visitor, stood Vice-Consul Fielding.

'Ladies and gentlemen,' he beamed. 'Please. You'll find name cards at each of the place settings.'

They shuffled around the table, hands shaken, the women kissed on each cheek, right then left, eventually locating their seats. Jack found himself next to

Fielding, opposite Rosalles and the architect, the Caballeros to his right.

'Mister Telford,' said *Señor* de Armas Gourié, 'I cannot tell you how pleased I am to see you safe.' Jack had forgotten the extent of the man's elegance. His charm. 'Such an ordeal. I admire the courage of you all. And my apologies that I could not join you earlier, as I promised. Perhaps, well...'

'All over now,' said the Vice-Consul. 'And, Mister Telford, please allow me to properly introduce *Señor* Caballero and his good lady wife.'

Jack muttered a greeting.

'Gerardo is quite a hero too,' said the architect. 'He led the Falange during the Movement in Oviedo. But he now has responsibility for the reconstruction. Three hundred towns and villages destroyed across Asturias. Three thousand dwellings gone in Oviedo alone.'

'And are you here to offer him your professional and technical assistance?' Jack enquired.

'No, Mister Telford. Gran Canaria keeps me fully occupied so far as architecture is concerned.' He looked to the Vice-Consul. 'Am I allowed to share our secret, Mister Fielding?'

'Oh, allow me, sir,' said Fielding. 'You'll be pleased to know, Mister Telford, that *Señor* de Armas Gourié has agreed to accompany those who are proceeding to Santiago.'

'And does that include *me*, Mister Fielding?'

'It seems so, Mister Telford. I explained to the General that Miss Carter-Holt has vouched for your integrity and, as a result...'

'How very decent of her,' said Jack. He still had too many questions about Valerie.

'By the way, Mister Telford,' said the Spaniard, 'you missed the excitement at Brooklands last week. Marjorie Eccles raced the Rapier again. But she say it is for the last time. For her, anyway.' Roy Eccles had died in April. A brain haemorrhage, Jack thought.

'Roy was a brilliant driver,' said Jack. 'That's quite a tribute she's paid him.'

'But she did not win.'

'No,' Jack replied. 'I was at Crystal Palace last year when she rolled the thing.'

'The London Grand Prix?' exclaimed de Armas Gourié. 'I was there too. Such a coincidence. My dear fellow! But that car has many good years still, I think. *¡Cielos!* That supercharger. The new dampers.'

'It needs them for the Brooklands track, doesn't it?' said Jack.

Caballero directed a question at the architect, and the Spaniard offered an explanation. The Civil Governor seemed incredulous. *He must think we're both mad*, thought Jack.

'My good friend, Gerardo, does not understand the English, I fear.'

'We barely understand ourselves, sir,' said Harold Fielding.

'You seem to understand us very well, *Señor*,' said Jack. 'It should be an interesting journey to Santiago.'

Food was served. Wine was poured. It was hardly a joyous occasion but it was more entertaining than Jack had imagined possible. An outpouring of relief, perhaps. Though he could not adequately have explained the bizarre way that he felt.

The waiters brought a silver tureen of *consommé* to the table.

'Ah,' said the architect. 'A good Asturian *cocido*.'

Jack nodded.

'Hey, Max,' he called, 'what's this fly doing in my soup?'

Max stood so that he could see better.

'Looks like breast-stroke t' me,' he replied. 'But 'ang about me 'ansum. What's orange an' sounds like a parrot?'

'A carrot?'

They laughed until tears rolled down their faces. They laughed until the Civil Governor, the *Falangista*, Gerardo Caballero, finally threw down his serviette, angered beyond toleration, exchanged protestations about them with the General, dragged the dowdy woman from her chair and stormed from the dining room.

General Latorre Roca waved a dismissive hand, as if to say that he had seen worse. At the Front.

What's small, red and whispers?

They laughed, Jack Telford and Max Weston, while Marguerite complained of headache, stomach cramps.

Why was the mushroom invited to the party?

They laughed through Catherine Kettering's furious outburst. There were tears in *her* eyes too, and Jack wondered why his own face was still so damp.

'Why should it matter what General Franco's press release says?' she yelled down the table at Vice-Consul Fielding. 'If Luis Bolín says that we're all still alive, the world will believe him, regardless of the truth. Won't it? Won't it?'

How do you approach an angry Welsh cheese?

Max and Jack laughed while the Holdens explained, in their fractured Spanish, how much they would miss the golf, the fly-fishing, the chamois hunt. But, no, they must return to England. So much work, they explained, to be done for the Anglo-German Fellowship. Chancellor Hitler so *badly* misunderstood. Germany *so* lacking in allies. The two men laughed until the Holdens also begged to be excused, looking at Jack in disgust as they passed his place, even though Jack himself could see them only dimly.

Somebody made an apology for him.

What happened to the cannibal that caught and ate the Chinese man?

They laughed while Carter-Holt and Sister María Pereda argued with General Rafael Latorre Roca that he was wrong to categorise all Republicans as *'Reds, Atheists and Freemasons.'* Why, their own driver was an excellent example of a devout Basque Catholic who had believed firmly in the Popular Front.

They laughed at the nun's outrage as she learned, for the first time, that Mikel Iruko Domínguez was now being given a further chance to renounce that heresy, now on his way to the Ebro.

Jack laughed. *Am I laughing?* He shook. He could not control the shaking. *Why am I so damned cold?*

They laughed while Laureano de Armas Gourié tried to explain how important it still remained that these tours should help to dispel the vile rumours, perpetrated by the Zionist press, of Nationalist atrocity and disregard for common decency. To explain the continuing menace of the Red Terror.

'Do you see now, Mister Telford?'

Do you see, Jack?

Do you…?

'Are you feeling unwell, Mister Telford?' somebody asked.

He was still laughing when Carter-Holt and Sister María Pereda helped him from the table.

He laughed as he saw Franco's favourite comedian lifted from his own chair by Marguerite and the Ketterings. The big fellow still had tears running down his face. Just wait until he had the chance to tell Sydney Elliott about this. Sydney would laugh too, he was sure of it.

'I must phone him,' said Jack, racked even now by his own laughter.

'Who, Jack?' said Carter-Holt, as they helped him into the lift.

'Oh,' he said in dismay. 'No lifts! I don't like lifts.'

'You must not worry, *Señor*,' said the nun. 'Everything will be better in the morning.'

'But I must phone…'

'Who, Jack? Who do you want to phone?'

'Elliott,' he replied.

'Maybe tomorrow,' said Carter-Holt, when they finally got him back to his room.

He laughed some more when Sister María Pereda modestly averted her eyes while the Reuters correspondent removed his white tuxedo, heaved him onto the bed and loosened the bow tie, tried to dry his face, removed his shoes.

Fred Astaire, he thought. *Very…*

'There's a coffee shortage,' he said.

'Yes,' replied Carter-Holt. 'It's terrible. Did you want coffee, Jack? Would it help?'

'I had one,' he muttered. 'At Fuenterrabía.'

Jack's world did not feel funny anymore. He was desperately tired.

'He'll be worried about me. When he reads Franco's press release.'

'Sydney Elliott?'

Jack tried to nod but the pillows seemed to have a grip on his ears.

The bells of the Basilica rang.

'You knew!' he said to her, remembering something vague and distant, spinning into empty infinity. 'But why can't you let me go home?'

She put a hand on his forehead, shifted some of the prematurely thinning hair.

'Because I need you,' she whispered, 'to protect me.'

Chapter Twenty-Four

Tuesday 27 September 1938

The driver was clearly under some instruction to make the short detour, back to the esplanade, past the Basilica, and then a tight circle at the end of the road which housed the Guardia barracks so that they had a privileged view of the five coffins. They stood upright against the whitened wall of the building, simple wooden crates. In the case of the *Jefe*, the box was not quite long enough to properly contain his frame, so that his head was tilted badly to one side. His hair seemed to have been combed, however, made presentable for the photographer who was now arranging final details for the required snaps. The fellow adjusted the *Jefe*'s bandoliers, straightened the pin-striped jacket, brushed away some dust from the darkly stained material. Encarna stood next to him, glazed eyes fixed on the hotel, arms folded across the bodice of her blouse, her shawl pulled tight around her shoulders as though to shield her from the early chill. Curly and Moe – he had already forgotten their real names, had made no note of them – lounged side by side, faces turned slightly towards each other as though sharing some last intimacy, arms ramrod straight, fingers stretched in an unnatural backward curve. And Larry at the farther end. Alfonso Toxo. *El Romero.* He was the smallest of the *guerrilleros*, Jack realised. The wiry reddish hair that had lent him extra height in life was now limp and flat, plastered down with some form of grease or oil. But nothing could disguise the damage that had been inflicted upon him. His left eye socket was so pulped that it was impossible to tell whether anything remained within. And his face showed small black marks that could easily have been burns.

Jack nursed the straw Fedora on his knee.

He had promised Frances that he would cherish the thing when the group had said their farewells fifteen minutes earlier, and he was fervently glad that she had been spared this sight. She had been brave, taken care of her appearance, the stylish black slicker restored to its former elegance, but she had needed no gardenia face powder to exaggerate the pallor of her features this morning. She had supervised the loading of Albert's coffin into the Abadal-Buick hearse and then taken her leave of them, one by one, before shunning convention and climbing into the front seat beside the olive-liveried chauffeur.

'Will you come to see me, Jack?' she had said, as he passed her umbrella into the car. 'When you get back to England? And come back soon, Jack. Don't stay too long in this terrible place. You must take good care of yourself.' Jack promised to do so, surprised by how much he was attracted to her, and she pulled him close, kissed him on the cheek, also with more tenderness than he had expected.

'Why did he do it, Frances?' he whispered. But she had no answers for him either. She shook her head quickly, there was an exchange of feeble smiles, and she was gone.

Then it had been the turn of the Westons and the Holdens too, each couple allotted a car to take them east as Fielding had explained at breakfast.

As it happened, Jack had hoped to escape everybody else by eating early. At seven. He had been awake at five, shaved once more, shocked by the sunken-eyed reflection that he saw in the bathroom mirror. He had smoked several cigarettes, having reclaimed the *Senior Service* taken from the cave. But they had not helped to relieve the deep shame that he felt from his previous evening's behaviour. He could barely explain it. The wine had played its part, naturally, but he had also felt desperately disorientated, consumed by a morbid sense of loss, palpitations in his chest that he could not control. A sense of profound and hysterical panic. But the others had all arrived at the dining room ahead of him. An uncomfortable silence. A silence not occasioned in the slightest by Jack's performance at dinner, it transpired, but rather by each of their own reactions to recent confinement, The Westons still felt physically ill, the Holdens haughty and distant, the Ketterings irascible with each other and with everybody else too.

So the parting, when it had come, was surprisingly brief.

Marguerite had treated Jack almost as though he were a stranger. He should have been pleased, of course, but found that he was offended. Max, on the other hand, was almost speechless with sadness.

'Marguerite says that if there be a war, I might get t' entertain the troops,' he said, though he could not bring himself to look at Jack directly.

'Good for you, old chap!' said Jack. 'Just make sure you stay out of the bloody army yourself. You may need to take up an instrument too. What about the ukulele? You should be able to pick up a good one in Mexico.'

Max smiled to himself, offered Jack his hand, though in a surreptitious, sideways fashion to hide that he was sobbing again. Then he was gone, away towards Santander where they would join Frances for the voyage home.

Alfred Holden, of course, had said not a single word, waiting in their own car, bound for the French border. Dorothea, however, had made a point of kissing each of those who were staying.

'Do you know,' she had said, 'that there's every chance we might not be able to catch a north-bound express until Friday? So we may all meet again in San Sebastián. I would so *dearly* have loved to go forward with you. Seems such a waste not to do so if we can't get home in any case. But Alfred has been *so* affected by his ordeal. Not himself at all. So you won't think badly of him?'

No, of course they would not. As if such a thing was possible…

And, finally, there had just been Fielding.

'What about you, Mister Fielding?' said Catherine Kettering. There seemed to Jack to be more than just a tinge of sarcasm in her voice. 'Shall we see you back in San Sebastián too?'

'I'm afraid not, dear lady. It appears that London requires my presence post-haste. Can't afford to wait for the luxury of Friday's express either. Damnable journey on the slow trains for me. And Murphy's corpse to be dispatched to Bilbao first. Still…'

'Need to explain your part in the murder of a British citizen, I imagine?' Jack had said.

'My part?' said Fielding.

'You lent them your suit and hat as I recall. Actively helped them with the pretence. Does that fall within your normal consular duties, Mister Fielding?'

'They were never going to let the *Machados* escape alive, Mister Telford. My task was to limit the damage, so to speak. London will understand. And sometimes there are larger issues at stake.'

Jack would have asked for an explanation, but the Vice-Consul had already moved on to take his leave of Carter-Holt.

'And you, my dear,' he had whispered. 'Are you sure that you want to continue with this?'

'Yes,' she had said. 'Quite sure. After all, I have Mister Telford to look after me now.'

So they had climbed aboard the bus, greeted by a nervous Laureano de Armas Gourié, head buried deep in pages of notes as they passed the corpses of the *guerrilleros*. The driver struggled with the unfamiliar gears and the passengers said nothing – though Jack imagined that they must all have shared the same thought: that Mikel had been infinitely the better driver. It was a grey morning but with the promise of better weather to come. Yet when they reached the main road and turned left, Jack could not help laughing once again.

'So,' he said, 'we never got to see Brendan's famous lakes after all!' Without Dorothea they had been free to sit wherever they liked. Carter-Holt had taken up the front nearside seat, the Ketterings just behind, Sister María Pereda across the aisle from them, and the Spaniard just behind her. So the double seat behind the driver was free, and Jack had occupied it. 'And you know, Miss Carter-Holt,' he continued, 'that I simply agreed to continue with the journey. I never made any commitment to look after anybody but myself.'

'And not especially good at that particular task either, I should say,' she replied. 'Still, we can discuss that later. How's the article coming along anyway? The *Machados* must have given you some original angles, surely?'

She was wearing the navy suit again, the one with the white trim. The darker blue beret too. No medal today though.

'It's fine,' he lied.

'Good,' she said, though she did not sound as though she believed him. There was a pause. 'D'you mind if I ask you something?'

'It depends. What is it?'

'I just wondered how you feel. After...You know what I mean.'

'Relief at one moment. And the most profound sadness at the next. You?'

'Humiliation.'

Jack was surprised, both by her question and her emotion. Fear he understood. Anger too. Relief. But humiliation? He must ask her to explain, though he would need to tackle the matter carefully or risk another bitter riposte. Anyway, he was still trying to resolve his other questions about Carter-Holt. And it was a growing list. What was it that had passed between her and Fielding in Santander? He had perceived mutual recognition when their eyes met. Then the strange business of the playing cards. Her timely warning to them when the attack began. Some strange link, too, with Brendan Murphy, unless he was much mistaken. But these things would have to wait, for they had arrived in Cangas de Onís and it was time for Laureano de Armas Gourié's *début* as a tour guide, rather than tour organiser.

'Ladies and gentlemen,' he said, shakily, and setting down his notes. 'Here we arrive in Cangas de Onís, first capital of the Kingdom of Asturias, Pelayo's capital.' The road had followed the River Güeña into town, to the triangular intersection with its distinctive church, a stepped tower, almost pagoda-like, with six bells. To the left was the market, stalls sheltered by tarpaulins, with cheeses, oil, olives, hams and wines for sale. Some small pens too. Goats and the fatter unshorn sheep of the region. 'Perhaps you would like to get off the bus? Take some air? And I will tell you the story of El Mazuco. The great battle.'

The passengers looked at each other in surprise. They had not expected further commentary. Nor had they sought any. Jack, for one, had simply assumed that they would be driven more or less directly to Santiago, admittedly with one final overnight stop, but with the actual tour now terminated. Although that was perhaps not the best way to phrase matters. But he was even more surprised to find that he welcomed the architect's attempt to resurrect the thing. It lifted his gloom, somehow.

'Have we time for a smoke?' Jack asked.

'Oh yes, of course *Señor* Telford. But here. One of mine, I beg you.' He offered his case, filled with the dark tobacco *Gitanes* that the French favoured. Jack took one. Carter-Holt also. 'Now, where am I? *Vale*, the Battle of El Mazuco. It is early September. Last year. The Reds are driven along the coast from Santander. Not far from here, to the north-east, there is Llanes. And near Llanes is the mountain called El Mazuco. Asturias is now surrounded. Alone. General Dávila attacks from the south and from the east. Llanes falls on the fifth day of September. But ahead, the Reds have fortified the Sierra de Cuera and the passes further inland. General Dávila had to advance along the gorge from Panes to Cabrales.'

'We came that way!' exclaimed Peter Kettering. 'On the way to Covadonga...' He fell silent.

'It is difficult. Narrow. Steep on both sides, like you have seen,' said the Spaniard. 'We expect no real resistance. After all, the Reds are now outnumbered by seven to one. Yes, seven to one. Impossible odds. Or are they, my friends?'

'I'm sure that Professor Holden,' said Carter-Holt, 'if we still had the pleasure of his company, might remind us of Thermopylae.'

'Exactly, dear lady,' beamed de Armas Gourié, straightening his cravat and settling more comfortably to his subject. 'The bold Leonidas!'

'You almost sound as though you admire the Reds' defence, *Señor*,' said Catherine.

'But of course! To recognise the valour of one's enemy makes the victory so much sweeter, does it not? There is no satisfaction to defeat an enemy that is weak, incompetent, is there? So, the attacks along the gorge are halted. General Dávila sees that he must first take the Sierra de Cuera. And the key to the Sierra is El Mazuco. He uses the German Condor Legion. Bombing and bombing, Shelling too. Then the advance. It takes us until the fifteenth of September to drive them from Pico Turbina and El Mazuco. But the devils still hold the ridges of Peñas Blancas. Rain turns to snow. In September! We need to bring up sixteen fresh battalions. Sixteen! We have to wait for better weather. The Germans bomb. We advance. The Reds beat us back. Once. Twice. Three Times. Four. It takes us five days before the Red flags fall. And the battle, in total, has taken eighteen days. It has cost us tens of thousands of lives. Yet nothing stands now between General Franco and Gijón, the last city left to the Reds here in the north. But we get to that story later, yes?'

The bus continued through Cangas de Onís to cross the larger Sella River. As they did so, they had a fine view of the old Roman Bridge, absurdly steep on both sides, before swinging north to Arriondas.

'What will we do for lunch, *Señor* de Armas Gourié?' said Jack. He did not feel especially hungry but he felt the need for conversation, wanted to avoid entrapment within his own morbid thoughts.

'Oh please,' said the Spaniard. 'That is such a mouthful. Surely we have all known each other long enough. You must call me Laureano. Really, I insist.' They all smiled. 'Good,' he continued. 'Now, about lunch. The Hotel has made some *bocadillos*. Ham and cheese. They are in the cold boxes. But I have suggestion. We are in Asturias. There is wonderful cooking here. So perhaps, when we reach Oviedo, we make a stop at a place I know. A good place. And I will tell you the story of Oviedo. Yes?'

Yes.

But it was two more hours to Oviedo, over some of the roughest roads that they had yet experienced. They followed the River Espinaredo as far as Infiesto and then west through Nava and Pola de Siero. And, along the way, the cooling system failed. The Moorish driver, it seemed, did not possess the talent of Mikel Iruko Domínguez for topping up the reservoirs every one hundred and fifty kilometres. The temperature was rising too. It was turning into a very fine day.

They stopped at a *fabada*, that peculiar style of Asturian eating house that specialises in the use of large white beans as its staple ingredient. And there were flagons of Asturian cider, sharp and strong, poured carefully from a height with the arms as far apart as possible to break the liquid – according to the locals.

'Is this good cider, *Señor*?' said Jack.

'Buznego?' said the Spaniard. 'It is a new one to me. But yes, good I should think. And you must call me Laureano, eh? Now. I tell you about Oviedo, yes?'

They agreed, kept eating the food, this wonderful food, while the architect told his tale. It took them back to the beginning of the war. July '36. Oviedo had been at the very heart of the Asturian Revolution two years earlier. The town's garrison was commanded by Colonel Aranda, seemingly a Republican sympathiser. So the *Generalísimo* did not consider that there was any prospect of a successful Nationalist rising there. The Republicans also thought that it was safe ground for them. Hence so many Asturian *milicianos* went east to help defend the Basque territories. To everybody's surprise, however, Aranda declared for National Spain, having first gathered all those on whom he could rely from all across the Region. Then he held Oviedo against tremendous odds all through August and September, into October. His losses were enormous. In the end, Aranda had to pull his five hundred survivors back to their only remaining barracks, sent a final message by radio that they would fight to the last man, and prepared to die. And then, by some divine intervention, a miracle. A miracle to rival Don Pelayo's visitation by the Virgin at Covadonga. For a relief column arrived from Galicia. The siege was broken and Oviedo was held until the rest of the war in the north was won, with the recapture of Gijón.

'I met him,' said Carter-Holt as she finished her stew. 'Aranda. He was at Teruel. Fearsome. A true warrior. Wonderful strategist.'

'But the town must have suffered badly,' said Peter Kettering.

'Weren't you telling us,' said Jack, 'that there were three thousand houses destroyed in Oviedo?'

'Ah, Mister Telford,' said the Spaniard. 'You remembered.'

'Yes,' Jack replied. 'I obviously wasn't quite so far gone as I thought. And if we're going to call you Laureano, should you not call me Jack?'

'Jack,' he said. He pronounced it *Jacques*. 'Yes, of course. And three thousand is correct. You will see. It is a terrible ruin.'

Indeed it was. Destruction everywhere. They paid a quick visit to the Town Hall, met the new mayor, and were shown the emergency accommodation in which thousands were still living. Food kitchens too.

'The Civil Governor certainly has his work cut out,' said Jack. 'Has he forgiven us for last night, d'you think?'

'I'm sure that *Señor* Caballero will have entirely forgotten you by now, Mister Telford,' said Carter-Holt.

'All sections of the Falange,' said Laureano de Armas Gourié, 'are working hard for Oviedo, ladies and gentlemen. And everybody has employment now. Everybody has something to eat.'

We've heard that before, thought Jack. *Monotonous.*

It was three more hours from Oviedo to the coast at Luarca, through Grado and Salas, then the tight hairpins to reach the sea.

'Can I ask a question, Laureano?' said Jack, woken by yet another pothole. De Armas Gourié said yes, of course. 'It's about the tours. Aren't you worried that the incident with Julia Britten, then the Covadonga thing, will damage their reputation?'

The Spaniard came to sit next to him. The Ketterings and Sister María Pereda were still asleep. Carter-Holt was writing.

'If I can speak in confidence,' whispered the Spaniard, 'we have taken steps to limit that damage. The Westons, I think, will return to find that they are being offered a chance to film the whole of *Mexican Max* in southern Spain, rather than going all the way to Mexico itself.'

I'm not sure that Marguerite will be very happy about that, thought Jack. *Denied her liaison with Jack Dempsey? Having to come back to Spain with all its attendant memories? But I suppose if there's enough money in it…*

'And Frances Moorgate?' said Jack. 'She blames Vice-Consul Fielding for her husband's death. Your General Franco too.'

'She must, of course, decide how she will take up any complaint about the Vice-Consul,' said the architect. 'But National Spain still has excellent relations with her late husband's bank. They want to open branches again, I understand. After the war.'

'And there are conditions on that, I suppose?'

Laureano de Armas Gourié shrugged.

'It is not for me to comment, Jack. You understand? But *Señora* Moorgate will be seeking some widow's annuity, I suppose. She would perhaps be more likely to receive such an annuity if she was prepared to say as little as possible about the circumstances of her husband's death.'

'She might not care about the annuity,' said Jack. 'She has her own job, after all.'

'As a librarian?' The Spaniard snorted. 'I think you know the good lady just a bit better than that. She has aspirations, does she not?'

'Yes, you're right,' laughed Jack. He had an image of Frances, her expensive tastes. He was tempted to ask about the Holdens, but knew that they would see it as part of their duty to the Reich and National Spain to raise nothing embarrassing. 'And the rest of us?' Jack continued.

Laureano shrugged again.

'The tour is not yet finished, *Señor* Jack. Not yet.'

Jack dozed again, awoke to the buzz of chatter between Sister María Pereda and the Ketterings. The Spaniard saw that everybody was alert once more, so reminded them that they had now left Gijón behind, just to the east. All the same, he said, it was important to remember that Gijón was where the Asturians made their own last stand. In a strange reversal of positions, Aranda had been promoted and given command of the Nationalist forces moving in to surround the city. The Reds fought well, but finally surrendered on the twenty-first of October, the previous year.

'The end of the War in the North?' said Peter Kettering.

'Thankfully, yes,'

'I feel as though we've lived through it,' said Catherine. 'It seems so impossibly long since we arrived at Irún. What was it? Eleven days ago? It feels like months.' She seemed angered by the thought, stared out of the window as though directing her comment to the passing landscape.

What did she mean, thought Jack, *when she said back in the cave that it was God's punishment? For what? Her affair with Peter?*

'Well, all over now,' said the Spaniard. 'Now you can relax at Ribadeo tonight. Then on to Santiago tomorrow.'

'And our meeting with *El Caudillo*,' said Sister María Pereda. 'Such a responsibility. To speak with him alone. Without Sister Berthe Schultz. I miss her so badly. Do you think that Our Lady will still protect me? Even after I shot that poor woman?'

'You acted like a true warrior of God, Sister. And Santiago will be a very important event,' said Laureano. 'A celebration. The first anniversary of our victories here in the north. The battles on the Ebro almost won. The end of the war in sight. There will be music.'

But not from Julia Britten, thought Jack.

They viewed Luarca from the hills above the town, close to the astonishing cemetery. The rectangular harbour was surrounded by white-painted houses to match these nearby dwellings of the dead. Jack glanced back at the similarly white-washed church as they headed down to the wide estuary which they needed to circumnavigate before reaching Ribadeo.

'You like the view, Mister Telford?' said Carter-Holt.

'Very much,' Jack replied.

'You have quite an eye for the beauties of the countryside, do you not? You should have your own camera. You'd make a good photographer.'

'Oh, I've got a camera,' said Jack. 'But not so fine as your own, Miss Carter-Holt. And not with me.'

'You hear that, everybody?' she shouted. 'Mister Telford has a camera too. But too shy to show it to us, it seems. He's hiding it from us.'

'To be honest,' Jack countered, 'I was looking forward to a swim.'

'Then perhaps I could be tempted to join you,' she said.

Jack almost allowed himself to become excited at the prospect, then remembered the last time this had happened to him. San Sebastián. Marguerite Weston. But then, a kiss from Valerie Carter-Holt would be an entirely different matter.

They passed through Vegadeo at the lower end of the estuary, then crossed the Eo into Galicia, Jack remarking that even here at its outer limit, the region's villages and towns looked like undamaged paradise compared to everywhere else they had seen.

'Yes, my friends,' said Laureano. 'Galicia. But be warned. These Galicians, practically Asturians themselves, are above all other things, Celts. More deep and complex than they like to pretend. Like all Celts.'

'And Franco hasn't banned the use of Galician?' said Jack.

'The Galicians are loyal to National Spain, *Señor* Jack. Why should they be repressed? *El Caudillo* may insist on *Castellano* for official business but he will not prohibit Galician for everyday use.'

Ribadeo itself, at last. A stately resort, many of its buildings in the Spanish Imperial style and, as they drove through, Laureano pointed out some of the architectural wonders, the occasional glimpse of the square lighthouse out on Pancha Island at the mouth of the estuary, linked to the cliffs by a precarious bridge.

They were staying at the Hotel Miramar, a converted manor house, a large *casona*, which looked directly onto the *ría*, overlooking the water with its array of sailing boats, large and small. For Ribadeo had somehow managed to cling onto its Golden Age of the previous century when traffic would leave here bound for the Philippines, the Río de la Plata, the Baltic, the Antilles. There was still a nautical school, many ship-owners continued to have summer residences here. So the walls of Miramar's lobby were lined with photos – sailing ships filling the bay and wharves of the port.

There was jasmine everywhere. Red carnations. Yellow oxalis *vinagrillos*.

Laureano promised them a private dinner. *Caldo Gallego* and *Pulpo a Feira*. No guests tonight. But Jack asked whether there was any possibility that he could take a swim beforehand and the Spaniard enquired at the reception desk after they had all checked in.

'They say, *Señor* Jack, that the very best beach on the entire coast of Spain is not far away. You would need a taxi to get there, but our timing is impeccable. It will be low tide soon. Just before sunset. Perfect for you. They will arrange a taxi, if you would like. Oh, and another thing. They say they will have an English paper here. Tomorrow, before we leave for Lugo and Santiago.'

Jack accepted the offer gladly, changed in his room, then came downstairs again to take a cup of *Queimada*, arranged by way of welcome from the hotel. It was a heady hot punch, lemon, coffee, burning spirit, and Laureano de Armas Gourié shared with them the secret of its ingredients, the *concurso* which was traditionally recited during its preparation.

Then he waited on the street. It was early evening. Galician musicians playing in the *plaza*. A monkey-faced piper with squashed uniform cap, bass and kettle drummers, a clarinettist – creased coats all in matching faded green. Old people had brought their chairs out to sit in the open, clamorous and loud. The deeply carved and stubbled faces of Finisterre fishermen.

The taxi arrived. Jack gripped the towel borrowed from his room, the bathing costume wrapped within. But as he told the driver his destination, he was conscious of somebody behind him. Carter-Holt, now wearing a pretty beige frock and matching Florentine hat.

'Well,' she said. 'I *did* say that I'd like to come along.'

It took thirty minutes for the taxi to cover the ten kilometres from Ribadeo to the beaches of Las Catedrales, the road sometimes no better than a grass-grown track. The driver kept up a continuous dialogue, some of which Carter-Holt seemed to understand, putting responses together slowly, but enough to prevent Jack from sharing his many questions. Some concerned his own sanity. Why should his mood still swing so violently? Between relief which bordered on hysteria at one extreme and a sadness so savage and desolate that it filled him, at the other, with a bleak winter wilderness in which his angry ghosts shrieked against cold injustice, repression, slaughter. Against all those forces that made human life so cheap. There were more practical questions too, that still plagued him from the *Cueva de la Santina*. What *had* happened to Brendan's Astra pistol? Then the *Jefe's* final admonition. *If you do not fight the fascistas here, you must surely fight them somewhere else.* But Jack had no intention of fighting. He wanted peace. Nothing but peace. And what had really happened in the cave anyway? At the end? Faulty wiring on the blasting box? Somehow, he could not associate such carelessness with the man he had come to know, albeit so briefly, as the *Machado*'s leader. Yet, in the end, he *had* been careless. He had known the danger, after all. *If the English tell you one thing it is better to believe the opposite.* But, finally, Eduardo Pinchón, *Guadalito,* had been fooled by the most simple of deceptions. Jack knew only one thing for certain. That they would never now discover his real intentions for the sniper rifle. He had hinted at assassination. But who was the target? Juan de Ajuriaguerra? The man who so many in the Republic believed had betrayed them by the Santoña Pact, the formal surrender of the Basques. Unlikely. Easier to have him killed in the prison at Burgos, surely? Or across the border somewhere. No. If an assassination target truly existed, it must surely have been General Latorre Roca. It was a mystery, Jack concluded, that had no resolution.

They stopped on the edge of a cliff top moorland of grass and fern, the driver promised Carter-Holt that he would wait for one hour, but no more, and the couple were directed to a flight of wood and gravel steps which ran steeply down the rock face to the beach.

'The driver says that you haven't long before the tide starts coming in again,' said Carter-Holt. 'I think he says it's dangerous to stay long after that. In case you get trapped.'

Jack nodded, trying to concentrate on the steps while, at the same time, looking at the remarkable rock formations below and ahead. There were isolated spires, columns, domes, some of them enormous. And archways in colossal buttresses to the cliffs, one after the other, the columns of nature's nave. Eroded slate and silvery schist. Magical. And he imagined the seascape at different states of the tide. But for now the sand looked fine, the evening warm. A surprising number of people still here.

'Have you got a book or something?' said Jack, as they slipped off their shoes and began to trudge down towards the water line.

'Oh, you needn't worry about me, Mister Telford.'

He stopped.

'This all right?' he said.

'As good as anywhere else, I suppose,' she replied, gazing around the beach appreciatively.

'You should have brought the camera,' said Jack. He removed his blazer, folded it carefully, set it down with the hotel towel. There was a self-conscious moment as he unbuttoned his shirt, then slipped off his flannels. Carter-Holt settled herself on the sand, shading her eyes with both hands, since her neat Florentine was insufficient for the purpose.

'You need feeding, Jack. Those ribs!' Self-consciously, he folded his arms across his chest.

'Well,' he said, 'here we go!' He made his way down to the waves, past the line of black-clad women gathering clams from the final stretches that the ebb would reveal. He waded up to his shins. It was damned cold. But he would get used to it soon enough. There was a shout from behind him.

'Hey!' called Carter-Holt. 'Aren't you going to wait? How very rude of you.'

He turned, saw that she was unbuttoning the back of the beige dress, though she still wore the hat. The frock fell, revealing a pale blue bathing suit, white and green stripes.

'I thought you couldn't swim,' Jack shouted.

'Teach me,' she said, tossing the Florentine to the sand and pulling back her hair, fastening it with some form of band. Then she ran down the beach, straight past him, impervious to the cold water over her knees, and threw herself into the sea with an ungainly splash, surfacing and thrashing like a stranded sea-bass, spitting out brine and rubbing her eyes. 'It's wonderful,' she spluttered. 'Why don't you come in?'

'I was planning to. But what about you? You seriously want me to teach you?'

'Oh, I was only kidding. I can manage some doggy-paddle. You go ahead. Enjoy your swim, Mister Telford.'

He was unsure. It did not seem altogether safe to leave her alone. And, anyway, Carter-Holt in a bathing costume deserved some further attention. Her figure was almost boyish, but Christ, she was lovely.

'Stay in your depth then,' said Jack.

'Yes, father.' She offered him a mocking salute, then ducked down pedalling around in a small clumsy circle.

Jack made his way past her, delighted when she offered him a warm smile, sank his shoulders below the surface, the cold biting at his belly and spine. He swam with long, easy strokes, parallel to the shore, front crawl but then changing to breast-stroke so that he could get a better view of the rock formations. As usual when he was in the water, time seemed to stop. He could not imagine a moment beyond this one. He did not want to. His usual solitary state seemed relieved, just now, by Carter-Holt's presence. But he would not delude himself into believing that her decision to join him, to come prepared with bathing costume, to give him that alluring smile, meant anything at all beyond the purely superficial. And even her presence only barely repressed the gloom and anger, the loss, which had settled upon him since Covadonga.

Suddenly, he saw his father standing on the beach. It was the usual image. The old army uniform, the flat hat, the rifle. Jack looked again, unsure whether he was actually seeing some patrolling Nationalist soldier. Then he heard the scream.

He turned in the water, catching a small wave full in the face, fingers clearing his vision.

She was a long way from the shore. And floundering badly. How far? A hundred yards? More?

He struck out towards her, sea water blinding him once again. He kept lifting his head, trying to see her, to keep on course. But most of the time he could not see her at all. Sometimes he suspected she was hidden by the small waves. But other times he knew, categorically, that Carter-Holt had slipped beneath the surface. Jack fought back against his instincts, knowing that, more often than not, by the time it became evident that swimmers were in trouble, it was already too late to save them. But he had to try. Desperation drove him forward, yet his limbs felt like lead. He was frighteningly aware that he was making slow progress, the tide turned, perhaps.

Jack trod water. There was no sign of the woman. None. He turned. Then again.

Nothing.

Christ, Jack, he thought. *Not another one! And, please God, not Carter-Holt.*

He looked towards the shore. His father was still there.

A seagull screeched.

Panic seized him. All the pressure of the past few days returned to haunt him as surely as his father was doing.

And then she broke the surface. No more than five yards away, coughing, spitting, arms flapping, exhausted. But Jack doubted that he had enough strength to get her back to safety.

Chapter Twenty-Five

Wednesday 28 September 1938

In the waxed moonlight of her hotel room, Valerie Carter-Holt's slim body was alabaster white, an ivory pallor that would have made Frances Moorgate most envious.

Jack had brought her ashore more easily than he might have imagined, pressed through the line of spectators who had gathered along the water's edge. These bystanders had been engaged in an animated discussion, presumably about the respective merits of whether this was, or was not, a good time to be swimming at the Playa de Las Catedrales. They were Spanish spectators, of course, so the views would have taken account of all previous similar incidents in recent history, each family's own experience of drownings, the dangers of the sea in general, the attributes needed by successful rescuers. And, whatever these might have been, Jack had seemed to be lacking. There had been one or two who had come forward to help him as the couple staggered from the water but, overall, they had been met by pursed lips, the condemnation of shaking heads.

The crowd had still been there, the debate continuing, while Jack wrapped the towel around Carter-Holt, picked up their bundle of clothes and led her back up the steps to the cliff-top. She had apologised frequently for her foolishness, but never thanked him. Rather the reverse. She had been brusque, snatched her own hat, dress and shoes, shaken off his protective arm.

'How do you expect me to get up these infernal stairs,' she had said, 'when I am constantly tripping over your feet?'

The taxi driver had been less than pleased with the prospect of wet bodies travelling in his pride and joy, but had become more amenable to the situation through the offer of ten additional Burgos *pesetas*. He had taken some sacks from the boot of the Model Twenty-Nine Elizalde and spread them thickly over the back seat while Jack, putting his jacket around Carter-Holt's shoulders, had used the towel to shield himself, behind the vehicle, to change.

Safely returned to the hotel, she had testily thanked him for his attention, no mention of the rescue, and excused herself from joining the party for dinner. She had roundly rejected his suggestion that he might check on her later while Jack, on the other hand, had been pressed for an account, telling the story several times while they ate, earning the admiration of Laureano de Armas Gourié, the blessing of Sister María Pereda and the reproach of the Ketterings for having undertaken such a foolhardy venture in the first place. But Jack's own thoughts, when they had not been dragged in confusion once more to Covadonga, had been entirely for Valerie Carter-Holt. He found himself completely besotted. Some peculiar gratitude that it had been he, rather than anybody else, granted the opportunity to save her from the sea. No matter that she had not shown the slightest appreciation. That was just her manner, he had thought. The price one must pay for the privilege of her company. And, having so recently swum in the Cantabrian currents, he had now bathed in self-satisfaction, played again in his mind every fraught word exchanged between them on the bumpy road back to the Miramar. Played them over and over, uselessly rehearsing every response that he might have made if only he had possessed the wit to think of it at the time.

So his heart had skipped several beats when, returning to his room near midnight, he had found a note slipped beneath the door.

Jack, it had said. *You must forgive me. I was too upset to thank you properly. Now feel like a prig. Of course you can check on me if you feel it necessary. VC-H.*

He had looked at his watch. It was late. How could he tell when she had written the thing? Did he have the nerve to knock on her door at this late hour? No, he had decided, he did not. He had undressed, climbed into bed, read a paragraph of *The Hobbit*. Then read it again, realising that he had not absorbed a single word. Out of bed again. A *Senior Service* smoked. A great deal of pacing. He had seen her go into her own room when they arrived. Just two doors along the corridor. Would it harm if he knocked gently on the door? She had invited him to do so after all. But what time *had* that been?

Jack eventually changed into his shirt and trousers. No more. He had closed his door quietly, then padded the short distance to Carter-Holt's threshold, tapped on the oak panel. There had been a noise from within.

'Who?' Valerie had whispered from the other side.

'Jack,' he had replied. 'Telford. Just checking that you're dry.'

He had heard her laugh, opening the door to let him in.

She had been wearing an apricot silk gown that trailed on the carpet.

'Mister Telford,' she had said. 'You got my note then?'

'I thought you might be asleep.'

'No. Writing.' She had pointed to the small table near the half-open window. There had been a *chaise-longue* just next to it, against the farther wall, covered in her notes, a couple of books.

'Listening to the sea?' Jack had replied. 'Thought you would have had enough of that.'

'I love the sea. It helps me to concentrate. To think clearly.'

'And have you?'

'What?'

'Thought clearly.'

'Yes, Jack.'

She had walked to the table, switched off the lamp, swept all her paperwork from the sofa, then turned to him, allowing the silk gown to fall and standing naked before him, illuminated only by the moon's full glow. A portrait by Émile Vernon.

Jack fumbled with the buttons of his shirt, then his trousers, almost tripping as he kicked them away.

Carter-Holt settled back against the pillows of the *chaise-longue*, her knees spread wide, her head turned to one side, eyes closed with a smile playing on her lips. Her breasts were almost non-existent now, the merest of mountains, though the nipples were astonishingly long, upstanding.

How long since his previous sexual encounter? Two months? With...

The truth was that he had always felt embarrassed by sex. He felt clumsy, uneducated. As though the Royal Grammar School Worcester had omitted an entire subject, a crucial one, from its curriculum. So he must be careful. Not to show his lack of expertise. To bring into play those few skills that he *had* developed. Not to make a fool of himself.

And above all, Jack, he thought, *do not be premature. You must not be premature.*

So he knelt, lifted her buttocks just a touch higher, reached over her thighs to caress the soft bush, and pressed his tongue into her. He felt for the tiny mound, just as a Parisian whore had taught him, felt her shudder slightly, then kept the tip of his tongue in place, moving it only slightly. She tasted still of salt water but he was stiff now, achingly so.

Careful, Jack. Think of something else.

But, to his surprise, Carter-Holt placed a hand on each side of his head, shifted him to a new and unfamiliar section of her private anatomy.

'Here, Jack,' she murmured, and after only a couple of minutes he felt a new dampness on his tongue, her excitement building towards a peak.

Or, at least, Jack hoped so.

Time to risk all, he thought. And he lifted himself, hands on the cushions of the *chaise-longue*, his erection intelligently finding its own way to the ultimate destination. He tried to kiss her, but her head was still turned, the eyes still closed. So he settled for the right nipple, took it in his mouth. Then he straightened, almost like performing press-ups.

'Oh Christ, Jack!' Valerie cried as they came together.

Thank God, thought Jack, as the waves of relief shuddered through him. And they would not stop. Not for a while, anyway.

He tried to kiss her again, but she pushed him gently away, out of her, so that he sat back on his haunches.

She slid from the *chaise-longue*, turned onto her hands and knees, pulled the dark hair away from her face to look over her shoulder, offering her backside towards him. It was bigger than he imagined. Out of proportion, somehow, to the size of her breasts.

'You can have anything you want, Jack,' she murmured. 'Anything at all.'

'What's on the menu?' he asked, thinking that it was a clever answer but realising, as soon as he had spoken, that it made him sound like an idiot. All the same he found himself aroused again, took her from behind. And, while they failed to reach a climax together this time, Jack was pleased to find that he had apparently outlasted her. She had come before him, loudly, great sobs as she buried her face in the oriental rug.

He withdrew carefully, emotion filling him as he crawled alongside her, placed his arm around her, stroked her hair, kissed the livid scar which he discovered on the back of her right shoulder. It was the first time that he had felt human and whole since their capture by the *Machados*.

'There,' he said. 'Nothing to worry about now.'

'Humiliated, Jack. It was the first time in my life that I ever felt humiliated. At Covadonga. That bloody cave.'

'It's all over now. You're all right.'

'No, Jack. It's not over.'

'Of course it is! What do you mean?'

'It doesn't matter. Maybe I'll explain later.'

'Seriously though,' said Jack. 'You're fine now. And I find, to my surprise, Miss Carter-Holt, that I am more than a little fond of you. I'll look after you. If you'll let me.'

'What, Jack? Should you like me to love you?'

Jack blushed. He might imagine that every woman who took an interest in him must somehow be attracted. But love?

'Yes,' he said, almost without thinking. 'More than anything in the world.'

He was entranced, captivated.

'Then I shall give it my best shot,' she replied. She lifted her head, wiped the tears from her face. 'But you'll need to be patient with me, Jack. And we must find something else for you to call me. *Miss Carter-Holt* no longer seems appropriate. I cannot stand *Val*. And *Valerie* is little better. Now, I must run a bath.'

She kissed him for the first time. On the cheek. But it was a beginning.

Jack began to gather his clothes as Carter-Holt went into the bathroom, swivelled the tap levers, the water thundering into the tub.

'Maybe you could leave it in for me. The water. When you've finished,' he shouted, then wondered whether she might take this as a sign of ill-breeding. 'Or shall I just climb into bed and wait for you? I'm intrigued by what else might be on offer. If I can *have anything*, I mean.'

She put her head around the door, frowning.

'Oh, Jack,' she said. 'I'm not very good at sharing my bed, I'm afraid. You don't mind do you, darling? I snore. Need my sleep too. Don't cope well with the bodily odours of others, that sort of thing.' She grimaced.

He was taken aback, had assumed…

But, then, she *had* called him 'darling'. He felt himself falling.

'Not a problem,' he said. 'Shall I see you at breakfast?'

'Of course you'll see me at breakfast. Silly! But perhaps we should keep this to ourselves. Just for now. As I say, Jack, there are things I need to explain. But tomorrow, yes? Now, be a sweetie and leave me to my bath.' She smiled at him. Quite divine. The head vanished and then reappeared. 'By the bye,' she said. 'I've had a brain-wave. Why don't you call me *Carter*?'

Carter? Yes, he liked it. He pulled on the trousers, left the shirt unbuttoned, moved to the door.

'Goodnight,' he called, his fingers on the handle, still hoping that she might call him back.

'Goodnight.'

'Carter it is then!' he said, and opened the door.

'Yes,' she called. 'But only when we're alone, naturally.'

Naturally.

He did not see her, as it happened, at breakfast. In fact, she only appeared at the very last moment when the bus was about to depart for Lugo. But at least it departed with a copy of Monday's papers. *The Manchester Guardian* and *The Times*. Just as well, since Carter-Holt treated him as though he were a total stranger.

Jack settled in the front seat while the others fussed over Valerie's brush with death, enquired whether she had suffered any ill-effects, protested that she should have eaten, thanked Our Lord for her safe deliverance, wondered that providence should have frowned so badly on this particular tour group, praised Mister Telford once again, though questioned his judgement in allowing the poor girl such exposure to danger in the first place.

Meanwhile, Laureano de Armas Gourié outlined the day's schedule.

'Such a pity,' he said, 'that you could not spend more time on the *rías*. And not enough time to visit Gijón. All the same, this day should be enjoyable.'

Jack turned over *The Manchester Guardian*, studied the front page.

HITLER'S NEW DEMANDS
Prague Decides That They Are Unacceptable
France and Britain Confer

The situation seemed to have grown worse, Hitler now not only wanting the Czechs to give him those territories where the Sudeten Germans were in the majority but also those areas where there were *any* such folk. And all this by Saturday. The *Guardian* correspondent then went on to speculate about what might happen next. Still more ultimatums, he predicted, this time aimed perhaps at the French, the surrender of the Maginot Line, plebiscites in the Flemish districts of Belgium. And all set against the threat posed by a German *Luftwaffe* already vastly superior to anything possessed by France or Britain. The Czechs, naturally, had rejected Hitler's demands, described them as preposterous, had mobilised one million men. War, it seemed, was inevitable.

Jack skimmed the other pages. The Home News. Gas masks being distributed and fitted, more than in the entire previous six months. Trenches being dug in Hyde Park, Green Park, St James's Park. Not just in London either. But Birmingham. Other large cities.

'The Civil War continues, I see,' remarked Laureano, peering over his shoulder as he came forward to issue fresh instructions for the Moroccan driver.

Jack was confused.

'No,' he said. 'The Sudeten Crisis.'

'Yes,' smiled Laureano. 'The Civil War is not Spain's alone, don't you think? The whole of Europe has been fighting it since '14. We may pretend to be different nations, but we are not, are we?'

Jack put down the paper. It was an interesting thought.

'That can't be right, surely?' he said. 'How can you say that the French, the Greeks, the English aren't different from each other?'

'Yet if you put those same people in the United States, then add Russians, Poles, Italians, anybody else you like, they all become Americans. So nationality is not a matter of ethnicity, is it? Perhaps more to do with ideology.'

'You should tell that to Hitler and the Sudeten Germans.'

'That is my point, *Señor* Jack. The Führer is establishing a border for National Socialism, not for Germany. He knows that the Czechs have a propensity for Bolshevism. When the people of Europe are finally persuaded of the political ideology that they need to share, only *then* will there be peace in Europe.'

'And that ideology will be National Socialism, you think? Fascism?'

'Of course,' said the Spaniard, as though Jack were an idiot to even ask the question.

The countryside slipped past. Or, rather, it shuddered past. They had all long since become accustomed to the peculiar motion evinced both by Spain's roads and the bus itself. It was akin to finding one's sea legs. But Jack had lost his appetite for the scenery now, he found. The weather was warm, bright, but he sensed rather than saw a shadow permanently cast upon both himself and the landscape. The River Eo was their constant companion, of course, for over twenty miles, first retracing their estuary steps back to Vegadeo, then rising steadily again, through valleys and narrow passes, the waters tumbling down to meet them, until they said a final farewell to the stream near Vitamea. The Moroccan driver swung the Chrysler clumsily around the twisting hairpins towards Puerto Marco as though he were still in the Atlas Mountains, then eased them down into the wider grasslands and pastures for a quick break at Meira, and the final twenty mile leg to Lugo and lunch.

The town lay on a hill surrounded by the rivers Miño, Rato and Chanca. But its remarkable feature was the Roman wall and round bastions that entirely enclosed the place.

'It looks contemporary,' said Catherine Kettering. 'Almost as though the Romans were still here.'

'Well, perhaps they are,' replied Laureano. 'The only city in the world, they say, with completely intact Roman walls. The Celts were here first, of course. They name the town after their deity, Lugos. Their god of light, I think. And in the Middle Ages, it is protected. Like Santiago itself. It has great religious privilege. In '36, there is little fighting. It quickly embraces National Spain. So no damage. Good, yes? Later, we will walk the walls. It is the practice here.'

They made a quick inspection of the Santa María Cathedral, with Laureano expertly pointing to the mixture of styles. The slender bell towers. The clever way in which they framed that triple-arched, double-storey main block. He was enraptured. Even more so with the interior. He led the Ketterings and the young nun to see the Blessed Sacrament, perpetually exposed here, twenty-four hours each day, to the wonderment of the faithful. But Jack followed Carter-Holt as she walked around the cloistered aisles to inspect the icons and statuary.

'So what is it?' he whispered. 'This thing that's still not over.'

She looked quizzically at him.

'Is that some clever way to remind me about last night, Jack?'

'Just concerned about you.'

'I told you that you'd need to be patient with me. But patience alone is hardly adequate in this case. It would take another quality in you entirely if I were going to even attempt an explanation.'

'And this magical quality would be what? Trust?'

'Of course. As it happens, I don't think we've ever been less than honest with each other, have we?'

'Almost to the point of brutality, some might say. You made it perfectly plain that you despised me.'

'We must all sometimes play parts that we find distasteful, Jack. And I never despised you.'

'What then? Marguerite Weston has already done the *we're not really so different bit*, Carter. Not that chestnut from you too, I hope?'

'Would it *really* surprise you, Jack, to find that we're really on the same side?'

'*Surprise* would hardly do it justice, my dear. But go on. Try me.'

She smiled.

'I went up to Lady Margaret Hall in '31. Daddy had warned me about the place, of course. I was reading Philosophy and Politics, you see.'

'They always attract a certain class of revolutionary, don't they?'

'Exactly. And in my case it was the visiting lecturer, Arnold Phelps. He could turn Marxist Economics into pure poetry. Shelley or Byrom. A dear friend. And one who could recognise an eager disciple too.'

Jack was incredulous.

'*You*, Carter?'

'Yes, Jack. Me. Arnold introduced me to the *Federation for the Relief of Victims of German Fascism*. Bit of a mouthful, isn't it? But they opened my eyes. I couldn't believe what Hitler's Nazis were really doing to ordinary workers, Jews, anybody that they chose as a scapegoat. I met Müntzenberg.'

'Willi Müntzenberg?'

'Yes. You know him?'

'No. Only by reputation. But he organised the Federation as a Communist front, didn't he?'

'*Front*, Jack? What does that mean? Communists have been one of Hitler's principal targets. The only real hope for Germany is that the Party can mobilise and stop him.'

'You're a member? Of the Party?'

'Yes, darling, I *am* a member. More than just a member. You remember now what I said about trust?'

'I remember. But you'll forgive me if this all sounds a bit far-fetched? What about all that vitriolic stuff you've written about the Popular Front? Your reports from Teruel? Your father – he's...'

She shook her head.

'You can believe what you like. When I got the job with *Reuters*, it was the perfect cover. Arnold Phelps helped me land it too. The Comintern showed an interest in me through Arnold. When I got an assignment in Vienna, they put me in touch with the underground there. I helped them to get some refugees out of Germany. There was a boy. Kurt Tiebermann.'

She looked away.

'What happened to him?'

'Oranienburg happened to him, Jack. They call it Sachsenhausen now. It doesn't matter how many times you change the name of a concentration camp, does it?'

'He's dead?'

'Of course he's dead.'

Carter-Holt turned to him, bit her lip, her eyes filled with tears.

'Ah,' said Laureano de Armas Gourié, rounding a column towards them. 'This place always affects me in the same way. These statues are *so* beautiful, are they not? But we must go for lunch now.'

The Ketterings asked whether Valerie was quite all right. But yes, she said. Just the after-effects of last night's little drama.

Jack's mind was in turmoil. It was ludicrous. Valerie Carter-Holt undertaking work for the Comintern? She was one of the country's most die-hard right-wing journalists. Upper class family. And now she was ignoring him once more. All the way through the meal. He barely tasted the lemon-soaked meat of the *vieras*. He barely heard a word of Sister María Pereda's spirited account of Froilán, Patron Saint of Lugo, whose festival would begin in a few days.

'Christ,' he muttered, thinking still about Carter-Holt, 'is *nobody* what they seem?'

'Oh, *Señor*,' Sister María Pereda said to him, 'San Froilán was very much what he seemed. When he died, he was mourned deeply. By all the peoples of the Region.'

They left town by the old Puerta de Santiago, then crossed the Miño on the Roman bridge. Their walk on the walls had been brief, to say the least, and particularly frustrating for Jack since he had been convinced that it might provide an opportunity for some more private discussion with Carter-Holt. But he was to be disappointed. Indeed, the whole journey to Santiago de Compostela was a disappointment. It began to rain again, driving against the windows, so that Laureano had to shout constantly to make himself heard. He had made the point that it was a shame they could not all return to San Sebastián for the coming weekend. There was, he said, to be a spectacular *corrida* at the Plaza Cubierta de Martutene.

Jack thought of that other San Sebastián bullring, at *El Chofre*.

'Domingo Ortega will fight,' said the Spaniard. 'He is the authentic master of *toreo*, my friends.'

'Is it true,' said Carter-Holt, 'that when the horses of the picadors are gored, they are left to drag their own intestines around the ring?'

'Yes,' Laureano replied, 'but they are always poor horses to begin with. Thin, half-starved, so they are no great expense. No great loss. And after all, we treat the horses no worse than the English treat their Hindus.'

'The British believe that they are much more enlightened now, *Señor*,' said Valerie, 'in the way that they deal with their minions.'

'Yes,' said the Spaniard. 'Presumably that is the reason there are riots in Delhi, Bombay and Allahabad. Hunger-strikers in just about every town and village of India protesting about their conditions. But back to the *corrida*, Miss Carter-Holt. Do you know, my dear, the thing that kills more matadors than anything else?'

'Bulls?' she offered.

'No, *Señorita*. It is sweat.'

'What?' said Catherine Kettering. 'It runs into their eyes?'

Jack smiled. Max Weston could not have done better. And he missed Max. There was the vision of a sweat-blinded matador turning around and around, sword and cape extended in the hope of finding his target before the beast should find *him*.

'Oh, how amusing!' said Laureano. 'No. The sweat dries cold, like ice, on his back. It turns to pneumonia. Consumption. That is the normal fate of the matador.'

And so it continued. Tales of the bullring's blood and sand, *sangre y arena*, its heroes, the almost religious fervor of its *aficionados*. But, for Jack, it prompted memories of Picasso's *Guernica*. The bull. The horse. The pain. He saw Spain, suddenly and clearly, perhaps as the artist had done. The enraged Republic, tormented by the *banderillas* of Córdoba, Jarama, Teruel, standing at bay, still dangerous but waiting for the inevitable death thrust. Two years already gone. The longest of all possible *corridas*. Now the *faena* had begun. The final flourishes before the death thrust. The most cruel in Spain's history.

He turned to his note-books, the confused scribbling, annotations, directional arrows and asterisks which, to Jack, and he alone, made perfect sense.

I've got enough, he thought. *Regardless of whatever Sid Elliott might say about it.*

And he assembled the constituent parts in his mind, as clear and sure as though he had put the typeset to bed himself, cranked the levers, printed the text.

Our guide, he would begin, *a member of the fascist Falange, admitted that the town had been held against Franco's professional soldiers by a cluster of working class militiamen, a group of local miners, and the people of the Basque country defending their own homes from those who sought to destroy their new-found freedom.*

He would tell the story that he had learned from the *Machados.* He would tell it through the eyes of the *campesinos,* their revolution against the landowners who had kept them in slavery for centuries. A people's revolution, exactly as Sydney had described it. The violence with which that revolution had been put down by Franco, by the Church, by the Privileged. A violence inflicted not soldier upon soldier but against the civilian population. And there would be his conclusion.

That has been the suffering of Spain. It has already been the suffering of Abyssinia. Tomorrow it will be the suffering of Czechoslovakia. And, after that, France. Britain too, in all likelihood. Yet there is still time for us. Time for all the free people of the world to apply those sanctions against Herr Hitler that will prevent him plunging our nations into war yet again.

And the link between Spain and Britain? It is this. That, long before the insurrection of General Franco and his fascist friends, the British Embassy in Madrid knew about the plot then hatching against the Republic. Let these diplomats deny it. We, the British, could have warned the Spanish Government about the peril that would imminently engulf it. We could have prevented this ghastly Civil War.

Instead, we have brokered the so-called Non-Intervention Pact. But then, instead of enforcing it, we have allowed Italy and Germany to breach every clause and condition. To kill and maim innocent Spanish civilians. Indeed, to sink British shipping and never lift a single finger in defence of our own Merchant Marine.

Worse, we have allowed the Germans to be rewarded by General Franco for these violations. A reward of minerals, raw materials and resources. All that Hitler could possibly desire for the completion of his re-armament programme. From this, loyal reader, there can be only one conclusion. That a further global conflict now seems inevitable. And, when the conflict erupts, we Britons will not be the innocent victims. We shall have been the instigators.

Chapter Twenty-Six

Wednesday 28 September 1938

'My great friend, *Señor* Bolín,' said Laureano de Armas Gourié, 'believes that one day there will be an entire network of *Paradores*, all across Spain. Including here in Santiago de Compostela.'

He had already explained the idea, first conceived twenty-five years previously. But it had not begun to reach fruition until the Marqués de Vega Inclán opened the first such establishment in '28. The Gredos Parador. Nine more already. State-run. Investment in some of the country's crumbling architectural jewels to convert them into quality hotels.

'Here?' asked Peter Kettering.

'Perhaps, *Señor*. Perhaps.'

Their luggage was taken inside the Hotel Compostela, in Calle Hórreo, just along from the Plaza García Prieto. It was a long building, ten years old, modern in style with an almost Mudéjar tower at the corner and a balcony of similar design running the length of the third floor. It stood, according to the Spaniard, on the very site occupied by the Inquisition until the abolition of that supremely Catholic office, just a century earlier.

Inside, there were grand staircases, endless corridors, each corridor an endless art gallery.

Jack's room had a polished block floor, a pair of four-poster beds rather than just one. A Savonarola chair, its cross-frame inlaid with Moorish ivory, the loose cushion in green velvet. Double doors opened onto the balcony, and the balcony looked out onto the street, across to the square itself, entirely occupied by the Castromil building, home to the bus and transport company. Its twin cupolas, thought Jack, would have done justice to a very significant basilica. The square was busy too. It seemed to form a natural boundary between the old town immediately to his north and the newer developments to the south, Santiago's *ensanche*. It appeared also to be something of a terminus for buses arriving in Compostela, constantly disgorging passengers, suitcases, men clambering down from roof-mounted seats, mothers with children, into the streets on each of *Edificio Castromil*'s four sides. There were other hotels too. Cafés and bars. Workers carrying ice blocks on bent backs. Car horns, bicycle bells, the roar of motorbikes, cartwheels on cobbles. The vague, indefinable pungency of Spanish streets, seasoned here by essence of gasoline, a dash of cigar.

The journey from Lugo to Santiago had been uneventful. Dominated by Laureano's frequent anecdotes about the peculiarities of Galician society. A better road for once though. At least, generally good enough for Jack to transmute his mental notes into ink on paper. Disjointed scribble, some lines of shorthand, but enough to capture the main elements. Yet he left the note-book itself in his day bag when the small group set off with the Spaniard for the inevitable tour of the main sights.

They followed the line of the old town walls though most had now been demolished, past a couple of convents. Then the university buildings to the market square and the Puerta Francígena beyond, the gateway and cross which would meet pilgrims following the Camino de Santiago from the east. From the Puerta de la Peña they crossed to the new School of Medicine, down the Calle de San Francisco to look at the impressive Monastery of San Martín Pinario, the ancient fountain, and thence into the enormous square, the Plaza del Obradoiro, with its old Royal Hospital and the Palacio de Rajoy – the Town Hall. But they were, each of them, dwarfed by the Cathedral.

This latter rose tier upon golden tier, from the opposing stairways to the double doors, thirty feet or more above ground level, the tall baroque central feature crowned by arched pinnacles and its statue of Saint James, the whole flanked by two square towers, and these topped by twin spires which climbed, impossibly, to a height of well over two hundred feet. Laureano believed that they should still be able to see the interior, but Carter-Holt excused herself. Not feeling quite the thing, she said, after her ordeal the previous night and, of course, the length of today's journey.

Jack, of course, volunteered to accompany her back to the hotel, earning him a suspicious glance from Catherine Kettering and a blessing from Sister María Pereda for his chivalry and thoughtfulness.

The couple headed south, back towards the Plaza García Prieto, or so they thought, not a word exchanged between them despite Jack's efforts to initiate a dialogue. They found themselves off course, however, outside the Church of Santa Susana or, rather, in the Alameda Gardens which stood between the church and the Calle de la Senra. Valerie sat on a bench and Jack joined her. She begged for a *Senior Service*, rose-pink lipstick staining the white tip as she lit the cigarette, but only on one edge, turning it so that it would burn more evenly.

'Well,' said Jack, chancing another line that he thought might entice her into conversation, 'I managed to finish a decent draft of my article. It's a bit wordy. You'll like my conclusion though. But I stole your script a bit, I'm afraid.'

'Ah, plagiarism. I would expect no better from *Reynold's News*. And which particular bit of my right-wing ramblings did you purloin exactly, Mister Telford?'

'The bit about the British Embassy. Our failure to warn the Popular Front that the *coup* was coming. Then I move on to talk about Britain's lily-livered approach to the Non-Intervention Pact. And, finally, the concluding paragraph. It should make everybody sit up and take notice. That we've effectively helped Hitler to re-arm. That when the war comes...And it *will* come, Carter, won't it? That Britain won't be the innocent victim. That we shall have caused the bloody thing. By failing to act sooner, better.'

She looked at him sadly.

'Yes, darling,' she said. 'There *will* be a war, I'm afraid. But you are a ninny. Do you *really* think that the British Government is so naive?'

'More naive than Stalin, that's for sure. At least the Russians have been giving technical support to the Republic. It may be part of their drive to disseminate world revolution, but it's *something* that they're doing their bit to halt fascism...'

'Jack,' she stopped him. 'The Comintern has no interest in disseminating world revolution. Wherever do you get your ideas? The Comintern's only policy consideration is the protection of Mother Russia. Comrade Stalin knows that sooner or later he must fight Germany. But not yet. He's not ready yet.'

'And Spain...?' he began to ask, but remembered another of Sydney Elliott's lectures. *Think, Jack,* he had said at the beginning of the Civil War. *Why is it that in every country with a formal alliance to Soviet Russia, the Communist Party is pro-Government? No matter how dirty the politics of that Government might be. And you can't blame them, Jack. The Comintern has been struggling to survive every year since the Revolution. Spain is no more than a sideshow for them, I'm afraid. A delaying tactic. A distraction to keep the eyes of the West off Moscow for a while.*

Carter-Holt smiled at him.

'You know, Jack,' she said, 'that despite everything, you're still correct. Spain *is* special. This war is special. Regardless of any damned views that governments may hold. You wouldn't know it, of course, by the way that the press depict it. Left *and* Right. And the worst crap is always spouted by those who haven't fought here. But *we* have, Jack. You and I. Haven't we?'

He thought about the shrapnel scar on her beautiful shoulder.

'*You* have, Carter. Though God only knows whose side you were on at the time. But not me.'

'Stuff and nonsense,' she said. 'What do you call Covadonga? Let alone having to tolerate the Holdens for so long.'

'Marguerite Weston too, remember,' laughed Jack. 'Does that count towards a battle honour?'

'Oh, a special commendation at the very least.'

But mention of Covadonga settled a shroud about him once more. He thought about Carter-Holt's words. It was all so much clearer now. There were certainly many in the British Government who had seen the Nazi threat plainly enough at the time of the Munich Games. Earlier. But would Britain, France or Russia have considered themselves strong enough, in '36 or '37, to openly oppose Hitler? Probably not. *A delaying tactic.* That was it, he supposed. They had each chosen to buy time in a different way. Britain chose appeasement and Non-Intervention in Spain. France followed along. While Russia chose the Spanish buffer. And did they know, these super-powers, that both strategies served, in practice, to strengthen rather than neutralise Herr Hitler's influence? He rather suspected that they might. That they would have seen this as inevitable consequence. Reasonable collateral if, in the longer term…

Yet what about the alternative? If Britain, France and Russia had stood united from '37 onwards? Could not a balance of power have been maintained? *Of course it could, Jack. But they don't trust each other enough for that. And, anyway, the Comintern seems to have other cards up its sleeve.*

'You're going to think this is a really stupid question,' he said.

'Try me, Jack,' she replied.

'It's just that, if you're not actually here to write yet more rubbish about Red atrocities, what *are* you here for?'

She frowned, shook her head.

'No,' she said. 'You can't ask me that, darling. Anything else. But not that.'

'What?' he laughed. 'A plan to kill Franco?'

'For Christ's sake, Jack,' she hissed, looking frantically around the gardens. 'Don't be so bloody obvious.' She grabbed his arm, dragged him further towards the fountain.

'Oh, come on, Carter. I'm not falling for that one!'

'Believe what you like, Jack. But I'm saying no more.'

He stared at her, incredulity melting like butter as he saw the fear in her eyes. What had Fielding said? Something about larger things at stake? But did that mean…?

'It's not as easy as that, Carter, is it? What the hell was the lecture on trust all about?'

'It's for your own good, darling. Believe me.'

'You're nervous and edgy,' said Jack. 'You're up to something, aren't you? But please tell me that you're not really planning to kill him. I was only joking.'

She said nothing and he felt his guts tighten.

'I told you, Jack. I have nothing to say.'

She stood. He snatched at her hand.

'It doesn't make sense,' he said. 'They only announced the Franco thing when we got to Fuenterrabía. To us, that is. Though the Ketterings and the two nuns were obviously invited. The Holdens must have been in the loop too, I suppose. Julia Britten. Oh, and the Westons…Christ, there must have only been me that *didn't* know!'

'Yourself and the Moorgates, I think. It was Daddy who told me that the Westons had been invited to meet Franco. It might not have been confirmed until the group was actually here, but the plans were all in place.'

Sir Aubrey Carter-Holt, thought Jack. *Secretary to the First Lord of the Admiralty. If only you knew…*

'But Carter, this is madness.'

'Is it?' she said. '*This* is madness, Jack.' She gestured around the park. 'You and me on a holiday to visit the scenes of Franco's so-called victories. We've had a taste, Jack, just a taste, of all the innocent people he's butchered. Starting in Asturias four years ago. Just imagine if he could be stopped, my darling. The chance that it would give to the Republic. The chaos it would cause. Not just here but to all of Hitler's plans too.'

'And a strengthened buffer for Comrade Stalin?'

'Is that so very wrong? Does it matter so long as it gives the Republic a lifeline?'

'You really mean it, don't you? Have you been sent here by the Comintern, Carter?'

'None of that matters either, Jack. But you see, don't you? That I can't involve you in this. It's too dangerous.'

'But you'll never get away with it. Have you *any* idea what they'd do to you? You can't. I won't let you.'

She sat down again.

'You can't stop me. But at least there's no Inquisition here now, Jack. They abolished it, remember?'

'A hundred years ago. That's all. And it's no laughing matter. What does that tell you about this place, Carter? That they only abolished the bloody Inquisition in the middle of the last century. They still use the garrote to execute people here. Did you know? They tie you on a stool and tighten a metal band around your neck with a turnscrew until you choke or your spine snaps.'

'I don't intend to die, my darling.'

'What, you think they'll let you walk up to their *Caudillo*, shoot him and walk away?'

'Yes. More or less.'

Jack laughed, on the verge of that now familiar hysteria again.

'Don't be a fool, Carter. You can't.'

'I don't think you're in any position to stop me, Mister Telford,' she snapped. 'What will you do? Inform the authorities? Then go back to your comfortable *bourgeois* life in London?'

If you don't fight the fascists here…

'Inform? On you? Carter…'

'What, Jack? More protestations of love? I may have let you shag me, Mister Telford, but I see now that it was a mistake. I should have kept you out of this altogether.'

'Then why didn't you?'

She stood again.

'Give me another cigarette, why don't you?'

He stood too, lit a smoke for each of them, put an arm around her camel-coloured coat.

'Why didn't you, Carter?' he asked again.

'You know why!' she whispered, but he was not sure that he *did*.

'Then you might as well share your plan with me. It's the least you can do. We can both be mad together.'

'I'm not sure. Jack, if it places you in danger too…'

'Trust, remember? And how can I tell how risky this all is unless you share it with me?'

This feels like something Lewis Carroll might have written, thought Jack. *Some Looking Glass nonsense. She can't possibly be serious about this.* But he could feel a chasm opening before his feet. Not a rabbit hole but a great yawning void into which they were both likely to slip. He kept imagining that in a moment or two, when the madness had left her, she would apologise, kiss him, return to the hotel and perhaps, God willing, let him love her again.

He realised that she had been talking and that he had not heard a word.

'So I picked up the automatic from the floor of the cave. Look, Jack.'

She opened the saddlebag purse, allowed him to peek inside. And there, sure enough, was the shining black metal of an Astra pistol.

'Christ, Carter,' he hissed. 'Close the damned thing. You mean you've been wandering around with a loaded gun? In the middle of Franco's Spain. What about the *Civiles*?'

'Why on earth would they suspect *me* of anything, Jack?' she snapped. 'I was awarded the Red Cross of Military Merit, remember? By the good General himself. Now it's my turn to present *him* with something in exchange.'

'Don't make light of this, please,' begged Jack.

'You think that's what I'm doing?'

'No, I'm sure you're not. But what happens, Carter? You wait until we all get presented to him, get out the gun and shoot him. Is that it? And why didn't you do it last time he presented you with a bloody medal? No. You don't need to answer that. But you'll never get away.'

'When we get presented, Jack, there'll be a distraction in the crowd. I shoot Franco but without taking the gun out of the bag. They'll have no idea where the shot came from.'

'Distraction? And how did you know that you were going to lay your hands on a gun anyway?'

'You don't need to worry about it. Comrades from Madrid. They would have provided the gun *and* the distraction.'

'And then we walk away?'

'Then we walk away.'

'It sounds simple.'

'The best plans are always simple. Unfortunately, it won't now have quite the safeguard that I'd originally intended.'

'Which was?'

'We wanted to avoid reprisals, Jack?'

'There'll be reprisals? Even with Franco dead?'

'*Especially* with Franco dead. They'll kill anybody else they can find that's ever been associated with the Left. You know that.'

'Then you can't avoid it. But Christ knows how you make the calculation,

Carter. How many martyrs does it take to tip the balance of Franco's assassination?'

'Don't be a fool, Jack. You know how many people will die if this war goes on. Any price, *any* price, is worth paying to see that monster dead.'

'So how did you plan to avoid the reprisals?'

'Perhaps not avoid them entirely. But to minimise them, Jack. It's a worthwhile aim, don't you think?'

'Of course. But how?'

'We'd planned that, at the moment I shot him, somebody else close to Franco would use my camera to take a photograph of him. Once escaped, and hopefully safe across the French border, the picture would be developed, publicised, along with my confession. You can circulate it, Jack. Your very own scoop. So it's clear that the assassination was carried out by a British citizen, acting independently.'

'You seriously thought that would avoid reprisals?'

'Perhaps not. But worth a try, Jack, don't you think?'

'And who, precisely, did you imagine was going to take the picture?'

'Brendan Murphy.'

'Brendan…?'

'Yes.'

'But Brendan wasn't…?'

'Part of the plan?'

'I was going to ask if he was another secret Communist.'

'If it wasn't disrespectful to the man, fascist though he may have been, I would have laughed, Jack. Brendan Murphy was exactly as he seemed. But what better man to get close enough with the camera?'

'And Fielding?' said Jack. 'Is he working for the Russians too?'

Carter-Holt stood again, stubbed out the remains of her cigarette.

'You shouldn't ask, Jack,' she snapped, and walked off towards the hotel, leaving Jack to weigh her words. He sat on the bench for a long time. *It's impossible*, he thought. *Absurd*. It seemed even more so now that Carter-Holt was no longer present to give the thing credibility. *I can talk her out of it. Surely. But then, do I want to?*

Jack met his fellow-travellers again one hour later in the hotel foyer, a broad smile from Sister María Pereda, a light kiss on his cheek from Catherine, a handshake from Peter, not even an acknowledgement from Carter-Holt. She was wearing Dietrich-style flared trousers, dark blue Falange shirt and a man's tie, bright red, a thin grey cardigan.

'Did you go far, Valerie?' said Catherine. 'This afternoon.'

'Far enough,' Carter-Holt replied.

They ate in the hotel's dining room. Guests, of course. A fine old lady, in widow's black, *Señora* Baladrón, who was praised for having donated twenty thousand *pesetas* to the funds of the Falange locally. The Dean of the Cathedral with one of his officiating priests, a rotund fellow with a propensity for cigars. The Mayor, naturally infantry commander Manuel García Diéguez, still sporting his uniform. The Mayor's wife. The Mayor's deputy, and leader of the Falange, *Señor* de la Riva, also present with his wife, an aristocratic type who could have been Dorothea Holden's double. And, throughout, the gathering maintained a steady chatter. About the Cathedral: the story of Saint James told once again. The first miracle associated with the return of his martyred body to the Peninsula. About the prospects for Spain's future: the war must conclude soon, surely, and even the most fanatical of the Reds must now simply want it to end. About the *Reconquista*: the original *Reconquista*, naturally. Tales of the Battle of Clavijo, where Saint James had appeared on horse-back, sword raised, to lead the Christians in their fight with the Moors. *Santiago Matamoros.* Saint James the Moor-slayer.

'*¡Santiago y cierra España!*' Saint James and strike for Spain. The war-cry adopted by Franco's fascists and rasped out here tonight as a toast.

'*¡Arriba España!*' responded Laureano, beaming at his five charges.

'*¡Arriba!*' replied Peter Kettering, though without great enthusiasm.

Talk of the *Reconquista* also brought tales of the campaign's close, seven hundred years after it began at Covadonga, with the surrender of Granada to Queen Isabella of Castilla and King Ferdinand of Aragón, those most Catholic of Monarchs.

Carter-Holt outraged them a little. Surely, she had suggested, after seven hundred years, the Moors must have had something of a legitimate claim to the territory, and whilst the Galicians and Asturians might have native Iberian blood, most of those who took part in the Christian Crusade to drive out the *moros* were themselves Frankish newcomers. Or did she have that wrong?

Jack was astonished by her *sang-froid*. He took virtually no part in the discussions. But then, neither did the Ketterings beyond a few initial comments. They had become morose once more, withdrawn, while Jack suffered more from an inability to focus. He re-lived his conversation with Carter-Holt over and over again. It was too much. First having to come to terms with her politics. Then with the reality that this elegant young woman seriously intended to take Franco's life.

'Well, *Señorita*,' said Laureano, 'whatever the facts of that particular episode in Spanish history, there can be no doubt that, for the *past* five hundred years, at least, we are being a Christian Catholic country with a strong tradition of Monarchy. In *this* case, it is the Reds who are the newcomers, the invaders, and General Franco drives them away for us.'

'*¡Arriba España!*'

'With the help of the British Government, of course,' said Carter-Holt.

'Of course, *Señorita. ¡Arriba Inglaterra!*' He raised his glass. The other guests followed suit. 'Though I should say that *El Caudillo* is disappointed in the new British Ambassador to Madrid. He does not understand Spain, I think. He says that everything that happens here is unexpected. He is a fool. Nothing could be further from the truth, eh?'

Dessert arrived. *Tarta de Santiago*, of course, with the Cross of Saint James emblazoned on its almond-flavoured filling.

'*¡Arriba Galicia!*'

And a discussion about the Region's natural support for National Spain. Bred in the bone.

'The more recent *Reconquista* must have been almost a matter of course here, then?' said Catherine. Don Laureano put the question.

'The *Alcalde* says that even here there was a strong Committee of the Popular Front. Fifty-eight of them. Party activists. Union leaders. That sort of thing.'

'All Reds and Freemasons, *Señor*?' said Peter.

The *Alcalde*,' replied the Spaniard, 'says that was precisely the worst of it. Here, the Republic had infected even the Church. The leader of the Socialist Party was one of Father Quiroga's parishioners. The *sacristán*. How do you say this?'

'The sexton,' said Carter-Holt.

'Yes, thank you. The sexton. And a strong member of his *confradía* too. Their *Llamador*. Their cryer. Leading the *braceros* who carry the great sculpture of Our Lady in the holy procession. How can such a man stand alongside the atheist? The heretic?'

'There was fighting then?' said Carter-Holt.

'*¡Qué va!* Not a shot. Within three days, Santiago de Compostela is firmly in the hands of National Spain. How can it not be so? Here, at the heart and soul of the original *Reconquista*.'

'No problems from the workers?' said Jack. 'The local *campesinos*?'

'*Señor* García asks them to return peacefully to their work. He promise that there will be no reprisal. So everything is peaceful.'

Jack saw himself ripping up the entire imagined article. But what did it matter anyway? If Carter-Holt succeeded in her madcap plan, there would be no space for analysis of the war's origins. Not for months. It would all be about Franco's death. About those involved. Would he be mentioned? And how? As the eye-witness journalist first on the scene like George Steer had been in Guernica? As the heroic correspondent who brought his scoop to the waiting world? Praised by a saved Republic? Or mourned as the innocent bystander mown down in the aftermath? Or murdered in the reprisals as Franco's successor simply continued where the *Generalísimo* had left off? In either case, how could Carter-Holt possibly hope to survive? And without her, how would *Jack* survive?

'It would be super news for the *Caudillo*,' said Valerie, 'if we could interview some of those people. Just imagine how easily we could dispel this nonsense about White Terror if we could only publish statements of former Reds who've now embraced National Spain. Lord, what about the local Secretary of the Spanish Communist Party? What about him?'

Don Laureano translated while Jack tried to remind himself that she was only acting her part, to fight down his old feelings of animosity towards her.

She is frighteningly good at this, he thought.

There was silence. It continued for a seemingly long time. Then the *Alcalde* coughed, spoke briefly.

'That was *Señor* Parrado. He has moved now. Gone from the town.'

'What about the former mayor?' Carter-Holt suggested.

'Ánxel Casal. Active in the Galician Nationalist movement. The *Partido Galeguista*.'

'Is that part of the Popular Front?'

'Yes.'

'Then we should speak with him.'

'Apparently, *Señorita*, he has left town also.'

'The President of the Popular Front Committee then?'

'That would be the Socialist. Fernando Barcia.'

'Left town?'

'Yes.'

'Union leaders?'

'I am afraid...'

'Do we know where they went?'

'The *Alcalde* says he has no idea. He say that he is not his brothers' keeper.'

'You said that the Popular Front Committee had fifty-eight members, *Señor*,' said Carter-Holt.

'The *Alcalde*, *Señorita*. He said that.'

'Very well. The *Alcalde*. Could you ask him whether he knows the whereabouts of even *one* such member?'

Laureano de Armas Gourié put the question, and Manuel García Diéguez took a cigar from his pocket, rolled it between his fat fingers, lit the tobacco, blew out a long curl of smoke.

Into the silence, Sister María Pereda directed a question to Father Quiroga. There was an answer. Another question.

'I ask the *padre*,' she said after a moment or two, 'well, these are all working men. Perhaps they have found employment in Lugo. In Vigo. In Ferrol. But were there no professional people on the Committee? No intellectuals? Surely my friends could find somebody like that, I say him. For your newspaper, *Señorita*. He say yes, of course intellectuals. Doctor Dehesa. A famous doctor, though he think perhaps a Communist. And the artist, Camilo Díaz, who was also Anarchist. So I ask how you can find either of them...'

They've all gone in the ground somewhere, thought Jack. *Worker or middle-class. Catholic or atheist. It didn't matter to these murderers.*

'Not a shot fired in anger, did you say, Laureano?' he murmured. That now familiar blackness settled on his soul once more. And the subject was changed.

Later, having turned Valerie's disclosure over in his mind a hundred times, he knocked lightly on her door. She opened it a little, then wider once she was sure that it was him.

Carter-Holt closed it again, leaned against the back of the door, still holding the handle.

'I've been thinking...' said Jack, turning towards her.

She was still wearing the shirt and tie from dinner, but the trousers now lay folded on the back of a chair. She wore French knickers, white, and a matching *porte-jarretelle* garter belt for her stockings.

'Not the quality that I need from you just now, Mister Telford.'

She planted her feet slightly further apart.

Jack felt himself harden at the sight of her, moved back to the door, cupped her tiny breasts and tried to kiss her. But she turned her face, forcing him instead to nuzzle her neck while she unfastened the buttons of his trousers. He shook himself free of his jacket, slid the braces off his shoulders so that the flannels and underpants pooled around his ankles. Then, swiftly and easily, she pulled aside the crotch of the knickers, lifted herself on tip-toes, an invitation to which Jack responded by gripping her buttocks, lifting her bodily, back still against the door, until he could enter her.

'Jesus, Carter,' he whispered, as her weight settled, forcing him deep inside, the satin almost biting at him.

'Just shag me, Jack,' she said. So he did, gripping the underneath of her thighs. It was fast and wild. And he held her there, just about, while he later shuffled across to the bed, dropped on top of her in an ungainly mess. She giggled, harsh but mirthless, so that his further passion was dampened, and he rolled away from her, lifting up his knees so that he could get rid of the shoes and, after them, the trousers and underpants.

'At least you weren't wearing combinations, Jack,' she laughed. 'Or what a pickle, eh?' He crawled across the bed so that he could take her in his arms, but she pushed him away. 'I need some air,' she said.

'But listen,' said Jack, 'I *have* been thinking...'

'Me too, my darling,' she murmured. 'I've been thinking about my promise.'

'Promise?'

'That you could have anything you wanted from me. I've decided where we should start. You've been such a good boy. Something new. Something that you won't have tried before. Have you ever done it with somebody else watching, Jack?'

'No, I...'

She's just trying to shock me, thought Jack. *Isn't she?*

'Just listen to Carter, Jack. You'd like it. I know you would. And I've got the perfect person. What about Laureano? He's rather attractive, isn't he? For an older man, I mean?' Jack was shocked and alarmed, both by her suggestion but also by his renewed arousal. They made love again, if that was the correct way to describe it. Then they lay side by side. 'You see?' she said. 'I knew that you'd like the idea. Now you, my darling. What have *you* been thinking?'

'That I want to help you,' he whispered. 'Tomorrow.'

Chapter Twenty-Seven

Thursday 29 September 1938

Jack sat in the gloomy booth of the *Telefónica* exchange near the Post Office. He had waited almost an hour for the connection, only to find that there was no answer from Sydney Elliott's number. So he had been forced to start the whole process again. Back to the desk, this time Sheila's number. Another wait until he had been directed to booth number six.

'Hello, Sheila. Is that you?' he yelled, when the crackling at the other end finally settled.

'Jack? My God, Jack, is that really you? We've been so bloody worried.'

'Did you say worried?'

'Yes. Was it your tour group involved in the Covadonga thing?'

'It's in the papers?'

'Yes. Today. Hardly any details. But it says a nun was killed. A banker. Oh, and an official guide. Is that right?'

'Yes. A bit more to it. But yes.'

'Christ, Jack. I thought Sydney was sending you on a holiday. Are you all right?'

'Yes. Well…Yes. Fine. I was trying to reach Sid as it happens. Do you…?'

'He called me. To see if I'd heard anything. Said he was going off to find out what was happening.'

'Tell him I'm…Look, it doesn't matter. To be honest, I have an article for him. I promised. Sheila, it's a big favour I'm asking but would you take it down for me?'

'What d'you think this is, Jack Telford, a bloody wire service for *Reynold's News*?'

'I was going to send a cable, but you know how much I hate not using punctuation.'

'Teletype then?'

'They've got an old Creed here, I think.' He peered through the glass panels of the booth doors, back towards the desk. 'But I wanted to speak to you.'

'You don't sound too good, Jack. You sure you're all right?'

'Yes. Yes.'

In truth, he felt terrible. Nausea had plagued him since the middle of the night. He had been warned, of course, before he came away. About the possible effects of such a dramatic change of diet. Or perhaps it was a bug of some sort. That would explain his frequent trips to the toilet. Except for the palpitations. Those familiar bloody palpitations. It was panic that gripped him. Panic and fear.

'How long *is* the blasted thing anyway?'

There, she was hooked. Good old Sheila. He owed her a great deal. But should he tell her about Carter-Holt? No, probably not. Time enough when he got home. That is…

He recited the whole article to her. And she liked it.

'Thanks, Sheila. I needed *somebody* to comment favourably.'

'Well, I don't expect you'll get very much out of Lady Carter-Holt, will you? I take it you've still got the fascist bitch with you?'

'Yes. But she's not so bad when you get to know her.'

'Jack, are you *sure* there's nothing wrong? Are we talking about the *same* Valerie Carter-Holt?'

'Yes, but never mind about that now. I need another favour.'

'What is it?'

'After you get the article to Sid Elliott, would you mind popping a note in the post to mother? Just let her know that I 'phoned and was thinking of her.'

'Christ, Jack. Now I *am* frightened. What…?'

The doors behind him folded back. It made him jump, then annoyed.

'I haven't finished…' he began to snarl, and then saw that it was Carter-Holt.

'What are you *doing*, Jack?' she hissed.

He put down the handset.

'Dammit, Carter. I told you I needed to file my article.'

'That's why I went to the telegraph office. You weren't there.'

'I wanted to 'phone it through,' he replied, picking up his note-book and pencil, pushing her out of the booth.

'All of it?'

'Yes.'

'It will cost a small fortune. What did Elliott say?'

'It wasn't Sydney.'

'Who then? Oh, I see. Grant Duff. Still carrying a torch for her, I suppose? You didn't tell her anything?'

'That I wasn't supposed to? No, Carter, I didn't. And I never did *carry a torch for Sheila*, as you put it.'

And he had not. But it was really only because Sheila had laid down the ground rules for their friendship almost from the first time they met. It had been important to her, she had said, since they would be travelling together all the way to Germany. A serious professional who would never allow her career to be marred by personal relationships. And, leaving aside a modicum of jealousy that it was *she* who received all the plaudits for the *Observer*'s coverage of the Saar Plebiscite, Jack adored her for it, working alongside her all through that long year of '35, through the General Election campaign, as she handled all the publicity for Hugh Dalton, the Party spokesman on foreign affairs.

He returned to the counter.

'Número Seis,' he said. *'Por favor.'*

The attendant checked with the telephonist, gave Jack a figure that he could not understand. The figure was repeated, then scribbled on a piece of paper. One hundred and forty-seven *pesetas*.

'My God, Jack,' said Carter-Holt, 'how much is that?'

'About two pounds, I think. Can't keep track these days. Value's dropping like a stone. Not the point though. That's all the Burgos money I've got left. Apart from a few *céntimos*.'

She offered to lend him some cash and they went out to the street, caught immediately in a swelling stream of people heading for the Puerta del Santo Peregrino, Franco's name apparently on everybody's lips. They were almost swept past San Clemente, along Calle Trinidade with its ancient houses, the back of the Town Hall, stopping at last on the corner of Calle de las Huertas outside the Church of San Fructuoso.

'Do we want to do this?' Jack shouted above the deafening babble.

'We don't seem to have much choice,' replied Carter-Holt.

'What time do we meet Laureano?'

'Ten-thirty.'

'It's quarter-past already,' said Jack.

'Five minutes?'

'It's academic. We'd never be able to push our way through this crowd anyway.'

Jack had never seen so many flags. Except maybe the scenes from the coronation. Or, rather, the coronations. For they had been coming thick and fast these past few years. Flags of National Spain, of course, but far outnumbered by banners and emblems of the Falange. And they sang...

Cara al sol con la camisa nueva,

...until the motorcycle outriders appeared, forcing a passage through the crowd...

¡Arriba, escuadras!

...for the cavalcade of cars, a Rolls-Royce amongst them, and a magnificent Fiat Twenty-Eight Hundred State Phaeton...

¡España una, España grande!

...from which stepped General Francisco Franco y Bahamonde...

¡España libre!

...forty-five years old. Son of a naval postmaster. Graduated from the Toledo Military Academy at the age of eighteen. Commander of the Spanish Foreign Legion by the time he was thirty-one...

¡Arriba España!

...and today, as always, accompanied by his wife, Cármen Polo, member of an extremely wealthy merchant family.

She was instantly recognisable. Black coat, white pearl necklace, a black *mantilla*.

The citizens of Compostela went wild, especially when Franco reminded them that *he* was also present by taking hold of her hand. Jack had expected that he would be taller, felt that he was absurdly unexceptional. The barely perceptible moustache, the plain cavalry boots, the slightly worn jodhpurs, the military cape and the plain forage cap of the Legion. But there was little time to assess the *Caudillo* much further since, no sooner had his Generals and Ministers, the Ministers' wives, climbed from their own vehicles than Franco and *Doña Collares* led them off towards the Town Hall.

The *Civiles* seemed almost surprised that the *Generalísimo* was among them, but they held back the cheering masses easily enough. All the same, Jack was astonished. Franco hardly seemed protected at all. He had thought to see a strong bodyguard, élite troops. This was home ground for him, certainly, but he had still expected a heavier security presence. Yet if this was normal, why had nobody bothered to simply kill the monster before this? He began to think that Carter-Holt's plan might not be so foolish after all. And, for the first time since the middle of last night, his stomach cramps began to ease.

They were carried by the tide around the corner into the Plaza del Obradoiro, disentangled themselves when the flags and fanatics crowded before the façade of the Town Hall, allowing Jack and Carter-Holt to cross the square and find Don Laureano waiting for them, with the Ketterings and Sister María Pereda, at the Cathedral steps.

'Ah, you have been following the faithful, I see!' beamed the Spaniard. 'We were going to try and get a glimpse too but there are *so* many people. You think the General has had a safe trip from Coruña?'

'It seems so,' Jack replied. He could feel himself shaking again. *What the hell have I talked myself into?* he thought. *There's no way I'll be able to go through with this. Yet Carter's as cool as a bloody cucumber.*

He determined to talk her out of it again. As soon as they were alone. There must be some other way.

'Well, good morning, my friends,' said Laureano. 'And what a memorable day for us all. To be presented to the *Generalísimo* himself!'

'What time will that be?' said Catherine.

My God, thought Jack, *she seems even more nervous than me.*

'The presentations are scheduled for one o'clock,' replied the Spaniard. 'New banners and standards to the Party first. Then some cadets going off to the Academy. Finally, the medals and commendations. So perhaps one-thirty.'

Sister María Pereda spoke to him excitedly in Spanish.

'Forgive me,' she said. 'I say to Don Laureano that I must buy flowers this morning. To present to *El Caudillo*. But I feel afraid. I wish that Sister Berthe Schultz is here.'

'I think we all feel a bit edgy,' said Carter-Holt. 'We could come with you, perhaps. Help you choose the flowers.'

'*¡Ay, Señorita!* That would be so good of you. I would like that.'

Carter-Holt beamed at her.

'And perhaps, Don Laureano,' she said, 'it might be possible for all five of us to be presented together?'

He looked taken aback.

'Oh,' he said. 'I doubt if that is possible, *Señorita*. There are protocols to be followed. And…' His glance fell on Jack.

'Is there a problem with me being there?' Jack asked. *Oh, I hope so. I* do *hope so.* 'I don't want to cause any problems.'

Carter-Holt glowered at him.

'Mister Telford is too obliging,' she smiled. 'But it would be such a pity if we can't all go up together. Mutual support. That kind of thing. Especially after everything we've been through. At Covadonga.'

'I mean no offence to anybody, Mister Telford,' said Laureano. 'But you have a certain reputation…' He was uncomfortable.

'It may be unusual for National Spain to tolerate Left-leaning reporters like Mister Telford, Don Laureano,' said Carter-Holt, 'but he *has* shared our dangers on this trip, has he not? And he is not one of those who've played both ends to the middle. Purporting to be on *our* side and then going over to the Reds with their distorted lies. Those people deserve whatever comes to them, *Señor.* But Mister Telford is not such a man, I believe. Why, you would vouch for him yourself, wouldn't you?'

'Well, yes, but…'

'And I'm sure that your good friend, *Señor* Bolín, would be happy to press our case? More positive publicity. *Red journalist on War Routes tour converted to the truth of National Spain.* That sort of thing.'

Jack regarded her with horror.

'Perhaps,' said Laureano, 'though Luis does not have the General's ear as he once did.'

'It would mean such a lot to us,' Carter-Holt continued, then turned to the others. 'Oh, you don't know, do you? I've persuaded Mister Telford that he might take some snaps of us. When we're presented. He has a camera, as you know. Is it better than my Box Forty-Four, Mister Telford?'

'Remarkably similar,' Jack found himself replying.

'There,' said Carter-Holt, 'it all seems to be arranged, Don Laureano. You *will* try to help us?'

'It is irregular, dear lady. But, yes, I will ask.'

'Such a sweet man.' She offered him the most alluring of smiles. *What had she said? Attractive. For an older man. She couldn't have meant it, surely? All that nonsense about…*

'And your travel arrangements, ladies and gentlemen,' the Spaniard continued. 'Exactly as I thought. Sister María Pereda will remain here until we can transport her back to Covadonga. You four good people will leave by train at six for Coruña. There you can catch the ten o'clock overnight sleeper and will reach San Sebastián early tomorrow morning. The Hotel María Cristina will be happy to look after you until the *Sud Express* from Lisbon leaves just before noon. You change at Irún, naturally. Like I say to you, it is a shame that you cannot stay there for the *corrida* but…'

In the Plaza del Obradoiro, loudspeakers were being wired to lamp posts, the square filling with even more people as groups of pilgrims gathered. Women in coarse home-spun with white headscarves. Priests and lay travellers in robes of brown, black or cream. Fifty young people who had walked the route from Calahorra. A whole regiment of folk from Navarra. Walking staffs, knapsacks, conch shells.

Laureano did not take them inside the Cathedral, as they had supposed. Instead, he led them on a short walk to the Calle de la Troya, stopping at last before a simple boarding house. He looked pleased with himself.

'*¿Ésta es la casa?*' beamed Sister María Pereda. This is the house?

Don Laureano returned her smile.

'The house?' said Peter Kettering.

'It is very famous,' replied the nun. 'Do you not know the book?'

'I don't think so,' said Peter.

'*La Casa de la Troya*,' said Laureano. 'One of the most famous books in the Spanish language. It tells the story of Gerardo Roquer, a young man with more interest in chorus girls than textbooks, whose father sends him from Madrid to Compostela so that he can concentrate on his studies. Gerardo comes to stay in this very house, run by Doña Generosa, but falls in love with the beautiful Carmiña Castro.'

'Which is how the silly boy's problems begin,' said Sister María Pereda. 'He is soon involved in all sorts of foolishness trying to prove to Carmiña that he is worthy of her.'

I think I know how he felt, thought Jack.

He politely declined Laureano's offer to guide them around the Cathedral, opting instead to join Carter-Holt and the nun in their quest for a flower shop, and finding just such an establishment in a nearby square. *Flores Azabachería*. But they did not return with her to the hotel.

'Let me buy you a drink, Jack,' said Carter-Holt. 'You look awful.'

'Christ, I need one, Carter. You're not planning to go through with this, are you?'

The bar was dark, almost deserted. She ordered *cognac*. The waiter brought a bottle.

'You know what the troops in the trenches call this stuff?' she asked.

Jack did not. He was not sure whether he even cared.

'Just pour, Carter. And what d'you say? Call it a day, yes?'

She swilled the amber rotgut around the glass.

'*Saltaparapetos*,' she smiled.

'What?'

'At Teruel. They'd get themselves tanked up with cheap brandy before going over the top. It means *Parapet Leaper*, something like that. That what you need too, Jack? Because, whatever happens,' she whispered, 'Franco dies this afternoon. With your help or without it. But remember, Jack, if you don't help, more innocent people will die in the reprisals.'

'Because we don't get a photograph?' said Jack.

'Keep your voice down, can't you? I've told you, Jack. The photograph is important. But if you haven't got the stomach for it...'

'And why pretend it's my camera, not yours?'

She laughed, slapped the table and stood.

'I think you're right,' she snapped. 'Time to call it a day, Mister Telford.'

'You're not going ahead with the plan?'

'Of *course* I'm going ahead. What d'you think this is? A game? Just without *you*, Jack. I thought you had a bit more about you.'

'And you're treating me as though I'm one of your bloody agents. Is that how you see yourself, Carter? As my Control?'

'Your *what*?'

'Control. Isn't that what they call it? Spies?'

'Too many cheap novels, I'm afraid. I have a case officer. Not that it's any of your bloody business. Goodbye, Jack.'

She slapped the required number of *céntimos* on the counter, shouldered her bag and walked to the door.

Jack put his head in his hands, then stood also.

'Carter!' he called. 'Wait.'

He wondered about the whole process. It was far from being simply spy stories. He knew so many colleagues who talked of London as though every third person was an agent for one country or another. Communists. Nazis. Yanks. Japanese. And where did Carter-Holt fit in with all this exactly? He knew that he was infatuated with her. But a spy for the Comintern posing as the arch pro-fascist? How far might she hope that this disguise could take her? Supposing, of course, that her plan succeeded and she survived in one piece. Would she also be able to ingratiate herself with British Intelligence? A mole for Moscow worming her way into the SIS itself? It was feasible, he supposed. And then? Where did that leave *him*? A complicit traitor? What?

He caught up with her at the hotel.

'Well?' she said. 'Are you in or not?'

'Yes,' he replied, slowly. 'I'm in.'

They sat in her room and she produced the Agfa from its canvas carrying case.

'Here,' she said. 'It's simple. This is the viewfinder.'

He picked it up.

'It's heavier than it looks.'

'Yes,' she replied. 'It's a nice solid camera. It's why I chose the Agfa. Well, this model, anyway.' Jack aimed the thing in her direction, peering down into the tiny mirror image of Carter-Holt. Indistinct reflection. 'Can you see, Jack?'

'Er...Yes. Got that. Make sure I don't miss the top of anybody's head, eh?'

'This isn't a holiday snap, Jack. The point is that we must prove how close we were to Franco. So make sure that the viewfinder is focused on Franco himself. Only Franco. His head or his chest maybe. And here's the shutter button. You have to check that the lower lever is set here. Then the upper lever just so. Need to press it quite hard. Get as close as you can and...'

'What about winding on the film? It's already loaded with film, I assume?'

'Of course, Jack. But you needn't worry. There won't be time for more than one snap, will there?'

'And the light? Do I have to think about that?'

'I'm sure it will be perfect.'

'Carter, are you absolutely sure about this? The distraction that you talked about...'

'All arranged, my darling. As soon as we're all on the platform. You mustn't worry about a thing. We'll be quite safe.'

'Don't worry? Are you being serious? We're going to stand on a platform with Franco. You're going to shoot him and I'm going to photograph...'

'The other way around, my love. When the commotion starts, Franco is distracted, you take the snap and *then* I shoot. Have you got that, Jack?'

'Do I need a dry run? Take a couple of pictures?'

She snatched the camera back from him, packed it in the canvas case, handed him the carrying strap.

'Don't be a fool, Jack. Just stick this over your shoulder and keep your nerve. We'll be fine. By tonight, Mister Telford, you'll be a hero.'

'Or one of the martyred dead, Carter,' he whispered.

'Come on,' she said. 'Just time for another brandy before the Pilgrim's Mass.'

They spent a few minutes in the hotel bar, met the others and made their way back to the Cathedral. The Pilgrims' Mass was due to start, as it always did, promptly at noon. But the number attending today was of such magnitude that it was obviously never going to begin until much later. So they edged their way slowly in the press, up the quadruple flight of front steps, below the towering granite Obradoiro façade, statues of David and Solomon flanking them. They passed through the outer doors to the inner Pórtico de la Gloria, a triple entrance, the fabulously intricate carvings depicting the Last Judgement. And below the Christ figure, on the central column, a statue of Saint James while, at the bottom, a self-portrait of the sculptor, Maestro Mateo. Between them, the branches, trunk and roots of the Tree of Jesse.

They could go no further, so numerous were the pilgrims, the quick and the lame, who pushed forward to bury their fingers in those petrified radicles, praying to the blessed Saint for whatever favour they sought, or touching their forehead to old Mateo in the hope that they would garner just a whisper of his wisdom from the act.

Jack had no idea how long he stood, jostled by the throng, trapping him here. But eventually they did move forward again, almost imperceptibly, until they finally stood at the back of the packed nave. Light streamed through the windows of the dome, illuminating the stone, the gold, the silver. And Laureano cleared a way for them, past the side chapels with their statues and reliquaries, until they were almost at the transept, the barrel-vaulted ceilings high above them.

'Look,' said Laureano. 'The altar. And below that, the silver coffer with its sacred relics of Saint James himself. You cannot see them from here but perhaps later. If we have time to visit the crypt. But there is his statue.'

But Jack was too busy with the preparations being made in the transept itself.

'Is that a censer?' he said, pointing at the almost man-sized burnished container hanging from a spider's web of ropes, each the thickness of Jack's arm, and surrounded by eight red-robed priests.

'The *Botafumeiro*,' said Laureano. 'For the incense, yes. What do you call it? In English?'

'A thurible,' said Carter-Holt. 'Though I've never seen one so big.'

She caught Jack's eye, nodded towards the north door of the transept where a solemn procession was led towards the reserved seats before the altar, placed in the centre of the nave's main aisle. Seats with red velvet cushions.

'Archbishop Muniz,' Laureano said. 'And the Marqués de Figueroa. They say he will be appointed as the town's first civilian mayor. Soon.' The man's bird-like skull bobbed like a chicken taking seed. 'The *caballero* behind him is the Civil Governor.'

A couple of Franco's Ministers too. Dark blue gabardine, white shirts, dark ties. Accompanied by their wives. *Señora* Baladrón again, from last night's dinner. *Señor* de la Riva. The current mayor. *The killer without his wife today*, thought Jack. *That fellow deserves to die every bit as much as Franco.* They all took up their reserved places on either side of the *Caudillo*, *Doña* Cármen Polo, their aides and generals.

The organ trembled and thundered into life, deep, shaking their souls, while the Archbishop stepped up, surrounded by his priests, to light the thurible. The lid was replaced and the clergymen took up position with their backs to the altar. One of the red-robed acolytes came forward while the other seven hauled on their ropes, jerking the *Botafumeiro* to head height.

'We call them the *tiraboleiros*,' whispered Laureano, as their chief gave the thurible a push, set it swinging, while a soprano voice began the *Himno al Apóstol Santiago*, the rest of the congregation slowly taking up the song, printed service sheets in their hands.

The eight thurifers heaved now, jerking and clumsy at first, but very quickly causing the *Botafumeiro*, belching smoke and incense, to swing back and forth like a wrecking ball, seeming as though it must surely hit the ceiling at the top of its arc by the time it had made its sixteenth or seventeenth pass, hurtling downwards again at incredible speed to pass only a couple of yards in front of Franco's imperturbable features.

If only it might deviate a little off course, thought Jack. *A divine accident. And I'd be free of all this. Let my prayer rise like incense before you, Lord,* he remembered from somewhere.

Finally, its own momentum began to slow the thurible. But it took a long time. The hymn went on, then died away, but the organ continued in resonant chords until the huge censer had almost stopped. The *Generalísimo* glanced at his watch and the chief *tiraboleiro,* presumably assuming some impatience on the *Caudillo*'s part, came forward to halt the pendulum movement. Like trying to halt time itself, and perhaps made nervous by Franco's presence, he gripped the thing, only to be lifted from his feet and swung around. Twice. Three times.

As the last chords faded away, the pilgrims jostled happily forward for the spiritual climax of the Mass. The Rite of Communion. And the Sacrament of Penance, Confession, administered in as many languages as the assembled priests could manage. The pilgrims, for their part, thus completed the required indulgences, fulfilled the canonical conditions of their spiritual and physical journeys.

Thirty nerve-wracking minutes later, Jack stood below the steps, still trapped, Carter-Holt at his side, as they looked up to see the Caudillo accepting the rapture of the crowd. The Archbishop was beside him, *biretta* and a cigarette in one hand, Nazi salute delivered with the other. From here, Franco looked even smaller, made rotund by his military cape. He began the descent, at the head of his personal entourage, while the *Civiles* pushed back the multitude, made a path across the square to the podium erected outside the Town Hall, its pediment crowned by a mounted figure of Saint James, sword raised in the now familiar pose of *Santiago Matamoros.*

Fitting, therefore, said Don Laureano, that the *Generalísimo* should now stand in triumph in the shadow of the Apostle. To the strains of a military band. The square itself packed, and every window surrounding the space crowded with spectators as well, banners slung along the length of each building. The smell of roasting chestnuts, vendors selling the season's first crop.

Cries of *¡Santiago y cierra España!* and *¡Arriba España!*

Press photographers were hard at work, flash bulbs shattering all around them.

Children laughed and sang.

The bells of the Cathedral peeled as though the whole town would burst with pride. And, from the podium, Franco spoke into a Fountain moving-coil microphone. Jack knew the equipment well. He had recommended it to Dalton during the Election Campaign. This particular one was attached by a thick cable to the sound amplifier system, rigged to stand on a table, but the *Caudillo* preferred to hold it in his hand, voice booming around the *plaza.*

Jack could not clearly hear the alternating translations of Laureano de Armas Gourié or Sister María Pereda. The nun made valiant efforts to keep her bouquet from being crushed in the press while, at the same time, providing her friends with a running commentary. But Jack was trying to settle his nerves with a cigarette. One of the *Lucky Strikes* that Fielding had delivered to the *Cueva de la Santina,* as it happened. He looked frequently towards Carter-Holt, fully expecting that, at any moment, she would whisper to him that he was excused. That something had gone wrong. That the plan was aborted. But she barely gave him a glance. Unlike his father's ghost, smiling at him from the stage. At Franco's right hand.

'...That under His protection,' he caught Laureano's translation, 'our Faith may be reborn but that, on the new path that God has set for Spain, we may have men with more sanctity and women with less lipstick.'

There was wild applause.

Then the presentation of new banners to the various sections of the Falange, replacing those destroyed by the Reds, or those simply lost in the chaos.

Jack thought about Mikel Iruko Domínguez. *What's become of him, I wonder?* And he thought about Julia Britten. She would have played tonight at a reception for the *Caudillo*.

What would she have chosen? he wondered. *And would Carter still have been planning this assassination? Would I have been involved then too?*

He turned to her once more as the presentation of medals began. She was wearing her own, of course. The Red Cross of Military Merit on its white and red Ladies' Ribbon. And this time she acknowledged him. A smile of such depth and devotion that it filled his heart. He prayed that the clocks would stop now, the moment held back. But time is a deceitful wretch and where, earlier, he had wished the hours and minutes away, only to have them slow to a ponderous slog, they now raced past him.

The *Caudillo*'s voice still echoed around the square. Another announcement.

'...And through the guidance of *La Santina*, now restored to her rightful place at the Holy Shrine of Covadonga through the sacrifice of these heroic friends of National Spain...'

A subaltern appeared at Laureano's side. There was a brief exchange. And the five heroes in question were directed to the steps at the podium's side, through the cordon of *Civiles* and up into the midst of the seated platform dignitaries. Carter-Holt's hand flitted nervously between shoulder strap and fastener of her large leather bag, while Jack's rested on top of the Agfa's canvas cover. Sister María Pereda stroked the flowers, surely the most blessed of God's creations. The Ketterings' fingers entwined, squeezed.

The subaltern gestured for them to halt, the calloused skin of his palm surprisingly pale.

Franco's First Lady touched the pearl necklace, twisting one of the beads around its string.

The *Caudillo* thumbed his meagre moustache, stared briefly at the waiting group, turned to listen as an aide provided a briefing sentence. He nodded, just once, sniffed, glanced at the microphone and swung towards them.

His eye caught Jack's. *Dark and distant as a bird of prey*, he thought. He imagined that he could see all the dying agony of Spain in that one glance, all the cruelty and suffering. And he knew that there was no turning back, not now. Even then, he doubted that he would have had the strength, as Carter intended, to pull the actual trigger, to end the despot's wicked life. Yet he would play his part in the thing. For Carter's sake. For everybody's sake. Though his insides heaved and quaked, he would play his part, take the photograph.

Franco's thin lips stretched slightly into the mockery of a smile, the ebon gaze fell to the flowers, and the *Caudillo* himself beckoned that Laureano's party should approach. That most Spanish of gestures, palm down, the four digits moving in and out.

The tension amongst the five travellers was palpable.

There was a moment when Sister María Pereda looked up at Jack, a puzzled question in her eyes.

But his only concern was for Carter-Holt. She lifted the flap of the saddlebag purse. He saw the stitching unnaturally sharp and clear, opened the cover of his own canvas bag, pulled free the Agfa Box Forty-Four, gripped it through the carrying handle, checked for the position of the shutter levers as she had shown him.

The crowd's roar was a confused echo in his head, surf breaking on the Galician coastline.

The *Generalísimo* had been handed a medal on a blue velvet pillow. The *Medalla de Sufrimientos por la Patria.* To be presented to the family of *Cabo Primero* Donald Kettering in recognition of his sacrifice on behalf of National Spain.

Another wave of noise. What was it that Catherine had said in the cave? God's way of punishing her? The unfaithful wife, now posing as sister-in-law? He remembered the hills above Irún. Why had she been afraid? Because she might have to confront Donald's final resting place? Because she may discover that, sometimes, heroism is simply another word for suicide?

Jack looked up to see his father's ghost at the *Caudillo*'s side. *And is it possible,* he thought, *that sometimes suicide requires a heroism of its own?* He had always considered himself abandoned. By a father who so feared and hated his experience of war that he had killed himself rather than confront it again, with little thought for the family he left behind. A selfish act, as suicides tended largely to be. But what if his father had simply weighed the odds? No real prospect of an imminent end to the slaughter. Only the slightest chance of returning whole in mind and body to his wife and son. The massively more likely prospect of some undignified and excruciating alternative. And, at St Albans, the option to inflict upon them a modest pain in the short-term rather than some greater grief in the future.

The Ketterings were being ushered forward to receive their honour, fingers still entwined, and Jack caught the subaltern's eye, lifted the camera slightly, seeking approval to take the snap. The officer nodded...

Rap! Rap! Rap!

Flash powder firecrackers, deafening at the far corner of the square. *Carter-Holt's diversion,* Jack assumed.

Rap! Rap!

All heads turned. Dignitaries rising from their seats.

Rap! Rap! Rap!

The merest hint of panic. A protective arm across the *Caudillo*'s chest. Jack hoped that it would not spoil the photo, that the arm would not hinder Carter-Holt's assassination attempt.

If you don't fight the fascistas here, you must surely fight them somewhere else.

Rap! Rap!

And Jack edged forward with the Agfa, his eyes trying to focus on the viewfinder until, finally, he was satisfied that the reversed image of Franco's face was sufficiently clear, sufficiently close.

Rap! Rap! Rap!

Chapter Twenty-Eight

Thursday 29 September 1938

In the Plaza del Obradoiro, heart of Spain's most sacred city, *Generalísimo* Francisco Franco y Bahamonde had taken the medal, passed the cushion back to his aide, moved to pin the award upon Peter Kettering's lapel, then stopped in mid-gesture at the sound of the firecrackers and, much worse, at the unusual intimacy of somebody touching his person. He glanced across the square, then at Peter, then finally at the arm which had been thrust across his chest. The dignitary who had so foolishly placed it there very quickly withdrew.

Carter-Holt's hand was inside her leather shoulder bag. She turned to Jack, eyes wide. There was dread in them, a wild madness too, almost a snarl on her lips as she nodded to him, more a convulsion of her head.

His own ears rang. The noise of the square had become a distant thing, as though he were about to faint. But he held the camera steady all the same, unable to desert Valerie at the moment when she needed him most. Comintern spy or not, at this moment she was the instrument of execution for the monster who had conspired to overthrow the Republic, who had directly caused the deaths of countless thousands. Executioner or assassin? He did not care.

But something stood in his way.

It was the young nun, Sister María Pereda. Directly in his path, flowers still cradled in one elbow, her free hand on Jack's own chest.

'*Señor* Telford…' she said, her eyes imploring him.

Yet she did not finish whatever moral admonition she intended. Had she divined his intentions? Had she somehow suspected them? He never discovered the answer since, at that moment, Catherine Kettering stepped in front of her lover, at the very instant when Peter should have been receiving the *Medalla de Sufrimientos por la Patria*. She held the decoration on her fingers for the briefest moment, glanced at the small gold castle on its blue enamel setting, the surrounding edge of laurel leaves, the dark ribbon.

And she spat in Franco's eye.

'*¡Asesino!*' she shouted. The Spanish was clumsy but clear. She had been rehearsing for long enough, it seemed.

All hell broke loose in the Plaza del Obradoiro.

Civiles appeared from nowhere. Franco, the assassin of so many good

Republicans, was instantly surrounded by a sea of his protectors, his assailants seized.

Carter-Holt moved quickly to Jack's side.

'The camera,' she mouthed. 'Put it away!' Jack looked at the thing, still poised absurdly in mid-air. He pushed the Agfa back into its canvas bag just as he, Sister María Pereda and Valerie Carter-Holt were pressed towards the podium steps, dragged down into the square, through the jeering crowd, and bundled into a side entrance of the Town Hall, down several flights of rough steps to some ancient white-washed prison cells.

It was all over in an instant. The cell door slammed behind him and he was alone. He could hear Carter-Holt for a while, her shrill protests. A distant sobbing too, that he assumed must be the nun. But after a few minutes, silence settled on the whole corridor. The cell was empty. Neither bed nor chair. Not even a bucket. So he stood in the centre of the paved floor, looked up at the curved brick ceiling. And he felt like a fool. Exposed. Angry. Relieved, of course. Yet cheated.

Now that he was out of immediate danger, he cursed Catherine Kettering for her useless gesture. It was an act as futile and pointless as Albert Moorgate's had been. And he began to imagine how things might have turned out if Carter's attempt had been successful. Franco dead. Nationalist morale destroyed. The victory parades in Madrid. Carter-Holt the heroine. Jack at her side, fêted as Robert Capa had been. The photographer who had found himself in the right place at precisely the correct time. The main praise would be reserved, naturally, for Carter-Holt herself. Or would it? He was suddenly doubtful about whether an agent of the Comintern would be allowed such publicity. But they would still have turned the tide of the civil war, surely. Carter-Holt's war. Jack Telford's war.

But these dreams of what might have been deserted him quickly, left him still exposed to his fears.

The featureless dungeon caused his imagination to see himself naked, revealed to watching eyes, scrutinising him, interrogating his deepest thoughts. So he moved to a corner, where the ceiling arched down to the floor. He sat shivering on the cold flagstones, waiting...

When the door opened, it startled him. He felt a tremor of fear as a Guardia officer and corporal entered, both armed, serious, deadly. But the fear evaporated to relief when they were followed by a troubled and apologetic Laureano de Armas Gourié.

'*¡Señor!*' he said. 'How can we ever make amends? *¡Madre de Diós!* Such a mistake.'

Jack was tempted to apologise in turn, for being a nuisance, for his association with the Ketterings. Anything that would allow him to escape this place more quickly. But he said nothing. Just picked up the camera as Don Laureano helped him to his feet, escorted him outside where Valerie was holding Sister María Pereda, though with little affection.

'The flowers...' the nun said to him, tears trickling down her face.

She had failed in her duty, must return to the Sanatorium with her mission unfulfilled. A sin so severe that Sister Berthe Schultz could hardly have contemplated its enormity. Yet Jack was incapable of thinking of anything beyond Carter-Holt.

'Carter...' he began, but was rapidly deterred by the bitterness with which she regarded him. She reached out to him. Hope flickered within his chest, extinguished instantly when she snatched the camera strap from his shoulder. She refused to speak with him when the car took them back to the Hotel Compostela, would not open her door to him when he knocked, half an hour or so before they were due at the station.

So he went down to the lobby, met Laureano, accepted a brandy from him, enquired with some trepidation about the Ketterings.

'They will be held in custody, naturally,' said the Spaniard. 'But you must not fear for them, *Señor.* The Consulate has been informed. And to be honest,' he whispered, 'I think that the *Generalísimo* is more embarrassed than enraged by the incident.'

Jack was less than certain. But there was nothing to be done. Yet he felt a deep sorrow that he had been unable to bid them goodbye.

Sister María Pereda, however, now recovered from yet another ordeal, promised to watch over the couple as best she could, and would certainly pass on *Señor* Telford's regards. It sounded like such a casual commitment, as though the Ketterings would simply be extending their holiday for a few days rather than facing the immediate prospect of Franco's prolonged hospitality at the prison in Burgos. Or worse.

The yellow Dodge bus was waiting to take them to the train, naturally, though it seemed eerily empty now. So few passengers left. No Mikel to drive them. And Jack could not resist stroking the bonnet with affection, a rueful farewell, as he handed Sister María Pereda down, just outside the main station entrance. She had stood next to Don Laureano on the platform, tiny, black-robed, that elegant face framed by her coif.

'In the square...' Jack began. But she stopped him.

'You are a good man, *Señor* Telford,' she said. 'And there was such fear on your face. I did not know why. I do not need to know. You remember? When we first met? I told you about the sin of curiosity. About straying into the forest's edge.'

Don Laureano looked from one to the other, clearly confused by the conversation.

'Yes,' said Jack, 'I remember.' He rummaged in his day bag for a moment, flourished his copy of the *Beano.* 'And you know, Sister María Pereda, that I can't think of a single reason why you shouldn't have this now. Call it a keepsake. But would you do me a favour in return?'

'You want me to pray for you, *Señor*?' she said, accepting the comic and gazing at its cover pictures of Eggo the Ostrich.

'I think that might be a good idea,' Jack replied. 'But I was thinking of something else.' He had intended to say a few words about the nature of fascism, about Hitler's Germany, about her need to see the evil. But the words would not come. They choked him. Palpitations again.

'Anything, *Señor* Jack,' she said. 'What is it?'

He took a moment before replying.

'Oh, nothing,' he murmured. 'I just wanted you to light a candle. In Covadonga. For Sister Berthe Schultz. Can you do that for me?'

She touched his hand, nodded, bit back a tear.

'I will make sure that she gets there safely,' said Laureano. 'And next time I am in England, I shall call on you. Perhaps we will visit the Grand Prix together.'

'Perhaps,' said Jack.

They had both still been standing on the platform as the locomotive pulled out, shrouding them in steam as Jack peered through the window, watched them recede into the distance, these two fascist acquaintances that he had made. Carter-Holt, however, had barely even offered them a goodbye, had chosen a separate compartment, remained aloof even when they reached Coruña and changed trains for the overnight journey to San Sebastián.

So, for the second time in twelve hours, he found himself alone, the wooden bunk of the sleeper little better than the cell floor, staring through the gloom at the compartment's ceiling. But sleep was impossible. There seemed to be a constant stream of vagabond musicians along the corridor, the door opening and closing as they asked for *céntimos*. Lottery ticket sellers too. Food vendors. Crippled beggars. He switched on the lamp, found the scrap book that Nora Hames had left in his care. He thumbed quickly through the first pages, those that he had already perused at San Sebastián and, later, at Galdakao. Julia's childhood. The onset of blindness. Her admittance to the Guildhall School of Music. The debut. The Royal Academy. Her early career. Jack turned more of the papers. Photographs and clippings. Celebrated performances. Presentations. And the tours. Provincial concerts. Then the foreign tours. France. Italy. Austria. Germany...

Jack turned back to the previous page, held the picture closer to the light.

He sat up, swung his legs from the bunk, stared at the article again. It was in German, completely unintelligible. But it was Vienna. '34. A grainy photograph of Julia surrounded by members of the audience following a performance, receiving flowers, polite applause.

And there, at her right shoulder, stood Valerie Carter-Holt.

He looked at the picture for a long time, then locked the compartment door and walked along the corridor, squeezing past a variety of vagrants.

'Carter,' he tapped hard. 'I need to talk to you.'

'Go away, Jack,' she called. 'I need my sleep.'

'But I need to talk with you about Vienna. And Julia.'

There was a pause. Then the door slid open. It was turned two in the morning.

The train rattled across another set of points.

Carter-Holt was wearing the apricot silk gown over her travelling clothes.

'Cold?' he said.

'Yes,' she replied. 'Cold. I failed, Jack. Have you any idea how this makes me look?'

'Tell me about Julia Britten.'

'She's dead, Jack. How much do you need to know?'

He opened the scrap book, set it down on her bed.

'That's you, Carter?'

She studied the photograph and he thought, for a moment, that she would not answer. But at last she smiled.

'Yes. It was an incredible performance. I wanted to congratulate her.'

'You spoke to her? Afterwards?'

'Yes. And we met later. For tea. I was with Kurt. Willi Müntzenberg too. She knew who he was, of course. Fascinated by the work he'd done with the Federation, exposing Hitler's attacks on the Jews.'

'She remembered you, Carter, didn't she? In San Sebastián.' He was trembling inside, hoped that it did not show. 'Was that why you kept putting the extra plum in your mouth whenever she was around?'

Carter-Holt pursed her lips.

'Only a few people knew I'd been to Vienna. And the link with Willi, it was careless. Dangerous.'

'But she spoke to you about it?'

'Yes. She'd heard that Willi had deserted the Party. He always had Trotskyist tendencies, you know. Julia thought that this must have had some influence on my own politics. But she couldn't believe that they'd changed so much. And she wanted to know about Kurt.'

'When was this?'

'On the morning that she died, Jack. She came to my room.'

'And then?'

'What do you mean, Jack?'

'Well, what did you say to her?'

'Nothing. Not really. I just told Julia that it was all a bit delicate. A personal matter. I asked her to keep the thing just between the two of us.'

'And…?'

'Jack, what the hell is this about? Are you now a private detective? Exactly what are you playing at?'

'I just needed to make sure.'

'Let me put this plainly to you, Mister Telford. Julia Britten and I had a quiet chat and then she left. That was the last time I saw her. I had a passing concern that my cover might be compromised, but I trusted her integrity. Why would I not? The more immediate question, Jack, is what the hell did that bloody Kettering woman think she was about?'

Jack sensed that she was deliberately trying to change the subject.

'I don't know. Something about the way her husband died, maybe?'

'Her husband?'

'Yes. You didn't know? Peter's her lover, not her husband. She was married to his brother. She blames herself for his death, I think. But she blames Franco more.'

'You didn't think to tell me this? Before?'

'How the hell was I supposed to know she'd spit on him? For Christ's sake, Carter…'

'She's probably some sort of Anarchist.'

'I doubt that.'

'You don't know them, Jack. They mess everything up. *Everything.* If it hadn't been for all those random killings in Barcelona back in '36 we would never have had all this *Red Terror* nonsense to confront. It's them who cost the Republic this war, Jack. Sodding Anarchists. And now this. Christ, I was humiliated enough already!'

'Maybe if the Comintern hadn't kept such a tight grip on the army command. On the Popular Front as a whole…'

'If the Popular Front had *really* been dominated by the Comintern, Jack, there'd never have been such a free-and-easy approach to the conduct of this war. It was discipline that the Republic needed. And foreign support that the Anarchists stopped us receiving.'

'If you say so,' said Jack. 'But what about *us*, Carter? What happens now?'

'Jack,' she said, 'I really don't know what you expect of me. I never promised to love you. Simply that I would try. But I know that it won't work, my darling. It never does.'

'I thought that it all worked very well. The sex…'

She laughed.

'Exactly, my dear boy. Sex. A shag between friends. And what *is* a shag between friends anyway? Why, no more than sharing a good bottle of wine. A fine meal. A performance at the opera.'

'How can you be so casual about it?'

'Casual, Jack? Please don't be insulting. I have never had casual carnal relations with anybody in my life. But with friends, yes, of course. Why not? It sometimes seals a bond, meets a particular need, satisfies a curiosity. No more than that, though.'

'And love, Carter?'

'Don't be a fool, Jack. You shall never find love by starting with a shag. Nobody ever does.'

'And is your curiosity about me now satisfied?'

'I'm not sure yet. I had hoped that we might remain friends. Enjoy ourselves from time to time. But that would be quite impossible if you insist on this foolish notion of love, Jack. Good heavens!'

Jack thought for a moment, jealousy rising within him.

'Have you shagged any other friends during this trip, Carter? Well, have you?' She made no answer, searched for a cigarette in the saddlebag purse. 'What about Brendan Murphy?'

She turned, glowered at him.

'Yes,' she spat. 'In San Sebastián.'

He bit his lip in an effort to stop his voice from shaking.

'And Fielding?'

'Santander.'

'Both friends then?'

'Murphy was something of an experiment. But Harold? Yes, we are old acquaintances. Colleagues, you might say.'

'He works for Stalin too?'

'That's childish, Jack. Now, if you'll excuse me, I need my sleep.'

'Fine,' he said. 'Please yourself. Maybe we can talk some more in the morning.'

'If we must. Now goodnight, Jack.' He nodded, turned to go. 'Oh, by the way. D'you have any cigarettes left?' she asked. He reached into the top pocket of his shirt. Half a pack of *Luckies* left. He handed them over. 'Don't want to smoke in here though. Pokey little place. Might walk up to the vestibule and open a window.'

'Then you'll get even colder.'

'In that case, Jack darling, I may come looking for you after all.'

She pushed him out into the corridor, slid the door closed behind her.

'Not going to lock it?' he said, glancing at the people still lurking in the passageway.

'They're all asleep,' she said. 'And I'll only be five minutes. Goodnight, Jack.'

'Goodnight,' he said, walked back to his own compartment, then realised that he'd left the scrap book behind. 'Hey!' he called, but just too late, as a waft of apricot silk disappeared around the farther end of the corridor. He wondered what he should do for just a few seconds, then decided that he must retrieve the album.

He opened her door, picked up the book and was about to leave again when he noticed the leather shoulder bag open on the small table beside the bunk.

Jack rubbed his chin, glanced towards the door, then stepped across the compartment. He peeked inside, saw the black barrel of the Nine Millimetre Astra, lifted it gently. *If she gets caught with this...* He was tempted to take it, heave it through one of the windows but, in the end, he let it fall back into its place. In doing so, however, he disturbed some of the other contents including, he saw, the edge of a playing card. He took it between his thumb and forefinger, pulled it free from the bag. It was a Seven of Cups, the number in each of the opposing corners circled in red and, in smudged ink down the centre, somebody had written the words *'All fall down!'* He slipped the card into his shirt pocket, went back to the door, the hairs standing on the back of his neck and a nervous shiver down his spine. He opened the door slightly, looked outside and then slipped into the corridor, closing the door behind him and returning to his own bed.

He studied the card for a long time, expecting at any minute that she would come storming along to demand its return. But she did not.

So she slept with them both, he thought. *The bitch. No. Hang on. It's a free world. You don't own her, Jack. And at Santander there was nothing between us. But old acquaintances? Colleagues?*

Was it possible that Fielding had been a Russian agent too? He had no idea. But, one way or the other, the card was proof, if proof was really needed, that he had sent her the message. It was a bit obvious but a simple warning that the attack on the cave would start at seven. And it had. So what were the implications? That she had connived in the plan to send the *Machados* to their deaths? Yes. That, if she could help it, she must not allow the *guerrilleros'* plan to succeed since that would have scuppered the timetable for the attempt on Franco's life? Yes. That, if she had not kept the attack to herself until the last possible minute, Bertie Moorgate might have been warned earlier, saved perhaps? He glanced at the Fedora, on the seat opposite. Yes. And, when all was said and done, like all the best laid schemes of mice and men, the assassination attempt had gone badly wrong. Otherwise...Well, who knew?

And then there was Brendan Murphy. *What did she mean? An experiment, she said. But she'd already told me she'd wanted him to use the bloody camera. Was that how she planned to bribe him? And, if so, what does that say about me? Dancing to the same tune. Christ! And all that stuff about a shag between friends. Was that all it meant to her?*

But he refused to believe it. *She's lying,* he thought. *Still trying to protect me. There's not much future in the damned thing, after all. The journalist and the spy? I must be mad.*

And so he was. He knew it. Yet he imagined a dozen possible happy outcomes for them, almost slipped from imagination to comfortable dream, except that, as he lapsed into sleep, he thought he heard her voice again.

'You hear that everybody? Mister Telford has a camera too!'

Chapter Twenty-Nine

Friday 30 September 1938

They arrived in San Sebastián at six-forty, checked that the train for Irún and beyond would depart at eleven-fifteen, debated whether they should leave their cases at the station, finally decided against, mainly because neither of them relished struggling with their Spanish at such an hour, then took a taxi to the Hotel María Cristina.

Carter-Holt spoke little, claimed that she had slept badly, was unhappy that he should have interrogated her in that way, but did not mention the Seven of Cups.

For his own part, Jack had mixed feelings about returning here. The hotel manager seemed pleased to see them, made some apologetic noises that Jack assumed must relate to Julia, but showed them personally to their respective rooms, both on the top floor this time with views of the river and its estuary. They agreed to meet for breakfast, seven-thirty, and Jack enjoyed a good shave, a wash and brush-up, changed his shirt. He could not resist walking down to the landing where Julia's body had been found and surprised himself by being shocked that there was no obvious evidence of the incident. It made him feel foolish again, brought back memories of Frances Moorgate. Fond memories, he decided.

As he reached the ground floor, he was met once more by the manager. The fellow was excited, waved a newspaper at him. It was *The Times*. Wednesday's edition.

> *BRITISH FLEET TO BE MOBILISED*
> *Reported German Threat of Full Mobilisation*
> *Prague Must Accept by 2 p.m. Today*

He carried it to a table in the dining room, ordered bread, jam, tea, without waiting for Carter-Holt to appear, and settled to the paper. He felt as though he had missed an entire episode of the crisis. The deadline was supposed to be Saturday, was it not? But *The Times* made it clear that a new deadline had been set by the Germans. Otherwise, Germany would begin to marshal its forces. There was a great deal more. Air Raid Precautions. Gas masks. Shelters. The nation edging towards war. It brought him close to tears again.

If you don't fight the fascists here…

He skimmed the letters page. *God,* he thought, *look at the length of this one.* There were columns of it, a detailed argument on the side of appeasement, based mainly on the view that the Germans were pursuing nothing other than the policies set out in the Nazi Party's original manifesto from eighteen years before. *Oh well, that's all right then. Who is this idiot, anyway? Fleming. Ian Fleming. Never heard of him. Seems to know a hell of a lot about the Nazi manifesto though.*

'Ah, you've seen the news then?' said a familiar voice. It was Alfred Holden, bobbing up and down, the unmistakeable scent of Anzora hair tonic wafting from his every movement.

'Oh, Mister Telford,' cried Dorothea, 'how good to see you again. How did things go in Santiago? I so wish we could have been there.'

Jack could have laughed. *Of course,* he thought, *there's no way that Franco will have allowed any coverage.*

'It was quite a day,' he replied, being unable to properly conjure any more original description. 'And yes, Professor, I've seen the news.'

'Well, couldn't expect you to support the Germans' claim, I don't suppose. Anyway, may see you on the train, old boy. I'm off for a breath of fresh air, my dear.' And he pecked his wife on the cheek.

'He doesn't change, does he?' said Jack.

'Whatever do you mean, Mister Telford?' she replied.

'It doesn't matter, Mrs Holden. Feels a bit strange to be back though, don't you think?'

'Of course. Memories of poor Miss Britten.'

'Yes. Speaking of which, do you mind if I ask you something? You made a comment once. That you'd had quite enough of something or other from Julia. Do you recall? I'd mentioned the Anglo-German Fellowship.'

'Do you intend to start yet another political row, Mister Telford?'

'No, not at all. I was just interested in Julia's final conversations. Trying to pull the threads together really. Find out about her last few hours. That kind of thing.'

'I see. Well, to be honest, I *don't* see. You're not still chasing Miss Hames's potty idea that there might have been foul play, surely?'

'I suppose not.'

'I should jolly well think not either. But if it puts your mind at ease, Mister Telford, I can tell you that Miss Britten and I had several conversations about Herr Hitler. We'd both met him, you know. But she simply did not see eye to eye upon the importance of the Fellowship, I'm afraid. Nothing more mysterious than that, however.'

He thanked her, agreed that he might take coffee with them on the *Sud Express.* At least, she said, they would be able to enjoy decent coffee again, once they were safely back in France.

I don't know why I even bothered asking her the question, he thought.

Jack finished breakfast, still without Carter-Holt having made an appearance, so he decided that he would go back up to her room. He needed to clear the air, he concluded. To get a straight answer from her. About whether they had any sort of future. About whether she might allow him once more to…

At the reception desk, this morning's newspapers were being delivered. The *Gaceta*. Several others. And *ABC*.

What did happen on Wednesday then? he wondered.

He picked up the *ABC*, attracted by the front page picture of four smiling faces superimposed against a backdrop of Munich. Chamberlain, Daladier, Mussolini, Hitler. He turned the pages to find the developments which must have inspired this collective satisfaction but he stopped almost immediately, for his eye was caught by the words *'Ruta de Guerra'* in bold print, and a set of accompanying photographs. He put the broadsheet on the desk, ran his finger along the lines of text, attempting his usual decipher. The article was written by a member of the Spanish Royal Academy, *Señor* Fernández Flórez, and concerned the War Routes, praise for the organisation which had established them. The comfortable transport. The attentive guides. The quality hotels. The incredible prices. There was mention of the itinerary. Something about the Red Terror. An education for the many Belgian, Portuguese and Italians who had undertaken the trips. But especially the English, it said. More English than any other country. And, just yesterday, in Santiago de Compostela, one more group of English friends had been presented to the *Generalísimo* himself. With friends like these, Jack thought it said, and the Grace of God, the war would soon be won, and Spain saved from its sorrows.

The photographs showed the *Caudillo* on the steps of Compostela's Cathedral, in company with the Archbishop, the Generals, the Ministers. Then a panorama of all the pilgrims gathered in the Plaza del Obradoiro, the workers, the nurses, the soldiers, special mention for the gatherings from Calahorra and Navarra. And, at the bottom, Franco in the very act of extending the *Medalla de Sufrimientos por la Patria* to Peter Kettering, the precise instant before Catherine's protest. *A Distinction for the Family of a Foreign Hero*, read the caption.

Jack was unsure whether to laugh or cry.

He turned more pages. And there it was. Easy enough to translate.

> *In Munich, the peace of Europe is assured by four gentlemen of good faith: Hitler, Mussolini, Chamberlain and Daladier. From the 1st to the 10th of October Germany will progressively take control of the Sudetenland. Last night, at twelve-thirty, the protocol was signed which solves the Czechoslovakian conflict.*

So, while Jack had been feeling sorry for himself in the confines of his railway carriage, the Czechs had been forced to sign away a significant part of their territory to satisfy Germany's ambitions. And he knew, with all the certainty that it was possible to possess, that nothing could now stop the fascists from following those ambitions to the bitter end, that the promise of peace for the rest of Europe was a wicked deception.

He was overcome with a most profound grief, needed comfort and company more than he had ever done in his life.

Jack gestured to the receptionist, asking if he could take the paper, then he walked the corridors until he came to the paternoster lift, stepped into the ascending car.

At Carter-Holt's room he knocked but there was no answer.

Was she in the bath? He put his ear to the panel. Nothing.

Gone to breakfast perhaps.

He decided to try the handle. It turned.

'Carter?' he called, putting his head around the door. No response.

Jack closed the door again. Would she have gone to breakfast and left the door unlocked? He was doubtful. But he decided to wait for her return. In the corridor? No, he decided. Inside. Why not? They were lovers now, weren't they?

He slipped into the room, settled in a chair by the window, looked at the Sudeten article again, feeling the mood of depression settle upon him anew.

Carter-Holt's travelling trunk stood just next to him on the webbing of a luggage table.

'You hear that everybody? Mister Telford has a camera too!'

He glanced at the door, then stood before the trunk.

Jack opened the lid. This was becoming a habit.

The contents were neatly packed. Items of clothing that he had seen her wear during the trip. The shirt, the tie, the Lyle and Scott twinset. Three tidy mounds of folded familiarity. He felt underneath each one of them until his fingers came in contact with the canvas fabric, covering a hard square box. Jack eased it free from the clothes above, took the Agfa from its carrying case. What had he missed? He turned it over, saw the German advertisement for Rollfilm, eight exposures. The Box Forty-Four had a tiny window that registered the number of exposures already used each time the winder was operated. The window was blank. So Carter had clearly removed the film. He flicked the catch that opened the camera's back. No film across the rear of the triangular exposure chamber, as he had expected. But, instead, an extraordinary mechanism.

At the level of the lower shutter lever, a fine steel bar ran from one side of the case to the other. Half-way along the bar was a stud that keyed into a flywheel and ratchet held firmly between two metal plates less than an inch apart. A sturdy spring ran from flywheel to the sloping floor of the casing, and the upper section of the mechanism was attached to a spring-loaded hammer which, in turn slotted into a chambered barrel running forward to the back of the lens. At the level of the upper lever, a second bar operated a trigger system which would release the hammer. Inside the casing, several bullets had been taped. Small calibre but deadly enough. Hollow-point bullets, designed to expand on impact and cause horrific wounds. Banned under the Hague Convention of 1899 – at least for use in international warfare, although Jack had seen several reports from International Brigaders about their use here, in Spain, by the Nationalists.

He recoiled in horror, looked again at the door and clumsily reassembled the Agfa.

Christ, he thought. *What has Sister María told you about curiosity, Jack?*

His immediate instinct was to put the damned apparatus back where it belonged. But it was easier said than done. So he decided to remove the entire mound that had covered the camera. He felt gingerly beneath, making sure that he should disturb the clothing as little as possible, then he lifted the whole lot cleanly from the trunk, setting it down on the chair. He tried to remember the exact position in which he had found the Agfa, replaced it in the same way, then noticed the corner of another black box protruding from a rag in which it was wrapped.

Though it was not a rag at all but, on further inspection, a pair of widely flared trousers similar to those that she had worn in Santiago, though paler in colour and with a dark stain splatter at the bottom of one leg. Rolled inside them was another camera, almost the twin of the first, the advertisement slightly different. And significantly lighter.

He was nervous now. On dangerous ground, he knew. His hands were shaking and his stomach felt hollow. If she came back…

Jack looked around the room, hoping that the shoulder bag with its Astra pistol would still be here, but it was missing.

'You hear that everybody? Mister Telford has a camera too!'

Jack folded the second camera back inside the trousers, set it once more on the bottom of the trunk, the canvas case alongside it. Then he gingerly placed his hands under the bundle of clothes and set them back on top of both Agfas. He examined the top layer, smoothed things back into place, closed the lid. Picking up the paper, he patted the seat cushion until he was satisfied that there was no obvious trace of his visit, then slipped out of the door and back to his own room, searching in a pocket for his key.

'Oh, you're there!' cried Carter-Holt, and Jack felt himself jump in alarm. 'Lost your key?'

Oh shit! he thought. *The key. Did I…?*

He imagined it fallen on the chair in her room. Or worse, in the trunk itself.

'Well…' he stammered.

'Whatever's the matter with you, darling?' she said. 'You look like you've seen a ghost. Have you checked your other pockets?'

He had not, but he did so now, relief pouring through him as his fingers found the ornamental bow inscribed with the hotel's name and his room number.

'Here it is!' he said. 'I'm sorry, Carter. Did you want something?'

'Well, Jack, I could be tempted in several ways but we may not have time for what I had in mind. So I wondered whether you'd settle for a swim instead?'

'Swim? Now? The train goes just after eleven.'

'It's only nine. We could get there and back easily. I've spoken to the desk. They'll send a boy along with some towels and the key for one of their huts.'

Jack had an uncomfortable memory of Marguerite Weston again.

'But after last time?' said Jack.

'Oh, I've learned my lesson, darling. I shan't do anything silly, I promise.'

It was the last thing in the world that Jack wanted to do at that moment. As much as he loved swimming, he needed time to think just now. The cameras. The gun thing. His brain felt as though it would burst. But Carter-Holt looked beautiful. And perhaps a swim might help him to get things straight in his mind.

'When?' he heard himself saying.

'Five minutes? At reception?'

Inside his room, Jack stood by the window, looked down on the waters of the Urumea where they flowed under the María Cristina bridge, away to his right. *I forgot to show her the paper,* he thought, then realised the stupidity of it.

Two cameras, one of them containing an assassin's gun. But which had she given to *him*?

'This isn't a holiday snap, Jack. The point is that we must prove how close we were to Franco. So make sure that the viewfinder is focused on Franco himself. Only Franco. His head or his chest maybe. And here's the shutter button. You have to check that the lower lever is set here. Then the upper lever just so. Need to press it quite hard. Get as close as you can and…'

And Valerie Carter-Holt, holder of the prestigious Red Cross of Military Merit would have been free as a bird.

No, thought Jack. *Better than that. How about this headline, old man? Reuters correspondent kills Franco's assassin.* He could envisage the scene even now. The monster shot down upon the podium. Chaos reins. The Red murderer stands rooted to the spot, looks puzzled. And Franco's avenger steps forward, takes a concealed Astra Nine Millimetre pistol from her bag and exacts justice on behalf of National Spain.

If it hadn't been for Catherine…

But would the price have been worth paying? The monster would, perhaps, have been dead after all. Wasn't that what he had thought? He had calculated the possibility of not surviving the attempt, had he not? So what was the difference? In all likelihood he would not even have been aware of Carter's betrayal. And what was the value of his life now? She had taken the damaged part of his soul, briefly warmed and nourished it, then returned it to him shattered, destroyed.

He thought again about the Seven of Cups, still in the top pocket of his dirty shirt, tucked away now inside his own case. The five *Machados*. Albert Moorgate.

Not everybody is what they seem…

Jack picked up *The Hobbit* from the day bag. He had almost finished it. Just a few pages left. He had not really enjoyed it very much, thought that the author would never amount to much beyond his Pembroke College career, but there were parts that had certainly amused him.

"'So comes snow after fire, and even dragons have their ending!' said Bilbo, and he turned his back on his adventure."

He rummaged some more, picked up the scrap book, decided to leave it prominently on the bedside table before finally finding his swimming costume and carrying it to the paternoster.

'Tell me about your conversation with Julia Britten again,' he said, as they walked towards the Playa de la Concha.

'Have you been in my room, Jack?' whispered Carter-Holt, turning her head to admire herself in a shop window. She had pinned up her hair. It made her look different.

'No,' Jack lied. 'At the hotel, d'you mean?'

'Never mind, Jack. I'm glad that we're going for a swim, my darling. And then we can talk about the future. On the way back.'

'Future?'

'Exactly. Now what about Julia Britten, Jack? Is she always going to stand between us?'

'You said she came to your room, Carter. But left on her own?'

'Yes.'

'Then she went down in the paternoster. Alone. It never made sense.'

'So shall I tell you the truth, Jack? The whole truth?'

'Yes. The whole truth.'

'I was with her, Jack.'

'In the lift?'

'Yes. She'd asked me about Vienna. Whether we'd met. There was no disguising the fact, so I said yes. That I hadn't been sure whether she'd remember me, so I'd not mentioned it myself. She talked about Willi and Kurt, like I told you. She said that she'd always felt an affinity with the Party, couldn't understand how my politics could have changed so dramatically. And then she asked me the strangest thing, Jack. She said to me in that superior voice of hers, *Tell me, Miss Carter-Holt, why it is that you never wind on your film after you've taken a snap?* Can you imagine, Jack?'

He felt panic welling up inside him.

'And...?' he said.

'And it confused me so much that, while we were going down, I realised I'd forgotten my bag. I asked her if she'd mind coming back up with me. So we stepped out on the first floor. Everything was fine. But when we got into the car going up, she stumbled somehow. Fell on her knees. She dropped her cane and as we came past the second floor she turned to look for it. She crawled forward and...'

'Christ, Carter,' Jack felt sick. 'And you never told anybody?'

'How *could* I, Jack? Don't be silly.'

They reached the beach hut. Jack changed, an unconscious act, his mind in turmoil.

Together in the paternoster? he thought. *And then lied about it? My God, for somebody who claims to write nothing but the truth as she sees it...I doubt that Carter would know the truth if it slapped her in the face. I'm not sure how much more of this I can take.*

And what's wrong with me? Jack wondered. *I know what I'm against alright. All the things I see at home and hate. The unemployment. The poverty. The privilege. The injustice. The bullies. Those who abuse their power. And all those in Germany and Italy that want to impose Nazi principles everywhere else. But what do I stand for? Some sort of social democracy, I suppose. Yet when you look to the future, Jack Telford, what do you see? You see war. If we can't stop them here, we'll have to stop them somewhere else. In Abyssinia maybe. Or Greece. Or Copehagen. Christ, maybe Paris or London. If we can beat them though, I guess there's a chance that we could build something better.*

'Are you ready, Jack?'

'Almost.'

But what will that something be? Those who've inherited wealth won't give it up. Not ever. And they can always buy or cajole others to fight for them, to help them keep it. So what do we get, Jack? A compromise? They agree to steal a bit less so we can get a morsel more? That's what social democracy will bring us. I know it. But it's not enough.

'Come on, Jack. Or I'll go in without you.'

It wasn't enough here. Courage hasn't been enough either. Being right hasn't been enough. Knowing that the pen is mightier than the sword hasn't been enough. Christ, Jack, it takes blood sacrifice after all. Blood, and more blood.

He came out of the changing hut, gave her a weak smile.

'Ready?' he asked.

She nodded.

On the shoreline there were just two deckchairs at this early hour, one of them occupied by Jack's father, the other by a younger man, scarlet tunic, a shako upon his lap. *Colonel F.C. Telford, I presume,* thought Jack. *Or is it? He looks a lot like Pinchón too. And something of Brendan Murphy about him.* Jack heard them calling. *Will you fight now, son? Or still the pacifist coward?* It was unfair. So bloody unfair. He had volunteered to help kill Franco, had he not? Was that not enough? He glanced involuntarily towards the slopes of Monte Urgull but he thought about the camera. Julia Britten had made some sort of connection in that agile brain of hers. About the camera, Vienna, Carter-Holt, her links to the Communist Party. And how would the rest of the plan have been feasible if Julia had still been around by the time they reached Santiago? What had she said? *I had a passing concern that my cover might be compromised, but I trusted her integrity.* A fortuitous accident then. Or was it?

They reached the water, some distance away, the tide still going out. It was cold but tolerable, though there were no other swimmers yet.

'You killed her, didn't you?' said Jack.

He felt completely empty. Entirely void of any emotion. Simply a bottomless black pit in his stomach.

'For God's sake, Jack. Did she mean that much to you?'

He was unsure. Perhaps it had nothing to do simply with Julia Britten.

'I suppose not,' he said.

'Fine. Then yes, I killed the bloody woman. She crawled forward trying to find the stick. I just helped things along. Are you satisfied, Jack? I had to do it. I thought it was necessary. If we were going to kill Franco.'

'We?' said Jack. 'Who do you mean by *we*?'

'Me. The Republic. The Party. What the hell does it matter, Jack? Julia Britten was just one more casualty in this awful damned war.'

She plunged into an incoming wave and, even now, he felt a moment of panic for her. But he need not have worried. Carter-Holt broke the surface a few yards away, swam confidently away from him. Nice style. She swam like a dolphin.

He imagined once more the stained trousers wrapping the second camera. The dark stains of Julia Britten's blood. And his mirror vision of Carter as the impressionable university rebel seduced by Moscow shattered as surely as that possessed by the Lady of Shalott.

'Out flew the web and floated wide – the mirror crack'd from side to side.'

He counted the elements of the curse which had now come upon him also. Carter's attempt to conceal her identity from Julia Britten. Her brutal butchery of the poor woman when Julia had smoked the deception. Her *shag between friends*, first with Brendan Murphy, then with the Vice-Consul. And what *was* her connection to Fielding? The part she had played in helping to betray the *Machados*. Her own side, in theory at least, Anarchists or not. The pretence at drowning. The vulnerable little woman. She had played Jack like a fiddle. The story of her recruitment by the Comintern. The tale of her lost love, Kurt Tiebermann. Had he even existed? But it had all been enough to drag gullible Jack Telford into the web itself. And then the cameras. When had she picked them up? In Paris, probably. Or delivered to her by Fielding in San Sebastián perhaps. It did not matter. But could he now have any doubt about the plan? If it had not been for Catherine, he would have pressed the shutter button, killed Franco but likely been killed in turn. By dear, sweet Carter. No longer the assassin's assistant, but rather her dupe. Her chump. Her mark. And now, he feared, she knew. She knew that *he* knew.

Jack swam after her.

She had stopped, the sea just above her waist. She looked around.

'Shall I let my hair down for you, Jack?' she said. 'I think you prefer my hair down, don't you?' She fiddled with the ornamental pin that held her bun in place. 'And have you ever had a shag in the sea, my love?' She held the pin carefully, but eased down the straps of her own bathing suit. Those tiny breasts.

Jack was aroused. He waded towards her.

Carter-Holt's arms reached out to twine around his neck.

The pin, Jack. Why has she got the pin? Is it poisoned? Another gadget of the NKVD?

But he caught the wrist that held it before she could properly embrace him. In fact, he caught both wrists, raised them high. He squeezed her flesh, his eyes filling with tears, anger and fear building within him in equal measure, holding the pin as far away as possible, taking just the quickest glance at the tip until, finally, she was forced to drop it.

'Jack, what's the matter?' she cried.

He looked once into the seductive eyes then switched his grip, quaking with despair and bitterness, taking hold of the dark mass of her curls, wet now with salt water. Jack held two handfuls of that lustrous hair, dragged it down, holding Valerie's head below the surface, listening as every gasping vestige of air to escape from her lungs competed for attention against the cymbal breaking of waves upon the shore.

Her nails tore at his belly, her fist beat weakly against his groin.

It will be winter here soon, he thought. *A winter for the Spanish like none they have ever known. But at its end? And there will* be *an end, Jack. Christ alone knows when it will come. Yet when it does, then maybe, just maybe, they will finally find their Golden Age. Not the colonial lie again, but something which all of them can share. The century of civil war finally at an end. The people's revolution secured at last. Prosperity. Democracy.*

Carter-Holt's head broke free from the water. Her eyes were wider than he could have imagined possible, almost starting from her head, huge and frightened. She coughed, gagged, tried to say his name.

'No!' she shrieked.

He summoned up the last of his strength, dragged the head below the surface once more. He saw the dark tresses, spreading medusas below the water. He felt surprise that the process should be so difficult, their natural buoyancy causing his energy to drain fast in the effort to keep her submerged, could only succeed by holding her head close against him. He pressed down on her, treading water furiously at the same time to keep his own face above the surface. He watched as she looked up, the distorted eyes imploring, begging, pleading. He felt the sting of salt in the wounds as she clawed and scratched one final time at his legs and stomach. He could both smell and taste the ozone carried on possibly the last warm wind of Cantabria's coastal summer. Eventually, she became still, but Jack did not release her even then. Not for a little while. Not until her mouth involuntarily burst open, the sea rushed inwards and she jerked back, pulled free from his grip at last.

He took a final glance along the hills of Cantabria, the Path of War in the North, and he watched as Valerie Carter-Holt's corpse drifted slowly away on the ebbing tide. He swam towards deep water. And peace. He so hoped to find peace.

Postscript

Sunday 2 October 1938

Nora Hames read the news for the third time, still trying to grasp whether she had understood the words correctly.

The headlines had been difficult enough. The papers yesterday had been so unanimous. Praise in every one of them for Mister Chamberlain. Such a spruce-looking gentleman, she thought. And now returned from Munich with an agreement signed between himself, Monsieur Daladier, Herr Hitler and Signor Mussolini. The Sudeten Crisis resolved. The Czech State guaranteed. Or, at least, those parts not wanted by Germany, Poland and Hungary.

And then, today, her copy of *Reynold's News* had been delivered.

She had thought instantly about Jack Telford. Dear boy! He had already been much in her thoughts. There had been the astonishing snippet earlier in the week about Covadonga. Mister Moorgate. But it had been such a busy seven days. Poor Julia's funeral to attend. In Romford, of course. Sir Michael had played Albéniz, but not a patch on one of the sweet girl's own performances.

There was the familiar title. The paper's *Late Edition* symbol to one side of it, the advertisement for *HP Sauce* on the other. The trademark sub-text. *Government of the people, for the people, by the people.* Price thruppence. And then the banner…

> *MUNICH AGREEMENT OR MUNICH BETRAYAL?*
> *A day of infamy dawns as we fail to honour the military alliance between Czechoslovakia, France and Britain. Prime Ministers Chamberlain and Daladier must hang their heads in shame at the document they have signed, destroying Czech sovereignty, a disgraceful sacrifice of third parties in the name of appeasement.*

Whatever did they mean? What was all this talk about *'next time'*? Next time for what? Herr Hitler had everything he wanted now, surely? And *'Peace for Our Time'* was such a nice turn of phrase.

But her cherished *Reynold's News* was telling her that even the League of Nations was unhappy about the Council of Munich. Yet what on earth would they have Britain do instead? Commit yet more generations to terrible violence, like the last show?

Well, at least the nation as a whole was grateful.

All those people who might otherwise have spent the coming weeks practising Air Raid drills. Why, the papers yesterday predicted a proper spending spree this weekend. Children would not need to be evacuated any more in such large numbers. And there would be special thanksgiving services all over the country today.

'I shan't buy it any more unless they buck their ideas up,' she said to herself. 'I'm sure young Jack would never allow it.' She thought about the yellow bus, that lovely young man, the driver – Mikel.

Ah, this was more like it. Picasso's painting, *Guernica*. After the Paris Exhibition, the painting had been on tour, first to the Scandinavian capitals, then coming to London, where it arrived on Friday.

I wonder if Jack and the others ever got there? she wondered. *To Guernica. Is that before or after Covadonga? I can't remember. I do hope he's kept the scrap book safe.*

But this was more distressing. Fighting on the Ebro all but finished. According to this report, the Nationalists had suffered sixty thousand casualties. The Republicans had lost seventy-five thousand, including thirty thousand dead, many of whom still lay unburied on the rocky slopes of the Tierra Alta and the high sierras. Barely enough weapons left to defend Cataluña and, with the war all but finished, there was every indication that Franco's Government would be officially recognised by Britain within a few months.

Poor Jack will be so disappointed, she thought. But here was another appeal from the Editor, for funds to help the Republican refugees. Tens of thousands of them, apparently. Sydney Elliott's United Peace Alliance Campaign Fund. *I shall send them ten shillings. For Jack's sake. And poor Julia would have wanted it too. I must remember to apologise to the poor boy as well. He must have thought I was quite batty. Asking him to find out who'd killed the wee lamb. You're a silly old fool, Nora Hames.*

Nora could only cope with such heavy news in limited doses, however, and she determined to turn the pages, looking for the *Young Ernie* cartoons. But something caught her eye towards the bottom of the front page. It was an obituary.

How odd, she thought. *The Obituaries are normally on page ten.*

STOP PRESS. Obituary.

The Editorial Board of Reynold's News must report, with great sorrow, the information received yesterday evening from San Sebastián in Spain. The British Consulate there has been informed about the tragic death of renowned Reuters correspondent, Valerie Carter-Holt, drowned in a swimming accident. The Consulate is also concerned about the continued disappearance of our own journalist, Jack Telford. Jack has been writing copy for this newspaper over the past year. He is a talented and committed professional par excellence and we have printed the full contents of his latest article on page five of today's edition. Mister Telford had been travelling on assignment through Northern Spain so that he might expose, at first-hand, the lies still being perpetrated by

General Franco's propaganda team in relation to the legitimate Republican Government. According to the British Consulate in San Sebastián, Mister Telford has not been seen since shortly after his arrival in the town and the Authorities fear that he may also have drowned during an unsuccessful effort to save the life of Miss Carter-Holt. Our deepest condolences to her family and we sincerely hope that the Authorities' concerns about Mister Telford may prove groundless. But wherever you are, Jack...God speed. Sydney Elliott. Editor.

Acknowledgements

I was lucky enough to stumble across the research undertaken by Sandie Holguín for the American Historical Review, entitled *'National Spain Invites You': Battlefield Tourism during the Spanish Civil War.* This set me on the track towards the remarkable tale of the Chrysler bus tours across the northern battlefield sites organised by Franco from mid-1938 onwards, the itineraries of which were broadly similar to the one portrayed in this tale. My thanks to Sandie, to the AHR, and to the University of California's Mandeville Special Collections Library for allowing me 'fair use' of the relevant materials.

My thanks also for two other significant sources. First, the website 'Airminded', compiled by Brett Holman, a study of Airpower and British Society, 1908-41, and which – for the purposes of this book – analyses the Sudeten Crisis of 1938 through the contemporary accounts of the world's press. And, second, the readily available archive copies of the Spanish newspaper *ABC*, the Sevilla edition of which serves as a day-to-day account of the Spanish Civil War from the Nationalist side.

So far as the story itself is concerned, I originally planned a novel specifically about the withdrawal of the International Brigades from the conflict, driven in part by the time that I had been privileged to spend with real-life *Brigadistas* Jack Jones (former General Secretary of the Transport & General Workers' Union) and Frank Deagan (former Liverpool dockworker and author of *No Other Way*). But the discoveries detailed above led me irrevocably instead towards this different tale, for which I borrowed the early espionage career and experiences of a certain Kim Philby and used them to shape the character of Valerie Carter-Holt.

I also only intended to write a work of fiction. There are some remarkable factual histories of the Civil War penned by non-Hispanic academics like Paul Preston and Antony Beevor, both of whom I greatly admire.

It would have been impossible to develop any real sense of Guernica's appearance in late-1938 without the help of the staff, archives and publications of Gernika-Lumo's Peace Museum, and many thanks to them for their kindness during our visit to the town. From a fictional viewpoint, of course, the definitive novel about that particular tragedy, for me, must be Dave Boling's excellent *Guernica*, which I had read when it first appeared on bookstore shelves.

So far as Britain's involvement is concerned, I owe a huge amount to the works of Spanish historian Ángel Viñas, whose fine book *La Conspiración del General Franco* gives the most compelling account that I could find of the British Government's at least questionable role in the affair, and particularly in relation to the help provided to Franco which allowed him to travel so easily from the Canary Islands to Morocco in order that he might launch the so-called *Reconquista*.

Following the collapse of the Republicans' Ebro Offensive, Franco's forces succeeded in capturing Cataluña in the first two months of 1939. Madrid fell on 28 March, Valencia on the following day, and Alicante on 1 April, the last of Spain's loyal Republican cities taken by the fascists. Franco's death-squad reprisals continued for many years afterwards against supporters of the Republic in what Paul Preston has described as *The Spanish Holocaust*.

Finally, therefore, an acknowledgement for the people who really helped to bring this story to life. First, to my wife Ann who, apart from her more usual role as my 'ideal reader', was this time forced to endure a lengthy camper van re-enactment – now as my 'ideal travelling companion' – of the entire route just so that we could verify the 'feel' of its various locations, speaking with endless numbers of archivists, librarians, book-sellers, school children and hotel staff while, at the same time, forcing ourselves to regularly sample the fine food and wines available along the admirable northern coast of Spain. Second, to Tony Roberts, a former driver of ancient Dodge trucks who provided detailed technical advice about vehicles of the period. Third, to our great friend, Mónica García Irles, from the University of Alicante, who gave me an especially constructive critique of the original drafts. It was Mónica, incidentally, who famously suggested that she had never read a book which made her so hungry, and I should probably admit that, apart from the many wonderful "food" experiences that we enjoyed while following the War Route ourselves, I also drew heavily on *Rick Stein's Spain* to confirm the nature of various dishes. Fourth, to Tim Owen at the Esperanto Association of Britain. And, finally, to my editor, Jo Field. As during our previous collaboration, Jo has been an invaluable source of guidance and inspiration to me.

Lightning Source UK Ltd.
Milton Keynes UK
UKHW010629220721
387590UK00001B/153